Tainted

By Brooke Morgan

Tainted

Tainted

BROOKE MORGAN

AVON

An Imprint of HarperCollinsPublishers

TAINTED. Copyright © 2009 by Cindy Blake. All rights reserved. Printed in the United States of America. No part of this book may be used or reproduced in any manner whatsoever without written permission except in the case of brief quotations embodied in critical articles and reviews. For information, address HarperCollins Publishers, 10 East 53rd Street, New York, NY 10022.

HarperCollins books may be purchased for educational, business, or sales promotional use. For information, please write: Special Markets Department, HarperCollins Publishers, 10 East 53rd Street, New York, NY 10022.

FIRST AVON PAPERBACK EDITION PUBLISHED 2009.

Designed by Diahann Sturge

Library of Congress Cataloging-in-Publication Data is available upon request.

ISBN 978-0-06-185337-1

09 10 11 12 13   WBC/RRD   10 9 8 7 6 5 4

For Keith Barnes, with love.
It's always the right kind of stormy.

ACKNOWLEDGMENTS

With special thanks to Siena Colegrave, Sam Shaw, Charlie Viney.

And if medals were awarded in their fields of expertise, David Miles, Hisham Hamed, Andrew Tutt, and David Ross would walk away with all of them—no contest.

1

Holly liked to sit at the front of the bus. The wide windshield gave her a feeling of space and a view forward which quashed any potential travel sickness. And she liked watching the bus driver swing the heavy front door open and closed. There seemed always to be big men driving the route between Boston and Cape Cod; heavyweights with gruff voices and a palpable command over their vehicles. Sometimes they'd crack jokes and talk to her. "This is my ship of the road," one had once commented. "I'm the captain, sailing her over the highways." He must have been in his fifties and over three hundred pounds, but there was such a wistful romance in his voice as he said it, she gave him a nickname: the Poet. Every subsequent time she boarded a bus, she hoped she'd see the Poet again, but he'd disappeared. To another highway, another ship.

She was early enough for the eight-thirty a.m. bus to be the first on and snag the front seat, the one beside the window. If she was lucky, no one would come and sit beside her and she could stretch out, have the front all to herself. People trickled on behind her: an elderly couple who went straight to the back, a lone middle-aged woman who took a seat a few rows behind her to the left, two teenage girls who wandered down the aisle toward the middle. *Keep going*, she thought. *Keep going past and down the aisle. Maybe I'll get lucky.* But then she looked out the window and saw a line beginning to form. It was going to be pretty crowded, she gauged. She probably wouldn't get away with two seats to herself.

She almost didn't see him. He had been stooping over, pushing his bag into the cavernous luggage holder and she had almost turned her gaze away from the queue of people when she caught sight of him as he straightened up. *Faintworthy*. That was the expression Anna had come up with to replace "drop dead handsome." "Look—" Anna had pointed at a guy in the bar the night before. "Look, Holly—there's a faintworthy over there. At least, he's close to being faintworthy. Let's go talk to him." Holly had laughed and told her to be quiet. She wasn't going to go talk to some stranger in a bar. Anna could, and Anna usually did. But last night Holly had managed to rein Anna in and they'd stayed where they were, finishing their drinks and then leaving to get some supper.

He was tallish, dark, thin and tanned. He'd rolled the sleeves of his white shirt up over his elbows. Clean-shaven, straight-nosed, strong-chinned. Wearing khaki trousers and loafers. No sunglasses. An old watch with a leather strap. Looking serious and nonchalant at the same time. So, so handsome she felt his looks hit her in a punch of pleasure. Like the first sight of a beautiful painting. He was staring ahead, not up. He couldn't see her looking at him, so she allowed herself to and was reminded of the time she'd been sixteen, in Friendly's, waiting to get an ice-cream cone and seeing, suddenly, at the front of the line, a man she thought she recognized as Noah

Wyle, one of the actors in *ER*. She'd stared and stared, taken aback by his looks. He was more attractive in person than on TV and for a second, when he'd bought his cone and turned, he'd caught her eye and she'd blushed. He'd smiled and walked out. Later, she'd learned he was filming a movie around Buzzards Bay, so it was definitely him. When she'd told Anna, all Anna could say was, "Why didn't you get his autograph, Holly? God, how could you let that opportunity slip?" and she'd thought she was much happier with that one fleeting smile than a tangible piece of paper.

Faintworthy had handed the driver his ticket and was climbing the stairs. Quickly, Holly turned her stare to the floor of the bus, feeling that same blush she'd had at Friendly's begin to rise. *A blush is like being sick to your stomach*, she found herself thinking. *You can't stop it. You have no control. It just happens. But he'll walk by and not notice me and as long as I keep my eyes down, I'll be all right.*

"Do you mind if I sit here?"

"Sure." She had to look at him. "I mean, I don't mind, no. You can sit here. I don't mind." She knew she was sounding supremely inarticulate. Her whole body was blushing.

"Thanks." He sat down.

Her eyes dived back to the floor.

"I know there are other seats, but I like to sit at the front," he explained. "I like to see out."

"Right."

He had an English accent. So his voice was as attractive as his looks. It wasn't fair. She'd have to spend an hour and fifteen minutes with him beside her and she'd doubtless be hot and sweaty and monosyllabic the whole time. She hadn't brought a book, she had nothing she could do to pretend to be engrossed. He was empty-handed as well, sitting there quietly, his arms crossed.

Holly had yet to meet one person who didn't say he or she was shy as a child; even the most outgoing, rambunctious personalities, even someone like Anna, would say, "Oh, but I was such a shy kid. You wouldn't believe it." And Holly always felt like saying, "No, I don't believe it. Because I was a shy child and I'm still shy and I don't see how you grow out of being shy, ever."

The last passengers were boarding the bus. A woman came on holding a toddler in her arms and sat down in the seats behind them. She looked tired and stressed and so grateful for a chance to sit down she hadn't even noticed this impossibly handsome man she'd just passed in the aisle. *Children do that*, Holly thought. *They make you concentrate on the really important things—like collapsing into a seat and taking a break from the constant demands for an hour or so.*

She could feel her blush finally subsiding as the bus driver climbed into his seat and swung the door closed. *Pretend you're Anna*, she told herself. *Say something feisty and funny. Make him think you're completely comfortable in this situation. As if it happens every day. A gorgeous man sits beside you and you start a scintillating conversation.*

As if.

She remained mute.

"It's interesting. The word 'mind.' In England, in London, at tube stations, they say, 'Mind the gap,' meaning, 'Watch out for the gap.' Between the train and the platform. And then there's 'mind' in the sense of, 'Do you mind me sitting here' like I just asked. And then there's 'mind' as in 'brain.' Not that . . ." he paused. "Not that you're interested in me banging on about a word. Sorry. I'm going for a job interview. I'm a little nervous."

"No. It *is* interesting. I promise." His anxiety immediately wiped out hers. She allowed herself to look up, into his eyes. They were a dark shade of blue, the same color as the sweater Billy had worn when she'd danced with him. *Bad memory. Cancel it out and move on.* She smiled and he smiled back, offering his hand.

"Jack Dane."

"Holly Barrett."

A brief, strong squeeze.

"My grandfather always shakes hands with his left hand. He says it's closer to the heart."

"Makes sense." Jack Dane nodded. "But it might be difficult to retrain the entire Western world."

"I don't think he's trying to convert anyone. In fact, I think he likes it being his private idiosyncrasy. Anyway, what job are you interviewing for? Or is it bad luck to talk about it?"

"Bad luck? No. I hope not. It's not a big job. Just a waiter at a new restaurant in a small town. But it's by the sea and I've always wanted to be by the sea."

"Where by the sea?"

"A place called Shoreham."

"You're kidding. Figs? Is that where you're interviewing? That's where I live. In Shoreham."

"That's the place."

"Figs is the first fancy restaurant we've ever had. It's big news in town. We're used to diners and clam shacks and Dunkin' Donuts and pizza places. I looked at the menu in the window just a couple of days ago. It's seriously grown-up."

"Seriously?" Jack Dane laughed.

"Very, very seriously. They have exotic sauces. They have pomegranate cocktails. I think I even remember some herb-encrusted salmon dish."

"The restaurant I used to work at in Boston has salmon cocktails with herb-encrusted ice cubes."

"That's ridiculous. What are they think—" Holly saw his sly smile and another blush started. "Oh, God. I can't believe how stupid that was."

"No—it wasn't stupid at all. Yes, I was teasing, but I wouldn't put salmon cocktails past that place. Or herb-encrusted ice cubes either."

"You're just being nice."

"No way. I worked there, remember?"

"You're from England, aren't you?"

"Yes. But I've never met the Queen, Prince William, Prince Harry or David Beckham. I'm such a disappointment to Americans. I'm beginning to think either I should pretend that I *have* met them or I should lose my accent. Not raise false expectations."

"Oh, no, you shouldn't lose your accent, it's—"

A child's wail came from behind them and then a woman's voice saying wearily, "Stop it, Tom." But Tom wasn't stopping. His cry moved up a pitch and Holly could hear him pummeling the seat—Jack Dane's seat—with his little legs. Jack turned and rose, putting his face over the seatbacks.

"Could you control your child, please?" he asked.

"He's tired and irritable," the mother replied. Holly could hear her exasperation. "I'm sorry. Tom—stop that now."

Jack Dane turned back and sat, frowning.

"What were you saying?" he asked.

"Only that you shouldn't lose your accent."

He flinched as another bout of flailing legs hit the back of his seat.

"Tom, Tom, stop. I mean it."

Holly peered through the crack between the seats and saw the mother struggling to keep hold of the squirming little boy, but he was determined to keep kicking. "You're bothering that man, Tom. Stop it or I'll put you to bed as soon as we get home. Do you hear me?"

"Bloody useless," Jack Dane muttered.

"She's trying."

"Not hard enough."

Whack, whack, whack—unrelenting tiny feet pounded the seat.

He stood up.

"This is really annoying and it's not going to stop. I'm off."

Don't go. Please don't go. Can I say I'll move with you? No. I can't. I'll sit here like an idiot and you'll be sitting beside someone else, teasing someone else as this bus hits Route 128.

"Come on." He leaned over, took hold of her hand and pulled her up. "There are two seats in the middle back there. Let's go."

She followed him as he led her down the aisle, not looking at the mother and child, knowing how embarrassed that mother would be. He motioned for her to go in first and take the window seat, a row behind the two teenage girls she'd noticed before.

"That's better." Settling in beside her, he immediately relaxed. "I hope you don't mind me dragging you with me."

"I don't mind," she smiled. "And we're right back where we started—with that interesting word 'mind.'"

"The secret of a good dinner party is a running theme—or two. Some story or joke the table shares and then can refer back to, embroider on. Food and drink count, but it's the conversation that really matters."

When had her father told her that? She had to have been young, maybe eleven or so. He'd been sitting with the *Boston Globe* on his lap; it was in the morning and her mother was in the kitchen. Preparing for a dinner party? Holly didn't know. She remembered thinking she'd have to try to create running themes when she gave dinner parties. Whatever running themes were. Now that she did know what they were, the other part of the equation was missing. She'd never given a dinner party. She couldn't imagine ever giving one.

"So tell me. What's Shoreham like?"

"Wonderful. At least I think it is. It's basically a one-street town. You know, like you see in old movies. A bank, a fire station, a hairdresser's, a grocer's, a liquor store, a diner and that's it—we used to have a movie theater but that was ages ago. And now of course we have Figs."

Shut up, she told herself. *You're babbling. You're so used to being the one who listens, you get nervous when someone asks you a question.*

"So he's like asking me out on a date, but I don't know if it's a date date or just a going-out thing. It's so not clear. And I'm like trying to figure him out."

The obnoxiously loud voice came from one of the teenage girls in front of them. Holly waited for the other one to reply but the first one kept talking.

"You think so? I mean, I'm with Teresa on the bus here and she's been saying it's a date date but I'm not so sure and what does that mean anyway? I mean, what do I wear?"

"Oh, no." Jack Dane shook his head. "We know how to pick them, don't we?"

"No way. The pink top sucks."

"They have cellphone-free places in the trains, but not in the buses," Holly said apologetically, thinking, *And I'm just as bad as she is. I'm acting like a teenager too. When you asked me to move seats with you, when you just said "we," my heart did a little dance.*

"OK, OK, I hear you. Look, I gotta go. Teresa is handing me a sandwich and my stomach's like empty. Talk later. Yeah."

Jack Dane scrunched down in his seat so his head was level to hers; he leaned over and whispered, "She's going to eat. We're saved."

His breath was warm, clean, so intensely male, she held it inside her as if it were a drug.

"Which is worse?" she whispered back. "The little boy kicking the back of your seat or the cellphone screamer?"

"It's a tie. Although I should be used to cellphone screamers. They inhabit restaurants too. Someone like me who hates noise shouldn't work in restaurants—but I do, so I should be used to it. Anyway, tell me, Holly Barrett. How old are you?"

"Twenty-three."

The tones of their voices, the softness of the whispers and the proximity of their heads made Holly feel as if they were side by side in bed, plotting something. Except she'd never been side by side with a man in a bed. But this was how she'd imagined it would feel.

"I'm twenty-six, so those days are even longer ago for me—but what were you like when you were a teenager?" he asked. "Did you have a group of friends who all talked too loudly and too fast?"

"No. I didn't have a group. Aside from one friend, I was pretty much a lone wolf."

"I doubt it." Jack Dane was studying her face so intently, from so close up, it took all the courage she had not to turn away from him. "No, you weren't a lone wolf. Lone wolves are the ones who get kicked out of the wolf pack. They straggle along behind, at a distance, hoping to gain re-entry into the pack. Whereas you, Holly Barrett, were the quiet, shy one who was serious at school, who studied hard and who didn't go in for silly teenage stuff. Which may have set you apart from the pack, but it wasn't a pack you wanted to join. You had a different world, a world of your own, a much more adult one. You're an old-fashioned girl."

"Yeah, it's me again. Yeah, it was a fucking tiny sandwich. So what do you think? If I wear that black top with the pink pants—you think that will send the right signals?"

He threw up his hands in a gesture of surrender and drew back from her.

"It's useless. No one knows how to put a sock in it. Wankers. Listen, I think I'm going to take a kip for a while—a nap, I mean." He put his hand in his pocket, pulled out a small iPod. "We can't talk properly with the cellphone screamer in full flow, so I'm going to tune out. I don't mean to be rude. But I had a late night last night. I need to recharge. Sorry."

"You don't have to apologize," she said quickly. "No problem."

"You don't mind?" he smiled.

"I don't mind."

Putting his earphones in, Jack Dane leaned back in his seat, fiddled with the iPod controls and closed his eyes.

Holly was still feeling his physical presence, the closeness of him. She'd felt something almost like it once before, the time she danced with Billy. Billy's sweater had smelled of autumn leaves; he'd held her close to his chest, she'd breathed in the scent, she'd felt herself melt into him. When they'd had sex a few weeks later, there'd been no melting, only his rank desire and her desperation.

Looking out the window, she saw that they were passing the Foxboro racetrack, so they'd reach the junction with Route 495 soon. Which meant they didn't have that much farther until they arrived in Shoreham.

There were certain types of people who took pleasure in telling you about yourself, Holly knew. Anna being a prime example. "I saw this great ad for white-water rafting. I might go. You'd hate it though, Holly, I know. You never take risks," or, "Hey, Holl—I was going to buy you a skimpy top for your birthday but I knew you'd never wear it."

Exactly how, Holly wanted to ask, did Anna know? Maybe Holly would have liked white-water rafting, or the skimpy top. *I took a risk,* she'd wanted to yell. *I took a huge risk with Katy.* But Anna had her typecast as a mouse from the age of thirteen and nothing Holly could ever do would change that.

Jack Dane was different. Out of nowhere, he'd looked straight into her and pulled out the truth of her early teenage years. Aside from her unlikely friendship with Anna, Holly had been apart from the pack. She had had her own world— with her parents, her books, her imagination. And yes, it had been largely an adult world, although she'd never thought of it in that way before.

The only part Jack Dane was wrong about was her not wanting to join the pack. She'd wanted to, all right. But she hadn't known how to. She was so self-conscious, she felt paralyzed. Other girls could be wild and fun and funny, but she felt as though she was outside herself, watching, and would appear foolish if she tried to join in. Every time she had worked up the courage to make an effort, she'd been ignored. Not rebuffed exactly—no one bullied her or was mean. They just didn't notice her, except as Anna's friend.

"I can't figure out why Anna hangs out with Holly Barrett," she'd overheard a girl named Debby say in the gym one afternoon. "I mean, what's the deal? Holly Barrett isn't exactly a winner. What's Anna doing with her?"

"She probably does Anna's homework for her," another girl, Wendy, had replied.

And Wendy had been right.

"Hey." Jack Dane nudged her, offering her one of his earphones. "Listen to this."

Holly took it, placed it in her left ear. It took her only a second to identify the song: Coldplay's "Fix You."

"Brilliant, isn't it?" he said when the song ended, holding his palm out. "It's possible, you know."

"What's possible?"

"To get fixed. Hang on, don't look so frightened. I didn't mean drugs. I meant, it's possible to feel better. You looked sad staring out the window, that's all."

She put the earphone into his outstretched hand, smiled. "Thanks."

He rearranged the earphones in his ears, closed his eyes again. Was he going to sleep for real this time? Holly wondered. Or would he be watching her as she stared out the window?

She wasn't wearing nice clothes; instead she had on her usual worn jeans and black T-shirt. No make-up. No jewelry. No perfume. Dirty white sneakers. Who dressed up for a bus trip? Holly wished fervently she had. She wished even more fervently that she had figured out somewhere along the way how to flirt, but most of all, she wished she knew what was supposed to happen next. Would he ask for her phone number? If he didn't, could she ask for his? No. Definitely not. It would be way too embarrassing. The odds were he was already going out with someone anyway. "Spoken for" as Henry, her grandfather, would say. He'd been making conversation, he'd been having a little fun. He'd probably call his girlfriend in Boston straight after the interview and she'd meet him at the bus station when he got back.

Closing her eyes too, Holly tried to recapture the smell and texture of his breath when he'd whispered to her. She wanted to put herself back into that moment of intimacy and stay there for a while, savoring it. Instead, images of him walking hand in hand with a tall willowy blonde appeared. Her eyes flew open and she turned to look out the window again.

Way too quickly, the Mill Pond Diner was in sight. The bus driver signaled, braked and pulled into the car park.

Holly touched him on the arm; his eyes opened, he disengaged the iPod.

"We're here?"

"Yes."

"Excellent."

The pneumatic door swung open with a swishing sound of air and Holly and Jack both stood. They appeared to be the only two on the bus getting out at this first stop. Jack Dane stepped into the aisle, motioned for Holly to precede him. She did, conscious of her sloppy clothes. Neither spoke as they climbed down the bus stairs then grabbed their bags from its underbelly.

"Nice meeting you, Holly Barrett." He extended his right hand. No "Can you give me your cell number?," no other words followed. Once again, they exchanged a brief, strong shake.

I can take a risk, Anna. I have to take a risk.

"If you need a lift into town, my car's here. I can drive you to Figs."

"Thanks, but the manager said he'd meet me." He put his hand over his eyes to shield them from the summer sun. "There's a man over there, by that blue car. Looks like he could be waiting for me."

"Charlie Thurlow. Yes, I heard he's the manager." Wanting to say more, but knowing he was anxious to leave her, Holly said, "Good luck, Jack Dane. I hope you get the job. It was nice meeting you too."

By the time she had reached the "It was nice" part of the farewell, Charlie Thurlow had waved to Jack, Jack had started off toward him and her final words ended up directed to his back.

I don't mind, she said to herself, hoisting her bag on her shoulder and walking to the other side of the car park where her car sat baking in the heat of the sun. *I was crazy and deluded to hope for anything more. I don't mind at all.*

2

After the ten-minute drive from town, Holly arrived back home in Birch Point and found a note on the kitchen table: *We've gone down to the Back Beach clamming. Join us if you feel like it. All is hunky dory, H.*

She put down her overnight case, went up to her bedroom and changed into a black one-piece bathing suit. "Old-fashioned" Jack Dane had called her. Before not asking for her number and walking away without a backward glance. At least this bathing suit wasn't flowery with a ruffled skirt at the bottom. But if he'd known how old-fashioned she really was, he'd probably have sprinted to Charlie Thurlow's car.

Today was a perfect one for him to come to Shoreham; one of those June mornings with endlessly clear skies and just enough warmth to make swimming an attractive prospect. In the dog days of late July and August the heat could be wet, muggy and stifling. She would go to the beach for relief only to be attacked on the way by swarming mosquitoes and find the water invaded by jellyfish when she got there. Jack Dane might want to live by the sea, but he might not know there were times when the sea was as uninviting as city pavement.

Grabbing a towel and a baseball cap, she left the house and

walked the fifty yards to the beginning of the dike. Each time she reached the rusty gate where the dike began, she silently thanked whoever had come up with the incredibly brilliant idea all those years ago to make the Cape Cod Canal.

In the process of digging out a channel cutting through Massachusetts to shorten the shipping route between New York and Boston, the U.S. Corps of Engineers had inadvertently given her family a two-mile, effectively private, beach. Holly still hadn't figured out the mechanics of it, whether they'd simply dumped the sand in one long stretch or made some kind of rock foundation for it first, but whatever the logistics, they'd fashioned the dike—a long sandy finger sticking out from the end of Birch Point—built a small lighthouse at the far end and declared it government property.

The left side of the dike fronted the canal; the right side created a bay and met up with the original beach at the end of the point. Holly's family had always referred to the canal side as the Back Beach, the bay side as the Front Beach. On the Back Beach the water was colder and there could be dangerous undertows from passing boats, so most people swam on the Front Beach. But Holly liked the Back Beach better: as a child she'd spent hours watching the boats go by, inventing stories of where they were going, where they'd come from, and what the people on them were like.

Because parking on Birch Point was illegal unless you lived there, the only way to access the dike was by foot or boat. Holly's house was the next to last on the Point, so it took her approximately one minute to get to the beginning of the Back Beach. She headed off down a small path leading to the shoreline, careful not to touch any of the red-leaved poison-ivy plants which bordered it. She could see that the tide was low, the only time it was possible to dig the clams out of their hiding places in the sand. Henry and Katy would be having a field day digging in the area of sand on Widow's Cove to her left, so she sped up, anxious not to miss any more time with them.

Within a minute, she'd caught sight of Henry, bending down, and Katy, squatting beside him, her little hands clawing up mounds of wet, gray sand. Stopping, she watched them for a moment, her heart melting with pride and love and a yearning to halt time and keep everything exactly the way it was for eternity. Her happy blonde little daughter digging sand in the sun with no worries, no fear, nothing difficult or sad or bad ever happening to her.

"Hey," she called out, waving, and Katy turned, looked up, waved frantically.

"Mommy! Come here. Look at all the clams!"

"Wow!" Holly ran over, picked up Katy, hugged her. "Let me see the bucket."

Putting her back down, she peered into the bucket beside Henry.

"Monster haul! There's been some serious clamming going on today. Looks like I'm not needed."

"Hi, sweetie," Henry gave her a kiss on the cheek. "How was Boston?"

"Fine." She pulled Katy to her, gave her another hug. "Thanks for taking care of her."

"It's a great-grandfather's privilege. We had a whale of a time. You should leave us to our own devices more."

"A not-so-subtle hint, Henry."

"Subtle or not, you should take it. You need to get out more. And I'm perfectly capable of looking after Katy."

"I know you are." She squeezed his arm, turned her attention back to Katy. "So what are we going to do with all these clams, chicken?"

"Henry says we're going to make clam chowder."

"Excellent."

"But it has to be perfect."

Holly shot Henry a look. Katy had been, for the past month, on a mission to make everything "perfect." It was her new word and had become like a mantra to her. At five years old, she wanted perfection in everything: the "perfect" amount of milk in her cereal, the "perfect" bedtime story, the "perfect" day. Henry shrugged and rolled his eyes.

"We'll try, Katy. That's the best you can do with perfect—try."

"I think we have the perfect number of clams," Katy said, staring into the pail. "Don't we?"

"Definitely." Henry stretched, rubbed the small of his back. "She's a taskmaster. Wouldn't let me take any breaks. She kept saying, 'Don't stop, Henry,' and I kept telling her what's easy for a five-year-old isn't necessarily easy for a seventy-five-year-old."

"But she didn't listen."

"She's a serious girl, you know. No fucking around."

"Henry."

"Oh, come on. She'll hear it in the playground."

"We're not in an inner city, Henry. We're in Shoreham."

"And people don't swear in Shoreham, do they, sweetie? God forbid." Henry laughed and picked up the pail. "I'm going back to the house. Why don't you come by after lunch and we'll start on the chowder?"

"OK—and thanks again for having her last night."

"My pleasure." He put his hand on Katy's head. "She was the perfect guest."

"Bye, Henry," Katy said. "See you and Bones later."

"You will indeed see us both, young lady." He walked over to where the beach met the long grass and picked up a light jacket. "Meanwhile I'll look up recipes for perfect clam chowder on the Web."

"Any excuse," Holly smiled, picturing Henry hunkered down at his desk, surfing the Net. She was constantly amazed at how computer-friendly he was and figured he spent at least three hours a day on his Apple. When he had gone, she crouched down in the sand so that she was Katy's height.

"What do you want to do now? Would you like to spend some more time on the beach or go back up to the house?"

"Can we stay on the beach and look for shells?"

"Absolutely. Let's take a walk."

They strolled down the beach, picking up the odd shell, until Katy asked if they could stop for a while and watch the boats go through the canal. Holly spread her towel out and they parked themselves on it—a front-row seat for the canal traffic. Tugboats, speedboats, yachts and cargo ships passed by, heading from New York to Boston or vice versa.

Henry had told her that in the old days boats would pass on

their way through the canal at night with people in evening dresses and tuxedos dancing on board. Now there were whale-watching trips in a nearby town called Onset and day cruises, but the glamor of those overnight trips from Boston to New York had gone. People flew, took trains or drove.

"Look, Mommy. There's an Australian flag." Katy pointed to a beautifully sleek racing-green yacht. She was right about the flag, but then Holly knew she would be. Henry had given her a book of national flags for Christmas and Katy took the task of learning which flag was which seriously; also she had a phenomenally good memory for a five-year-old.

Holly wasn't one of those mothers who saw signs of genius in every single thing her child accomplished, but she knew Katy's ability to remember verged on the "special." For a while, she even feared that this was a sign of autism and started to research autism on the Web, until Henry caught her doing it and told her she was being an ass. But still, she worried whether Katy was normal and totally adjusted. Did she laugh enough? Was she too introspective? Too serious?

She'd obviously had fun digging the clams, so she was clearly capable of joy; she just didn't jump up and down and let herself go wild very often. Was that bad? Holly looked at her daughter staring intently at passing ships, searching for the flags.

How do you ever know as a mother? There are landmines everywhere, waiting to blow up in your face. Am I too strict? Not strict enough? Should I tell Henry, for example, that he really has to stop swearing in front of her or is that being overprotective and silly? Will Katy be sitting in a shrink's office some day, blaming me for everything wrong in her life? Will she make the same mistakes I did?

Holly turned her gaze to the lighthouse at the end of the dike and beyond. The skies were so clear she could see all the way to Martha's Vineyard—or at least she thought she could. She was never sure which islands in the distance were which on days like this.

"God, Holly, you don't have any idea, do you? I mean, how long have you lived here—and you don't know whether that's Martha's Vineyard or Nantucket or whatever out there?"

"I'm not very good at geography."

"Oh, come on—you're good at every subject."

She was seventeen, he was eighteen. They were sitting on the cold hard sand, on a tiny beach carved out amidst rocks three-quarters of the way to the end of the dike. The Thanksgiving had been one of those crisp, clear ones. Holly's parents had come down from Boston to install winter heating in the house and Billy's had come to check out the November cut-price motorboat sales. Billy had dropped by to say hello and they'd decided to go for a walk.

Billy Madison, who had danced with her two weekends before, a few days after her friend Anna had ditched him; who had held her closely to him when a slow song had come on; Billy, whom she had had a desperate, unrequited crush on since she was fourteen and saw him on the Front Beach for the first time. He was beside her now, wearing the same dark blue sweater he'd worn to the dance, his cheeks pinkish in the cold.

"*I study a lot, that's all. I guess most people think I'm a geek.*"

"*I don't think you're a geek.*"

He'd put his arm around her shoulder, drawn her in to him. She didn't remember how it had gone from there, how exactly he'd kissed her or how he'd taken off her jeans: what she remembered was the unyielding sand, her back driven into what felt like concrete as he entered her; the surprise and fear and longing and hope she felt. This was Billy Madison and they were having sex on the sand and her life was going to change forever afterward. She wouldn't be a virgin, she would have a boyfriend, she would know what it felt like to be loved back. What was happening to her now, as her back was being smashed into the sand, wasn't romantic or intimate, but it would be in time. Because Billy Madison was perfect.

"Yuk."

Holly turned to see Katy with a shell on the palm of her outstretched hand.

"You know what that is—an Indian coin."

"It looks like a yukky toenail. A gross yellow old horrible toenail."

"At some point whatever the Indians used for money must have looked like that and that's why it's called an Indian coin."

"I wouldn't want to have much money if I was an Indian and my money looked like this." She dropped it and buried it in the sand. "Wow—look at the tugboat coming." Katy pointed down the canal to the railroad bridge, toward Boston. A massive hulk of cargo was being pulled by a tugboat. "How can something so little carry something so big?"

"I don't know."

"I don't know too."

"Henry put sunscreen on you, didn't he?"

"Yup," Katy nodded, still staring at the little red tugboat.

"But you've been out a long time. I think we should go in now."

"OK."

"Did you have a fun time with Henry last night?"

"Yes. I love Bones so much."

"And he loves you." Getting up, Holly retrieved the towel, shook the sand off it and draped it over Katy's bare shoulders.

Was it normal for a five-year-old to spend hours lying beside an old black Labrador, patting its head and whispering in its ear?

"She's not pulling wings off butterflies, for Christ's sake," Henry had said when she'd professed her worry about Katy's attachment to Bones. *"Will you please relax, sweetie? She's a wonderful child and you're a wonderful mother and all you really have to do is love the hell out of her—which you do."*

They were walking on the edge of the sand, their feet just touching the incoming water. When Katy held her hand out, Holly grabbed it, then pulled her up to her chest and hugged her tightly.

"I love you, chickpea," she whispered.

"I love you too, Mommy. And I missed you."

Holly switched Katy's body to the side so she rested on her hip. They came to the path that led back up to the road and the house and Holly stopped to look over into the small field of long grass that began where the sand stopped. There was no marker or memorial stone, but somewhere in that field lay the ashes of her parents.

I love you both. And I'll never stop missing you.

As soon as they reached the road, Holly put Katy back on the ground and they walked past another little path cut out from the wood, leading to Henry's house on the left. Henry's was at the very end of Birch Point, and looked straight out over the dike, with a magnificent, unobstructed view, while Holly's, about fifty yards away, was hidden in the trees. It was possible to see a sliver of ocean if you looked closely from Holly's side porch, and in winter, when the leaves fell off the trees, the view improved, but she could get a guaranteed view only from the second-floor windows. At times she wished she could hack all the trees down and have the vista her grandfather did.

She knew she wouldn't, though. Not only because it might affect the wildlife, but also because she didn't want to change anything. Her parents had lived here; she wanted all her memories intact. She'd kept all their weather-beaten old furniture; perversely, she liked the way the cushions absorbed damp on wet days; the musty smell that permeated the house matched the low tones of the foghorns in the Cape Cod Canal. The kitchen, aside from a dishwasher her mother had installed a year before she'd died and a new electric coffee-maker Holly had bought recently, was pretty much antediluvian.

A 1950s refrigerator was always seemingly on its last legs, making continual rumbling sounds of protest at having to keep working well past its prime; there was a separate, chest-shaped freezer which would have the starring part in any mystery story as the natural place to hide a murdered body, cupboards full of faded, chipped china, a toaster so ancient it was now retro-chic, an old, battered oak table and an oven with four electric hobs on top—two of which no longer functioned.

After they reached the house, Holly went into the kitchen and rummaged through the cupboards for peanut butter and jelly to make a sandwich for Katy's lunch. She thought of Jack Dane's face beside hers on the bus, his breath, the smell of him. And she saw yet again his back as it receded into the distance.

Yes, I'm old-fashioned, Jack Dane. I wonder what I'd be like if things had been different. If we hadn't come here that Thanksgiving weekend, if there hadn't been that boat sale, if Billy hadn't come here then too.

"Mommy—do dogs like clams?"

"I don't know, chickpea. Maybe. But clams might make dogs sick."

"Then we shouldn't give any chowder to Bones. In case. I don't want him to get sick—ever."

Her little face looked so worried, Holly almost wished Henry didn't own a dog, especially a fairly old one. How would Katy cope when Bones died? She knew Katy had picked up on her own overwhelming grief when her parents had died so un-expectedly. She'd been almost two years old at the time, yet children absorbed the atmosphere, and Holly was sure that Katy knew in some unarticulated, profound way that her moth-er's heart had been broken.

And she suspected that Katy's serious nature also stemmed from that week when Holly's world had imploded—when her father had had a heart attack at work and died instantly; when, three days later, her mother had fatally crashed her car into a tree after viewing her husband's body in the funeral home.

Grandparents who had been there all Katy's short life suddenly disappeared forever. The fact that life was precarious and arbitrary must have seeped into her tiny brain. No wonder she was more restrained than most children her age: there had not been a whole lot of joy around Katy when she was a toddler. But Holly and Henry were making up for it as best they could. In the oasis that was Birch Point, they swam and went clamming and built sandcastles and watched the plovers nesting on the dike and identified foreign flags on boats and found shells on the beach and read her stories and gave her all the love they both had.

I can keep her safe. I can cushion any blows. I'll be there with her when Bones dies and I'll never let anything bad happen to her— ever.

"Why does Henry keep saying you have to get out more, Mommy? Does he think you need more air?"

"Probably," Holly laughed. "But I've got plenty of air. I've got all the air I need right here with you."

3

In the past, residents of Shoreham used to refer to Birch Point as "Barrett Point" and joke about its similarity to the Kennedy Compound in Hyannis. During the 1880s, Holly's family on her father's side had colonized a hundred-odd acres on the southern Massachusetts shoreline, buying up all the land and building summer houses on it.

"Not quite the Kennedy Compound," Henry would say. "We never had any presidents, senators or absurdly brutal touch-football games."

Holly had spent her childhood summers on Birch Point with cousins and second cousins, swimming and sailing, in a kind of genetic cocoon. A private, winding, dirt-sand road cut through woods for a mile and a half before reaching the start of the dike; branching off that road were driveways leading to houses of people she was related to, people like her parents who lived in Boston in the winter and came down to Shoreham from June to September.

The dismantling of the Family Compound had been remarkably swift: as soon as one of their cousins broke the unwritten law and sold his house to a "stranger," others felt free to follow. Money was the issue: what had once been an assumed WASP privilege—a summer house—became something to trade in order to sustain a better lifestyle throughout the year. Those who hadn't sold up for financial reasons bridled at losing "their" point, the terrible prospect of meeting people they didn't know on the beach. They sold out and left.

Holly was thirteen when the exodus from Birch Point started; she missed seeing her cousins but was relieved her parents kept their house. Henry and Granny Isabella had given it to them as a wedding present, at the same time buying the house closest to it, at the very end of the point, which had belonged to a female first cousin who had never married. Now both Holly and Henry lived there year round. So one branch of the Barrett family tree remained in Birch Point, carrying on the tradition.

Except Henry Barrett was not traditional, not in the Bostonian sense of the word. He may have gone to Groton and then to Harvard, done a stint in the Marines, been a lawyer, but he wasn't the typical WASP. No typical Bostonian WASP was a Democrat with a flair for racy language who didn't join any of the socially prestigious Harvard clubs, who had himself taken out of the Social Register on principle.

Henry hadn't been a huge part of her life while Holly was a child; he and her grandmother, Isabella, came to her parents' house often, but her grandmother took over all the interactions with Holly while Henry kept a distance. To Holly he was both a glamorous and imposing figure: tall, bald, with perfect posture and a forthright manner. He didn't hold back or change when children were around; he said whatever he wanted to say and there had been times, when she was very young, that she'd been frightened of him.

"Are you going to eat the goddamn peas on your plate, Holly, or are you going to let them rot there?" he'd barked at her once, sending her into a cowering state of anxiety.

But there were other times when a distant cousin might say something silly and he'd give Holly a look as though she and he were the only ones in the room who understood each other. Or Holly's mother would tell Holly it was time to go to bed and he'd say, "She can sleep when she gets old, Julia," which made her feel they had a special link. While Isabella was called Granny Bella, Henry insisted she call him Henry because, as he put it, "Gramps or some such word makes me sound like a baby. And 'Grandfather' makes me sound ancient. So let's leave it at Henry."

As she grew older, she'd watch him at family parties, study him from afar. He could be gruff, but most of the time he was just teasing—and, she began to notice, people actually talked to him. Invariably, he'd be in a corner with one person and the conversation would be serious. She could tell, from the expressions on their faces, that it wasn't social chit-chat or family gossip. Henry, without making it explicit, demanded more than the mundane.

In his kitchen, however, Henry was nothing but explicit: he divided up chores as if he were back in the Marines. By the time Holly and Katy arrived, he'd already assigned tasks for the chowder-making: Holly was detailed to the sink where she peeled potatoes, Katy's job was to separate the bacon slices from the pack and lay them out in wait for Henry to chop up after he'd finished peeling and chopping the onions, then she could take the clams off their shells when they'd finished steaming open—meanwhile, the strict "No Talking During a Red Sox Game" rule was in play. Working away silently, they listened to the radio as the first game of a double header finished and the Sox beat the Minnesota Twins 2–1.

"Good start—but we need to take the second. We need to pound them into the ground in the next game. What do you think, Katy? Do you think we'll sweep this one?"

"Yes. We have to win when we play at Fenway."

Holly, just as she was about to pick up another potato, found herself saying, "Henry? You know that new restaurant in town—Figs—Charlie Thurlow's the manager, isn't he?"

"That's what I've heard. You know I'm not averse to change. But it looks way too fancy-shmancy to me. Yuppie heaven." He wiped his onion-streaming eyes with the sleeve of his plaid cotton shirt. "A fancy-shmancy restaurant, the new goddamned mall, Jesus H. Christ—I never thought I'd see the day that Shoreham had a Starbucks, but believe me, it's coming."

"The mall is going to be gross," Katy pronounced.

"It certainly is. And I hope, Katy, that you are as tasteful when you're a teenager as you are now."

"What do I taste like now?" she asked.

"Like a little nutcase," Henry laughed, then went to open the fridge. "Damn it all, we don't have any light cream. But we can use milk."

"I don't have any cream at home but I can go into town and get it," Holly said quickly.

"Milk would be a healthier option."

"But will milk make it not perfect?" Katy asked.

Henry sighed. "Hard to say."

"It will be better with cream, and light cream won't kill us. I'll go into town. It won't take me long." She put down the paring knife. "Make sure Henry doesn't mess things up while I'm gone, OK, Katy?"

"OK," she nodded. "I know the mall's going to be gross, but I don't know why the mall is going to be gross. Does that matter, Henry?"

"Not at all. I'll be happy to tell you why the mall is going to be gross while your mother is getting the cream. But honestly, sweetie, I'm sure milk will be fine. You don't have to go into town."

"No problem. I'm gone—and I'll be back before the second inning of the next game."

Holly waved, walked out of the kitchen and then sprinted to her house and the car. She didn't even try to pretend to herself that she had no ulterior motive for insisting on the cream and volunteering to get it. The Cumberland Farms was almost next door to Figs and she could park and walk by, glance in the plate-glass window, just check if he was there. She didn't have to go in or speak to him; she could walk by and keep walking. That's all she wanted. A quick look.

Zapping the windows down on her Honda, she turned up the radio and drove down the road, thankful that as yet the Birch Point residents hadn't had it paved over. If Henry was upset about the prospect of a Starbucks, he'd be apoplectic were cement to replace the sand and grass. And so would she. This had always been a magical road: as a child she'd sat on her father's lap, steering, while he controlled the accelerator and brake. It had been a scary wonderful adventure to be in control of the car for that mile and a half: she'd clench her teeth and hunch her shoulders and stare straight ahead, gripping the wheel with intense concentration. Every bend had felt like a massive arc. Now she rushed down it, avoiding potholes and the odd rock. Going too fast. Going to see Jack Dane.

Just as she pulled into the Cumberland Farms car park, a song came on the radio—"New Kid in Town." Holly's mother had loved the Eagles and used to play their Greatest Hits album on the car CD when she picked Holly up from school. They'd sing along together, and her mother once said, "Someday we'll enter a karaoke competition at that Chinese restaurant near Shoreham and your father will not believe how great we are. But they serve alcohol there so we have to wait until you're twenty-one. We'll have a big party there, a big karaoke party. How much fun will that be?"

Julia Barrett wasn't alive when Holly turned twenty-one. There'd been no party, no karaoke; instead Henry and she had shared a bottle of champagne and Holly had brought Katy in to sleep with her that night.

"Hopeless romantics, here we go again . . ."

She had been happily singing along to the lyrics until this line. Until its meaning slammed into her head and ricocheted around her consciousness so hard she felt no brain cell had been left untouched.

Hopeless romantics.

Here we go again.

Here *you* go again. Here you go effectively stalking someone you have a crush on. Here you go again making one encounter mean more than it ever could or did.

Billy Madison had been the new kid in town once upon a time. When his family had moved from New York to Boston, and bought a summer house on Birch Point. When she'd been fourteen and first set eyes on him: a teenage boy on the beach pushing a sailboat into the water, his blond hair whirling in the wind. When she'd then seen him at school in Boston in the autumn and spent all her time trying to find out where he would be and "happen" to be there herself. When she'd finally realized that she could have dropped a bowling ball on his foot and he wouldn't have bothered to ask who that girl was who had maimed him.

It was amazing what you could convince yourself of when you were desperate, Holly knew too well. She'd made herself believe that when Billy asked her to dance that night after Anna had ditched him, he'd actually wanted to dance with her—not that this was his way of getting back at Anna. And that perfunctory screw on the beach? It wasn't revenge sex or "take it when you can get it" sex; it had meant something special. Billy cared. And he would have showed how much he cared for her if his parents hadn't been so controlling and disapproving.

Tell your heart lies enough times and it will fashion them into the truth.

The song ended; Holly pulled up to park, turned the engine

off and remained sitting, an elbow on the car windowsill, her fingers raking her temples.

"The definition of insanity," she'd heard on a random TV talk show not long before, "is doing the same things and expecting different results." A twenty-three-year-old woman walking past the window of the restaurant where a man she'd just met might be was perilously close to a fourteen-year-old girl walking by classrooms trying to catch a glimpse of a boy who was already clearly smitten with her best friend.

Holly left the car, went into Cumberland Farms, bought a small carton of light cream, got back into her car and drove home.

She was a mother now. She might never lie beside a man in bed or find out what it meant to have real, intimate sex, but none of that really mattered. All that mattered was Katy.

As she turned into her driveway, she saw another car parked there, a black Audi. People sometimes drove down the Birch Point Road and parked at Holly's or Henry's in order to get to the dike. They were trespassers on private property and Holly could have called the police and had the car towed as the owners frolicked on the beach, but she never did. Instead she'd write a note informing them politely that this was not allowed, and then make a note of the car license in case they ignored it and came again. If people hiked or bicycled down the mile and a half of private road to the dike, she would never complain, but if she didn't take any action on the cars, on sunny summer days her driveway would end up like a Red Sox parking lot.

She got out of the car, went to the house, opened the screen door, and stepped into the living room.

There was a man standing by the table, his back to her.

Just as she screamed, he turned, holding up his hands in a gesture of surrender.

"Holly—it's OK, it's me. Billy."

Paralyzed by fear and confusion, she stood staring at him. Because it couldn't be Billy. She hadn't seen Billy in over five years. Billy was at Stanford. He was in California. Billy didn't exist, he wasn't supposed to exist, much less be standing in her living room. Some wire had crossed in her psyche: she was imagining his presence because she'd just been thinking of him.

"The front door was open. I came in. Sorry. I should have waited outside."

"Billy?"

"Yes. Billy."

A guy in a J. Crew advertisement. That's what he looked like. Pink polo shirt, chino trousers, Gucci shoes. Billy Madison, the boy she'd desired so much for so long, the one who had changed her life irrevocably, still looked like a fresh-faced blond boy. As if life hadn't touched him, had made no dent on the teenager who had taken that walk with her on a cold Thanksgiving Saturday.

"What are you doing here?"

"I wanted to see you, talk to you."

"Why?" She could hear the fear in her own voice. *Katy. This is about Katy. I don't want him within a thousand miles of Katy.*

"It's obvious, isn't it?" He gestured to the photographs on the table—pictures of Katy. Beautiful pictures of a beautiful daughter he'd never acknowledged.

"I don't understand."

"Do you think we should sit down?"

"No."

"OK."

They stood facing each other, Holly trying to control her shaking body. This couldn't be happening. This was too random. Too absurd. But he was standing and looking around the room in the same way he'd stood and looked around this room when he'd come to ask her out for that walk. With a kind of nonchalance, an expression of vague interest bordering on boredom.

It hadn't been revenge sex, she suddenly understood. It hadn't been "take it when you can get it" sex either. What it had been was "I don't have anything better to do right now" sex.

"You haven't changed anything, have you? The furniture, anything. The place looks exactly the same."

He was here all right. This was Billy Madison, not some specter.

"Everything has changed, Billy. Every single thing."

"Of course. I didn't mean—look, Holly, anything I say is going to sound wrong, I know. I screwed up. I should have contacted you. I should have done a thousand things I didn't do. I know I can't make up for that. But I'd like to see her. That's all. I thought we could talk about it. I'm back now. I'm going to Harvard Law School in September, so I'm back."

"You'd like to see her? Do you even know *her* name?"

"Katy. My parents told me."

"That's great. Your parents told you."

"You see? Everything I say will come out wrong."

Holly walked over to the window. She couldn't look at him any more. Why hadn't she prepared for this? Why had it never occurred to her that he'd come back? How unbelievably stupid could she be?

And why couldn't she see the ocean? Why was she hemmed in by the trees, the stupid trees she should have cut down years ago? It was crazy to live here and not have a clear view to the water. Stupid and crazy and awful.

"She looks stunning in the pictures."

"Don't. Don't keep looking at the pictures. You have no right. You walk into my house without telling me you're coming. You say you're back and you want to see Katy. You must be joking, Billy. You haven't seen Katy, you haven't contacted Katy, you don't know anything about her. You just can't—" her fear was turning to rage "—suddenly show up and think you can see her. I won't let you hurt her."

"I wasn't planning on hurting her, Holly. Why won't you turn around and face me?"

She wasn't used to being angry. She hated confrontations and arguments and normally did anything she could to avoid them. Anna had once said, "Holl, if someone slammed the door on your hand, you'd apologize, wouldn't you? You'd say, 'Oh, I'm so sorry, it's my fault I put my hand there.'" But this wasn't about her: this was about Katy. And when it came to Katy, Holly wasn't Holly any more. She was Katy's mother.

"Why won't—?" She turned. "All right, I'll face you. And I'll ask you exactly what it was you were planning. To come down on the occasional weekend and take her out for ice cream?

Until you get tired of that or caught up in your law school life? It doesn't work like that. Being a parent doesn't work like that. You have no idea."

"Did you tell her I was dead? Is that it?"

"I wish. No, Billy, I didn't tell her you were dead. You know when she first asked me about her father? In the car. On the way to kindergarten. 'Do I have a daddy?' she asked. I wasn't prepared. I almost crashed the car. I had thought I'd tell her when she was older, I kept putting it off. I thought when she started real school, I'd tell her then. But I hadn't thought *what* to tell her. And she was sitting in the back of the car in her child seat, so innocent. So sweet. I couldn't tell her her father had run away and left her. What was I supposed to say? 'Sorry, sweetheart, but your father's just not that into you?' I couldn't. I said the first thing that came to my mind. I said, 'Your daddy is an explorer. He goes around the whole world all the time exploring places that are really far away.'

"How ridiculous is that? Of course she asked me if you were ever coming back and I said I didn't know. For a while she asked me lots of questions about where you explored and what explorers do. And it was too late. I had to stick to the lie. I made up so many lies, I can't even remember half of them. Now she doesn't ask me any more questions because she knows I get upset when she does. So she asks Henry. And Henry has to lie. We both have to lie. To cover up for you, Billy."

The phone rang. Holly didn't move. On the second ring Billy said, "Go ahead—answer it. I'll wait."

"I'm not going to answer it. And I don't want you to wait. I want you to leave—now."

He didn't move. On the third ring the answering machine kicked in. They stood; Billy now staring at the floor, Holly staring directly at him, wanting him to look up and see just how much she meant what she'd said. He couldn't mess up Katy's life. She wouldn't let him.

"Hello, Holly Barrett, this is your traveling companion, Jack Dane. I went off without getting your number. Fortunately for me, you were listed in directory inquiries. Anyway, I have the job, so I'm in your town now—don't start until Monday though, so I was wondering if you'd like to have dinner somewhere with me tomorrow—Sunday—night. I think I should leave where to have dinner up to you as you're the native here. If you'd like to, please call me at 617 495 7783. I should hang up soon or I'll use up all the machine time. If you're otherwise engaged, I apologize for asking. Right. Goodbye."

"Traveling companion?" Billy's eyebrows arched. "Have you been in England?"

Her cellphone rang; Holly reached into her pocket, retrieved it and saw it was Henry. She punched the answer button, spun away from Billy.

"Hi."

"Are you OK, sweetie? You've been a very long time."

"I'll be there in a minute."

"Is something wrong? You sound—"

"I'll be there. One minute." Shutting it off, she stated, "I have to go, Billy. And so do you. Now."

"Listen, please. Please try to understand. I didn't know what I was doing. We went on that walk and it happened, suddenly you were pregnant, and Holl, I really didn't know you. I mean, we were friends. When I was with Anna the three of us would hang out together. And when Anna broke up with me, I turned to you. Yes, I guess I used you. But I never thought for one second of what could happen—that you might get pregnant."

"You should have."

"I know. Obviously. I should have. But I was stupid and I didn't. The next thing I know you're telling me you're pregnant. We'd never even gone out on a date. It wasn't as if we were a couple. And my parents were telling me that I should go ahead and live my life and not get caught up in being a father so young—that your decision to have the baby shouldn't wreck my future—and I listened to them. I'm not saying it's right, but can you try to begin to understand my position? I knew you as my girlfriend's friend and presto—you're my child's mother. I didn't mean to hurt you. Look, I can see how angry you are. I'll go now. I have to go away for two weeks but toward the end of June I'm back here—and I want to talk everything over with you. Try to figure this out."

She had been watching his face as he spoke, how his cavalier attitude had shifted; his eyes nervous, his teeth biting his lower lip. A little like Katy when she'd say, "Please don't turn off the light," at bedtime. And what he'd said wasn't untrue. She wasn't the only one blindsided by her pregnancy. He must have been terrified too.

If only he'd actually talked to her then. Instead of running down corridors to hide every time he saw her in school, like some kid about to be taken to task by the headmaster. If he'd just phoned her once, come over and asked her how she was. Or why she had decided to go ahead and have the baby. The last words she'd ever spoken to him were, "Billy, I'm pregnant." His mouth had gaped, his hands fluttered briefly, he'd said, "Shit," and then he'd climbed into his car, started it up and driven off, leaving her standing in the school parking lot. Alone.

"What do your parents think about you coming to see me?"

He pushed his hair off his forehead with a little flick. At which point Holly heard the "click" of a gear shifting into place in her mind. Every single thing in her life *had* changed. Nothing had in Billy's.

"You didn't tell them, did you?"

"Not exactly."

"What does that mean? They must know you're in the house or they would have rented it out. They've rented it out every summer since—since I had Katy. So what's the deal, Billy? Did you promise them you wouldn't see me?"

"I didn't promise."

"Whatever." She closed her eyes, shook her head, opened them and allowed herself a wry smile. "You know what my father used to call your father? Dumpy—the eighth dwarf. Dumpy being an acronym for Dumb, Unpleasant, Mealymouthed, Patronizing Yuppie."

"This isn't getting us anywhere, Holly. Be logical, though. I'm bound to run into her on the beach or pass you two in the car on the road. It would be better if we worked out together what the best way of me seeing her is."

"It would be best of all if you left now."

He rubbed his hand over his mouth, took a step toward her,

then pivoted and walked away. Out of the room, out of the house. The screen door slamming shut as he left.

When she heard the sound of his car engine starting, she walked into the kitchen, turned the cold tap in the sink on full blast and threw handfuls of water on her face. Her rage had left her shaking and in tears. Always—she always made excuses for people, tried to figure out what the other person's point of view was and why they might have done whatever it was they'd done. There was always a reason to forgive people. But not Billy. She couldn't forgive him. If she hadn't gotten pregnant, if they'd just had that one brief moment on the beach and he'd never talked to her again, she would have found a way to excuse his behavior. But he'd walked away from Katy, from the most beautiful person in the world, a girl who deserved her father's love. There were no excuses for hurting an innocent child.

Yes, Billy, I'll be logical. And responsible. And adult. All the things you've never had to be and I've been for the past five years. Oh, and by the way, thank you so much for your kind words about my parents' deaths. Thank you for being you and not changing one little bit.

"You seem preternaturally calm about this whole situation," Henry remarked.

As soon as Holly had returned to his kitchen, she'd told Katy that Bones looked lonely in his dog bed on the living room floor, knowing Katy would rush off to be with him and she could then tell Henry what had happened.

"I'm not. But I don't want Katy to see me upset. Besides, I don't believe for a second Billy has thought anything through. The idea of seeing Katy is an impulse of his. It will pass."

"You think so?"

"Yes, I do," she answered quickly, but wanting to say, *It's the same for him as having a quick screw on the beach. A whim with no thought for the consequences.* "As soon as he gets back into his life in Boston, reconnects with his old friends, he'll forget about her. Plus, at some point he'll have to tell his parents and they'll go ballistic about not letting this ruin his future, and that will stop him. He's a coward, Henry. I understand his confusion when it happened, but he hid behind his mother and father the whole time. He never spoke to me once, not once after I told him I was pregnant. He's a coward. Cowards don't want little children. And anyway, he still looks about sixteen. He's still a child himself."

"And you're positive you have no feelings for him? Did seeing him bring back any memories?"

"Only bad ones. I know I was crazy about him—crazy being the right word. I know I put way too much on him, or the idea of him. That's not his fault. But he's arrogant. I don't know—" She shrugged. "Let's stop talking about him. Let's finish making this chowder and then play card games and listen to the end of the baseball. Let's get everything back to normal."

They sat out at a table on Henry's porch playing Spit, playing Fish, playing Old Maids, playing Crazy Eights. Henry and Holly would, very occasionally, let Katy win on purpose while at the same time competing wildly with each other. His old transistor radio sat on the window ledge, giving them good news as the Red Sox proceeded to hammer the Twins.

Henry's house was as ramshackle as hers inside, as weather-beaten as hers outside. They were both gray clapboard with peeling paint, both had dusty old attics with crawl spaces. But his porch, unlike hers, was in pristine shape, possibly because this was where he spent so much of his time. When he wasn't clearing dead wood from his land, hunkered down in front of his computer, or off in his boat fishing, he'd invariably be sitting on his porch—reading, or simply staring out over the water, smoking his pipe.

When Holly first heard the expression "walking tall" she thought of Henry. He was straight and upright without being smug or patronizing. On the day her father had died, Henry had spent all night staying up talking to her mother. He'd lost Isabella two years before, to cancer—now he'd lost his son. He knew too much about grief. Until three a.m., Holly had been at the kitchen table with them, but she finally left them to get some sleep, worn out by shock and sadness. The next morning she'd come downstairs, seen them both still sitting there, drinking coffee. When Henry finally got up from the table and headed back to his house, her mother said, "Henry has an inner compass that points true north. Like your father."

Henry wouldn't let anything change, she knew. They were happy in the world they'd created on Birch Point. Henry adored Katy. Billy couldn't touch them, not when Henry was there. Billy would go away and leave them the way they were and everything would go back to normal. Like it was now.

"Time for our perfect chowder," he announced after Katy won a game of Concentration.

"I'll go get it and bring it into the dining room." Holly rose, made her way to the kitchen past a myriad of old photos of her ancestors. Each time she walked by them, she'd stare into their unsmiling faces, wondering what their lives had been like, whether the stress of daily life had been the same for them or whether the age they'd lived in had been less complicated, easier.

After the first spoonful, Henry pronounced the chowder was, indeed, "perfect" and shook Katy's left hand with his. She beamed, her smile so contagious, Holly and Henry grinned with her.

"You know, I used to play Ping-Pong on this table with your grandmother," he said. "I must still have the net somewhere. I should teach you how to play, Katy."

"Here we go again." Holly shook her head. "Your pet projects. Get me out of the house more and get Katy playing more games."

"She's a child. Children like to play games. You're an adult. Adults like to get out. It's normal for a great-grandfather and grandfather to give sage advice."

"As if you were a normal grandfather." Holly gave him a smile. "Or a normal great-grandfather, for that matter."

"Are you saying I'm abnormal?"

"No, just different."

"Well, shit, I certainly hope so."

"Henry."

Katy yawned volubly and Henry said, "Quite right, young

lady. Your mother's attitude to the infinite variety in the English language is very boring."

"It's time for her bed." Holly stood up. "See you for coffee tomorrow."

"Same time, same place." Henry was about to light up his pipe. Holly took Katy's hand and pulled her up from her chair.

"Come on, chicken. I know you love the smell, but no passive pipe-smoking for you. Go say goodnight to Bones and I'll be right with you."

"Henry," she said after Katy had left the room. "Do you think you could have Katy to stay again tomorrow night? The thing is, I might have kind of a date and I'm not sure when I'll be back—it would be easier for her if you could keep her with you."

"Kind of a date?" Holly could hear the pleasure in his voice. "You've been holding out on me."

"I haven't. I met someone on the bus and we may be going out to dinner, that's all. He's new to Shoreham. It's nothing serious."

"Kind-of-a-date dates are never serious, are they?"

"Stop teasing."

"I was only kind of teasing."

"Goodnight, Henry."

"Goodnight, sweetie. And you know we'll deal with whatever Billy throws at us, don't you? I won't let him hurt you—or Katy."

"I know." She went and kissed his cheek. "That's exactly what I was just thinking. I love you, Henry."

"Ditto, sweetie."

Katy was quiet for the minute it took them to walk back to their house. After they went inside and Holly had changed her daughter into pajamas, Katy asked, "Why are Bones's eyes always so sad-looking?"

"I don't think they're sad, Katy. I think he's a little old and maybe he's thinking about his life and remembering when he used to run around more, like when he was a puppy."

"But that's sad. That he can't run around so much any more."

"But he has you, chicken. You make him happy."

"I hope so."

"I'm sure so. Now, which story would you like me to read to you?"

"I think I want to go to sleep now."

"OK."

"Can you leave the light on?"

"You know I can. I always do."

"Love you, Mommy."

"Love you too. Sleep well."

"Can we get clams again tomorrow? And make chowder again?"

"We'll see. Henry might want to teach you how to play Ping-Pong."

"That's good." Katy turned over on her stomach, her arms stretched over her head. "I like Ping-Pong. I think."

Holly pulled up the covers and kissed her on the head.

When she'd found out she was pregnant, she'd looked at the line on the stick she'd peed on and felt a rush of pure fear travel through her. What was she going to do? How was she going to tell her parents? What would people at school think? What would Billy think? Billy, who, for the past six weeks, had been acting as if that walk on the beach had never happened. Curling up in bed, she began to weep, burying her face in the pillow.

Anna thought Holly had gone ahead and had Katy because Holly believed in some romantic dream—that Billy would accept the baby and they'd live happily ever after. Anna was wrong, though. She kept Katy because in the middle of her crying fit she'd suddenly seen her. Pictures of a girl came running across her brain, one after another: a little baby dressed in pink asleep in a cot, a toddler running on the beach, a scared little first-grader on her first day at school. The images were so vivid, so real, Holly knew this child already existed as a person, waiting to be born, that there was no way she could ever not have her.

Holly looked at Katy now, as she lay in bed. She resembled uncannily those images she'd had that afternoon. Bending over, she whispered, "Thank you," in her sleeping ear. "Thanks for coming to me early and showing me how unbelievably special you are."

The memory of Jack Dane whispering to her in the bus came back and Holly straightened, left Katy's room and went downstairs into the living room, to the answering machine. She listened to his message again and took down the number he'd left. Looking down on the pad of paper, she hesitated before taking the phone from its cradle. What was the point of having dinner with him? Was he calling her because he didn't know anyone else in town?

Care factor? He's asked you out, Holl. He's Faintworthy and he's asked you out. Go for it, she heard Anna's voice. *What's the worst that could happen?*

Holly picked up the receiver and dialed. On the third ring Jack Dane answered with, "Hello."

"Hi. It's Holly Barrett."

"Hello, Holly Barrett. Thank you for calling me back."

"You're welcome."

"So—are you going to tell me to get lost or are you going to go out to dinner with me tomorrow night?"

"I'm going to go out to dinner with you tomorrow night. There's a place called the Lobster Pot on the road to Buzzards Bay. The seafood is great."

"Excellent—should I meet you there, then? At eight?"

"Can you get there on your own?"

"I hope so. I have to get to know my way around. This will be good practice."

"OK."

"Does this place have exotic cocktails?"

"It has cheap wine and beer. Do you mind?"

"Not one bit. I'm looking forward to it. It will be, like, really, like cool."

Holly laughed.

"So goodnight, Holly Barrett. I'm glad I have the chance to see you again."

"Goodnight, Jack Dane. And I'm glad too." She hung up the phone, but kept looking at it, smiling, remembering a line from a Fred Astaire movie her parents used to love: *Chance is the fool's name for fate.*

4

The Lobster Pot was anything but a fancy-schmancy restaurant. Midway between Shoreham and Buzzards Bay, it was squeezed in between an abandoned cranberry factory and a Waterslide Park on a road that had once been the only way to get over the Bourne Bridge to Hyannis and beyond. In Holly's youth, this road had been full of knick-knack shops, cheap motels, a mini golf course, and a variety of restaurants with names like Mamma Mia's Pizza and Surf 'n' Turf Delight. Amazingly enough, it still was full of them: Holly couldn't work out how these little businesses could survive now that a highway bypassed them, avoiding all the traffic lights and stores and delivering all those potential customers straight onto the bridge.

The planned mega-mall that Henry so loathed was half an hour's drive away. Gap, Starbucks and their ilk were waiting to descend, but at least they wouldn't be wiping out the Windmill Mini Golf Course or the old faded, falling-apart yellow house next to it, the one with a cardboard sign saying "Nancy's Fortune Telling" in the window. Only recently, Holly had told Henry she'd always wanted to have her fortune read at Nancy's but was too afraid. "I'm scared of it for some reason, I don't know why."

"Possibly because it *is* scary," Henry said. "I've been told Nancy has a wart on her face the size of a cauliflower. I've also heard that if you're a man and fold a twenty-dollar bill the right way, you'll get a lot more than your fortune told."

How old was Nancy now? Holly wondered. And would she be visiting the new mall, checking out Victoria's Secret, maybe?

She pulled into the Lobster Pot parking lot, took a brush out of her bag and tried to tease her curly, dark, shoulder-length hair into some form of cohesion. Rain had arrived in the morning after a mass of clouds had moved in overnight. It hadn't stayed long, but had left behind a misty, wet air—the kind that made hair go wild. When Anna was visiting in weather like this, she'd spend most of her time with a ceramic hair tongs, ironing her long hair back into its perfectly straight shape.

Holly had put on a little lipstick and a little eyeliner, a white blouse Anna had once said really flattered her and a nice pair of black jeans. There was no point in dressing up too much for the Lobster Pot, which was part of the reason she'd chosen it. This was the first "date" she'd ever been on. She tried not to think of the novelty of it and decided it wasn't really a date, anyway. Just two people having dinner together.

No big deal, Holly. Stop worrying, just get out of the car and try to act like a normal person who isn't scared out of her mind at the prospect of spending a few hours with a man. Go. Open the door and walk to the restaurant. Now.

Five past eight. Would he be there or would she have to wait?

"Hey."

She heard the voice and felt a hand on her shoulder simultaneously.

"Hey." She turned. Yet again his good looks hit her, so hard she stepped back a pace. "Did you just get here? I didn't see you in the parking lot."

"I should tell you I smoke the occasional cigarette. Very occasional, I promise. I was smoking over there at that picnic table when you drove in." As he pointed, she thought of how she had brushed her hair in the car. At least she hadn't put on any make-up using the rear-view mirror.

"I'm sorry if smoking bothers you."

"It's not a problem. My grandfather smokes pipes."

"The one who shakes hands with his left hand because it's closer to the heart?"

"Good memory." She smiled and he opened the restaurant door for her, waving his hand in a signal for her to go in first.

The Lobster Pot was like a large shack, harshly lit, with long wooden tables and a few booths. Soft rock music played loudly, nets and lobster pots hung on the walls, people wearing shorts and flip-flops drank beer from plastic cups. Another reason Holly had picked it: there was no way Jack would think she was expecting a romantic evening. The food was delicious, but the atmosphere was only a few steps up from McDonald's.

"Wow—great place. Puts Figs to shame, but promise you won't tell anyone I said that."

"I'm calling Charlie Thurlow tomorrow."

"You wouldn't do that, would you?"

Flirt, you idiot. At least try to flirt.

"Of course not."

OK, don't flirt. But at least try to relax.

"Look, there's a table free." She led him to a fortuitously empty booth in the middle of the room and they sat down across from each other.

"OK—this is how it works. Over there, in the back on your left, is where you order lobsters and steamed clams if you want them—see where they have all those Lobster Pot T-shirts hanging up? Over the tank full of live lobsters? Right behind the tank, there's a counter."

"I see." He pointed to a counter at the other end of the room. "But people are queuing up at that counter too—why?"

"That's for other types of food like scallops, haddock, fried clams, coleslaw and stuff. If you want wine or beer, you get it in the back room with the lobsters. Soft drinks are at the scallop and other stuff counter."

"Very complicated; I'm not sure I could work here."

A voice on a microphone said, "Number 128, your order is ready," and a large woman in pink polyester pants with a "Wild Women Are Necessary" T-shirt rose from the neighboring table, made her way to the counter and collected a red plastic tray heaped with food.

"If you want a lobster, they can take it out of the shell for you. They call it a Lazy Man's lobster—no work. Otherwise you have to crack it open yourself."

"I don't want to be typecast as a Lazy Man straight off the bat here." He put his elbow on the table, his chin on his hand, and narrowed his eyes. "So I'll go the Alpha Male route and get a lobster and crack it open myself. How about you?"

"I'll do the same. They drown the Lazy Man lobster with so much butter it's hard to walk to the car afterward."

"Right, then." He stood up, took off the blue windbreaker he was wearing and placed it on the tabletop. "This will save our place. Let's go foodwards."

They ordered two boiled lobsters and two glasses of white wine. When he said what he wanted, the young girl behind the counter couldn't take her eyes off him to write it down.

"Jeez. Are you English or something?" she asked.

"No. I just pretend to be."

"You sure sound English."

"Thank you. It's taken years of practice."

She stared for another thirty seconds then managed to put pen to pad. When she then handed over the bill, Holly opened her bag.

"No—this is on me," he said. "No arguments."

After picking up their numbered ticket and their glasses of wine, they headed back to their table. Jack stopped at the tank with the lobsters in it and peered in.

"You have to wonder when they know," he said.

"Know what? That they're about to be taken out of the tank to be eaten?"

"No. I mean before. When they're in the sea. How long before they know the bait they've just headed for has trapped them?"

"Somehow I don't think they have brains."

"Somehow I think you're right."

"Which makes it fine to eat them."

"Completely fine," he nodded.

She was back on track with him now, finding it easy to talk again. How did he manage to put her at ease? She didn't know; what she did know, though, was that other women always looked at him. When he passed by, females inevitably stared. She could see with peripheral vision that many even turned their heads to keep looking at him. Yet he didn't respond at all. In fact, he didn't even seem to notice. Because he was so used to it or because he didn't see it happening or because he didn't care?

They settled back down in the booth. Jack was wearing a pale blue shirt with the sleeves rolled up above his elbows. This was all beginning to seem so normal, so relaxed, Holly felt giddy.

"So, how was the interview? Good, I guess, seeing as how you got the job."

"Great, actually. It's a nice restaurant. I start tomorrow so I have to get a move on. I've rented a little flat—apartment—just by the boatyard, so it's an easy walk."

"Pretty much anything is an easy walk in Shoreham."

"I've noticed. You described it perfectly on the bus: a street like a street in old movies. It looks like it hasn't changed much in decades."

"It's changing now, though. More people are moving here year round; they're figuring out that the commute to Boston isn't that bad except in the summer and that it's a good place for families. Pretty soon there'll be a lot more than that one street. And there'll be more upmarket places like Figs to cater for everyone. Plus there's a new mall going up just half an hour away down Route 495."

"That's a shame."

"My grandfather would agree."

"And you?"

Holly recognized her chance and took it.

"I'm not hopelessly old-fashioned."

"That's a shame too."

"Why?"

"I'm not a big fan of modern, that's all."

"Why not?"

"Because it's out of control. You should see the young people in Britain now. They go binge drinking as often as possible, make as much noise as possible, get sick on the pavement, get into fights and end up in hospital. And that's supposed to be fun." He shook his head. "No one has any self-control, but that's fine because they're all modern and that's the way of the modern world. I don't understand it."

"Number 157, your order is ready."

"That's us."

They both got up and went back to collect their food.

So I misunderstood that comment on the bus. It was a compliment, not derogatory. I was so worried about it and I didn't need to be. He actually likes old-fashioned. But how old-fashioned is it to be a single mother with a five-year-old? What will he think when I tell him about Katy? Why haven't I told him yet? Because I'm waiting for the right time. It will come. I just want him to get to know me as Holly before he knows me as a mother.

When they sat back down, their trays were laden with red lobsters, plastic cups of butter, forks, knives, water to dip their hands in and implements to crack the lobsters open.

"A feast." Jack picked up his glass of wine. "Here's to brainless lobsters and a perfect choice of restaurant."

Holly clicked her plastic glass against his.

"I'm glad you like it." She took a sip, watched as he began to work on pulling his lobster apart. "Do you miss England?"

"Sometimes." He was looking befuddled as he picked up the shears, put them down, picked up a claw and tried to wrench it off with his hands.

"You must miss your family—hold on—you're doing it the hard way—let me show you."

She took the lobster, used the shears to cut it down the middle of the tail, pulled the chunky white meat out. "This is the best part, in my opinion. I'll show you how to do the claws later."

"Guess I'm not a real Alpha Male." Cutting off a piece, he dipped it in the butter and ate it. "Mmmmm, delicious. Thank you."

"You're welcome." She did the same with her own lobster and had a huge, buttery mouthful. "Are your parents upset that you moved over here?"

"My parents are dead."

She was wiping the butter off her mouth with a napkin when he said it.

"I'm so sorry. Oh, God." She put the napkin down, her stomach turning. "That's terrible. I'm so sorry, Jack."

"They died in a car crash when I was eighteen. It's a conversation stopper, I know." He pulled off one of the little side legs, stared at it. "I've never worked out whether you eat these things or not. What's the idea? Are you supposed to suck them?"

"My parents both died too—when I was twenty."

He looked up at her then, held her brown eyes with his blue ones, his gaze so compassionate she felt they were trading worlds of unspoken emotion.

"I'm sorry too," he said softly.

"Thanks. You must miss them horribly."

"There's something you should learn about Englishmen, Holly Barrett. We don't talk if talking involves any emotion. We change the subject or we make a joke or we order another drink."

"Really?"

"Absolutely. But we can talk about books or movies or sports. Who's your team in the Premier League?"

"What?"

"A bad joke. OK, what's your favorite movie?"

"*Notorious*—it's an old Hitchcock movie with Cary Grant and Ingrid Bergman."

"I know it. Great choice. Mine's *A Beautiful Mind*. Have you seen it?"

"No, I always wanted to, though."

"Russell Crowe's brilliant. He was once on an Australian soap that has a kind of cult following in England—called *Neighbors*. Anyway, what about books? I know it's an obvious topic of conversation, but films and books are a shortcut to getting to know someone, aren't they?"

Bryan Adams was belting out "Summer of '69" in the background, numbers kept being shouted out, but Holly and Jack managed to have an intense conversation about books and movies. She was surprised by how much he'd read, embarrassed that she hadn't heard of some of the authors he mentioned.

"Did you major in English at college?"

"Didn't go to college—university. I had to work. But listen, you know what I'd like to do?" He was leaning back against the booth. One hand was resting on the top edge of the seat. "Do you know somewhere we could take a walk by the water? I'd really like to get out by the sea. Oh, I'm sorry—that's rude—I haven't asked you if you'd like dessert."

"No, I don't want dessert, thanks. And yes, I know a place we could walk by the water. There's a beach right next to my house."

"Excellent. Can you drive me? I caught a lift here."

"Absolutely—we can go together in my car. I've only had one glass of wine, so I'm fine to drive."

"We've already paid so we can go now, can't we? That's one of the advantages of a place like this—you don't have to wait around for some recalcitrant waiter like me to bring you the bill."

"Recalcitrant?" Holly slid across the booth and got out. "I guess with all the reading you do, it's natural to use a word like recalcitrant."

"I'm just trying to impress you." He grabbed her hand and held it as they walked out.

"Hang on a second, will you?" he asked just as they reached her car. "I've forgotten something. I'll be right back."

Holly watched as he jogged back into the Lobster Pot, wondering what he could have forgotten, then turned her gaze to the sky. There were no stars visible, but she kept looking up anyway.

Six months after her parents' deaths, she'd seen an ad in the local paper for grief counseling. There was a weekly meeting of a group of bereaved people in a room in the Town Hall. "It might help" was the tag line on the announcement. The tentative "might" made Holly trust whoever had written it, so she showed up at six o'clock the next Wednesday.

She couldn't remember now most of what the twenty or so people had said. They were all distraught, though some were more accepting than others. Not one of them had lost two loved ones within days, and though Holly knew it wasn't a competition, she felt set apart from the others. She listened without taking much in, never spoke herself and decided halfway through she wouldn't return. Yet something one man said did make an impact. He was in his forties, she guessed, wearing a suit and tie, as if he'd come straight from work in a bank. His twin brother had died from a heroin overdose two years before.

"I know this is going to sound really bizarre," he'd stated. "But I have this theory. People we love who die can give us presents. What I mean is, they can make something good happen or not happen or send the right person into our lives at the right time or keep out the wrong ones. They're allowed to give us three gifts from wherever it is they are." He looked embarrassed then and squirmed in his chair. "It's just my personal theory. Be aware of it—that's all I have to say."

Where'd he come up with that? she'd wondered. And why three exactly? "Bizarre" was the right word.

Or was it?

Have you sent me Jack? Smart, funny, handsome, compassionate Jack? she asked the sky. *Is he your present?*

Jack came out of the restaurant, holding something. When he was a few feet away he said, "Catch," and tossed it to her. It was a Lobster Pot T-shirt and when she looked up to thank him, she saw he was wearing one over his shirt.

"I almost bought us the pink ones with the garish lobster smoking a cigar plastered all over the front, but then I calmed down and decided the more restrained plain blue one with the discreet logo was better."

"Thank you, and good choice. The cigar-smoking one is a little scary."

Opening the car door for her, he asked, "Where exactly are we going?"

"To Birch Point—it's where I live. I have a flashlight in the glove compartment. When we get there, we can go down the path to the beach and walk there."

"Sounds perfect." He closed the door, went to the other side and got in.

On the way, he asked her about Shoreham and she told him all she could think of, including the story of Nancy the palm reader and her alleged interest in folding bills. As they were crossing the railroad track, she said, "Lift up your feet, Jack."

"Excuse me?"

"We're going over a railroad track. It's bad luck if you don't take your feet off the floor."

Dutifully, he lifted his feet as they crossed the track.

"And you do this too? While you're driving?"

"Yes, it's a family tradition. I've done it forever."

Katy would always say, "Mommy, quick, pick up your feet," with such urgency Holly sometimes laughed and sometimes frowned. She could tell Jack about Katy now. Or she could wait until they got to the beach.

"Isn't it dangerous? Driving with no feet?"

"It would be more dangerous if I didn't. Bad luck."

"Right. Of course. I see. Bad luck. I'm not even going to ask what happens if the car stalls while it's *on* the tracks, when the ability to use feet might be crucial."

"That hasn't happened yet," she smiled over at him. "But if it did, I might jettison the tradition."

"Jettison. I guess with all the reading you do, it's natural to use a word like jettison."

"I'm just trying to impress you," she said, thinking, *If this is flirting, maybe I can do it after all.* "In a few seconds we're going to pass the graveyard. You have to hold your breath while we do—when we've cleared it, you can make a wish."

"No bad luck *and* a wish. Any more traditions? Do we get out and crawl around the car when we pass the third lamp-post on the left so we can have certain good luck and another wish?"

"There, look, the graveyard's coming up. Take a deep breath."

"Whatever you say."

They inhaled together. After they'd passed the last grave, they exhaled together.

"Whew. I should stop smoking."

"The cement road stops ahead here, see. And the road to Birch Point begins. That big white building on the left is a Catholic retreat, right at the beginning of the Point. We're lucky it's there; if it weren't I think there'd be a huge development of condos."

"And that 'No Trespassing' sign? I assume that means the road is private."

"Yes."

"Look at all these trees. It's a little paradise here. God—was that a deer I just saw bounding across the road up there?"

Holly had seen it and was thankful that it hadn't leaped out in front of the car in the dark. It was so easy to run into one at night and she dreaded the thought of badly hurting an animal, a Bambi, bounding through the woods. Henry had given her a small handgun and taught her how to use it in case she ever ran over one and had to put it out of its misery. The prospect of actually having to use it terrified her; having it in the house, even though she'd hidden it on the top shelf of her bedroom cupboard, was scary enough. She wasn't about to tell Jack about it: he'd think she was another crazy, gun-toting American.

"There are tons of deer around here. We have to be careful because they have ticks, and ticks carry Lyme Disease. We have to check constantly to make sure we don't have a bite with a little red ring around it: that's one of the signs. It's a dangerous disease to get."

"But how can you possibly get it?"

"It's easy, you can get it walking through—"

"No, I mean you're all lucked up after the railroad track and you can make a wish that you don't get it every time you drive by the cemetery. I don't see how you could possibly catch a disease."

"Do you ever stop teasing people?"

"I'm English, remember. We don't talk much and when we do, we tease. And look, there's yet another 'No Trespassing,

Private Property' sign. That's the third I've seen in the space of a hundred yards. It has to make you wonder. At what point do they think it will sink in? I mean, if someone isn't deterred by the first sign, why would they be by a second? Or a third? Is repetition the key to control?"

"I suppose it is a little overzealous."

She drove by a wooden sign posted on a tree with the name "Madison" on it. If she'd turned right then and gone on a few hundred yards, she'd be at Billy's house. For the past five years, she hadn't had to think about him as she drove up and down the road. The house was empty in the winter, rented out in the summer. Billy was right, though. They were bound to pass each other in their cars or see each other on the beach. She'd have to work out how to deal with him soon. But not yet.

Jack Dane was silent as they drove the next half-mile to the house. When they pulled up into her driveway, he let out a small whistle. "I like those gables."

"They make for a great attic. Although there's nothing up in the attic at the moment except for a couple of old beds. Come on, let's go to the beach." Holly grabbed the flashlight from the glove compartment, got out of the car, turned the beam on. "This way."

Jack, hands in the pockets of his windbreaker, followed her.

"So you inherited your house when your parents died?"

"Yes. We used to live in Boston in the winter and come here in the summer. After they died, I moved here year round. OK—we're going to the left down this little path to the beach. Be careful—there's poison ivy around."

"Oh, great."

As she shone the light, he lifted his feet up in exaggerated steps.

The stench of low tide mingled with the mist, making it even more powerful a smell, but Holly liked it. It was so clearly a smell of the sea; and on a warm night like this, with the buoys rocking in the canal making gentle ringing sounds, there was a melancholy romanticism in the air, making her think of whaling ships and old schooners plying their trades. Jack was leaning down, untying his shoes; she did the same, following him too when he rolled up his trousers. He strolled to the water, waded in up to his knees.

"There's a massive amount of seaweed here."

"Yes." Holly walked in and stood beside him. "At low tide it's really seaweedy on the Back Beach. That's what we call this beach, the one that fronts the canal. The other one, on the bay side of this dike here, is the Front Beach." She explained about the dike coming into existence when the canal was built, then said, "You can swim in low tide over on the Front Beach. It's pretty disgusting here."

Retreating from the water, they began to walk along the shoreline, toward the lighthouse.

"Why did you come to America?" she asked.

"A new beginning. A new life. I needed to get away."

"It's the opposite for me; I needed to stay. I wanted to surround myself with memories and the familiar. I knew I couldn't pretend it hadn't happened, but I wanted to have my parents around me, so to speak."

"There's a point at which you have to . . ." he paused. "Jettison the past. Otherwise it never lets you go. I think—hang on . . ." He had stumbled and grabbed her arm for balance. "Sorry, I didn't see that piece of wood. Not a very smooth move."

She heard the soft slap of a small series of waves hitting the beach, a subtle undertow from a passing ship. *Even noise was quiet on nights like this*, she thought. *The crickets didn't chirp as shrilly, the hum of boat motors took on a lower tone. Everything was dampened down by the moisture and darkness.*

"Someone once told me that you can't move forward if you're looking over your shoulder at the past. It sounds trite, I know." Jack took her hand in his. "But trite works sometimes."

"But the past can't help but affect you. At least, I can't really escape it. I don't answer the phone any more. When my father had his heart attack, I was the one who answered the phone when the hospital called. And then when my mother had her accident, I answered the phone when the police called. Now I let the answering machine take a message—always. I'll answer my cellphone, but never the phone at home. Never again. I guess I think if I don't, nothing bad will happen." Holly closed her eyes for a second; when she opened them, she said, "I've never told anyone that."

"You're full of superstitions, aren't you, Holly Barrett? Come on." He stopped walking. "Let's race."

"What?"

"I challenge you—let's race."

"To where?"

"I'll count to twenty as I'm running; whoever is ahead when I say 'twenty' wins."

"But you might trip again. And I'm holding the flashlight."

"If I trip, I lose. And think of the flashlight as a baton. Come on. One . . ."

Jack Dane took off, Holly shouted, "Cheat," then took off after him, the beam of the flashlight jiggling up and down as she ran.

"Twenty!"

He was yards ahead of her, had turned to face her, with a huge smile on his face.

"Jack . . ." she panted, when she reached him. "That was completely, totally unfair."

"Yes, it was. But I win."

Putting his hands on her shoulders, he leaned down and kissed her. It was an easy, slow, kind kiss. A thoughtful kiss. Holly's initial surprise at the fact he was kissing her gave way to a different type of surprise—surprise that a kiss could be so warm and go on for so long.

The last, the only, time she'd been kissed, the kiss had stopped quickly and the undressing had begun. This time, when Jack drew away from her, he stayed away. His hands went back into his pockets.

"Sorry," he said. "Couldn't resist tricking you into that."

"I don't mind." Holly smiled at him. "Honestly."

Take that shit-eating grin off your face, Holl. Anna had popped up in her brain again. *Play it at least a little cool, will you?*

I would if I could, Anna. But I can't.

"I'll challenge *you* this time." She tossed the flashlight at him. "One . . ."

Jack reached out to grab her before she could run.

"No way," he said, dropping the flashlight on the sand. "I'm not going to take the chance. You might beat me." He kissed her again, his hands moving from either side of her face, to her shoulders, to her waist.

Holly understood then. What it was like to be held and touched. What it was like to feel real desire.

And then he broke away from her, stepped back, out of their embrace.

"Uh-oh. Referee. Time out."

"What?" Her heart felt as if it had been slapped.

He put his hands up in the air.

"Time out. That's all. We're getting ahead of ourselves."

"I don't understand."

"Holly." He put his hands back on her face. "Come on—let's go back to your house and chill out and I'll have a cup of coffee before I go home."

"Right. OK." She wished she could shake her body the way a dog shakes itself when it gets out of the water, to try to rid herself of the feelings she was having, go back to where she had at least a modicum of control.

She picked up the flashlight and they turned around, headed back to their shoes and the path. Side by side but not touching.

Holly stared at the flashing red lights on the towers of the railroad bridge in Buzzards Bay. An ingenious edifice, its middle section, which ran between the towers, had a track on it; when a train needed to cross the canal the section was lowered. In its normal, upright position, it looked like a huge steel goalpost.

Time out, he'd said. *Referee*. As if this were a game. He must have had so many girlfriends. English girls with perfect complexions and perfect bodies. Outgoing and self-confident girls who knew exactly how to kiss and how to flirt and how to tease him back. Girls with names like Emma and Sophie who rode horses and played tennis.

"So . . ." She felt the weight of his hand on her shoulder. "Holly Barrett. What should we do next time we see each other? I was thinking bowling. Or maybe mini golf. I think we should take a pass on Nancy the fortune teller, don't you?"

Pleasure and relief coursed through her just as the blush had on the bus.

"That might be wise."

The rising tide had almost claimed their shoes. Holly slipped hers on, felt the sand crunching into her feet. Normally she wouldn't have noticed, but Jack Dane had thrown a physical switch on in her: her mouth, her shoulders, every place he'd touched her felt alert, wholly present. Waiting for more contact. She had begun this walk thinking they were going to talk and get to know each other more. She was ending it in a state of hypersensitivity, as if she'd taken a drug which had woken up all her nerve endings.

"I'd opt for mini golf," Jack said. He seemed to be in control, but then he always seemed to be in control; even when he was kissing her. "Bowling might be a little hectic. There's a lot of noise in bowling alleys."

"You're not a big fan of noise, are you?"

"No. No, I'm not."

"Sorry about the Lobster Pot. It's very noisy in there."

"Hey—don't knock the Lobster Pot." Unzipping his windbreaker, he pointed to his T-shirt. "I'm fiercely loyal to my brand. Uh-oh, I see we're coming to poison-ivy territory."

Again, he picked up his feet and tiptoed with ridiculously huge steps.

When they reached her house, Holly opened the screen door, flicked the living room light switch on. "I'll go make you some coffee. Sit down anywhere, I'll be right back."

Flicking another light on in the kitchen, she got the coffee out of the cupboard, poured the water in the coffee maker, stretched up to get the filters from the shelf above the sink. She hadn't made coffee here for anyone but herself and sometimes Anna since her parents had died. Every morning at nine o'clock, she and Katy would go to Henry's for coffee on his porch. Katy would get a mug like theirs, but hers would be full of apple juice.

Katy.

I haven't—

"Holly." Jack Dane was in the kitchen doorway. "Listen, don't bother with the coffee. I have to go. Can you drive me back into town?"

"You have to go right away?"

"Yes."

"The coffee won't take long."

His arms were crossed over his chest. He looked so distant she found herself stepping forward, trying to close a gap. He took a step back.

"You have a daughter, don't you?"

"Yes, Katy. I—"

"I saw the photographs. Where is she?"

"At Henry's—my grandfather's. Next door. I was going to tell you. In fact, I was just thinking how strange it was I hadn't told you yet. I was just about to. I'm a single mother . . ." She was aware her words were speeding up, her voice was sounding nervous. "She's five years old. And she's so sweet, Jack."

"I'm sure she is."

"Is this . . . I mean, does Katy . . . Do you still want to go to the mini golf?" Every word of that sentence was feeble, lame, desperate, she knew.

"I don't think so." He shook his head. "No. I'm really sorry, Holly, but I can't."

"Because of Katy?"

"It doesn't work for me. I'm sorry."

"But why not?"

"There's no big reason. Just that a child complicates things."

"But we could get to know each other and you could get to know Katy."

"And what if it didn't work out? That would be harder on everyone. It's better if I leave now. Really."

"Are you angry I didn't tell you about her right away? On the bus?"

"What makes you think I'm angry? I'm not." He rubbed his temples. "I should leave."

There was nothing she could think of to say in response. He turned, left the kitchen and she followed, into the living room, out of the house. When they got into her car, she grabbed the keys from under her seat and started the engine.

"This is really sad, Jack."

"I know." He nodded. "I just didn't figure you'd have a child. You must have been really young when you had her."

"Eighteen."

"And her father?"

"He left town."

"I'm sorry."

"It's not your fault." She switched on the headlights, backed the car up.

They drove in silence, down the Birch Point Road, past the Catholic retreat, past the cemetery where she turned left to go into Shoreham. The already strained atmosphere in the car became even more palpably awkward as they passed the cemetery. Neither inhaled.

"I'm in that building right beside the boatyard," he said when they entered the town.

"I know, you told me."

"I was lucky to get ahold of a flat so quickly. I'm going into Boston tomorrow morning to pick up the rest of my things. I start working tomorrow night." His tone was distantly pleasant.

"Well . . ." She pulled up beside the building, turned to him. "I hope you enjoy the job, Jack. And I know you're right for being honest with me. Katy's the most important person in my life. If you can't try to get to know her, there's no point in trying to get to know me."

"I really am sorry, you know."

"It's OK." She made herself smile. "You've apologized enough, really. No problem. As my grandfather often says, 'Worse happens at sea.'"

"Was he a sailor?"

"No. He just likes the saying."

"Right. Well, goodbye, Holly Barrett. I'm sor—OK,

enough apologies. I suppose I shouldn't say, 'Let's be friends,' should I?"

She shook her head.

He kissed her on the cheek, opened his door and left.

Holly drove off without looking back. Five minutes down the road toward home, she pulled over, put the car into park, reached down, took off her shoes, opened the door and shook them over the pavement.

Stay away from the damn beach, you idiot. Never take a walk with a man there ever ever again. The first time you get pregnant within seconds, the second time you get dumped within minutes.

She had to get the sand out of them. Every last grain of it. Before she pounded the steering wheel with her fists and cried.

5

"When's Mommy coming?"

Henry checked his watch. "In ten minutes. Just after I beat you."

"I don't think so." Katy lifted a black checkers piece, jumped it over his red one, and grinned as she took it off the board.

"Early days, young lady. Plenty of time for me to make a comeback."

"Where did she go last night?"

"She told you. Out with a friend."

"What friend?"

"A friend she met on the bus."

"Did she have a sleepover at the friend's house?"

"I don't think so, Katy."

"Then why did I stay here last night?"

"Because she thought she might be out late."

He moved a piece, sat back in the dining-room chair. Being cross-examined by a five-year-old wasn't easy, even with his legal training. But Henry was pleased that there was finally a subject, aside from her supposed "Explorer" father, about which Katy was asking difficult questions. How he had let Holly convince him that he had to go along with the ridiculous Explorer story she'd made up, he'd never understand. But at least now he wasn't trying to think of yet more faraway countries the Explorer had gone off to explore; this time he was trying to explain Holly's absence without saying the word "date" and having to then define to Katy exactly what "date" meant.

With age came wisdom, or so people said. But Henry knew better. With age came other people's inability to understand that age didn't change your mind, only your body and face. He didn't have to plumb the foggy depths of memory to recall what it was like going out on a first date: he knew exactly how nervy and exciting and awkward and promising it could be. And he hoped with every ounce of his heart that Holly's date had been a success.

Studying Katy's face as she puzzled over which move to make next, he was struck by how much older than five she appeared. She looked, when she was concentrating like this, as if she had the weight of the world on her little bony shoulders. She looked like her mother: an old soul in a youthful guise.

All that crap about loving yourself being the crucial element of every person's psychological happiness was bullshit, Henry knew. Holly was doing fine, certainly. But she'd be a different woman if she found a man to love who loved her. Human beings needed appreciation and acknowledgment from other human beings. They needed romantic words and wonderful sex and the whole nine yards of a proper relationship. Maybe some self-loving individuals could live blissfully in caves, but he had yet to meet one.

And if Holly were less stressed, Katy would be too.

"I'm going to get the ping-pong net out today and set the table up. You'd like to play, wouldn't you?"

"Is it hard?"

"It takes practice, that's all."

"Henry . . ." Katy took the piece he'd just moved. "You messed up again. You're not paying attention enough."

"You're right. I'm being foolish." He lifted his cap off his head, placed it on backward. "This is the new me. You won't be able to take another of my pieces now."

"You look silly," Katy giggled.

"I am *not* silly." He made a silly face, pleased beyond measure as her giggling increased. It was his job, he knew. His responsibility to bring silliness and games and fun into her life. "All right. Enough funny business. Now, let me see. Where shall my next move be?"

He alternated between making moves which would help her and ones which were neutral, knowing she was quick enough to work out if he was losing to her on purpose. Trying to let her win without being too obvious about it required a certain skill and was a game in itself.

"Ah, I see your mother coming across the lawn. She's a few minutes early. I'd better go put the coffee on."

"What about our game?"

"We'll finish it after coffee. Don't worry. Leave it right here on the table."

He put his cap back on straight, went to the kitchen, switched on the kettle and got Katy's apple juice out of the fridge. This was their morning ritual—coffee and apple juice—when he and Holly and Katy gathered to start the day. Before he'd heard about Holly's "sort of date," he'd planned to broach the subject of her getting a job. She didn't need the money, she had inherited a more than sizeable amount when John and Julia had died. But she needed something to do, a place to go where she could meet people her own age. Katy would be starting first grade in September. It was time that Holly thought about starting a different first grade, the first steps back into the real world. She would balk at the suggestion, would say Katy needed her to be a full-time mother; she'd come up with all sorts of reasons for staying hidden in Birch Point. But he would persist and coax her into at least thinking about it. Because that was his job too: to help Holly emerge from her hibernation and re-enter her own life. And he had to move her toward it as carefully as he had to pretend to play checkers.

Introducing the topic of a job had been his plan for this Monday morning; now that Holly had taken a different step, one on her own with this man on the bus, he would postpone the conversation. A little at a time—that was his game plan. Holly had been through so much in such a short space of time, she needed patience.

"Almost ready," he said when he heard her footsteps; then looked up from the cafetière to where she was standing at the threshold of the kitchen. "Sweetie, are you all right?"

"I'm fine, Henry."

But she wasn't, he could tell. Her face was anxious, her eyes tired. She looked defeated, as if someone had set her a task she couldn't perform. He could sense straight away that whatever was wrong was not anything he could tease her out of. And that he'd have to approach her obliquely, not head on.

"Katy and I are having a game of checkers. She's beginning to really get the hang of it."

"Good," Holly nodded. "That's good. I'll take the coffee out to the porch."

"Thanks." He poured out two mugs' worth, put milk in them both and handed them over to her. "I'll bring Katy's apple juice."

Careful, he told himself. *Tread carefully, Henry.*

The weather was veering wildly. After the rain of the day before, it was sunny again; sunny and hot. John had died on a day like this. In his office, working at his desk. He'd keeled over and died at the age of fifty-three. Henry had wanted to call God, to tell him he'd taken the wrong Barrett. *Take me, take me, take me*, he kept saying over and over; but no one listened. Then Julia died three days later. The natural order had gone haywire; he'd had to bury his son and daughter-in-law together. On another hot, sunny day.

The three sat out on the porch as they always did, whatever the weather. Holly cradled her mug in both hands, taking sips, avoiding his eyes. Katy was telling her mother about the checkers game, how silly Henry had been putting his cap on wrong and making funny faces. Holly, who usually concentrated intensely on whatever Katy was saying, was nodding and saying, "Mmm-hmm," with a preoccupied voice and look.

It was physically paining him, this sadness of hers. And baffling him as well. He'd had to admit to himself years ago that he had never been the kind of parent he was now. He had loved

John with all his heart, but Isabella had been closer to their son; she'd been such a natural mother, he'd taken a back seat. Now he was both mother and father, entirely hands-on, trying with all his might to give both Holly and Katy all that they could ever need or wish for. But he couldn't fix a date which had obviously gone wrong. He could only hope she'd tell him about it.

"Here, Katy." He rose from the wooden rocking chair, went to the side of the porch, retrieved an old tennis ball. "Why don't you play a little catch with Bones on the lawn?"

As old as Bones ever became, he'd always be able to chase a tennis ball. Katy jumped up, took the ball Henry handed her and called Bones down the porch steps to the lawn. Taking his seat again, Henry waited. At first Holly continued to avoid his gaze, watching Katy toss the ball to Bones, but after a few minutes, she turned to him.

"It's hard," she said. Stopping himself from saying, "What's hard?" he willed her to continue.

"We had a nice time. But I hadn't told him about Katy." She frowned. "It was stupid, I know. I should have. When he found out, he was nice, but he wasn't interested any more. I don't blame him. It's the way things are, that's all."

"And who is he?" Henry asked, softly.

"His name is Jack Dane. He's a waiter at Figs. He's English. His parents died too—in a car crash when he was eighteen. He was so easy to talk to. But I understand. It's hard, that's all."

Henry nodded.

"I think it's always going to be this way. I mean, it's too much for someone, a five-year-old. I'm a package. No one who doesn't have children . . . but then someone who does have children, that would be hard too. He'd love his child or children and I love Katy and how can that possibly work out?"

"I think you'll find it does, sweetie. Lots of people merge families. And lots of men wouldn't mind having a package, as you call it."

"I don't think so, Henry. Men are like Billy, you know. Men my age, anyway. They like their freedom."

"Yes, but at some point, when they fall in love, men understand their freedom is just that: their love, their families."

Holly shook her head.

"That's a sweet thing to say, Henry. But it's not really . . . I don't know. I only know that Jack can't deal with the fact of Katy. And I'm . . ." Henry could hear the tears in her voice. "I'm not, I don't know how to . . . I'm not exactly a catch."

"You're the best catch in planets full of seas, Holly."

"Yeah, right. You're slightly prejudiced on that one." She smiled thinly. "But it doesn't matter, not really. The only thing that matters is Katy. Anyway, I have to concentrate on this whole Billy situation." She straightened in her chair. "That's what's important. Making sure he doesn't hurt Katy in any way."

"Right."

He wanted to tell her not to let this one incident stop her from trying again; he wanted to tell her she had to stop hiding away, that the world wasn't as bad and scary a place as she had experienced it to be. He wanted to dispense advice that would make her listen and believe in herself. And yet he knew, if he pushed her too hard, she'd only withdraw further. Her one and only experience with men to date had ended in a teenage pregnancy. Her parents had died unexpectedly and she'd been left with a small child to bring up. What Holly hadn't done was to go crazy and run away from her responsibilities. She hadn't gone off on drug binges or been in any way, shape or form a delinquent mother. Retreating to Birch Point was not, given the circumstances, a wrong choice to have made. He only wished she could see that there were other options open to her, that her life, at such a young age, was not buried in these woods.

"Maybe you could talk to Billy, Henry. He might listen to you."

"I doubt that, sweetie, but I'll certainly try if you want me to."

"Let me think about it." She looked over at Katy again, who had rolled the tennis ball in front of Bones. Then her gaze turned outward, over to the canal. "You know, I think you would have liked Jack. He's funny. And he teases, like you do."

"I'm not a huge fan of his at the moment."

"Don't blame him, Henry. He was honest. Which is a good thing." She stood up. "We should get going. Coffee time is over."

"Katy wants to finish our game of checkers. Let her stay; I'll bring her over when we're through."

"OK. I wouldn't mind taking a quick swim to clear my head. See you later."

"See you." He watched her as she walked over to Katy, gave her a hug, then headed home. A young girl in blue jeans and a baggy white T-shirt, with a slightly pigeon-toed, hunched-shoulders walk. A young girl who always hid a face that was far prettier than she thought it was behind a mass of curly dark hair. A young girl who was self-conscious, sympathetic and shy. Above all, a young girl with a huge, generous heart. Any man, if he got to know her—any good man—would be lucky as hell to have her as his partner.

"Come on, bumblebee, time to finish our game." He waited for Katy to come up the porch steps, put his hand on her shoulder. "And be prepared for defeat."

Henry wasn't sure exactly when the plan popped into his head; some time during the afternoon. He'd let Katy win the checkers, taken her back to Holly's, spent time answering emails on his computer, gone for a swim, come back, reheated the clam chowder, picked up the chainsaw and headed for the trees by the path down to the Front Beach where some dead wood needed clearing. And sometime in the middle of sawing, he'd thought of it.

It was a slightly crazy idea, he acknowledged that. On the other hand, he didn't think it could hurt.

"There's no harm in it," he repeated to himself as he showered. "I'm not meddling."

Yet as he put on a suit for the first time in months, he had a twinge of guilt. This had to be the first time he'd kept any kind of secret from Holly. And he was aware that he'd have to lie to her if she came by or called for any reason. So he made a pact with himself: if she did call or come by, he wouldn't go ahead with this scheme. He could keep something from Holly, but he couldn't lie outright to her.

Figs was definitely not his type of restaurant. The older he became, the more he yearned for simplicity in all things. As he found a parking space a few feet away, he thought about the bait shop which had once been where Figs now was. It had been as basic as a shop could be; designed for fishermen who knew what they wanted and who didn't want to have to spend much time getting it. The owner had been taciturn, abrupt and extremely adept at finding whatever was needed quickly, ringing it up quickly and avoiding any small talk. *What had happened to him*, Henry wondered? *Had he been pleased to sell out or did he feel forced to?* Adjusting his polka-dot bow-tie, Henry got out of the car and took a quick look around before going into Figs. No sign of Holly, but then he knew there wouldn't be: her car had been parked outside her house when he drove by. *I would have made a lousy spy, if I was as nervous as this*, he said to himself. And then he opened the restaurant door.

There were only two occupied tables in the room, which had been fashioned to look like someone's living room. Plush curtains at the window, sofa-like banquettes with plump cushions against the wall, two standing lamps on either side of a fireplace. All very quiet and chichi and ridiculous. An attempt at European sophistication in the heart of small-town America. There were times when teenagers came up with perfect expressions. Henry wanted to say, "Whatever," and leave; instead he smiled at the maître d' who was standing at a little podium, looking oh so serious.

"I reserved a table for one," he said.

The floppy-haired man stared at a piece of paper in front of him, nodded.

"Yes, I see here—a table for one at nine o'clock. Let me take you to it."

Henry followed him for the three steps it took to reach a table on the right side of the room, with a place setting for one on a starched white linen tablecloth.

"Thank you," he said as he sat down.

"You are very welcome."

"I'm sure I am."

"Excuse me?"

"Nothing, I'm going deaf. Don't pay any attention to me."

The maître d' strutted back to his podium, returning with a large menu.

"Here. Your waiter will let you know the specials this evening. Meanwhile would you like a drink?"

"A glass of tap water would be fine, thank you."

Ordering tap water was greeted with the kind of disdain that ordering French fries and a Big Mac might be. Henry shrugged, picked up the huge menu, meanwhile scanning the room. A fifty-something couple sat at an intimate corner table in the back; the only other table taken was at the front, by the window: three thirty-something women, all with lots of make-up and revealing blouses, were talking and laughing loudly. The door to the kitchen opened and Henry turned to see a man carrying two plates enter. He placed them in front of the fifty-something couple and Henry heard him say, "I hope you enjoy your dinner," in an English accent. The sound of laughter from the table of women increased in pitch; Henry looked over to see them all staring at this waiter who was obviously Jack

Dane. Holly hadn't said how handsome he was. The type of good looks Henry normally associated with old movie stars. Gary Cooper, Gregory Peck. Classically male.

Shit, he thought. *She didn't stand a chance.*

He had gone back into the kitchen only to emerge seconds later with a glass of water. Placing it in front of Henry, he said, "Is there anything I can help you with on the menu?"

"The whole fucking thing," replied Henry. "In fact, why don't you choose for me? I want something simple and I'm having problems finding it."

"Do you like fish?"

"I do. If it's not smothered in some God-awful sauce."

"OK." Jack Dane smiled. "What if I ask the chef to broil a nice piece of bluefish and hold the God-awful sauce?"

"Sounds good to me."

"Would you like a first course?"

"Not particularly."

"Vegetables with your fish?"

"Yes, please. And I'll leave that choice up to you too."

"Fine—some broccoli, maybe?"

"Sounds fine to me."

"Wine with your meal?"

"A glass of dry white would be nice."

"Done." Jack Dane took the menu. "I'll get this out of your way."

"I'll hazard a guess that you're not from the area."

"You'd be right."

"But I won't ask you if you know the Queen or if you've ever met a friend of mine who lives in England."

"Now that's a huge relief." He smiled again. "You wouldn't believe how many people ask me exactly those questions."

"Oh, I think I might."

Jack Dane hesitated, as if he would like to continue the conversation, but he left Henry's table, going back into the kitchen. *Easy to talk to,* Holly had said. She was right; he had an engaging manner, was quick and had somehow managed not to let those looks of his make him arrogant. Not your average waiter in a small-town restaurant; but he was still young and he was foreign. And, as Holly had informed him, Jack Dane had lost both his parents at a young age too. The likelihood was that he was traveling the world to find himself, or maybe to shake off some of his grief. He watched as Jack came back, cleared the main courses from the table of the three young women. They were all giggling and rolling their eyes at each other, but he was merely polite, never betraying either pleasure or displeasure at their antics.

Henry bided his time. He'd brought a *New York Times* crossword puzzle with him and concentrated on that as he waited for his meal. When Jack served it to him, he thanked him, put away the puzzle, and ate slowly, taking the occasional sip of wine. The middle-aged couple left; the three women finished their desserts and left too, not without sniggering and making comments about coming back soon for the "really cute food."

His scheme was falling into place very neatly. Soon he was left with only the maître d' and Jack for company. As Jack cleared his cup of coffee away, Henry said, "You've done very well with a cantankerous old man tonight."

"Hardly cantankerous."

"It's not easy dealing with the public though, is it?"

"Some days are better than others."

"A tactful response. Is this a new job for you?"

"No. I was a waiter in Boston. But this is my first day working here."

"And what brought you to Shoreham?"

"The ocean. I wanted to live close to the water. Plus I like small towns."

"Do you know anyone here?"

A small hesitation.

"Not really, no."

"Well, that's very brave of you. Coming to a place like this without friends or family."

"I don't really see it that way. I like living alone."

"My name's Henry." He watched for any sign of recognition, but from the complete lack of response, he guessed that Holly had not told him her grandfather's first name. "I've lived in Shoreham for a long time. It's a good place. I think you'll like it here."

"And I'm Jack Dane." He held out his right hand; as Henry was going to offer his left, as he always did, he switched to the right, just in case she had told Jack about this habit of his. He'd come this far; there was no point screwing it up now.

They exchanged a firm handshake, and a second later the maître d' called out, "Jack. I need to speak to you. Right away." Jack raised his eyebrows and hopped to, quickly crossing the floor to the front desk.

The two had a huddled conversation. When he returned, Jack asked, "Would you like your bill now?"

"So what did Floppy Hair Faux French say? That you shouldn't fraternize with customers or that I might be some old goat trying to—what is it they say now? Hit on you?"

Jack just shrugged.

"If it's the latter, I should inform you that I am not of that ilk. I have no designs on you, believe me. I'm just an old man who likes the occasional conversation."

"I know. He didn't say anything about you. It was about my hours tomorrow night."

"I'm not sure I believe you, but yes, I'd like my bill."

When Jack then brought it to him, Henry pulled out his wallet, and took out cash to pay.

"Right, then. I'd like to invite you to take a fishing trip with me tomorrow morning. Early. And I mean early. Six-thirty. I have a boat at the dock here. Do you like to fish?"

"I never have. But I'd like to, yes. Very much."

"Good." He handed the money, including a tip, to Jack. "And I'll see you tomorrow morning—you know where the dock is?"

"Yes, I live right beside it."

"See you at six-thirty."

As he left, Henry gave Floppy Hair a pat on the shoulder.

"Nice place," he said. "But the bait shop was superior. The real air of France. Croissants stuffed with live minnows. Delicious."

6

Henry liked the fact that Jack was waiting for him when he drove into the dock's parking lot. He'd never understood people who couldn't be punctual; making others wait for you was rude, however you might try to excuse yourself. But Jack was standing there as if he'd been there for some time, wearing khaki trousers, a blue sweater and a windbreaker. He liked the way the boy dressed, too. Not showy, no flashy watch or designer labels.

"Hello there," he said as he got out of the car, reaching back in to grab the fishing rods. "Thank you for being on time."

"No problem." Jack walked toward him. "Can I help with those?"

"Punctual and polite, too. I won't be able to complain about the younger generation any more if you keep this up." Handing one of the rods to Jack, he opened the trunk and retrieved the tackle box.

"My boat is down there on the left. It's not big, but it works just fine."

They walked together to one of the jetties where the boats were docked, past huge fat motor boats with names like *Gone Fishin'* and *Piece o' Peace*.

"Here we are. No frills. No cabin. But enough horsepower to get us where we need to go."

The tide was high, so the boat was easy to board.

"At low tide, it's a pain to climb down for an old man like me," Henry said. "Of course, the best time to fish is when the tide's just turning. I think we may be in luck." Putting the tackle box on the jetty, he stepped on board with the one rod. "Hand me the box and the other rod, will you?"

Jack complied and Henry placed both rods in the stern, the tackle box a few feet away.

"Hop in."

Jack boarded the *Sea Ox*.

"You know, I've never been in a boat."

"First time for everything. I'll give you a lesson now on how to start this up."

Taking the key from his pocket, Henry put it in the ignition, pushed a button which lowered the motor into the water.

"See, this is in neutral now. But I have to give it some throttle to start it. Like this." Jack peered over his shoulder as Henry turned the key, revved the throttle, put it back in neutral. "Now we have to cast off. Can you untie those ropes at the bow and stern?"

When Jack had done just that, Henry put the boat in reverse.

"Now keep us away from those posts as we back out."

Again, Jack obeyed, helping to guide the boat backward and free of its berth.

"You're a natural," Henry said. "Hard to believe this is your first time on a boat."

Jack smiled, went and stood beside Henry as he pushed the gear into forward and headed out to the channel, keeping to the left of the red buoys and the right of the green ones.

"We have to go slowly to begin with. There's a speed limit to keep the wake down."

They passed by yachts moored in the harbor, making their way out of the Shoreham River toward the open sea. Each time he took the boat out, Henry felt his spirit lift. The salt air, the water beneath him, the prospect of casting loose, always reminded him of his childhood, the thrill and pride of a boy going to sea with his father. And when John was old enough, Henry had taken him fishing, carrying on a tradition of what would now be called father and son "male bonding." Back then it was just called fishing together.

"Here." Henry stepped aside. "You take the wheel and steer. We're out of the river now." He pushed the throttle gently forward, upping the speed. "Head straight."

A reddish sun was rising fast as the boat sped toward it. Henry didn't wear sunglasses on principle, though he could never have explained exactly what that principle was. Jack grabbed the wheel with both hands, concentrating intensely while Henry watched him, ready to take over if he had problems handling the boat.

"Keep a lookout for the lobster pots," he warned. "It can be hard to see them in the waves." A light wind had kicked up, creating a few whitecaps, but nothing serious. The boat swerved slightly as Jack veered around a lobster pot, doing so gracefully enough to make Henry confident of his steering ability. He was free now to switch his gaze to the horizon, scanning the skies.

"What are you looking for?"

"The fish chase the bait up to the surface of the water, the seagulls then dive down to catch that bait. So the bait is in a nasty sandwich, attacked by the fish underneath, the gulls up above. I'm looking for seagulls. Where the gulls are, the fish will be."

"It looks like there are some birds over there." Jack pointed ahead to the left. "See?"

"I think so. Wait." Henry shaded his eyes. "Goddamn it. You're right. There's a whole mass of them. I'll take over now. Hold on."

Stepping back behind the wheel, Henry pushed the throttle hard and the boat raced into action, speeding across the water toward the gulls, throwing spray back at them as it surged ahead. Jack was holding on to the top of the windshield as they bounced over the waves.

Henry didn't understand the pleasure so many men had driving fast cars. What was the point if you weren't outside, in the elements, with the wind ripping through you? When he was charging toward a pod of fish, he was entirely caught up in the pursuit; at the same time, he felt healthy, young, and free. Jack, he could sense, was enjoying this too; right along with him in the chase.

As they came closer to the gulls, Henry slowed down, pointed to the churning water underneath the birds.

"See them jumping? Those are blues. Bluefish. They're great fighters."

Unusually, there were no other boats in sight. They had the spectacle to themselves. Maneuvering the boat so they were up-wind of the circle of gulls, he then cut off the engine, not wanting the fish to be frightened off by the noise.

"God, look at them jump." Jack was fixated on the fish leaping into the air and landing with thwacks on the water. "Look at them. They're going mental."

"Now comes the hard part." Henry went to the stern, picked up the rods. "I'm going to give you the quickest ever lesson in casting." He handed one to Jack. "Watch me." He unhooked the silver lure from the rod. "First you reel this in so it's a few inches from the top of the rod. OK?"

Jack nodded, copying Henry's movements.

"Now . . . Think of the rod as a stick. Think of the lure as an apple at the end of the stick. You're holding the line with your finger—like this."

"OK."

"The trick is to throw the line as far as you can in the direction of the fish. But you have to let go of the line and release the lure at the top of your cast, as if you were throwing the apple off—watch." Henry executed a perfect cast into the roiling waters. "And now you reel it in—like this . . ."

When the bouncing little silver minnow lure was within six feet of the boat, there was a sudden splash in the water beside it.

"A strike," Henry exclaimed. "That was a strike—when the fish goes for the lure but misses it." He reeled the lure back up to within a few inches of the top of his rod. "Now you try. Go to the stern there where you have some room and practice.

Don't worry if it takes a while to get the knack of it. It'll come in time."

He was throwing Jack in the deep end, he knew. But in his experience this was often the best way to teach a beginner. Within seconds of his next cast, he'd caught one, his rod bending over double in a huge arc with the weight of the fish.

"Gotcha," he said. Jack looked over as he began to reel it in. "You have to give them some line, let them tire themselves out. This one's a real fighter." Turning the reel handle furiously, he made sure to keep the tip of the rod out of the water. "Shit!" The line had snapped. "Lost the bastard. I have to put on a new line. You keep casting. They're still here, they're still jumping."

He went over to the tackle box, careful not to get in Jack's way. The boy was struggling, he could see. Five times his casts ended with a plop a few feet away from the boat. Jack didn't say a word, brought the line back in, planted his feet farther apart as the boat rocked with the waves. He fixed the lure, took the line with his index finger, drew the rod back over his right shoulder.

"An apple off a stick," he said, and hurled it again.

This time the lure traveled farther, and Henry said, "Much, much better."

On his next try, Jack threw the lure so it landed right smack in the middle of the jumping fish.

"Excellent!" Henry grinned. "Now reel it in. Quickly. The fish have to think it's a minnow and minnows travel fast."

"Henry—look!" Jack had caught one. His rod was arcing over.

"Keep the rod up. Reel it in, then let some line go. Fantastic! Hold on. You're doing great." Henry put the rod he was working on down, went to stand beside Jack. "Take your time. Play him."

"It's so heavy."

"That's the boy. You're doing fine. You're a pro. Your seventh cast? Genius. It looks like it's going to be a big one."

"It feels big." Jack was panting. "It feels huge."

"Let the line out some more. OK. Now reel it in again. I'll get the net. Careful. Take it easy."

"Easy? This is a whale."

For ten minutes, the fish fought, swimming as hard as it could.

"It's tiring now. Bring it in. Slowly. Take it slow. Get it as close to the side of the boat as you can. Right." Henry leaned over the side of the boat, net in hand.

"OK. Reel in some more." He could see it surfacing, struggling mightily. With one quick swoop he reached out, put the net underneath it and scooped it up into the air and into the boat in the same motion.

The fish flapped wildly in the boat, jerking in spasms against the deck, a hook hanging out of its mouth.

"It *is* big. Looks like at least a three-pounder, maybe more. It's definitely a keeper."

"A keeper?"

"We unhook and throw back any that are too small."

The fish jumped, spun and hit the deck again, its gulls puffing out and in wildly.

"Shit!" Jack stepped back, staring at it. "Excuse my French."

"Don't worry. I swear all the time, in every language."

"So what happens now?"

"We have to whack it on the head. Kill it. I've got the club here." He reached over, pulled a large wooden club from the tackle box.

"You have to. I can't. I can't kill it." Jack shrank back.

"All right. But you know we're going to eat this, it's not just for sport. I never kill any more than I can eat." Henry raised the club; Jack turned away. After he'd bashed it hard on the head twice, the fish lay still. "I know. It's not pretty." He unhooked the lure from the fish's mouth, getting some blood on his sleeves. "But it has to be done."

"I suppose so."

"It was a nice clean catch, though. Sometimes they get foulhooked—through the eye sometimes. That's when I feel most sorry for the bastards. And I throw back any small ones."

"Right."

"Has this put you off fishing for good?" Henry asked, straightening up.

"No, no. I don't want to kill them but I do want to eat them, so if you're with me to do the dirty work, I'm fine."

"Good." He patted Jack on the back, with true affection. He'd been a good companion, a quick learner who didn't talk too much, who did what he was told, who didn't get in the way. For a beginner, Jack had done surprisingly well. He would have made a good Marine.

"They've disappeared." Jack had turned back to look at the water where the pod had been. "They've gone. No seagulls, no nothing."

"They do that." Henry checked the horizon for any other gulls, any other pool of swirling fish. There was no sign of even a single bird. "Sometimes they move on and you can see where they've gone, follow them. And sometimes they just vanish. Like magic."

"Wow. That was amazing. Really amazing." Jack laughed. "I never thought I'd be doing this. Catching a fish."

"Your first fish. It's always a big moment."

"It's kind of crazy how exciting it is. Out in the middle of nowhere, with all this space. It's so beautiful. I used to dream about this, this whole . . ." He swung his arm in the air. "OK, I'll shut up now."

"No, it's nice to have someone be so excited. Makes me remember catching my first fish when I was eight years old. Centuries ago."

"Yeah, right. Centuries."

"Almost. Anyway, the fish appear to have gone but I'll fix my rod and then we can both cast for a while; you never know, there might be some loiterers. And you can practice more."

They stayed where they were, casting, as the sun rose further. Jack was diligent, working hard at throwing and reeling, concentrating on improving his technique.

Most young men these days were more impatient, Henry thought. Casting with not much hope of catching a fish wasn't exactly thrilling, but Jack reminded him again of his time in the Marines: you followed orders and never complained. Perhaps he hadn't been fed a diet of video games growing up in England. He wasn't addicted to instant gratification; nor did he babble on just to hear himself talk.

Thank Christ he doesn't find it necessary to "share."

After almost forty minutes of solid casting, Henry reeled his lure in and hooked it onto his rod.

"I suggest we call it a morning now and head over to my house. I can anchor the boat on the beach and you can come up and I'll give you some breakfast and show you how to clean your catch. What do you say?"

"Sounds great. I have to admit, after all that casting and reeling, I'm feeling hungry."

"Let's go, then." Henry laid his rod in the stern, started up the motor, took off toward the dike.

This, of course, was the part of his plan that might fail. Holly might have told Jack about the dike, and if he recognized where he was going, he might protest. But as they cruised along in the sun, Jack didn't make any comment. He stood straight, occasionally looking back to the deck of the boat to see his fish, but otherwise gazing out toward the islands and the open sea. When he reached the bay and the Front Beach, Henry slowed down, timing his landing so he had enough speed to turn off the engine, raise it, and still get to shore. Jack hopped off the bow and held on to the boat, while Henry lifted the anchor, passing it over to him.

"Take this a few yards up and bury it. The tide is going out so we don't want to anchor it too far up the beach or we'll have problems getting it back into the water later."

"OK." Jack set off with the anchor while Henry gathered the rods and the tackle box, handing them to him when he came back to the boat. He lifted the fish from the deck and jumped onto the beach, grateful that he was still agile enough to make the leap.

"Here. I'll take the rods and the box—you take the fish. You put your finger inside the gill and out its mouth like this." He showed him. "It feels a little slimy at first; you'll get used to it."

"I feel like a hunter-gatherer, back from the wild."

"You look like one, too."

"I wish I could bring it into Figs, make it the special of the day."

"Catch a few more and you can some day." Henry led the way, up the path from the Front Beach to his house.

"Wow. What a view," Jack exclaimed when they reached the lawn. "Amazing. And the house, too. Do all the houses around here look alike?"

"Some." Henry led him to the side of the porch where he had set up a fish-cleaning table. Picking up a hose beside it, he washed down the fish, then took out a knife from the tackle box.

"You scale it first—like this," he said. "And then you slit it open and take the guts out."

Jack turned away again.

"I suppose this isn't pretty either."

Jack's sensitivity when it came to killing and cleaning the fish slightly surprised Henry; he hadn't struck him as someone who would have a queasy disposition. After finishing the job as quickly as possible, he washed off the fish fillets, hosed down the table as well. "Now we can have breakfast. I'll put these fillets in some aluminum foil and into the fridge."

"I like these posts," Jack commented as they climbed the porch steps. The porch was held up by old, whitewashed pieces of trees, with branches coming off them. "They look ancient."

"They are. It's an old house. But I would guess what's old to Americans is not old to you English."

Jack smiled. "We do go back a while."

"I can't find fault with him" had been one of Henry's mother's expressions. As if she were always looking for a fault to find. Which she may well have been: she had a highly honed critical side. But when she couldn't find any fault, she gave overwhelming approval, taking that person into her heart with an abundance of zeal.

Henry couldn't find any fault with Jack. Except his inability to accept Katy. Which was a major, huge fault. But a fault that might just be rectified.

"I'll make us some fried eggs and bacon," he said as he opened the front screen door. "Meet my dog, Bones."

The Lab rose from the living room rug and padded over to them.

"Hello, Bones," Jack said. "Nice to meet you." He reached down to pat him, but Bones turned around and headed back to the living room.

"That's not very polite of you." Henry gave Bones a disapproving look.

"I'm invading his territory. He's allowed to be suspicious. You know, I always wanted a dog when I was very young. My parents didn't want one, though."

"That's a shame."

"It was." Jack was behind Henry, following him into the kitchen. "They said I wouldn't walk it and they'd end up having to, but they were wrong. I would have."

"Well, Bones doesn't walk as much as he used to. He used to

be able to walk for miles. Old age." Henry grunted. "I know it's better than the alternative, but sometimes it's shit. A real pain in the ass. And the knees. And every single joint. Sit down. I'll get us our breakfast."

"Can I help?"

"No. Thank you. I'm a pro at after-fishing breakfasts."

Taking a seat at the kitchen table, Jack was silent as Henry prepared the eggs and bacon and some toast.

"Did you live in the country in England?" he asked as he took the orange juice out of the fridge and poured two glasses.

"No."

The abruptness of the answer made Henry decide not to ask any more questions. His parents had died tragically; not wanting to talk about the past was understandable. The eggs and bacon were cooked; Henry served them to Jack, took the toast from the toaster and put it on a plate in the center of the table. While they ate, Jack asked him questions about fishing: how he knew which lures were best, what other types of fish he caught, whether he ever fished on rivers. In the middle of a story about fishing for salmon once in Alaska, Henry snuck a look at his watch.

"Enough about my youthful exploits," he announced. "Let's take our coffee out on the porch in the sun."

Within minutes of sitting down outside, Henry saw Holly and Katy appear at the end of his drive. Holly shaded her eyes as she approached, peering at them; Katy broke into a run, then stopped at the foot of the steps. Jack half-rose from his chair, sat back down as Henry said, "Good morning, girls. Come join me and my fellow fisherman. Katy, come up and shake hands with Jack. Jack, this is my great-granddaughter Katy and my granddaughter Holly."

This time Jack stood up and stayed standing, staring at Holly.

"Hello," he said.

Holly, who had approached and was beside Katy, said, "Jack. What are you . . ." she looked up at Henry. "Henry?"

"I met this young man last night at Figs and we've just been fishing. He caught his first fish today. A very nice-sized blue. Katy—come shake hands."

She mounted the steps slowly, her eyes on Jack.

"Hello," she said, holding out her hand. Jack leaned down and shook it.

"Hello—again. Katy."

"Are you the Explorer?"

"Katy!" Holly ran up the steps, put her hands on Katy's shoulders. "What's going on?" She looked wildly from Henry to Jack, a blush rising so fast it engulfed her face in a second.

"No, I'm afraid I'm not an explorer, Katy." Jack kept her hand in his. "But it's nice to meet you. And it's nice to see your mother—again." He put out his hand to Holly. "Remember me? The bloke on the bus who can't crack a lobster open properly?"

Holly stood, speechless, still grasping Katy's shoulders.

"I didn't have anything to do with this, honestly . . . I had no idea . . ."

"Henry says we should shake hands with the left hand," Katy said. "Because it's closer to the heart. I forget sometimes."

"Ah, yes," Jack smiled, raised his eyebrows. "I remember

someone telling me that. I forgot too. Let's start again." He put his left hand out, shook Katy's, then offered it to Holly. "Should we start again too?"

Henry watched as Holly put her left hand out and shook Jack's, seeing how shyly she acknowledged his touch. She was her age, suddenly, had transformed into a twenty-three-year-old woman right here in front of his eyes. *By George, I did it!* He wanted to shout and do a little jig on the porch. Because he knew enough about men to know Jack was not going to run away this time. Not the way he was looking at her now. Jack, this time, was a keeper.

"I'll go get your coffees," he said. "You stay here and let Jack tell you about catching his first fish."

"Can I sit beside Jack?" Katy asked.

"If it's OK with him," Holly responded.

"Here." Jack pulled the smaller chair up beside his. "Please do me the honor, Katy," he said, in an endearingly serious tone. Henry could feel Holly's pleasure, her maternal pride almost tangible in the air as Katy smiled at Jack and sat down.

It could be, he thought as he went back to the kitchen. *It could work. A nice young man. Who was uneasy at the idea of a child, certainly, but when faced with the reality, with the sweet, lovely Katy, changed his mind. Even if it doesn't last forever, isn't this progress? A man who is not only attractive but also a good man, a thoughtful, polite one, one who understands, too, what Holly has been through. Not that smug coward Billy who knows fuck all.*

I could start a dating service. I could be an old Cupid, arranging love matches. A whole alternative career. Why didn't I think of it before?

True pleasure, those moments when all was right with the world, had, since Isabella and John and Julia had died, almost entirely vanished from his life. He could get snippets of it playing with Katy, or sometimes when he and Holly and Katy were sitting chatting on the porch on a beautiful day. But then the sad weight of what was missing crept into the joy, making him reflect on how much happier they all would have been if everyone who should have been there was. When he went back out onto the porch with Holly's coffee and Katy's apple juice, he didn't feel that lack, only delight in what he had wrought.

Katy was telling Jack about their clam-digging and chowder-making: every single detail of it. Jack was listening intently, occasionally interjecting a question. He got it right, too. Unlike many adult questions where children were concerned, Jack's didn't try to bring the subject back to an adult theme and they weren't patronizing. He was helping Katy with her story, not taking away from it. Henry could tell, by Holly's face, her posture, her whole being, that she was thrilled and amazed at how quickly Katy had taken to him.

As he handed the coffee mug to Holly, he winked at her. She gave him a quick "I don't believe you did this" shake of the head, but along with it a smile.

I'm a fucking genius, Henry told himself. *I rock.*

7

"Jesus, Holl. You're traveling faster than the speed of love."
Anna sounded incredulous. "You're breaking barriers. You met
him what? Three weeks ago? And he's moved in? Isn't that a
little—what's the word? Precipitive?"

"Precipitate. And I know it's fast. But we spend all our time
together except when he's working. It's stupid for him to live in
that tiny apartment. Besides, he paid rent in advance, so he has
it for two months and he can move back there if he wants to.
We spent a long time talking about it, Anna. It wasn't a quick
decision."

"Depends on your definition of quick. Katy really likes him?"

"They're down on the beach now, as we speak, having a
swim. You should see her with him. It's so amazing to watch.
He has this way with her, it's so sweet."

"I want to meet this guy."

"You will."

"When?"

"I don't know. Soon."

"You want to keep him to yourself, don't you?"

"Oh, please."

"Well, you're allowed to. But not for much longer. I—"

"They're coming in the door now. I have to go. Talk soon. Bye." Holly hung up the phone, turned to see Katy rushing in, Jack behind her.

"How was it? Was the water nice?"

"Beautiful." Katy stood in the middle of the living room, with her towel wrapped around her, dripping water onto the rug.

"No, princess. It wasn't beautiful. It was perfect." Jack rubbed the top of her head.

"Come on out, let's sit on the porch in the sun and you two can dry off."

They went out the side living room door to the porch. It wasn't as big as Henry's, but her chairs were more comfortable than his and you could actually lie down in two of them. Holly towel-dried Katy and put some sunscreen on her while Jack threw his towel over the rail and then hopped on beside it, facing them.

"Have you ever thought of clearing some of these trees?"

"All the time." Holly stretched out on her chair, luxuriating in feeling the sun on her face and the warmth of Jack's presence.

"I could do it for you. A little of it, anyway. It's a shame to hide the view."

"Feel free." She'd finally made the decision. It was time now.

"I'll consult with Henry about it."

He'd slipped into her life with hardly a ripple. One day it was she and Katy and Henry, the next it was she and Katy and Henry and Jack. The only requests he'd made were that they have a cooked breakfast at seven-thirty sharp every morning and lunch at twelve-thirty on the dot. For someone changing his life to accommodate a young child, Jack seemed to be asking for very little. Agreeing to stick to a schedule for breakfast and lunch was relatively easy. She kept waiting for the hard part to start.

My present. The gift of Jack. Who has come into the woods and woken me up from my stupor.

Holly closed her eyes, crossed her legs. She was thinner. Sex and happiness had made her thighs thinner and her hair shinier and her skin softer. There were probably magazine articles written on the benefits of wonderful, passionate sex, but she'd never read them. And now she didn't have to. She was her very own "Before" and "After": she could feel the transformation, she could see it in the mirror. The right kind of touching made miracles happen. Real sex. Nothing like the sex she and Billy had had on the beach, but making-love sex, when you felt excited, wild, out of control and safe, all at the same time; when, for the first time in your life, you felt attractive and desired.

The thrill of the beginning of a love affair might be a cliché but she didn't care if it was. Because she was walking around in a constant state of wonder. Small things amazed her: Jack taking out the trash, Jack making her a cup of tea at four every afternoon. Little gestures like this were infinitely touching, but then when he'd help her read a bedtime story to Katy on his night off, or when he'd come home late from work, climb into bed and pull her to him, whispering and teasing and embracing her, she'd lie in a haze of joy. At first she wouldn't let herself truly believe in it. It couldn't last. She'd wake up one morning and he'd be gone. Back to Sophie or Chloe or whomever he must have left behind in England. Now, though, she was beginning to believe in a future. After all, he had moved in, a decision prompted by Katy asking one morning, "Why doesn't Jack have any clothes here?"

"Because Jack has his own apartment where he keeps his clothes," Holly had replied.

"Why does he need his own apartment?"

Jack and Holly had exchanged a glance then, and she saw the question mark in his eyes, making her guess that, if she suggested it, he might actually welcome a move. Later that afternoon, he brought the subject up himself: "It makes sense for me to move in, you know. But only if you and Katy want me to."

So she'd told a white lie to Anna. They hadn't discussed it at length; but they didn't have to. Every step forward came naturally. He fit in naturally. Holly didn't have a flicker of unease when he said he'd consult Henry about the trees. Her body now belonged to him: every time they made love, he possessed her entirely. There were no boundaries in her life with him and she wanted him to know that.

Today was Sunday, his night off. She'd promised Katy a trip to Friendly's for an ice-cream cone; after that they'd go down to the beach and swim some more, maybe drop by Henry's for a glass of wine in the evening. She'd make something nice for supper, they'd put Katy to bed and Jack and she would watch a DVD together. He'd tease her about her love of old black-and-white films, he'd make funny comments as they watched, and then they'd go to bed.

Life plays funny games. When you're a child all you want to do is

stay up. And when you're a woman, with the right man beside you,
all you want to do is get back into bed.

"Holly?"

No.

Her eyes flashed open; she sat up instantly, recognizing the
voice even before she saw Billy standing on the lawn, beside
the porch, his hands in his pockets.

She moved with the speed of instinct, grabbing Katy from
her chair and up into her arms, against her chest, carrying her
back into the house, into her bedroom.

"You stay here, sweetheart. Just for a while." Placing her on
her bed, she reached wildly for a reason, some way to keep Katy
here and away from Billy. "I have to talk to someone privately
for a little while."

"You mean the man who just came?"

"Yes."

"Why?"

"Because it's a private conversation. OK? And anyway, you
have to get changed out of that bathing suit. You get changed
and stay here and then I'll come back and we'll go out for an
ice-cream cone like we said we would."

"Who is he?"

"I'll tell you later. I'll be back soon. Please, chickpea, just do
what I say. Please."

"You're scaring me, Mommy."

"There's nothing to be frightened of—I promise. We'll go to
the mini-golf place after the ice cream. We'll have a great time.
But you have to get dressed."

"OK."

Holly didn't care that she was bribing her way out of this, she just wanted to make sure Katy stayed in her room until she got rid of Billy. She imagined Katy piping up and asking Billy what she'd asked Jack, the "Are you the Explorer?" question. And then Billy might just say, "I'm not an explorer, but I am your father," and their world would implode.

He'd said he'd be gone two weeks, but three weeks had passed and he hadn't shown up. So she'd stupidly relaxed, thinking he'd given up on his desire to see Katy. How typical of him to come on foot a week late; to sneak up on her—and Jack.

Jack. Jack's here. I won't have to deal with Billy on my own. It's a whole different world now that Jack's here.

And it was. She realized just how much it was when she went back out onto the porch and saw Jack standing across from Billy, who had come up the steps and was sitting in the chair Katy had just vacated. Already, Jack had established his authority, as if this was a job interview and Billy was the applicant. Holly walked over and stood beside Jack, presenting a united front.

That first night after she'd seen him again at Henry's, she'd told Jack about her past with Billy. He'd listened, nodding occasionally, swearing occasionally. And when she'd informed him at the end that Billy had returned, he'd hugged her to him and said, simply, "Don't worry. We'll take care of that wanker if he ever comes back. I'll sort him out."

"Holly. Your friend here seems to think I have no right to

see Katy." Billy was facing into the sun; his eyes were squinting and his right leg, swung over his left knee, was jiggling. "I don't think this is any of his business. Can we talk alone?"

"No." She put her arm around Jack's waist. "Jack and I are together."

"Jack your traveling companion?"

He was dressed as if he'd just come off a golf course, in green shorts and white polo shirt. Everything about him, especially in comparison with Jack, looked weak and boyish; his tone of voice was snippy too, a child deprived of a toy.

"Hardly." Jack crossed his arms. "We're not traveling together, we're living together."

"Living together?" Billy paused, and Holly took some satisfaction from the surprise on his face. "Well, that's, as you would say, *hardly* the point. The point is Katy, don't you think?" He addressed his words to Holly. "I'm not only talking about my rights, I'm talking about her rights. Her right to see her father."

"I'd say you forfeited your rights, Billy," Jack said evenly. "And as for Katy, I think she has the right not to see someone who doesn't actually give a toss about her."

"Would you please tell this man to leave?" Billy's voice raised in pitch. Holly could see the struggle he was having as he tried to gain some control. "We used to be friends, Holl. Before all this happened. I honestly don't see why we can't have a civilized conversation with each other, alone. Now."

"Oh, bugger off," Jack muttered. She could feel the muscles in his back go taut.

"Billy—I've thought about what you said when you came

before." Holly made sure her voice matched Jack's in confidence. "And I might have considered what you were proposing. But look what you did. You said you wanted to see Katy and then you left. You took off yet again. You said you'd be gone for two weeks. Well, it's been three weeks. You can't even be bothered to call and say why you needed that extra week. I can't trust you to do anything you say you're going to do. And Katy won't be able to trust you, either. This is a huge, huge deal, Billy. And you can't even get the beginning part right. I refuse to have you disrupt her life on a whim."

"It's not a whim. A friend of mine got sick in California. I had to go back and see him in the hospital. He was having an operation. He used to be my roommate at Stanford. I couldn't let him down. And I didn't know how long I was going to be there. He was in the hospital longer than I expected. That's why I didn't call."

"So, Billy, your friend was sick. I see. And did the dog eat your homework too?" Jack was smiling; and he was using his teasing voice, the one Holly loved—except it wasn't one that Billy would appreciate, she knew.

"You're really pissing me off. Why don't you fuck off, limey." Billy stood up.

"Limey? That's a clever put-down. Learn that at Stanford, did we?"

"Where did you learn 'bugger off?' At Oxford, Cambridge? Where did you go to college, Jack?"

"Not some poncey place for cowards. Anyway, you haven't told us. What happened to your roommate? Did he break his leg running away from his responsibilities?"

"Oh, ouch. That really hurt. And what were your roommates like, Jack? Is it true what they say about English men? Were you all buggering each other? Is that how you learned the word?"

Jack took a step toward Billy.

"Don't." Holly was reaching out to grab his hand when she saw the door to the porch open and Katy come running out barefoot, in shorts and a T-shirt, heading straight into Jack's arms.

"Hey, princess." He picked her up, threw her a foot in the air, caught her, and held her so she was facing away from Billy.

"Time to go, Billy Boy. Holly and Katy and I have an ice-cream date."

Billy didn't move, his eyes on Katy's back.

"You really should go," Holly said, trying not to make it sound like an order. If he stayed as angry as he was, he might dig in his heels and cause havoc.

"I'm here now, you know. For the rest of the summer."

"I know," Holly nodded.

"I'm not going anywhere."

"I know." Katy was beginning to squirm. Holly knew her daughter: she wanted to be put down, she wanted to know who this new man was. "We'll talk. But not now."

"All right. But not if he's—"

"Please. Just go. Please."

Billy left, his shadow following him down the porch steps. Jack threw Katy in the air again, put her down after he'd caught her.

"Good riddance to bad rubbish."

"Jack."

"I mean it, Holly." He shook his head. "He's spineless."

"We'll talk about it later."

"Talk about what? Who is that man?" Katy tugged on Holly's shirt. "Why was he here? Is something bad happening?"

"No, nothing bad is happening, chicken. Something good is happening. We're going to get ice cream."

"Who is he?"

"He's someone I used to know at school."

"Then why don't you like him? And why doesn't he have a spine? Doesn't he need a spine to walk with?"

Jack laughed, ruffled her hair.

"What are you like?"

"What am I like?"

"I mean, you make me laugh, princess." He turned to Holly. "I need to get changed and we'll go to Friendly's. Be right back."

"OK. And I promised Katy we'd take her to the mini golf afterward."

"Excellent." He executed an imaginary putt. "Tiger Woods, watch out."

When he'd gone, Holly sat down, pulled her daughter to her. "Katy, why did you run into Jack's arms like that? I've never seen you do that with anyone but me and Henry."

"Jack's my friend." She said it with pride. "He's almost like me."

"What do you mean?"

"I mean, I forget sometimes he's not the same age as me. I forget he's a grown-up."

"So you really do like having him around? You really are happy with him moving in with us?"

"Yes."

"And you'd tell me if you weren't, right?"

"Yes. Jack doesn't like that man you went to school with. I could tell."

"He doesn't really know him, Katy."

"Do you like him?"

"Let's stop talking about him. What kind of ice cream are you going to have?"

Katy blinked, her brow furrowed.

"You know, Bones . . ."

Holly waited but Katy didn't continue.

"Of course I know Bones, chicken."

"I *know* you know Bones, Mommy. I'm not stupid. I don't understand why Bones . . ." She stopped, and bit her bottom lip. "I want chocolate chip. With jimmies on top. Two scoops. Can we go now? Please?"

"Sure."

"Race you two lazy girls to the car," Jack called out from the house. "At the count of three, go. One . . . two . . . three . . ."

Katy took off like a rocket.

Holly waited a second, watching Katy's churning little legs run as fast as they could, her blonde hair flying behind her.

She's happy. I've never seen her this happy. If Billy ruins her happiness, I'll kill him.

8

"William, you're not making sense." Henry sighed. "If you are intent on becoming a lawyer, you should attempt to be more coherent. I'm glad you've come to see me. Frankly, it saves me a trip to your house. But I have no idea what you want from me, or what, exactly, you're trying to prove with this verbal rampage. You don't approve of Holly's young man. I understand that much. But I fail to see how her choice of partner is your concern."

Get a life, he felt like saying. Once again, a teenage expression which was remarkably apt.

They were sitting opposite each other in Henry's living room, on either side of the fireplace. Henry had taken his pipe and his pouch of tobacco out but hadn't lit up yet. Ten minutes before, just after he'd finished his dinner, Billy had arrived at his front door, had asked politely if he could speak to him about the situation with Holly and Katy, had sat down with a serious expression—and then had proceeded to lambaste Jack Dane. Who was this guy? What right did he have to talk as if he owned Holly, as if he was Katy's father? Just because he had an English accent didn't mean he could be so superior, did it? On and on in such a wild manner, Henry wondered if he were on drugs. Until he finally interrupted him, addressing him as William on purpose, in an attempt to bring some formality into the proceedings.

"I'm sorry." Having been on the edge of his chair, Billy now sat back, looking abashed. "Something about him makes me crazy." He dragged his hands over his face. "I'm not usually like this. I'm usually calm. In fact, that's the whole problem. In all of this . . . in all of this . . . what I mean is, everything that's happened since Holly got pregnant. The way I've acted hasn't been me."

"Who has it been, William?"

"OK," he sighed, expelling a heavy sound of dismay. "Point taken. But haven't you ever done something you're ashamed of?"

"Sorry, but I don't think my behavior comes into this."

"I know. Of course not. I'm only trying to say I'm ashamed of what I did. Of how I ran away. I'm not someone who would normally do that. And I want to make up for it. I want to make things right. The problem is that everything I do and everything I say only seems to dig me deeper into the hole I've made. Is it so wrong to want to see my daughter? To meet her, to talk to her, to have a relationship with her? I'm not saying I wasn't wrong—I was. And because I was wrong I missed five years of her life. So I have paid a price."

"Katy and Holly have paid a price as well. A much heavier one."

When Billy didn't respond, Henry placed the pipe in his mouth, took his time lighting it. The complexities of this situation were daunting, exhausting. Billy was right: he'd done things in his past which he was ashamed of; not on the same scale as Billy, but still. No one was an angel. Perhaps Billy did have rights. If so, what did that mean for Holly and Katy—and Jack, for that matter? The thought of Katy shuttling back and forth from Billy's house to Holly's was disturbing. Yes, many children did exactly that these days, but this was Katy, his Katy, who loved routines and rituals. What would it be like for her to be shunted back and forth, how would she feel about having a father appear out of the blue? Especially a father like Billy. Who might be intelligent but who was essentially a weak man.

"The point is, Henry, I thought I could at least have a decent conversation with Holly. We used to be friends. I wanted to sit down and discuss this with her. I really believe we could have figured out a way to work something out if we'd been given some time. But this guy. Jack. I mean, who is he? How long have they been together? What does he do?"

Henry lit his pipe, dragged on it and watched the puffs of smoke float in the air.

"I'll find out one way or another, Henry. It's a small town. You know that."

"He's a good man."

"And? What does he do?"

"He's a waiter. There's no shame in that."

"Where does he work?"

"At that new restaurant. Figs."

"Charlie's new place? I see. And now he's living in Holly's house. He's certainly fallen on his feet, hasn't he?"

"Your implication is unbecoming, William. And grossly unfair. I'd prefer to end this talk now."

Sitting forward again, Billy eyeballed Henry, unblinking.

"The very first time I saw my daughter, she was running into the arms of another man. All I saw of her was her back, Henry. He deliberately threw her up in the air and held her to prove to me she was *his*, not mine. He was staking a claim. And he was provoking me, trying to start a fight. The Holly I knew wasn't someone who should be with a man like that."

"The Holly you knew shouldn't have been abandoned by the man who made her pregnant."

"There's no way, is there?" Leaning over, he put his hands on his knees, his head in his hands. When he raised his face, there were tears in his eyes. "I'm never going to be forgiven. Fine." He stood up, wiped the tears away with his palms. "But I will tell you what I told Holly. I'm not going anywhere. I'm not going to slink away and make it easy for you. I don't trust that man. I don't want my daughter involved with him. Believe it or not, I care about Holly too. This is all wrong. She must have inherited a lot of money when her mother and father died. And now some good-looking English waiter has moved in. Whether it's unbecoming of me or not, I'm daring to say what you must be thinking."

"That is so far from the truth—" Henry rose too "—that I won't even dignify it with a denial. Goodbye, William."

"Goodbye."

Billy stalked out, leaving Henry fuming. The gall, the arrogance of the boy. Did he think Holly couldn't possibly attract a good-looking man, that Jack was only in it for the money? It was convenient for Billy to believe Jack was a fortune-hunter;

casting Jack as a villain put him in a better light. Pathetic. Damn pathetic.

Henry crossed to the sofa by the window where Bones lay sleeping. Sitting beside him, he rubbed the dog's head between the ears, in an attempt to calm himself down.

And there you have it, Bones, you old dog. Billy may have gone to the best schools and the best university, he may turn out to be an excellent lawyer, but I would prefer to be with Jack any day. Waiter or no waiter, whatever his background may be. Lucky Holly to be rid of Billy, is all I can say. We'll protect her, won't we? Let him try to interfere. Just let him try. I'm a tired old man right now. But I have fight left in me. And so do you, you old thing. Don't you?

Opening his eyes, Bones rolled over onto his back, his paws in the air.

All right, I'll rub your stomach. But only for a minute. Then I'm going to bed. And we can both dream of the days when we could run for miles.

The moonlight woke him, his eyes opening to a clear white stream of rays. He hadn't drawn the blinds in his bedroom; after brushing his teeth and washing his face, he'd been too tired to perform even that simple a task. Instead he'd flopped on the bed, on top of the blanket, and nodded off immediately. Now he was alert, awake, and checking the clock radio to see what time it was. Midnight. And the moon was full. He sat up, telling himself not to slouch. No one could see him, but posture counted, always. Swinging his legs over the side of the bed, he debated with himself, but only for a few seconds. It was a perfect time to go fishing. Age was no excuse, his creaking knees were no excuse. In the old days, he wouldn't have hesitated even this long. He'd already be getting dressed and ready.

Stop dawdling. Turn the light on and get moving. Now.

He obeyed his own orders, pulling on a pair of trousers and a long-sleeved shirt. No wind, so the mosquitoes were going to be biting; he'd cover himself with anti-bug spray too, but clothes were the best protection.

See if you can bite through cloth, you little bastards, go ahead and try.

He pulled on a pair of thick socks, slipped into his shoes, tied the laces and made his way downstairs.

"We're going fishing, Bones," he called out, clapping his hands. "Wake up and get your ass in gear."

Bones stuck his head out of the living room as Henry went to the back of the hall, to the closet where the guns he once used for hunting were locked up. He grabbed one of the rods leaning on the front of the closet, reached down and picked up the net from the top of the tackle box. On the way out of the door, he stopped, doubled back.

Shit for brains. A knife would be a good idea. Having a functioning memory would be a good idea too.

"Come on, you silly dog. I'll get the flashlight too and we'll be on our way. Probably won't need it with this moon, but we'll bring it anyway. Won't we? And don't look at me like that. I know you're a dog. But I'll talk to you when I damn well please. And don't pretend you don't understand exactly what I'm saying, you little fucker."

He opened the porch screen door, letting Bones precede

him outside, into the hot July night air. On nights like this, fishing at the beach was glorious. As exciting as fishing during the day was, it couldn't compare to the magic of the sight of fish jumping under the moon, or the satisfaction of the sound they made when they hit the water, that *thwack* magnified by the stillness of the ocean. No need to drive to the dock and go through all the palaver of getting the boat out, only a simple walk down to the beach with Bones at his side. He didn't care if he didn't catch a fish. All he wanted was to be out with them, watching them, casting into the dark.

They made their way across the lawn, and started down the path to the Back Beach. He didn't need the flashlight; the moon was bright enough to guide them. Henry was the only person of his age he knew not to have been in awe of the first manned moon landing. "When we get to an inhabited planet, I'll sit up," he'd said to Isabella, as Neil Armstrong delivered his famous line. She'd shot him a withering look and told him to be quiet.

When he reached the bottom of the path, he stopped abruptly.

What the fuck?

There were people on the beach.

He put the tackle box down on the sand, grabbed the sheathed knife with his right hand and moved forward, trying not to make any sound.

And then he saw who the people were, and stopped again, shocked.

Katy was twenty yards to his left, at the water's edge. In her pajamas, her hands outstretched.

And Jack was ten feet away from her, throwing something.

Katy caught it. A tennis ball? She jumped up and down, threw it back, underhand. To Jack.

Henry placed his hand on top of Bones's head, making him sit.

What the hell is going on?

Jack tossed the ball back. Katy bobbled it slightly, fell to her knees in the sand, but hung on to it. She lifted the hand that held it into the air, waving it wildly. Henry could see her face bathed in moonlight, grinning, excited, proud, as she then got back up on her feet and prepared to throw it back.

"Katy." He threw down the rod he was carrying in his left hand and strode toward her. "Katy."

She turned, saw him.

"Henry! Wait! We're almost there. Wait!" With great concentration, she stood straight, drew her arm back and threw the ball to Jack, who had to dive into the sand to catch it.

"Yes! Twenty!" Katy cried out, jumping up and down and then skipping toward Henry. "We made twenty in a row!"

"Hello, Henry." Jack was brushing the sand off his clothes, following behind her. "What are you doing down here? We didn't wake you, did we? We were very quiet."

"No, you didn't wake me. But what in God's name is this all about? What are you doing here so late? Why is Katy up at this hour?"

"We were playing catch. Trying to reach twenty in a row without either of us dropping the ball—and we did it!" Katy did a little jig, then dropped down on her knees to hug Bones.

"And you're our witness," Jack said. He came closer to Henry, tossing the tennis ball from hand to hand. "I heard Katy wake up and I didn't want her to disturb Holly's sleep, so I brought her down here for a game. Isn't the full moon amazing?"

"I'm not sure this is appropriate."

"What?" Jack caught the ball, held it.

"I don't think it's a good idea to bring Katy out here so late at night."

Katy leaped up like a little frog. "We weren't doing anything bad, I promise. We kept quiet. I was awake. I didn't want to wake up Mommy. It's like the day only later. Because of the full moon. We got up to twenty. If we practice enough we can get up to two million."

"That's a tall order, princess."

Jack laughed and the disquiet Henry felt subsided. Not the least perturbed by Henry's appearance on the beach, Jack seemed, on the contrary, to welcome him. And, more importantly, Katy wasn't acting at all oddly—in fact, she was clearly having fun. Still, he wasn't entirely sure he should condone this night-time game business.

"What if your mother woke up and you weren't at home? She'd be so worried, Katy."

Jack put a hand on Henry's shoulder.

"We haven't been here long and we were going to go back up soon. Besides, how often is there a moon like this? Katy should get to see it in its full glory. Isn't that what brought you down here?" He pointed up at the sky. "Were you going to take a moonlight swim?"

"I was going to fish." Leaning over, he picked up his rod. "Down by the rocks."

"Sounds wonderful. I'd like to join you. But I guess I'd better get this little one back to her bed, right?"

Henry nodded.

"Actually, I think I'll skip the fishing. I'll walk back to the house with you. Come on, Katy." Henry held out his hand, conscious that he was feeling suddenly proprietorial. Up until this point, he'd been pleased by the closeness which was obviously developing apace between Jack and Katy, but now he thought that perhaps Jack had overstepped himself. While there had been something quite magical and lovely in the scene of the two playing catch in the moonlight, it was also odd. That's the only word he could think to describe it. Odd.

Henry collected his tackle box, but Jack took it from him, saying, "Allow me." They went back up the path, Jack in front, Henry and Katy hand in hand behind. Henry didn't turn up the path to his house, but kept going along with them to Holly's. When they were outside Holly's front door, Jack said, "Why don't you run inside, princess? I'll be there in a minute."

"OK. Night, Henry. Sweet dreams."

"Same to you." He let go of her hand. "Ping-Pong tomorrow."

"Can you teach Jack, too?"

"I know how to play Ping-Pong. In England we call it table tennis."

"You're so weird in England."

"I know. Now get into the house."

Together they watched Katy run into the dark house.

"I hope she doesn't wake Holly up," Jack commented.

"Well, Holly might like to see the full moon too."

"That's true." He scratched his forehead. "Bloody mosquitoes. I lathered myself in bug stuff and they still bite."

"Relentless little bastards."

"Exactly. Listen, Henry, I can tell you're not sure about this little excursion Katy and I took. I can see how it might seem strange. But it's a way for us to get to know each other and now that I've moved in, I want a good relationship with Katy. It's important. Besides . . ."

"Besides what?"

Jack didn't answer immediately. He looked up at the sky, then at the ground, shifting from foot to foot.

"Besides what, Jack?"

Again, he didn't respond, but held out his hands as a signal for Henry to give him time.

"I don't like to talk about it. But I had a little sister when I was growing up. She died when she was four and I was ten. Her heart was wired wrong—it beat too fast and no one knew about it and she just dropped down and died one afternoon when she was running around in the garden. When I was playing catch with Katy, it was like being with Miranda again. She reminds me of her sometimes. I don't talk about it. I haven't even told Holly about her yet." He paused. "There's too much death around us as it is."

The tears in Jack's eyes, real tears, so different from the self-pitying ones in Billy's just hours before, made Henry reach out and put his arm around him. "I'm very sorry, Jack. You've had such sadness in your life. It's not right."

"No. It's not. But everything has changed now. I met Holly. And thanks to you, I had a second chance with her. You've been brilliant, Henry. Honestly, I can't thank you enough. I love her, you know."

"I guessed." He squeezed Jack's shoulder. "It wasn't too difficult a guess, either. You should tell her about your sister."

"I will. When the time's right. And I hope you don't mind, but I'd prefer it if you didn't tell Holly about our game of catch. I want to surprise her, I want her to watch us when we get good enough to reach a high number."

"You plan to do this again?"

"Not if you disapprove. Of course not. I'll practice with her during the day if you think that's better."

"I think it's better not to keep her awake so late."

"But she was already awake—still, I see what you mean. I'm not exactly used to thinking of what's best for a five-year-old. Sorry."

"That's all right. Obviously it takes a while to get accustomed to having a child around."

"It's much easier than I'd thought it would be. Anyway, right now I'd better go and make sure Katy gets some sleep."

"See you tomorrow then."

"Absolutely. Ping-Pong. I'll be there." Jack handed him the tackle box.

As he and Bones made their way back to his house, Henry chided himself for being an old fool. It might not be entirely normal for Jack to be out with Katy at midnight, but what fun had normal ever been? He himself had flouted Bostonian conventions with pleasure. Nothing about Jack's behavior had been untoward. And the poor boy had had a hellish life. He couldn't object strenuously when there clearly wasn't any harm done.

Still, he might just get up the following night and go down to the beach again, to make sure Jack wasn't keeping Katy up late. New teenage expressions might be apt occasionally, but old truisms were always the most sensible. It was better to be safe than sorry.

9

Crisp slices of bacon were resting on kitchen paper, eggs were frying alongside tomatoes, the coffee was almost done, the toast had just popped up and Holly was sweating. It was as if Billy's arrival the day before had brought with it the start of a cloyingly muggy heatwave. At ten past seven in the morning, it was already sweltering, outside and in, and the heat from the stove was ratcheting up the discomfort factor. For one moment, Holly felt nostalgia for the days when she and Katy used to have cereal and orange juice for breakfast whenever they decided they were hungry. But Jack needed a cooked breakfast at seven-thirty sharp, just as he needed lunch at twelve-thirty on the dot. "I'll cook," he'd said. "But it's important to have a schedule and stick to it."

He was so insistent, she couldn't even tease him about it. "Everyone needs to know where they are in the day," he'd stated when she'd tried to wriggle out of him why he was quite so obsessively punctual. At first she'd thought he was joking and almost responded with, "What happens? Do you get lost if you don't know where you are in the day?" but she'd held back because the tone of his voice had been so uncharacteristically serious. And it wasn't an issue which was important to her. Until he'd moved in, though, she would never have thought of him as someone who would care so much about routines.

"Breakfast's ready," she called out. "Come and eat."

"Brilliant." He'd sauntered in, and, as he did every morning, looked at his watch before pouring himself orange juice from the carton on the table. "Smells delicious."

"I hope it tastes delicious."

And they had this same conversation every morning, too. Usually it made Holly smile internally, thinking what an old, stick-in-the-mud couple they'd appear to anyone else. Today she found herself saying, "We're beginning to sound like that movie *Groundhog Day*."

"What do you mean?" He looked up at her as he sat down.

"The way we say the same things every morning. You've seen the movie, haven't you?"

"Yes." He frowned. "And your point is?"

"Nothing." She took the eggs out of the pan, slid them onto a plate, put two slices of fried tomato and two pieces of bacon beside them, and placed the plate in front of Jack. "I'll get the toast."

The smell of soap that had wafted up from his skin as she leaned over to give him the plate was almost as strong as the one from all the fried foods.

Living with someone was like putting together a jigsaw puzzle, Holly was beginning to realize. She could see the whole picture from the start, but she didn't know the component bits; in what shapes and sizes they came. Jack's need for strict timing was one large piece; an equal-shaped one was his personal cleanliness. He was never late and he was never dirty. He washed and ironed his own clothes every day.

They fit together somehow, those two pieces, she knew. And she guessed they both had something to do with the need for control. Which made sense when you were orphaned at eighteen. She'd had Henry and Katy to keep her together when her parents died and even then she'd felt lost and rudderless. Jack, it seemed, had had no one.

Or he might have had someone. She didn't know. In the three weeks they'd been together, she'd talked and he'd listened. At first it had been natural for her to tell him about herself; she'd spilled out the details of her life as if she'd been waiting forever to share them. Yet when she'd ask him about himself, he'd block the questions by switching the subject and making a joke about something silly.

"You know something really weird about men?" Anna had asked once, a few years before, when they'd been watching *Friends* together.

"No, tell me," Holly replied, knowing Anna was about to make one of her pronouncements on the subject of the male species.

"They tell the truth at the beginning of a relationship. They tell you about themselves. Like they'll say, 'I don't like commitment,' or, 'I can't go out with anyone who doesn't like mountain climbing.' They tell you about themselves but girls don't listen. I mean, we hear it, but we don't believe it. We think we can change the guy, make him want to commit, or make him realize it's not that big a deal to go mountain climbing together. But we *should* listen. We should listen because they're being upfront and honest. They're telling the truth and they're not about to change—for anyone."

Jack had told her he didn't talk about emotions. Or his past. He'd jettisoned the past—he'd made that clear from the start, but Holly kept thinking he'd open up to her. She wanted to know about his past, she wanted him to share as much with her as she had with him.

One night, after she'd refused to be diverted and had pressed him to tell her about his school days, he'd stood up, stated, "If I had something interesting to say, I'd say it," and left the room. His tone matched exactly the one he'd used when he'd said, "That way everyone knows where they are in the day"—a tone brooking no further discussion, a tone which effectively closed the subject.

Her happiness with him was beginning to be tinged with a streak of fear. It had all happened so swiftly, she wasn't sure whether her heart was planted on solid ground or in quicksand. Why had Jack, so handsome, so smart and funny and eligible, chosen her, and chosen her so completely and comprehensively? They were sharing the same house, the same bed; their lives were now inextricably intertwined, but it was so sudden it felt precarious. Jack might make passionate love to her, spend all his time away from work with her—and Katy—but might he also, at any moment, drop her as quickly as he had moved in with her?

None of these worries entered her mind when they were in

bed together. As soon as their bodies connected, she felt she knew him wholly and completely, that words were unimportant, that his or her pasts didn't count. But once they had finished making love, as soon as they were physically separated, her anxiety returned. He'd told her he loved her, he *seemed* to be happy with her, but how could she be sure when she had to admit to herself that she didn't really know him?

With her fear came watchfulness. She was on the lookout for her own mistakes, in the hope that if she could spot them quickly enough, she could fix them just as quickly. She'd made sure she'd stuck to his rigid eating schedule, she'd stopped probing him about his past, she'd tried to strangle all her retroactive jealousy about the possible Sophies and Emmas in his life. She'd take whatever clues and cues he gave her and follow them, like a good dancing partner. Her mother had once turned to her father after watching a Fred Astaire and Ginger Rogers video and said, "That's us. Except I'm Fred and you're Ginger." Her father, Holly remembered, had laughed and said, "You wish." Holly didn't care whether she was Fred or Ginger, as long as she was in the dance.

"I suppose I see what you mean," Jack said, as she was buttering his toast.

"What?"

"About the film. *Groundhog Day*. I hadn't thought about the repetition."

His "And your point is?" had pained her. He must have sensed that and was now making up for it. Give and take; trade-offs, allowing the other person time and space: more aspects of the relationship puzzle she was gradually beginning to put together.

"Mommy, my ear hurts." Katy came running into the kitchen; her right hand up to her right ear, her face pained. "It really hurts."

"Oh, chicken, I'm sorry. There's nothing worse than an ear-ache. I'll get you some paracetamol."

"She doesn't need aspirin." Jack frowned. "Aspirin's bad for a child."

"It's not aspirin, it's paracetamol, children's paracetamol. It's fine." Holly went over to the cabinet where she kept it. "She's had it before."

"That doesn't mean it's good for her. You shouldn't give it to her."

She had the bottle in her hand but hesitated.

"What am I supposed to do? Let her ear keep hurting?"

"It will be fine. She's making a meal of it. You shouldn't give in to her."

"It hurts." Katy began to cry. "Ouch, Mommy. It hurts."

"Don't be silly, Katy. And stop crying. Sit down and have some breakfast."

"Mommy?" The cry turned into a wail. "Mommy?" She came hurtling toward Holly, throwing herself into her arms. "Make it stop."

"Holly."

"What?" She didn't know what to do with this sudden anger of his.

"Don't give in to this."

"Give in to what? She's in pain. Her ear hurts. Haven't you ever had an earache? Ssh, sweetheart." She hugged her tightly, but Katy kept crying.

"For Christ's sake. I can't stand this noise." Tossing his knife and fork down on his plate, Jack stood up. "You shouldn't give her aspirin and she shouldn't be crying. Sort it out, will you?"

He walked out of the kitchen without looking at either of them. Seconds later, when she heard the car's engine start up, she rushed to the kitchen window. Jack was at the wheel of her car, heading out the driveway.

For a minute she stood, holding Katy and the paracetamol bottle, floored by his departure. What was that all about? Had Billy's arrival on Birch Point upset him? The night before, as they were getting into bed together, he'd said, "Don't worry about Billy. He's a waste of space, but he's harmless. He'll go play in his sandbox and leave us alone," and that's all he'd said on the subject. He hadn't seemed in the least perturbed.

What have I done wrong? Have I done something wrong?

"Here, come on." She led Katy to the kitchen table, sat her down. "I'll give you a spoonful of this medicine and you'll feel better in a little while."

"Jack's mad at me," Katy said between sobs. "I shouldn't have it if Jack's mad at me."

"He doesn't like noise, that's all. He's not mad at you. Come on. Take this." She spoonfed her the paracetamol, picked her up again and carried her to the living room. "I'll turn on the TV and you can lie here on the sofa and watch a cartoon until your earache goes away."

Where had he gone? And why had he been so mean to Katy? After she'd found a good cartoon show for Katy and settled her down, she said, "I'll be back in a few minutes. I'll be in my room if you need me, OK?"

"OK."

"Anna?" She'd taken her cellphone into the bedroom, sat on the bed and dialed. "We've just had our first fight. At least, I think it's a fight. I don't know what to do. Jack's gone."

"Calm down," Anna said in her "I'm giving good advice here" voice, after Holly had told her what had happened. "It's natural."

"What do you mean?"

"Look, Holl. He's living with a five-year-old kid. This is a whole new deal for him. He's not used to crying kids with earaches. So he's gone for a drive to take a break. His clothes are still there, right?"

Even knowing he hadn't had enough time to clear out his clothes, she got up, went to the closet and opened it.

"Yes."

"So he hasn't driven off for good. You have to expect the occasional tantrum from men. More than occasional with most men. They're all babies."

"But he's always been even-tempered. Except with Billy yesterday. But that was understandable."

"Except what with Billy?"

"Billy showed up again yesterday afternoon. And Jack basically got rid of him for me. For a second I thought Jack might punch him."

"Good for Jack. See how right I was to ditch Billy? I still

can't believe you and he ever got together. You should have told me you had a crush on him, Holl. I would have told you he wasn't worth it."

She wanted to say, *"Do you have any idea how many times you've said that to me? If you ever say that again, I'll scream. And this isn't about you—it's about me, and Jack."* But she knew Anna wouldn't listen.

"Billy's not the point, Anna. The point is that Jack was angry with Billy, but not in the way he was angry just now. I haven't seen him angry like that before."

"You haven't seen all that much of him before, have you? There's practically no 'before' in your short knowledge of the guy. In any event, in the real world, the world outside Birch Point, everyone gets angry, Holly. And it sounds like he didn't explode—he just left. That's OK. It will blow over."

"He upset Katy too. She cares about him so much."

"Well, that's good too. I mean the caring about him so much part. In fact, it all sounds pretty amazing to me. You get this man with a cool English accent waltzing into your life, moving in with you straight off the bat, and you're complaining? Do you know how commitment-phobic most men are? You've hit the jackpot here, Holl. Pun intended."

"I know. I guess there's a lot I have to learn about living with a man."

"You'll never learn enough." Anna sighed audibly. "There's always another surprise waiting to ambush you. Anyway— when am I going to meet him? It's unbelievably hot here and it's supposed to stay this way all week. What about the weekend?

Give your friend a break and invite her down for the weekend, will you?"

"Of course." It would be churlish of her not to, she knew. And she couldn't keep Jack hidden away forever.

"Excellent. I'll see you Friday. I'll try to get off work early so I can miss the traffic."

"Great. And thanks, Anna. You've helped. A lot."

"Before you hang up, what are you going to do about Billy?"

"I don't know. The way he showed up like that shocked me. And then yesterday, well, the whole scene between him and Jack didn't help either. I know I'll have to face it, and soon. I'll have to tell Katy and I'll have to let him spend time with her. But I'm putting it off. It's been so wonderful these past weeks with Jack and Katy, so uncomplicated. I hate the idea of turning her little world upside down. But Billy says he's staying here and he's determined."

"Well, we can talk about that next weekend, too. Billy's an idiot, but he *is* her father, and I suppose he has some rights. It would be so weird to see him again after all these years. Hey—it just occurred to me. Maybe Jack's a Christian Scientist. They don't believe in anyone being sick, do they? You have to heal yourself or something crazy like that. Or is that Scientology?"

"No, you were right the first time. It's Christian Science. But he would have told me if he were one."

Or would he?

"I've got to go check on Katy now and see how her ear is feeling."

"OK, give her my love."

"I will."

They said goodbye simultaneously; after hanging up, Holly went over and sat with Katy while she watched cartoons.

Anna was probably right that she had nothing to worry about, but as time passed and Jack didn't return, she replayed the scene that morning over and over again, trying to figure out why he'd been so angry, why he'd walked out.

Was he a Christian Scientist? Was Anna right? Had she offended his religious principles with the paracetamol? Was Katy supposed to cure herself?

"My ear doesn't hurt any more."

"That's good, sweetheart."

"But I'm tired."

"Do you want to get into bed?"

"Just for a little while."

Holly carried her upstairs into her bedroom and tucked her in.

"Take a nap and then you'll feel all fine."

"OK. Tell Jack when he comes back that I'm sorry."

"There's nothing to be sorry about."

"Tell him I promise we'll get up to thirty next time."

"Thirty what?"

"Full moons."

It was a half-asleep answer, one of those sentences floating between consciousness and unconsciousness. The earache and paracetamol had sapped her of her usual energy; Holly couldn't remember the last time Katy had taken a nap in the morning.

She leaned down, kissed Katy's head and headed back downstairs.

"Is she OK?"

Jack was standing at the foot of the stairs.

"She's asleep."

"That's good." He held his hand out to her.

"Where did you go?" When she reached him, she took his hand and squeezed it. "I was worried."

"I needed to get out. It's so bloody hot."

"I don't want to fight, Jack."

"We're not fighting. Come with me. I have something to show you." He led her into the living room, picked up a bag from the floor beside the coffee table. "Look what I've done." Reaching into the bag, he took out framed photographs, one by one, and placed them on the table. They were pictures of her and Katy together, him and Katy together, him and her together, the three of them together. Some were beach photos, some were simple ones of them sitting in the house. He hadn't been an irritating photographer, snapping away constantly; she'd barely even noticed it when he'd taken his digital camera out.

"They're amazing, Jack. I had no idea you were going to get them framed. They're stunning. I love them. I love the ones you took with the timer of all of us together—especially that one on the beach."

She couldn't imagine a more perfect way of making up after an argument.

"So . . ." He threw his hands in the air. "Let's get started."

"What?"

"Here."

He picked up the now empty bag and began to walk around the living room, taking the photographs she had of her parents, of Katy as a baby and little toddler—all the pictures she had displayed on tabletops and bookshelves—and shoving them in the bag.

"Jack! What are you doing?"

"What does it look like?"

"But those are my pictures."

"And these are our pictures."

He dumped the bag on the floor, went back to the coffee table, took each picture and put it in the place of the ones he'd just removed.

"Those are pictures of my parents, Jack. I don't want to get rid of them. And the ones of Katy as a baby too. They're special."

"They're old. They're the past. You need to look forward." He was looking around at the new photos, admiring his work.

"I can look forward and still have reminders of the past." She picked up the bag of her photos he'd left on the floor and started taking the pictures back out. "We can have both. The old ones and the ones you took."

"No." He walked over and stood in front of her, his hands on his hips. "No. Put the old ones back in the bag. Now."

"This is crazy. I don't understand. Don't you have any pictures of your parents?"

"No."

"Why not?"

"Because I don't." Grabbing the bag from her hands, he began to put the photos she'd taken out back in.

"I want my pictures, Jack." She couldn't help it; tears began to run down her face. "They're important to me. Please understand."

He wasn't listening. He strode into the kitchen and Holly followed him, unbelieving, watching in despair as he took a garbage bag out from under the sink.

"You can't throw them away."

"Why not?"

"Jack. Please. Stop it. Those are my parents. They're what I have left of my parents."

Tears were now cascading down her face. This couldn't be happening. Not to them. They were happy. They were in love. Everything was going right. But the man who would hug her to him at night and tease her and excite her was staring at her with an impenetrable, unfeeling expression. She didn't know what to do, could only stand watching helplessly as he tied up the ends of the garbage bag and hauled it outside.

Holly could hear him take the top off the trash can, she could hear the sound of the bag full of pictures being thrown in. And the lid crashing back down.

She sank onto the kitchen chair, lay her head down on the table. When she heard him come back in, she couldn't look up.

"Holly, look at me. We're orphans. But we have each other now. And Katy. That's all we need. Look at me."

Her face was in her hands, hands wet with tears. She shook her head. When he pulled her hand away, out from under her face, she wouldn't look up. She couldn't.

His hand was over hers, separating her fingers. He was putting something on her fourth finger, slipping it over the tip and down.

"You really should look at me when I propose."

The weight of both the ring and his words hit her.

"Ah—now I have your attention. Now you're looking at me. Will you marry me, Holly Barrett?"

"What?"

"What's a question not an answer. I want us to have a life together. A new life. Starting from scratch. You've changed my life. You've made me believe in life again. I didn't think that was possible. But now I do."

"Jack."

"Jack's not an answer either. Do you want me to get down on one knee? I'll do it, Holly." He knelt beside her chair. "I had planned it differently. I was going to ask you tonight, I was going to take the night off work and ask you out to dinner, but then Katy had that earache and that might have meant we couldn't let Henry look after her so we could go out and all my plans had to change. So I'm doing it now. We can be a family. You and me and Katy. We can fix each other, Holly. We've both been wounded. But we can fix each other. Wouldn't you like that?"

His eyes were clear and blue and beseeching. He was squeezing her hand so hard the ring he'd put there was digging into her flesh. Her tears were still falling but they were coming out of a different place in her heart: the lonely hole that had been there for so long was filling up and spilling over and the deepseated anxiety she'd had for the past month was vanishing as she realized that this was her future, her forever future that he was offering her, and she put her arms around his neck and leaned down and kissed him with the kind of love for a man she never believed she'd have.

"Yes," she whispered in his ear when she caught her breath again. "Yes. That's an answer. Yes, I'll marry you, Jack Dane."

10

Billy sat in the white deckchair on the lawn, hoping for some breeze from the bay, even a small hint of a breeze, to cool him down. The air-conditioning in the house wasn't working and he'd spent the night tossing in damp sheets. At about three in the morning, when he'd finally managed to fall asleep, he was woken by the buzz of a mosquito. That irritating whine which wouldn't go away until he'd turned the bedside light on, got up and hunted it down; finally swatting it with a rolled-up newspaper he'd retrieved from the kitchen.

He'd almost forgotten the humidity of a Birch Point heatwave; California had been hot, but somehow never quite as bad as this. Could Katy sleep in weather like this? Could Katy swim? Ride a bike? His little girl with her long blonde hair and those questioning eyes. That's what had struck him most in the photographs he'd seen at Holly's the first time he'd gone: Katy's eyes. The way they seemed, in every picture, to be asking something. Like: What are you doing with that strange thing you're pointing at me? Or: What happens next? Or was it: Where's my father, the explorer?

An explorer. Yeah, right. An Asshole Dirtbag who'd run

away was more like it. He could spend all the time in the world making excuses for himself, some of them actually reasonable excuses, but nothing could change the fact that he'd treated Holly like shit and his daughter as if she didn't exist. He could hear himself try to justify to both Holly and Henry what he'd done, he could hear how pathetic and weak he sounded. "I was young," or "We were friends and suddenly you were pregnant." Ridiculous efforts to try to wipe away his negligence, his rank stupidity. No wonder Holly and Henry both thought he was a coward, hiding behind his parents. That's what he'd been, and that's what he'd done.

"Look, I was head over heels in love with Anna, she ditched me, I took advantage of Holly, but I hadn't been expecting I'd take advantage of her on that walk so I didn't have a condom and didn't think about using one, and my parents completely freaked out and I didn't know what to do so I listened to them and went to Stanford and I can't believe I never talked to Holly and I can't believe I spent five years in total denial, but I want to make up for it now."

Great speech, Billy. That will have them applauding in the aisles.

He wiped the sweat off his forehead, stood up and went back into the house. His parents had changed everything since he'd last been there; making it modern and rent-friendly, the antithesis of Holly's place. The kitchen was full of sparkling appliances, all state-of-the-art. He grabbed a glass of water and ice cubes from the ice-cube-making machine, sat down on one of the stools at the bar and picked up the cordless phone. This time he'd call, not arrive at her house with no warning.

He'd be smarter this time, more composed. And if he was lucky, Jack wouldn't answer. He'd have a chance of speaking to Holly on her own.

After three rings, an answering machine kicked in: *"Hi, you've reached Holly and Katy. Please leave a message at the beep."*

"Holly, it's Billy. I'd like to speak to you, please. Could you call me back at 508-295-6678? Thank you."

Well, at least the message hadn't included Jack's name. Billy stood, unsure of what he should do next. Sit and wait for her to call back? Not dare to go out in case she did and he missed it? Or go down to the beach for a swim? Maybe Katy and Holly were down on the beach. He went to try to find a pair of binoculars his parents used to keep in a cupboard in the hall, but before he'd gone ten steps, the phone rang. He doubled back.

"Hello?"

"Billy, it's me. I just got your message."

"Good. Great. Can we talk? I mean, can we meet up together and talk? I have some ideas about how we could work this out. I'd like to know what you think of them."

"Listen, Billy. I have something to tell you—"

"You can tell me at the Mill Pond Diner. Remember how we used to like it there? I thought that would be a good place to meet. Have a cup of coffee. Or you could have one of those black-and-white *frappés* you used to like. They probably still have jukeboxes on the tables. I bet they do. I bet the place hasn't—"

"I'm engaged, Billy. Jack Dane and I are getting married. Soon."

"Oh, fuck."

"Billy—"

"This is crazy, Holl. How long have you known him? This is ridiculous."

"No, it's not. Not at all."

"You're not thinking straight. He's a good-looking guy, I grant you that. But what else is he? *Who* is he? You have a crush on him, fine. But marrying him? What about Katy? Have you thought about her?"

"I honestly can't believe you just said that."

"OK, OK, OK." His fist was pounding the counter top. "Fine. I'm not allowed to say anything, ever, on the subject of Katy. Just tell me one thing. How long have you known him?"

"It's none of your business."

"So not long."

"Billy, I'd known you for three years before you got me pregnant and walked out on me."

"Why don't you bring up what an asshole I was at every single opportunity you get? If I was such a bastard why did you take that walk with me, anyway? You should have shot me when I came within ten feet of you."

"I'm going to hang up now."

"At least I'm not some foreign gold-digging waiter."

The line went dead at the same time as he was saying, "Holly, I didn't mean that, I'm sorry."

No. No, no, no. I did not just have that conversation. I didn't lose control again. I wasn't an asshole again. What the hell is wrong with me? It's the fucking heat.

He picked up his glass of water and poured it over his head.

He'd had it planned out. They'd go to the Mill Pond Diner, a place they'd spent fun times in together before. In the days when he was dating Anna. And maybe they'd find that friendship again, the laughter they'd shared at the bad songs on the jukebox. He'd ask her all about her life. He'd tell her how sorry he was about her parents' deaths, how much he'd respected them. He wouldn't mention Jack Dane. They'd gradually get around to talking about Katy and she'd tell him what Katy was like. And together they'd figure out the best way of telling Katy about the explorer who wasn't an explorer.

He'd be the Billy Madison he'd been at Stanford. The rational, hard-studying, well-behaved Billy. Not the dickhead who'd made her pregnant and disappeared.

A chance—that's all he wanted. The opportunity to sit down with her and start over. One huge mistake shouldn't turn you into a monster. People made mistakes, didn't they?

Jack Dane had made it abundantly clear that he would do all he could to keep him away from Katy. Billy had seen it in those cold eyes of his. He had seen it in the way Jack had picked up Katy—as if she were his possession. Had Jack Dane proposed because he thought Billy might be a threat to his plans?

Jack Dane had hoodwinked them all—Holly, Henry and even Katy. No one could dare to suggest that this English emperor who had conquered their hearts had no clothes. Worse, that he might be out to rip off Holly. Jack Dane was the handsome prince savior and Billy was a nasty, spoiled, selfish brat. That was the way the play had been cast.

So he's a waiter. What's wrong with that? You're being elitist, Billy. How dare you suggest he might have ulterior motives? Shame on you.

So Holly hasn't known him long. What's wrong with that? You're being hypocritical, Billy. She knew you for a long time and look what happened.

We love Jack because he's not you. Nothing he does can be wrong because he's not you. You showing up just reminded everyone how bad a man can be. You're a nasty piece of work, quod erat demonstrandum *Jack Dane is perfect. It's writ in stone. It's a fucking legal document.*

He stopped circling the bar and headed outside, down toward the Front Beach, slapping at divebombing mosquitoes with every step. The heat was so oppressive he was breathing in soggy air. No one was on the beach when he arrived. The smart people were in their air-conditioned houses or air-conditioned cars or stores or movie theaters. When he reached the sand, he stripped off, down to his boxer shorts, and ran into the water, finally diving in when it was deep enough.

He was in a sea of squishy, clear jellyfish. Each time he took a stroke forward, he felt as if he were swimming through a million small, slimy plastic bags. After a few seconds he gave up, turned around and waded back to the beach, away from the grotesque jellyfish and tepid sea.

"Charlie, glad I caught you. It's Billy. Billy Madison."

He was back, pacing around the kitchen bar, the Shoreham phone book open on the counter.

"Billy. Wow—it's been a long time."

"I know. I've been in California. But I'm back on the East

Coast now. In fact, I'm in Shoreham. I'm going to Harvard Law School in the fall, but I'm here for the summer."

"Wow. Harvard Law. Impressive, Billy. You know, a week or so ago I was thinking about that weekend we spent together when we were sixteen, believe it or not. Remember—"

"You're doing great too, Charlie. I've heard about Figs. Sounds amazing. I'll have to come in and check it out soon."

"Just tell me when. I've got the reservation book in front of me, as it happens. Glass of champagne for old times on me."

"I'm not sure of my schedule right now, but it will definitely be soon. I'll let you know and I'll collect that champagne for sure."

"Good news. And it was nice to hear from you after all this time. We have to catch up. Swap life stories. I'll never forget that party down on the beach. Remember when you—"

"Charlie—listen. I have a favor to ask you."

"Shoot."

"You have a waiter at Figs. An English guy. Jack Dane."

"Jack? Sure. What about him?"

"Do you know anything about him? I mean his past? What he did before he came here?"

"Heck, I have his résumé right here in my desk. I can look at it again, but as far as I remember there's nothing particularly interesting in it."

"Would you mind looking at it again? It's just I'd like to find out a little about him."

"Why would you—ah, I get it. He's living with Holly Barrett now. Wow. After all that mess, you're not starting up with Holly again?"

"I never—no. I just want to find out a little about him. That's all."

"Sure, Billy. Whatever. Like I said, I don't think there was anything. Hold on a minute—I'll get the résumé."

Billy waited, drumming his fingertips on the counter.

"OK, here it is. A waiter at John and Company on the East Side in New York for two years. A good reference from there. Then a year at an Upper West Side restaurant in New York. Good reference."

"What do you mean by good?"

"I mean 'Jack Dane is personable, quiet and good at his job' kind of good. And then we have another one-year stint at Lamington's in Boston. And another good reference. Everyone uses the word 'quiet.' I'd use it too. He's quiet and efficient and good at his job."

"What about his education? Is that down there?"

"Whoa—Billy. You're stretching things here. What can I tell you? It looks normal, but I don't know anything about schools in England. Let's see—it's some place called Compton Hall."

"What college did he go to?"

"Doesn't look like he went to one."

"And where did he live in England? What was he doing there? Was he a waiter there too?"

"That's it, pal. End of story. You know, you messed up big time with the whole Holly thing. I think you should leave them alone, let them be happy. To tell you the truth, it's kind of creepy you digging into his past like this."

"OK, Charlie. Point taken. And thank you."

"Yeah, well. Maybe I'll see you if you come into the restaurant. But I'm not always here. Gotta go now. Bye, Billy."

"Goodbye."

Kind of creepy. Well, that's how I'd describe Jack Dane.

A shower—that's what he needed. Cold water guaranteed. He'd take a long shower and cool down and figure out his next move. But how soon was soon? When was Holly going to marry Jack? How much time did he have before they were Mr. and Mrs. Dane?

Because when that happened, when they were formally a couple, things would change. He'd have a harder time having any kind of relationship with Katy. Jack would be her stepfather. He'd be an even bigger part of her life than he was now.

Just as he had reached the shower and turned on the cold water, he heard the phone ringing.

Holly. Holly's calling me back. She's forgiven me. She's going to give me a chance and meet with me.

He rushed back to the kitchen, naked, and picked up the phone.

"Hello?"

"Billy?"

Not Holly. A female voice but not Holly's.

"Yes. This is Billy. Who's this?"

"Anna. Remember me? The love of your life?"

"My teenage life, Anna." He sighed. "I'm not a teenager any more."

"Holly says you look like one still."

"You talk to Holly?"

"Absolutely. We've always been friends. Why wouldn't we talk?"

"I don't know." Strangely, he felt on the edge of tears. Now Anna had been added to the list; he could tell it from her voice. Anna hated him too.

"Of course we're friends. And she just called to tell me her big news. She also told me what a scumbag you were when she told you."

"Great."

"And I'm calling to tell you—this is without Holly's knowledge, by the way—I'm calling to tell you to back off, Billy. Holl's been through tough times, really tough times. She's happy now. So leave her alone, why don't you?"

"I can't leave her alone, Anna. Katy is my daughter."

"Listen. I probably have more sympathy with you than anyone else in this drama does. I didn't know Holly had such a crush on you when we were going out—"

"She had a crush on me?"

"Yes, lamebrain. Super-size crush, apparently. Which is one of the reasons she went ahead and had Katy. Somewhere in that innocent deluded heart of hers, she thought you might come back. When Katy was born, you'd show up at the hospital and defy your parents. Cue music, cue sunset, cue happy family. And then, oops, it didn't happen.

"In any event, now she's finally really making a life for herself and you're back giving her shit. So here's the deal: if you want to have a decent relationship with Katy, give Holly and

Jack some breathing space. Let them get married and have a little time together before you start in with the 'I'm her father' business. Holly will respect you for that. She certainly isn't going to if you call her fiancé a 'foreign gold-digging waiter.'"

"It slipped out."

"Yeah, right."

"How long has she known him, Anna? That's what I'm worried about. Does she really know him? Who is this guy? He could be anybody . . . Anna? Hello, are you there?"

"I'm here. I was thinking. Look, I'm going to Holly's this weekend. I'll check him out and report back to you if he's a mass murderer, OK? But only if you keep away for a while. Don't hassle them. Is that a deal? . . . Billy?"

"Sorry—I was thinking too. I don't see what other options I have right now. I don't want to get lawyers involved. Not yet, anyway. I want to try to make this as painless as possible—for Holly and Katy. You promise you'll tell me the truth—exactly what you think of him? And you'll try to find out a little bit about him? Who his friends are, things like that?"

"Sure. I'd do that normally. I mean, I feel protective of Holl. You're not the only one who wants to make sure she's not making a mistake."

"Excellent. But a heads-up, Anna. He's a handsome guy. Don't let that cloud your judgment, OK?"

"Shut up! How handsome?"

"Anna."

"OK. I'll drop by your house on my way back on Sunday."

"Good. Perfect."

"It'll be nice to see me again, won't it? But a heads-up for you too, Billy. I'm even more attractive than I was when I was a teenager. But don't let that cloud your judgment. I'm still a bitch."

Billy smiled for the first time in days.

11

It's all my fault Jack wasn't at breakfast. Jack's always at breakfast and breakfast is always at the same time. That's one of the
good things about Jack. Jack believes in alwayses. But with
some excepts. Like when he goes fishing with Henry. Then
breakfast is after fishing. I think it's OK to have some excepts
as long as you have alwayses too.

I'm bad because it's all my fault Jack wasn't at breakfast. I
was coughing really loudly last night. He hated that. He hates
noise. He especially hates it when I cry. Mommy came into my
room and tried to get me to stop coughing. She got into bed
with me and hugged me but it didn't work. I couldn't stop
coughing. It was like when my ear wouldn't stop hurting. My
room is next to Mommy's and Jack's. Jack came in and said,
"You're keeping me up. I can't sleep with all this coughing. I'm
surprised she hasn't woken up Anna too." He stops calling me
princess when he's mad at me. And Mommy said, "Anna can
sleep through a hurricane." Jack said, "Well, I can't. Get her to
shut up." He was mad and that made me cry so he got madder.

That made Mommy cry too. Especially when Jack left.
Mommy got up to go find him but she couldn't find him any-

where. When she came back she said, "He's gone." She was crying but the quiet kind of crying.

Mommy was happy before, when we had supper with Anna after Anna came to visit. Jack was working at his restaurant and Anna said, "I can't wait to meet him," and Mommy and Anna were talking about the wedding and drinking wine and laughing. They'd let me stay up with them for a while. They talked about dresses and how nice it would be to have the wedding on Henry's porch. "Can we put a bow around Bones's neck?" I asked and Mommy and Anna laughed.

But that was all before I woke up and started coughing.

Then Jack didn't come to breakfast. Anna didn't either but that's because she sleeps late in the mornings. "This seven-thirty in the morning routine sounds crazy to me. Count me out," Anna said last night. So me and Mommy had breakfast alone and Mommy kept looking to see if Jack was going to come into the kitchen but he didn't. She said, "He didn't take the car." She said it to herself, not me, and I didn't dare ask her if not taking the car was good or bad.

When Anna woke up, she had a glass of orange juice and we went down to the beach because of how hot it is. Anna has this funny bathing suit. It has pink polka dots and it's in two pieces but it's almost like she's not wearing anything.

I was make-believe looking at boats and flags. I wasn't really looking because I knew Mommy was sad and I was scared about that. Anna said something about the pictures Jack put up in the house. She said, "He's faintsomething." That's what it sounded like. I didn't understand. Then she said, "He's super faintsomething. How the hell did you catch him," and I wanted to say, "Mommy didn't catch Jack. That's stupid. Jack's not a tennis ball or a fish," but I didn't say it cuz I was make-believe looking at boats. Mommy didn't say anything too and Anna asked her, "So where is he? When am I going to meet him? Where are you hiding him?"

Mommy looked like she was going to cry again and said, "I need to talk to you" to Anna and I was scared she was going to talk about how to stop me coughing even though I wasn't coughing any more. I don't want to get sent to a hospital.

I saw Jack first. He was coming from where the lighthouse is at the end of the dike. I wanted to run up to him but I didn't because he might still be mad. Mommy must have seen him too. She jumped up and waved at him and he waved back and kept walking to us. I think Mommy couldn't find him because he was out on the beach all the night. He told me how much he loves the beach. When we were playing catch, he said he loves the beach because he loves the ocean and the beach loves the ocean too and when the waves come to the beach, they come because the ocean is talking to the beach. It's a funny thing to say but I think he's right.

Jack came up and Mommy kissed him and he gave her a hug. He said hello to Anna and shook her hand. He shakes hands now with the wrong hand like Henry shakes hands. He asked Anna how her trip was and Anna started talking fast and laughing a lot and waving her hands in the air. Jack and Mommy and Anna sat back down on the sand and Jack said, "And how are you today, princess?" so I knew he wasn't mad at me any more.

Then Anna did this crazy thing. She jumped up and said, "Come on, let's go for a swim," and ran into the water and jumped around in it and yelled, "Jack, come on. It's beautiful. Come in." Jack smiled a make-believe smile and shook his head and put his arm around Mommy. Mommy smiled a real smile and I got so happy I started to look for boat flags for real.

Anna jumped around in the water some more and then came back and sat down and started putting sun cream all over herself. She kept looking at Jack like he was a flag she'd never seen before. Then she lay down on her tummy and untied the string things of her top so her whole back was showing and she said, "Jack, I've got a good idea. Why don't we go for a picnic lunch later? Holly doesn't like picnics, but you and I can walk down the beach and find a good place for one and I can find out all about my best friend's fiancé and decide if he's good enough for her."

Mommy was bad then cuz she lied. She said she did like picnics.

Jack said, "Well, I don't like picnics. Let's have lunch all together at the house."

Anna told Jack that she and Mommy had been talking about the wedding and that they had to go shop for their dresses together soon and asked him when did he think the wedding would be?

Jack said, "I was thinking next weekend, actually." He kissed Mommy on the lips.

Anna sat up and she was holding the top part of her bathing suit to her chest so it didn't fall off into the sand. She looked really surprised. She said, "But you need more time to arrange things. You must have friends from England you want to come, Jack. They'll need some time to get their flights." Mommy looked surprised too but she didn't say anything.

Jack got up and came to me and picked me up and went and sat back down with me on his lap. "It's going to be a family lonely wedding," he said. I didn't understand so I asked him what family lonely means.

"Family *only*. It means just you and me and Mommy and Henry, princess."

"And Bones."

"Of course. And Bones," he said. "But no one else."

Anna didn't like that. She looked hard at him and then she looked hard at Mommy. Like now she was the one who was mad.

"No one from your family, no friends of yours?" she asked.

"Exactly. Holly and Katy and Henry are my family now. Oh, sorry, princess." He tickled my sides. "And Bones."

Jack says he's not ticklish. He says you can only be ticklish if you're afraid and he's not afraid of anything.

Anna said, "Holly. What do you think about this?" She sounded really mad.

And Mommy said, "I think it's perfect. I agree with Jack. Family only will be beautiful. And the sooner the better."

She kissed Jack back on the mouth.

That's when I asked if I could come here and see you. I was afraid I'd forget some things and I wanted to tell you everything. I tried really hard to remember everything cuz I know you want to know. Mommy said I could come because she knew Henry would be here in the house too.

She's happy again and Jack's happy too but I'm afraid. Cuz

what if I cough again or my ear hurts? You have to help me make sure I never cough again and I never cry. Ever ever. If I feel like I'm going to cry, I'm going to come here and see you and you have to help me not cry. I don't want it to be all my fault. I don't want Jack to get mad and go away again.

Jack has a secret, Bones, but we know what the secret is, don't we? It's why you don't go to Jack ever. It's why you stay away from him. I didn't know why at first because you can't talk so you can't tell me, but you don't have to talk because I know why now.

Grown-ups lie. Mommy told a lie on the beach when she said she did like picnics and Jack told a lie when I first saw him. He said he wasn't the Explorer but he is. He's the Explorer. And you're afraid to go near Jack cuz you're afraid you'll get to like him too much. And then what happens if I cry again?

If I cry, he'll go away and explore again and he won't come back ever and you'll be sad. Everyone will be sad and it will be all my fault.

12

"Look. She's teaching him how to sail. It's ridiculously sweet."

Anna was standing on the back porch of his house, holding binoculars and staring out into the bay. She hadn't changed much in five years. The sexy teenage girl he'd known and loved so much was now a sexy woman with the same long, thick black hair, the same mischievous eyes, the same ability to make him feel as if he was lagging behind somehow. Anna had always been ahead of him; she was so far ahead of him when she ditched him he hadn't even begun to see it coming.

"I can't believe they're getting married next weekend."

"Believe it." She continued watching the blue-and-white striped sail in the distance.

"So he has no family, no friends? What's with that?"

She shrugged. "Jack Dane's a mystery. I tried to find out something about his past, but he kept changing the subject. He did it in a funny way, though. It's hard to explain. I'm not sure if he was avoiding my questions or if he thought my questions were boring. I couldn't figure him out. At one point I asked him what he was like as a kid and he went on some riff about a TV show he used to watch—some Australian soap opera called *Neighbors*. One of the guys in it has been on *24* and *The OC* and

Ugly Betty and *Lost*—the thing is, he was really funny about it. So funny in that sarcastic English way I totally forgot my original question."

It's a game. You're ahead of me, Jack's ahead of you—but where's Holly?

"Anna—will you put those binoculars down?"

"Whatever." She lay them on the glass table beside her. "Your parents must have bought all this stuff at the same place. It's generic Cape Cod rental, isn't it? Lots of wicker and glass and tasteful watercolor paintings of sea scenes."

"It works for them." It was his turn to shrug.

They'd never belonged here, his parents. And he hadn't either. Because the joke about it being Barrett Point had a painful truth to it. Everyone else on Birch Point was an outsider, really. They could swim on the beach and walk on the dike and go fishing and sailing, but they missed whatever it took to have this Point in their blood because they weren't Barretts. They didn't swim and walk and sail and fish in the same way.

Billy remembered the day, a few weeks after they'd moved in, when his father had asked Holly's father John over to play tennis on their court. "Might as well get in with the locals," his father had said. When John Barrett arrived, tennis racquet in hand, he was wearing long khaki trousers stained with fish blood and an old blue T-shirt with a hole in the side. Billy's father had on crisp white shorts and a white Fred Perry tennis shirt.

But the strange thing was that Billy realized instantly John Barrett's clothing was clearly the right Birch Point choice.

John had brought Holly with him and Billy and Holly sat on

the grass together watching their fathers play. With pride, Billy saw his father win the first five games in a row. Yet as John walked by Holly when he was changing sides, he said, "Now I've got him exactly where I want him, sweetheart," and winked at her. Billy knew his father heard this, because he saw a big smirk on his dad's face.

What happened next was astounding. His father began to falter, making unforced errors, double-faulting, and finally losing 7–5. When his father then said it was too hot to play a second set, Billy blushed with embarrassment.

He remembered too bringing up the subject of that game with Holly, back when they were friends. They were sitting at the Mill Pond Diner and Billy felt he had to apologize for the fact that his father had never asked her father to play tennis again. "He couldn't stand the fact that he blew it like that. He cares a lot about winning and he just blew it after your father said that."

"Your father was probably trying too hard," she'd stated, as if, of course, trying too hard was bound to end in disaster. "My father once told me that there's no mastery without ease."

"Is that why your family are the only ones on the Point who never get a poison-ivy rash? Because they have mastered the art of avoiding poison-ivy easily?" he'd asked, and she'd laughed her shy laugh.

His parents had tried to convince him that Holly was after their money when she insisted on having the baby. "Look at that house of theirs," his mother had said. "It's shabby. Look at the clothes they wear. Thrift shop. They want you to marry her so they can get their hands on our money. She tricked you, Billy. You can't ruin your life in order to fund theirs. They know when we die we'll leave everything to you and their precious daughter will be secure."

Billy made himself believe them. Because he wanted his life to go on as if Holly's pregnancy hadn't happened. But he had to keep pushing away the knowledge that they were wrong, that the Barretts had a different take on money than his parents. They never wore designer labels, they didn't buy expensive gadgets, they drove old cars. None of which meant they didn't have lots of money; it meant they wore their money easily.

Anna had sat down on one of the wicker chairs, sprawling, showing off her short denim skirt and long tanned legs. Her top was sleeveless, pink, hot. She was holding a glass of iced tea to her chest.

"I really blew it with that gold-digging waiter comment, didn't I?"

"Yup."

"Is there any way back for me? I mean, can I make up for it somehow?"

"I don't know. But I would definitely steer clear for a while, if I were you. Let them get married, settle down a little. Maybe you could even congratulate them. Show you don't have any hard feelings."

"Yeah, right."

"What is it about Jack that bothers you so much, Billy? The fact that he's so gorgeously handsome?"

"I don't trust him."

"Well, you wouldn't, would you?"

"Come on, he has no friends or family, he's rushing her into this marriage—what's to trust?"

"Let me see." She fingered her lip. "How about trusting him because he loves Holly and Katy? They're a real little threesome, you know. He wouldn't even take a walk on the dike alone with me. It's all about Holly and Katy. He was polite to me, but that's it. I didn't count. Which kind of pissed me off, but hey. I have to admit I was pissed off because I was semi-flirting and he didn't take the bait. So I deserved it for being a shitty, selfish friend. Holly's a lucky girl. And God knows, she deserves some luck in her life."

"But why get married so quickly?"

"Why not?" Anna put her iced tea down on the ground, stood up. "Look, I have to go. I don't want to get caught in Sunday rush-hour traffic. As far as I can see, Jack is a hunk, and a decent guy. He may not have friends or family, but so what? Less hassle for Holly. He doesn't like to talk about his childhood? I say, fanfuckingtastic. He's not some wimp who can't stop talking about his past.

"Holly loves him and I'm sorry but Katy loves him too and Henry even likes him—he took him fishing at some ridiculously early hour this morning. If you want any chance of getting to know Katy and all that father stuff, you'd better accept Jack and stop making waves. Otherwise you're screwed. Katy won't like you either if you give Jack a hard time. She adores the guy."

"Great."

"Suck it up, Billy." Anna slapped him on the side of the

head, then kissed him on the cheek. "And be nice to the girl whose heart you broke." She walked out; he followed her to the front door.

"If you need to say something stupid again, call me and say it to me. My number's in the Boston phone book. But try and keep that mouth of yours shut, OK?"

"Right." He nodded, trying not to feel abandoned. She wasn't really an ally; he'd just hoped she'd be one.

"Holly loves him and I'm sorry but Katy loves him too and Henry even likes him—he took him fishing at some ridiculously early hour this morning."

Yes, I know he did. I went to the boatyard to take the Whaler *out early this morning and I saw them. Billy and Henry getting into the* Sea Ox *together, setting off for a trip. Like they were already family.*

I never dared ask Henry or John to take me fishing. I wanted to, but I didn't dare. I was worried I'd mess up somehow and they'd make fun of me in that Barrett dry way they had. I knew I'd try too hard.

But there was Jack, starting up the boat, backing it out of its berth. Jack who fits in easily. As if he'd been born here.

I turned around and came back home.

He threw himself on the large sofa in front of the flat-screen TV, picked up the remote control, switched it on, switched it off, put his elbow over his eyes. His dream of the night before hadn't left him; it lurked in his mind sickeningly, coloring his mood.

He'd seen Katy running through a dense forest, her hair flying behind her, barefoot and afraid and obviously in danger.

He was calling to her from behind, but she wouldn't turn around. She kept running and the forest turned into a swamp and she was sinking down into the swamp and he couldn't help her. She wouldn't turn around and look for him, no matter how loud he yelled. Instead she struggled forward, into the arms of a faceless man who'd appeared out of nowhere.

Then he wasn't behind Katy any more. He was standing behind the faceless man. He had a knife in his hand. But then it wasn't in his hand. It was in the man's back, up to the hilt. Blood was leaking out of the man's back. And he was holding the handle as tightly as he could.

13

The weather was glorious. The heatwave had passed and the temperature was in the low eighties, with no humidity and a bright, sparkling sun. Holly couldn't have asked for a more perfect day.

My second present, she thought, when she woke up. *My parents gave me Jack and now they've given me the best possible day for our wedding.*

In a token gesture to wedding rituals, Jack had stayed at Henry's the night before. She and Katy had woken up early, had breakfast together, gone down to the beach for a quick swim and then come back to shower, do their hair and get dressed.

It took a while to calm Katy down enough to get her dressed. She'd been running around the house after her shower; naked, dripping water, spinning around in circles like a little whirling dervish.

"Mommy's getting married," she kept chanting, clapping her hands.

"Not if you don't get dressed, chicken," Holly said, grabbing her shoulders mid-twirl and guiding her to the bedroom. "Nothing can happen until you get dressed."

She'd bought a pale green dress with white smocking for Katy, and had made a circle of daisies to go around the top of her head. When she'd finally managed to get her to stand still long enough to put on the dress and the daisies, Holly stepped back and looked at her daughter in the full-length mirror.

"Jack's right. You are a princess, sweetheart. You look like you stepped out of a fairy tale."

"I wish there was a castle. And snow." Katy looked up at Holly. "And a big church and horses and a long white dress I can hold the end of."

"It will be beautiful, chicken. You'll see. Just the way it is."

She'd once had dreams of a wedding with all the trimmings. A church full of people and flowers and music, a measured walk down the aisle in a long white dress and veil, the train of her dress trailing behind her. At first, when Jack had proposed, she'd pictured it happening like that and seen herself on Henry's arm. But she knew Jack was right as soon as he'd told Anna what he envisioned. A small, informal wedding was best. It was more intimate. They didn't need anyone else to witness their happiness. And it would have felt wrong anyway to have a church wedding when her parents weren't there to see her.

Besides, as pathetic as it might be, she had to admit to herself she'd prefer to get married without Anna, who would doubtless have worn some unbelievably sexy outfit, in attendance.

She went to the closet and took out a turquoise blue, sleeveless, empire-waisted silk dress which came down to just above her knees. It was simple, old-fashioned, and as soon as she'd seen it, she knew Jack would love it.

After she put it on, she took a string of pearls her mother used to wear for formal occasions and hung them around her neck. She had blow-dried her hair so it was straighter than it normally was, but she didn't put on any make-up. Jack didn't like make-up; he'd told her soon after they'd started going out that he thought women put on make-up for themselves, not men. "It's not necessary," he'd said. "It looks fake. Someone centuries ago thought it up for a marketing ploy and women have been buying into that ploy ever since. It's a sham."

"Mommy, you look beautiful," Katy said as Holly slipped on a pair of blue high-heeled sandals. "Do you want some of my flowers for your hair too?"

"No thanks, sweetheart. I'm fine. Look at us." They stood in front of her bedroom mirror, gazing into it. "We make a good pair, don't we?"

"We look perfect," Katy smiled. "And Bones will look perfect too in his white bow."

Holly leaned over and kissed the top of Katy's head. "Are you happy, chicken?"

"Yes. Jack's happy too, isn't he?"

"I hope so." Holly nodded. "Yes, Jack's happy too. I know so."

At noon, she and Katy walked over to Henry's, to find Jack and Henry and Judge Hearne waiting for them on the porch. As a teenager, Holly had imagined Billy as the man waiting for her as she walked down the aisle. After she'd had Katy, she'd watch a romantic movie or read a book and find herself day-dreaming about a wedding, but she had no image in her mind of what her husband would look like.

Seeing Jack standing on the porch beside Henry, dressed in a dark blue suit with white shirt and pale blue tie, she had exactly the same shock of pure pleasure she'd had when she first caught sight of him beside the bus, the visceral reaction to a breathtakingly handsome man. Except this time she wasn't looking at a stranger, she was looking at Jack: the man whom she loved, who loved her, with whom she was going to spend the rest of her life.

He smiled and she smiled back, while Katy dropped her hand and ran up the porch steps to him.

"I'd pick you up, princess, but I don't want to muck up your dress," Jack said.

"Can't have a mucked-up dress," Henry added, patting his great-granddaughter on the head. He had on white flannel trousers with a blue jacket, and was looking both paternal and distinguished.

Holly went and shook hands with Judge Hearne, a gray-haired avuncular man who was wearing a black robe, but one which didn't completely cover the red lobster motif of his blue trousers. Jack had joked that he should wear his Lobster Pot T-shirt to the wedding, and Holly decided the judge's trousers were yet another sign that this wedding was destined, that the heavens were looking down on them with a big nod of approval.

The service was straightforward. They'd debated about

creating their own special vows but finally decided against it. "You know me," Jack had said. "I don't want some trendy service; whatever we might say won't add to the traditional vows—they cover everything that needs to be said and there's a good reason that they've been in use for so long. Poems and our own words can go in and out of fashion; these vows are eternal."

When Judge Hearne stated, "I now pronounce you man and wife. You may kiss the bride," Jack gathered Holly to him in a huge hug, kissed her briefly, then pulled back and winked. The way her father used to wink at her sometimes. Katy jumped up and down, clapping, and Henry said, "Time to break out the champagne."

It had all been simple and beautiful and, as Katy inevitably announced, "Perfect." Henry poured champagne for the judge, Jack and her and a glass of ginger ale for Katy. When she begged to have a sip out of Holly's glass, Holly gave in, but stopped her firmly when she tried to glug down more.

Henry had made lobster salad for their wedding lunch and had set up a little table in the shade on the side of the porch where they could sit and eat, looking out over the water. Judge Hearne took off his robe, revealing a lobster-red golf shirt, and helped himself to a huge plate. He then proceeded to regale them for half an hour with tales of his fishing exploits, before stopping mid-sentence, checking his watch and announcing he had a golf match to play in.

After he'd wished them the happiest of marriages, he left and Henry chuckled, saying, "Nice man, the judge, but those fishing stories are fifty percent wishful thinking and fifty percent more wishful thinking. I took him out with me once and he was a nuisance. Managed to hook himself in the thumb and hook me in the ankle. A real liability on a boat. Anyway, what's the plan, you two? When are you off to Vermont?"

"We're leaving late afternoon." Jack had his arm around Holly and squeezed her shoulder. "Holly and I are going for a sail in the Sunfish after lunch. I'm going to show her what a good teacher she is and what a good learner I am. We'll go for a nice, long, relaxed sail and then come back and hopefully get going in time to make it to the inn for dinner."

"That sounds like a good plan. What do you think, Mrs. Dane?"

It took Holly a second to realize Henry was addressing her; when she did, she smiled, touched her gold wedding band with her left thumb, and reached up to put her hand over Jack's.

"I think it's an excellent plan. What about you, Katy? Are you all right with Jack and me going for a sail on our own?"

"Yes." Katy nodded, rhythmically patting the head of Bones, who was lying at her feet. "Bones, you can go see Jack now. Go on. It's OK now."

Bones didn't move and Holly was surprised to hear the anxiety in Katy's voice when she said again, "It's OK, Bones. You can go see him now."

"What are you talking about, Katy? Why is it OK for Bones to see Jack now? I don't understand."

"I thought now Jack can say."

"Say what?" Holly looked over to Jack, who raised his eyebrows and shrugged.

"Say about being the Explorer."

"What?" Holly's heart dropped from its great height with a crash.

"He is, isn't he?" Katy's eyes were beseeching.

"Sweetheart." She looked at Jack again, then at Henry.

"Princess." Jack went over to Katy, knelt down on the porch in front of her. "You've got the wrong end of the stick."

"What stick?"

"I mean . . ." He took her hands in his. "I'm not an explorer, I'm afraid. Just a waiter. A good waiter. A very good waiter. But I don't explore. I stay at home. With you and your mother. Remember I told you when I first met you I'm not an explorer. That's OK, isn't it? You like waiters, don't you?"

"But I thought . . ." Katy bit her lip. "I know you are. You are."

"I'm your stepfather now, princess. Which means I'm a special kind of father. Who loves you very much."

Holly thought Katy was going to burst into tears. Instead she made a funny face, screwing her lips to one side, and then looked over at Henry.

"Henry, can we play Ping-Pong now?"

"Of course, Katy." Henry went over to her, picked her up in his arms. "But I think we'd better get changed out of these fancy clothes first. I have your shorts and T-shirt in your room upstairs. Why don't you run up and change?" He put her down on the porch. "Off you go—skedaddle."

She ran to the screen door, opened it and disappeared into the house.

"Jesus H. Christ." Henry rubbed his forehead. "Did you know she thought that?"

"Of course not," Holly replied, bridling. "I had no idea."

"Jack?"

"Absolutely not, Henry."

"What a fuck-up."

"Actually, she didn't seem that bothered." Jack was up off his knees and back at Holly's side. "She seemed more interested in the Ping-Pong than my status as non-Explorer."

"You think so?" Holly turned to him. "Really?"

"She had an idea, that's all. And she found out it wasn't the right idea. She doesn't even know what a father means, not really. I'm sure she'll be fine."

"You don't think I should go up to her now, explain about Billy?"

"No way. You'd just confuse her. I bet you anything she'll be running through that door in a few seconds, desperate to get a Ping-Pong bat in her hand, with no thought whatsoever for the Explorer."

"I don't know." Henry shook his head. "This whole Explorer business has to stop. It's always been wrong. Holly, you should think about—" But he was interrupted by Katy, who bounded through the screen door in her shorts and with her T-shirt on the wrong way around. "Let's play, Henry. Come on." She grabbed his hand and tugged it.

"Chickpea, are you sure you're all right? Do you want me to stay for a while?"

"I want to be with Henry and Bones. You and Jack go."

"OK." Holly looked at her daughter, standing impatiently,

tugging at Henry's hand, and for the first time she saw Billy in her. Her blonde hair had probably come from Billy's side, but it had never reminded Holly of Billy—it was thicker and more platinum than his. Her eyes and nose had a slight twinge of Barrett to them, but Katy had been otherwise unmistakably Katy, her own individual genetic print. Yet when she said, "I want to be with Henry and Bones," something about her mouth, the straight line it made, resembled Billy's when he was being stubborn.

So Billy had managed to make his presence known, like in a fairy tale when the evil fairy godmother shows up at the party and casts a spell. For a second, when Judge Hearne had asked if anyone had any objections to the marriage, Holly had looked around, terrified that Billy might be hiding in a bush or behind a tree and would spring out and try to stop them. This unexpected reminder of him was like a thorn in her happiness, but only a tiny one, and one almost instantly removed. Katy's expression changed; as she leaned down to pat Bones, she became Katy again.

I'll have to talk to Jack. When we're in Vermont. We have to face this Billy business and decide on the best way to introduce him to Katy. But it will all be fine, because we're so happy now we can handle anything.

"Before we all go our separate ways—" Henry stood up "—I'd like to make a toast. To Holly and Jack. And Katy, of course. You deserve the very best in life, and I feel sure now you'll have it, together. I'd like to take some credit for this match." He smiled. "But you would have found each other again without me, I'm sure.

"Jack, I welcome you to our family. It's a real pleasure to have such a wonderful grandson-in-law. Not to mention one who can fish. I'm looking forward to many more fishing trips. But I want us to raise our glasses, too, to the people we love who aren't here. They're all still a part of us and I'm sure they're sharing in our happiness. Let's raise our glasses to you and to them."

They all stood, raised their glasses, and drank. Holly kissed and hugged Henry; he held her tightly, then pushed her away, saying, "Shit, sweetie, I'm too old to cry. Go. Get out into this beautiful weather and go sailing."

After they'd changed and Jack and she had walked down to the beach in their bathing suits, they began to drag the Sunfish down to the water. Just before they reached the water's edge, a memory of her mother calling out, "You forgot your life jacket, Holly. Come back," slammed into her heart. This intense, overwhelming surge of sadness she felt should have hit when she was putting on her wedding dress, or when she was saying her vows, not when the ceremony was over and she was doing something as mundane as getting a Sunfish into the water.

But Holly had learned that grief could ambush you when you least expected it. She'd be walking from the kitchen to the living room, have a sudden memory of her parents, stop in her tracks, and find tears running down her face, from the sheer force of missing them. Anniversaries of their birthdays and deaths would always bring sadness, but the most powerful emotions came out of the blue, catching her off guard.

"Holly?" Jack had the centerboard in his hand. "Are you all right? Hop on. We're going."

All she could do was to hold up her hand, signaling for him to wait while she tried to get her composure back.

"Holly?"

"I'm coming." She didn't want to tell him what had upset her, worried that it would make him sad about his own parents too, so she stepped forward into the water, splashed some quickly onto her face, and while Jack held the boat for her, she hopped on board and grabbed the sail's rope.

One of her parents' favorite movies had been *High Society* with Grace Kelly, Bing Crosby and Frank Sinatra. In one scene, Grace Kelly and Bing Crosby sail off together on their honeymoon in a boat called *True Love*. This Sunfish was too small to have a name; it had a blue-and-white striped sail and a fiberglass body which was as rudimentary as a sailboat could be. But as Holly watched Jack take command of the rudder, she thought of it as their own *True Love*.

They set off in the breeze, tacked a few times and headed for the end of the dike and beyond. Jack had picked up the art of sailing seemingly effortlessly, and Holly sat happily, soaking up the sun as they glided across the tops of tiny waves.

Sometimes when she'd go out on her own, she'd purposefully take the boat to the limit and beyond, riding the wind so hard that the hull lifted out of the water, the boat was almost perpendicular, and she was flying. There was always that moment of heady abandon mixed with fear as the sail went that one inch too far, toppling her and the boat into the ocean.

This was going to be an easy, relaxed sail, though. No

capsizing, simply meandering along, enjoying a few hours of sun, salt air and post-ceremony, pre-honeymoon time. When they reached the end of the dike, Jack said, "There's a little island up ahead and off to the right, isn't there? I've seen it when I've fished with Henry and I've always wanted to land on it and explore. Do you know the one I mean? I think Henry called it Little Bird Island."

"I know it. But I don't want to land there. Let's just keep sailing."

"Why don't you want to?"

"It's called Little Bird but it has another name too. I've always been scared of going there, ever since I was a child."

"Holly?" He shot her a quizzical look. "What are you on about? How can you be afraid of a little island?" He nudged her leg with his foot.

"Because it's the Bad Boy's Island."

"What does that mean?"

"It's what we've always called it. My mother told me about it. There was a bad boy who lived on the road into town, just after the Point Road ends; and he used to go to that island and camp out at night."

"A bad boy?"

"That's what we called him. All my cousins had heard about him too. We used to dare each other to go to the island but none of us ever did."

Jack pushed the rudder so the boat headed straight into the wind.

"What are you doing? We can't move when we're headed straight into the wind like this."

"What did this boy do that was so bad?"

Clearly, he wasn't going to move the tiller; she didn't know why this story interested him so much, but she went ahead and explained:

"That's the funny part. We were all terrified of him and thought he was a murderer and none of us dared ask what he'd done. You know how little kids are. We used to tell scary stories about him at night to frighten each other. One day when I was sixteen or so, I finally asked my mother what he'd done and she told me she thought he'd stolen a bicycle. But she wasn't sure."

"What's funny about that?"

"It's not funny exactly, but you know, like I said, we were kids and we'd built up this whole image of him as this evil, awful bad boy who'd done terrifying things and it turned out all he'd done was maybe steal a bicycle. Still—somehow it stuck. I mean, we kept calling Little Bird Island the Bad Boy's Island even when we knew he hadn't done anything horrible, and I know it's ridiculous, but I still have a thing about it. I don't want to go there. It feels like bad luck."

"Bad luck? Because some poor boy who may or may not have stolen a bicycle used to camp out there? And it's supposed to be funny that because he may have made one mistake, you branded him an evil monster for eternity? I can't believe how stupid you were and how stupid you're being now."

"Jack?" Holly reeled with shock and pain. "If you feel that strongly about it, of course I'll go there with you. It just wasn't something I wanted to do on our wedding day, that's all."

The boat wasn't moving and the sun was bearing down on

her and Jack was sitting with the rudder in his hand, staring at her with the same terrible cold expression he'd had those two times when Katy had been sick and crying. Holly pulled the sheet of the sail in a vain attempt to get them moving again.

"Come on. I've changed my mind. That's a woman's prerogative, isn't it? Let's go there. It will be fun." She was pleading with him now, hating the way his eyes had hardened, desperate to make amends for screwing things up. "You're right, I was being stupid and childish."

"Stupid and childish and worse. You were being cruel and judgmental, not to mention absurdly superstitious."

"I was being cruel? I don't think I was being cruel."

"Did you ever meet him?"

"The Bad Boy?"

"No, the President, Holly. We were talking about the President, weren't we?"

"Jack, please. I'm sorry, OK? And no, I never met him. Please can we just start sailing again and forget about him?"

"Absolutely." He pushed the tiller as far as he could to the left, maneuvering the boat back into a position to catch the wind and pick up speed. But just as Holly was beginning to hope he'd calmed down, he tacked; the boom swinging so quickly in the other direction, it almost smashed her in the head.

"Jack? What are you doing?"

"We're going home."

"What?"

"We're going home."

"I don't understand. This is silly. Can't we forget it?"

"We've done enough sailing, Holly. It's time to go back."

They'd never talked about the night when Anna had come to visit, the night when he'd gone off and hadn't come back. She assumed he'd slept on the beach, and had wanted to ask him why he had felt the need to leave. But Anna had been there and then they'd been busy planning the ceremony and that awful night faded into obscurity. She didn't want to bring it back to life by mentioning it.

Besides, she had decided that there was a gulf between their cultures she'd just have to get used to. The English don't like to talk about their emotions, and she would have to learn to accept that and be thankful that he didn't overanalyze everything the way Americans did. Going out and sleeping on the beach was better than staying in and being angry. It was preferable to say nothing than say something you might regret. And he might have admitted that he was having problems dealing with a small child who cried and coughed at night. In the heat of sleepless irritation, he might have said something about Katy which she wouldn't be able to forget.

But Katy's crying or coughing wasn't the issue now. The problem was, she had no idea what the issue was, why he was so angry and distant.

This was their wedding day and Jack wasn't speaking to her; he wouldn't even look at her.

She'd prepared herself for the possibility of Billy coming and making a scene. The fact that he'd been quiet in the past week, that he hadn't shown up at the house or called, didn't totally allay her fear of him making trouble for them somehow.

What she would never have imagined in a million years was that the old scary Bad Boy of her childhood would come back and ruin her perfect day. Maybe Jack was right. Maybe she had been cruel to the Bad Boy. If so, he was getting his revenge on her now. In spades.

14

No one had answered his knock on the door. Which didn't mean he had the right to walk in, but he did anyway. His purpose for coming to the house had been well-intentioned. He was going to congratulate Holly and Jack on their marriage, show them he could rise above his feelings and make a gesture toward some kind of harmony. Having taken Anna's advice about steering clear, he was going to go that one step further and hold out the proverbial olive branch or peace pipe or whatever it took to get himself back on track and in Holly's good graces.

So he'd knocked and no one had answered and then he'd found himself opening the screen door. This hadn't been part of the plan, but he couldn't stop himself from walking in. "Hello," he called out, but again, no one answered. He almost turned around then and walked out; he might have if he hadn't seen the photographs. They were dotted all around the living room: pictures of Holly and Katy and Jack—a whole gallery of them, framed and on display. And not one of the ones he'd seen when he'd been before. No Mr. or Mrs. Barrett, no pictures of Katy as a baby or toddler.

The new regime.

Jack's kingdom.

He walked around, picking each one up, staring at it, putting it back down. At the far end of the room, on the bookshelf beside the porch door, were two with just Jack and Katy: one beach scene with the two of them sitting on the sand, digging a sandcastle together, the second an indoors shot—at the kitchen table. Katy was sitting on Jack's lap, wearing a Lobster Pot T-shirt that swamped her, pulling a funny face for the camera. And there was Jack, looking like he'd won the fucking lottery. Proud Jack, the proud father of a daughter who wasn't his.

The smug fucking bastard.

He whacked the photo back down on the shelf so hard, the glass broke.

Oh, shit. This is all I need. Jack coming back to find his photo smashed. Holly going berserk. Oh, shit.

Picking up the pieces of glass from the shelf and putting them in the palm of his hand, he carried them into the kitchen.

Get rid of the evidence, bozo, then get the hell out of here and hope Jack and Holly don't notice the frame is broken.

He found a roll of paper towels on the kitchen counter, wrapped the shards of glass up in wads of them and then hunted around until he discovered the garbage can underneath the sink. Lifting a used coffee filter from the top of the garbage, he hid the wrapped-up glass underneath, put the filter full of grounds back on top of it and went to wash his hands in the sink. As he was drying them, he noticed a cellphone lying on the kitchen table.

It wasn't right, but then what was right any more? Was Jack

right to have rushed Holly so quickly into marriage? Jack, Billy's instinct told him, had been the one to get rid of the photos of Holly's parents and past. How right was that?

He picked up the phone, flipped it open.

Jack's or Holly's?

When he punched the key to bring up the contact list, Holly and Figs were the only names listed. So that question was answered.

Not one other name? Jack had no friends, no family whatsoever?

Clearly not.

He hit the "Messages" button.

Zero.

While he was at it, he decided he might as well check the "Recently Dialed" list. There were four calls to the same local number—he assumed Holly. But there was also one international one. So Jack did still have one tie to home. But what tie? With whom? Billy was about to look for a pencil and a piece of paper when he heard the porch screen door open. Immediately he memorized the international number, flipped the phone shut and replaced it exactly where it had been on the table.

"Jack, it's our wedding day," he heard Holly saying in a pleading, tearful voice. "Can't we sit down and talk about it? I didn't mean to upset you. I've apologized. I don't know what else to do."

There was no escape from the kitchen, no back door. Billy stood, holding his breath, hoping they would go upstairs so he could sneak out the front; at the same time he wanted to hear what Jack's response to Holly would be.

He didn't get a chance to do either. Jack walked straight into the kitchen.

"What the hell are you doing here?"

Jack's face looked as though it should have a bubble above it with the word "Snarl" written in it.

"I came to congratulate you two. No one answered my knock and then I had a coughing fit and I came in to get a glass of water."

"Where's the glass, then?"

"I was just about to get it when you walked in."

"Oh, no." Holly stood at the threshold. "Billy. What are you doing here?"

"I told Jack. I wanted to congratulate you and I had a coughing fit so I came in and was about to get a glass of water."

"You mean you broke in. You mean you trespassed on private property."

The snarl had turned to a sneer of contempt and disdain.

"Look—I'm sorry." He held up his hands. "I'll leave."

"Bloody well right, you'll leave. You have no business here. I don't want to see you in this house again."

"I have some rights, Jack. I *am* Katy's father."

"We'll see about that."

"And what does that mean?"

"It means . . ." Jack walked to the threshold, took Holly's hand, and led her with him until they were standing opposite Billy, only a few feet away. "I want to adopt Katy."

"Jack?" Holly looked up at him.

"Yes." He let go of her hand, put his arm around her. "We're a family now. I want to adopt her."

"You won't be able to. I haven't gone to lawyers yet out of respect to Holly. But if you push me, Jack, I will."

"If I push you?" Jack took his hand away from Holly's shoulder, stepped forward and pushed Billy in the chest—with enough force to send him staggering backward.

"Jack!" Holly cried out at the same time as Billy said, "Fuck you, asshole," regained his balance and clenched his hands into fists.

"Stop!" Holly screamed. "It's my wedding day. Stop! Please don't fight. Please."

Billy took a step back, away from Jack.

"All right. For your sake, Holly. But you know something, Jack? You're supposed to be this perfect man, but you've already screwed up big time. I heard her when you came into the house. I don't know what you did, but you managed to make her miserable. And you've been married for what? A couple of hours? I came here to make peace and congratulate you, but I don't think this marriage will last. I think Holly is smarter than you give her credit for and she'll come to her senses and get rid of you. But I'll tell you something, I won't hesitate to get lawyers involved if I have to. For Katy's sake. The last thing she needs is a psycho bully father."

Jack raised his eyebrows and smirked. Billy watched in confusion as he then walked over to the bread bin and opened it.

Please God, don't bring out a gun.

He brought out a cigarette and matches and proceeded to light up. After two long inhalations and puffs, he leaned back against the counter and shot a haughty look at Billy.

"You don't want to fight me—fine." He shrugged. "Can't say

I blame you. You're a loser, Billy. And I'm warning you now—you'll lose everything if you try to come between me and my family."

"A psycho bully who threatens people. And you love this guy?" Billy looked at Holly and shook his head. "What have you gotten yourself into, Holl? What would your parents think?"

"Yes, I love him." She wiped away her tears and straightened her shoulders. "And my parents would love him too. I know they would. I know they *do*. You're ruining everything, Billy. Everything. I knew you would."

"Let's play a little game, Bill. I'll close my eyes and count to ten. Let's just see what happens if you're still here when I get to ten and open them." Jack took another puff of his cigarette and closed his eyes. "One . . ."

"Jesus, Holly—where did you find him?"

"She found me on a bus. Two . . ."

"What station was the destination? Hell?"

"Three . . ."

"I'm going. This is stupid." He walked over to Holly and placed his hand above her elbow. "I'm really sorry it has to be like this, Holly. I'm sorry you're upset. I bet you looked beautiful in your wedding dress today."

As he walked out of the kitchen, he heard Jack's "Four . . . ."

Well, that couldn't have gone much worse.

The half-mile hike to his house seemed much longer, as he rewound the tape and played the entire scene over in his mind. Getting caught in the house was dumb, almost fighting Jack yet again was dumber. But Jack had provoked him when he'd shoved him. He'd been looking for a fight.

And what had he done to Holly to make her so upset before?

Your parents would have loathed the man, Holly. Even I can see that. Love has made you blind and I guess loneliness or age or grief has made Henry blind and all Anna can see is how good-looking he is. I'm the only one who knows there's something wrong with him. I'm crying wolf and everyone else thinks he's a puppy.

When he reached his house, he headed straight for the telephone on the kitchen counter, picked it up and dialed the international number he'd memorized. He listened as the phone rang twice in succession instead of the one long American ring. After four of the two-in-a-row rings, someone picked up and a female voice answered with a name. Eliza McCormack.

"Hi, sorry to bother you, but I was looking for Jack Dane. Do you know him?"

"Excuse me?" A clipped English accent. Like some woman in a BBC adaptation of a Jane Austen book.

"Jack Dane. I'm a friend of his and I was trying to get in touch with him."

"I have no idea who you're talking about. You have the wrong number."

"Are you sure?"

"Of course I'm sure. You have the wrong number."

"OK, well, thanks anyway."

"Goodbye." She hung up.

He hung up too, and immediately redialed the number he'd memorized, in case he'd punched in a wrong digit the first time. She answered on the first ring, this time with "Hello."

"Sorry, it's me again. I thought I might have dialed the wrong number before."

"You *did* dial the wrong number before. And you've dialed the wrong number again." A very upper-class, exasperated voice. He couldn't place an age—but she wasn't young or old. Maybe in her forties.

"OK, sorry."

"I suggest you find the right one and don't bother me again."

"OK, sure. Goodbye."

She didn't bother to say goodbye, obviously desperate to get rid of him. Which made sense if he'd dialed the wrong number twice and she didn't know Jack Dane. Still—he was sure he'd memorized it correctly. Maybe someone else lived at that number. And that someone was the one Jack had called.

Billy took his own mobile phone out of his pocket, scrolled down his list of contacts and hit Daniel. As he waited for an answer, he stared out across the bay; a huge tanker was making its way down the canal looking ancient, rusty and tired.

"Hello?"

"Daniel? It's Billy Madison."

"Hey, Billy. How are you?"

"Fine. Listen, I was hoping you could help me with something. You spent your junior year abroad in London, didn't you?"

"I was in Manchester, actually."

"Right, well, maybe you won't know this, but I have an English phone number. If I give it to you can you tell me where it's based, if you see what I mean? Whether it's a London number or whatever."

"I know some of the codes, but it's like area codes—there are tons of them. I know Manchester and I know London and Oxford. Anyway, try me."

Billy reeled off the number.

"That's a mobile number—a cellphone. Not a landline."

"Really?" .

"Mmm-hmm. I guess that doesn't help you. Sorry."

"No, that does help, thanks, Dan. I'm in a hurry but I'll give you a call soon and we can catch up with each other."

"Sure."

After they'd said their goodbyes, Billy grabbed a beer from the fridge, went outside and sat down on the wicker chair Anna had lounged so seductively in when she'd come over.

A cellphone was personal. Jack Dane must have called the McCormack woman personally. And she, for whatever reason, was pretending she didn't know him.

He had no proof, though. And his theory would hardly stand up in a court, much less in the minds of Holly and the people around her. Besides, how could he admit he'd surreptitiously looked at Jack's phone?

As his thoughts were churning away, he found himself staring at the dike, at the tiny beach three-quarters of the way to the lighthouse; but not until he'd finished his whole can of beer did he realize that he'd been unconsciously focusing his gaze on the exact spot where Katy had been conceived.

Holly had been a sweet, shy, seventeen-year-old girl. To this day, he couldn't explain to himself why he'd had sex with her. He was feeling hurt and rejected by Anna, and Holly was there; sure. Boys will be boys. But it had never really made sense to him—because Holly had been a friend and he'd never had one sexual thought about her. There were other girls he could have taken advantage of, more obviously attractive ones.

Yet he'd just said, "I bet you looked beautiful in your wedding dress." He hadn't expected to say it; it just came out.

What confused and surprised him was that he'd meant it.

Billy Madison stood up and headed back to the kitchen for another beer.

15

Henry took the Ping-Pong net off the dining-room table, put it in a chest in the hall and went to his living room, where Katy was lying on the rug in her pajamas, curled up alongside Bones. She looked so adorable, he hesitated for a few seconds before telling her it was time to go to bed.

"Can Bones sleep on my bed with me?" she asked.

"I don't see why not. But go and brush your teeth first. Bones and I will come up after you've finished."

She scrambled to her feet and ran off toward the stairs. He heard a thud and then "Ouch!" and when he ran to the hall-way, he saw her little body sprawled on the floor.

"Katy!"

"I tripped," she said, as he picked her up. "I'm sorry, Henry."

"It's not your fault, bumblebee. I'm sorry you tripped. Does it hurt?"

"I promise I won't cry."

He carried her back into the living room, sat down with her on his lap.

"You can cry if it hurts." She was rubbing her knee; her mouth was quivering. "Go ahead. Cry. Let the hurt out."

"No!" It was a wail, this "No!," a terrified wail. "I can't cry."

She wriggled out of his arms and rushed over to Bones, burying her face in the dog's neck.

"Katy. It's all right." He wasn't sure what to do, how to make her feel better. "Honestly. Come back to me and I'll give you a hug."

Her hand went up to cover her mouth, and her body heaved in spasms.

"Katy? Come over here."

When she didn't move, he rose from the chair and picked her up again. She hurled her arms around his neck and pressed her face against his chest. Her heart was thumping wildly.

"Katy? Sweetheart. What's wrong?"

"Jack hates it when I cry. I can't cry ever again."

"Jack's not here, sweetheart." He patted her back. "He and Mommy have gone on their honeymoon. I'm here, though. And I say it's fine to cry."

Lifting her tear-stained face and looking up at him, she said, "I'll stop now. It doesn't hurt any more. Don't tell Jack I cried. Please. Promise?"

"I won't." He frowned. "I promise. Let's get you up to bed."

He carried her upstairs to the bathroom, watched as she brushed her teeth and then took her hand and led her into her bedroom.

"Hop into bed," he said, and when she did, he pulled the covers up and tucked her in.

"I want Bones."

"Bones will come." He sat down beside her. "But first, Katy, will you tell me why you're so afraid of Jack finding out you cried? Is he mean to you when you cry?"

"He leaves."

"Leaves the house?"

"Yes. He hates noise."

"I see." Henry paused. "Are you frightened of him?"

"Only when I cry. It's my fault he leaves."

"And the rest of the time. When you're not crying. What's Jack like then?"

"He's fun. He's good at games. Like you are."

"What kind of games?"

"Like catching games and hide-and-seek games. Fun games."

"No scary games? No games you don't like?"

"I like them."

"And you understand them?"

"What does that mean?"

"It means are they games you would play with anyone else if they asked?"

"Yes." Her hair was splayed out on the pillow; her face was pale and questioning. "Why are you asking about our games?"

"Does Jack tell you to keep any of the games you play a secret?"

"Only the catch game—so we can show Mommy how good we are when we get up high enough."

"Right."

"Can Bones come up now? I'm tired."

"OK. I'll bring him up."

Henry trudged downstairs, mulling over what Katy had told him. Jack wasn't used to children crying—that made sense. But to leave? And to make Katy so damned terrified of her own tears? It wasn't right. And these games they played. He'd asked the leading questions and had no responses which pointed to the unseemly, but there was still that image of them on the beach in the moonlight in his mind. He'd gone down a few nights since then to check and the beach had been empty, yes. But he'd been remiss about following up: he should have asked Jack if he'd told Holly about his sister dying. He should have found out if Holly knew about the late-night game of catch.

The wedding had taken his mind off Katy; he'd been concentrating on Holly, and her happiness had been so contagious, he had allowed himself to bask in it with her.

I'll have a word with him when they get back. He has to understand he can't scare Katy like that. Poor little thing was in a state. It's not right. He just has to get used to noise, whether he fucking hates it or not. And I'll talk to Holly too. I'll talk to Holly first.

By the time he'd led Bones upstairs and placed him on the foot of Katy's bed, she was fast asleep. He didn't turn out the light because he knew she liked to have it on. Patting her sleeping head and Bones's head too, he left them.

It had been an eventful, emotional day. Holly was now no longer only his responsibility. She had a husband to look after her—and that both pleased and saddened him. As anxious as he was for her to move back into the world and find independence, he couldn't help but feel a loss.

At least they hadn't moved away: another man might have preferred living in a different place, a different state even. He had to admit that he would have hated not having them nearby.

Had that fact, too, skewed his thinking about Jack? Had he been loath to question him further or take him to task in any way because he was so relieved that Jack was happy to stay in Birch Point?

Deciding to make a cup of tea and sit at the computer for a little while before going to bed himself, Henry headed for the kitchen. When the phone rang, he had just settled down at his desk, with the tea in easy reach.

"Hello?"

"Hello, Henry. It's Billy."

"Hello, Billy."

"I'm sorry to bother you, but I have to tell you something. It's Jack. There's something wrong with Jack. I'm not talking about the whole waiter business. He doesn't have any friends. Or any family—supposedly he doesn't. Except he called someone in England. And I called her and she says she doesn't know any Jack Dane. Which is bullsh— I mean I memorized the number from his phone and I know I got the right one. So who is she? That's what I want to know. Who is she?"

"Billy, you're not making any sense."

"I looked at his phone. When I went over there. There was a number he'd dialed and I called it. And this woman, Eliza McCormack, answered and said she didn't know him. Which is crap but no one will believe me, will they? You don't believe me, do you? Do you believe me?"

"Young man—you're drunk."

"Yeah, OK, whatever. I've had a few beers but I'm telling the truth. There's something wrong with him. He made Holly cry today. I heard them when they came in and I was in the kitchen and they didn't know I was there. She was really upset.

Who makes his wife cry on their wedding day? There's something wrong with him."

"There's something wrong with you, William. Are you telling me you stole Jack's phone?"

"I looked at it. That's all, OK? I didn't steal anything. I broke a picture. That's all I did. But don't tell her. I threw the glass away."

"This behavior of yours is bordering on the obsessive. What are you doing? Stalking them? Your legal career will be in jeopardy if you carry on like this. Looking at other people's phones. Calling people randomly. Breaking pictures. It's unhealthy. And now, on top of it, you're drunk as a skunk."

"I knew you wouldn't believe me. I'm going to find a lawyer. I'm going to find out exactly what my rights are."

"Fine—you do that. But meanwhile I suggest you leave them alone."

"Do you know anyone else who doesn't have one single friend, Henry? Not one? Who won't ever talk about his past? There's something wrong and no one will believe me."

"Tell it to your lawyer, William. You should go to bed and sleep it off."

"He smokes, too. He shouldn't smoke when there's a child in the house. You know, when he went to get his cigarette I thought he was getting a gun. I'm not kidding, Henry."

"And I'm hanging up now."

He placed the receiver back on its hook and reached into his pocket for his pipe.

Billy was crazy. Stark raving mad. And drunk. Stuffing the bowl of the pipe with tobacco, he leaned back in his chair.

"Do you know anyone else who doesn't have one single friend, Henry? Not one?"

No, I don't. But that's not a crime. It doesn't mean that something is "wrong" with Jack.

"Don't tell Jack I cried. Please. Promise?"

All right, Katy. But I'll promise you something else. I'll find out more about Jack. I'll make it my job. If he really made Holly cry on her wedding day, he has a lot to answer for—and he'll have to answer to me.

16

The back porch of the Woodstock Inn looked out over a lake. Rocking chairs, a hammock and some tables were scattered on it in a seemingly random fashion, inviting guests to sit and relax in a comfortable, casual setting. Everything about the inn was informal and cozy: catering for all seasons. As soon as she and Jack had walked in, Holly pictured how beautiful it would be in the autumn, with the New England foliage in full flow, or in the winter, with gently falling snow and a big fire crackling in the sitting-room fireplace.

She'd found it online and was thrilled to see that it lived up to the pictures and the happy reviews from satisfied customers. They'd arrived in time to have a nice supper in the small dining room; and though the other eight tables were all occupied, no one was talking too loudly or interfering in any way with the intimate atmosphere.

They'd taken their coffees outside and were sitting in two rocking chairs, watching the moonlight bathe in the lake.

I'm a married woman. I have the best, most wonderful husband in the world and the best, most wonderful child in the world. I never thought I'd be so happy. I never thought I'd be so lucky. How did I get so lucky?

"The lake's nice, but it's not the sea, is it?" Jack asked in a low, hushed voice.

"I've always thought there were mountain people and water people and I'm a water person. A lake's not the sea, you're right, but it's still water. It has the same effect."

"There's no endless horizon, though. That's what I dream about—an infinite horizon. I wouldn't mind dying if I could look out over the sea when I did."

"Please don't talk about dying." She reached out and grabbed his hand. "I can't stand it if you talk about dying. My dream is to live forever, as happy as I am now, with you and Katy. Nobody's going to die. We're going to live happily ever after and ever after that."

He laughed and squeezed her hand.

"You're a hopeless romantic, you know that?"

"And you're not?" she shot back. "You're the one who loves old-fashioned, and there's nothing more old-fashioned than a happily-ever-after ending."

"True."

"You know, I thought when you first called me old-fashioned on the bus, you meant it as a criticism."

"You couldn't have been more wrong."

"Sometimes I think about how lucky we were—I mean, I don't think we would have gotten together again if Henry hadn't tricked you into coming to his house."

Jack stopped rocking.

"I have a confession to make. As soon as we landed on the beach and started walking up to his house, I figured out where we were and who Henry was, so I guessed I'd see you again.

I *hoped* I'd see you again. We would have found each other again without him—he just made it easier."

"Really?" Holly smiled.

"Really. We were made for each other, Holly Barrett Dane. Don't you know that?"

"I guess I do—now."

He began to rock again, and she timed her own rocking so it matched his. Their hands were still entwined; his was warm and strong and comfortable. An elderly woman came out onto the porch, looked over at them and went back in.

"She's very tactful, leaving the honeymooners alone," Jack stated.

"Do you think she knows we're honeymooners?"

"I think we have 'honeymooners' written all over us. We're a walking ad for honeymooners. We radiate honeymooners."

"I love the way you always make me laugh."

Again, he stopped rocking.

"But I made you cry today. You didn't love that."

"Let's forget that. It doesn't matter."

"But it does. It matters hugely. I hate hurting you, Holly. I hate upsetting you. I want you to know that. You have to know that."

Unaccountably, the seriousness with which he said this scared her slightly.

"I thought the English didn't like to talk about their emotions. Watch out or you'll be on Oprah soon."

Why was she trying to lighten the mood when he was doing exactly what she'd always hoped for—airing his feelings? On the car trip, she'd been walking on eggshells, careful not to bring up the scene with Billy or even his desire to adopt Katy. She'd kept on safe territory, fearful that she might set off his anger again if she said the wrong thing, or said the right thing in the wrong way. Now that he had broached the subject of that terrible sailing trip, she should have felt relief. Instead, she wished she could put it off, defer discussing anything too serious until they'd had a few days all on their own. They'd never been together like this before; they'd always had Katy with them. She wanted to wallow in this feeling of being a young couple at the center of each other's universe before she let the world in again.

He sat forward, his elbows on his knees, his arms crossed.

"Wolves mate for life, you know. Once, there was a male wolf who'd been caught in a trap. His mate, his wife, came every night to see him. Every night for weeks. He was becoming weaker and weaker and she was more and more distressed. Until she finally lay down beside him and stayed there with him and they died together."

"I asked you before—please don't talk about dying."

"I'm not talking about dying, Holly. I'm talking about enduring love. About sacrifice."

"Do you feel you've sacrificed a lot for me?" A different fear hit her. "Too much? Do you want to go back to England?"

"No." He shook his head. "No. And I haven't sacrificed for you, you've sacrificed for me. I know there are times you're not sure about me, times when you don't understand me—and that's my fault."

"What are you saying?"

"I'm saying the past always catches up. You think you're beyond it, that it's behind you. But it's not. I hate it."

"I don't understand." Holly stared at him. "You always talk about the future, about not looking back. We're going forward, aren't we? You said you wanted to adopt Katy today. You meant that, didn't you? That's a huge step forward."

"I can't adopt Katy."

"Jack?" She didn't want to cry—not again. But he was looking so sad, so wistful, and she was feeling so lost, tears started to form. "I thought you wanted to. I don't understand."

"Holly, listen to me. It's not that I don't want to. I do. But it would be too complicated. Too many people would have to get involved. People who ask questions. People like Billy."

"What questions?"

"I should have told you before. I should have told you and given you the choice."

"What choice?"

"The choice to stay away from me. I was selfish—and frightened that if I told you the truth, you'd leave me. But we're married now. We're going to spend the rest of our lives together—I hope. You need to know about me. And I need to tell you."

"Tell me what? Jack, you're scaring me."

He got up, picked up his chair, moved it so that it was facing hers and sat back down.

"Put your legs up on my knees."

When she did, he put his hands on her ankles and began to rub them.

"Don't be afraid. Never be afraid of me. It's a long story, though. So get comfortable."

"Does it have a happy ending?"

"I hope so." He nodded. "If you love me enough, it does. That's all I want, Holly. I want us to be all about a happy ending. I want 'happy ending' to be written all over us."

17

I can tell you my secrets because you can't tell anyone so it's not like I'm breaking my promise, is it? It's a really special secret so I'm going to whisper really softly. You have to listen hard.

You know Jack and Mommy came back from the honeymoon last night. And Mommy picked me up from here and then she and Jack and I had a late supper together. Then I went to bed. But then Jack woke me up. I didn't know what time it was, but it was late and really, really dark. He had a flashlight and he told me to be quiet so I was.

I thought maybe we were going to the beach again to play catch even though it was cloudy and the moon wasn't showing. But we didn't go outside. He took my hand and put his finger to his lips and said, "Shhhh," and we went to where the stairs go up to the attic.

I don't like the attic. It scares me. It's all dusty and there's nothing there except two old beds. I was scared to tell Jack I was scared in case he got mad again. He told me to sit down on one of the old beds and I did and then he sat down too and put the flashlight between us.

"Are you glad I'm back, princess?" he asked me and I said, "Yes."

"You're not frightened of me, are you?" he asked and I said, "No." I almost said I was frightened of the attic but I didn't.

"I'd hate it if you were frightened of me," he said, so I said I wasn't.

"People can be so bloody stupid," he said. I didn't know what to say back and then he said, "But you're not stupid." And that made me happy. He was quiet and didn't say anything. He crossed his legs underneath him so he was sitting on them and he put his elbow on his knee and then he put his hand on his chin.

"Some people might think it's wrong that we play games."

"It's not wrong," I said really, really quickly because it's not. It's fun.

"I like playing games."

"So do I," I said again really quickly.

"I love you, princess. You're what makes the world a good place." He smiled at me and I smiled back. It made me feel really special when he said that. Like I was really important.

"Do you want to play a game now?" he asked.

And I said, "Yes," but I didn't know how we could play catch in the attic because the roof comes low down and a grown-up can't stand up all the way.

"Good!" He slapped his knees with his hands. "That's excellent. We'll play hide-and-seek. You close your eyes and count to ten and I'll go hide and you can come find me. But you have to be really quiet, OK?"

I didn't dare tell him I didn't want to play hide-and-seek in the attic. It was so dusty and scary and dark there and I wanted to go back downstairs but I didn't dare say so.

It's like he can tell what I'm thinking because he told me I shouldn't be afraid. He said he'd give me the flashlight and that's all I needed not to be scared.

I always want to do what he says. It's hard to explain but when we're together on our own it's like we're the only two people in the whole world and he and I are best friends. I used to have made-up friends. Mommy calls them imaginary friends. But Jack's real and that's different. I know that you're real too. And so are Mommy and Henry. But Jack is different. When he's with grown-ups he's a grown-up too but when he's with me alone, he's my age. And he makes me feel like when we're together nothing bad will ever happen. Like he has magic.

I didn't want to play hide-and-seek but I couldn't say so. I took the flashlight when he gave it to me and when he told me to close my eyes and count to ten, I did. I wanted to open them and to peek but I was afraid he'd see me open them and then it wouldn't be a real game any more and it would be my fault.

I was sitting on the bed all alone when I got to ten and opened my eyes. I didn't know where to start looking but I got up and I waved the flashlight around. I couldn't see him anywhere and there were all these scary shapes on the walls. I was more scared than I've ever been and I knew the only way to get unscared was to find Jack.

I walked around the bed and then I walked around the other bed and I waved the flashlight some more. It was so quiet and I wanted to call out his name but I knew that I wasn't supposed to. The way the roof is in the attic makes these spaces Mommy calls crawl spaces. She took me up to the attic once when she was deciding if she should put an old chair up there. She told me a cousin of hers used to come up there with her and they'd play in the crawl spaces the roof made. They're like tunnels. You get on your hands and knees and crawl inside them.

She told me her cousin used to crawl really far into the tunnels but she never did. She said boys did things like that and weren't scared and her cousin would come out looking like a ghost because he was covered by all the dust inside the tunnels. I thought maybe Jack had crawled into one of them so I went over to one and I put the flashlight on the floor and lay down so I could look inside but I couldn't see him.

And then I heard this knocking sound. It knocked once and then stopped. And then it knocked again. I thought it was a ghost knocking, and the ghost was about to come and get me. I was so afraid I crawled inside the tunnel so the ghost couldn't find me. But I forgot to take the flashlight and the tunnel was all dark and I tried to get out but I got stuck. I couldn't move and I was breathing so hard and I was so scared I wanted to scream but I couldn't because I opened my mouth but no sound came out. And then the ghost grabbed my legs and started pulling me out of the tunnel and I kept trying to scream but no sound would come out. It just wouldn't come out no matter how much I tried and the ghost was pulling me out and I was sliding on the floor trying to kick and to scream but the ghost was holding my legs and I still couldn't make any sound come out.

And then the ghost put its hand over my mouth and was

smothering me and I couldn't look. My eyes were shut because I knew the ghost was going to kill me and I didn't want to see it kill me.

"Sshhh, princess, it's all right. Ssshh. It's me," a voice said. It was Jack's voice. His breath was all warm and clean in my ear. I opened my eyes and I saw his face right next to mine. His hand was still on my mouth.

"That wasn't a very good game, was it?" he said and he shook my head back and forth with his hand so my head was saying no. "I'm really sorry, princess. I didn't mean to frighten you. I was standing right behind the door. I thought you'd find me straight off."

He took his hand away from my mouth. I said, "Where is the ghost? Is the ghost gone? Did you kill it?" and he said, "There wasn't any ghost, princess."

"But I heard it knocking."

"That was me knocking—trying to tell you where I was. Giving you a hint."

"OK," I said but I was still scared and I still thought there was a ghost.

"Come on." Jack picked up the flashlight and then he picked me up in his arms and carried me back down the attic stairs. "We're going for a treat. A midnight feast." He kept on carrying me, past my bedroom and down to the kitchen.

We sat in the kitchen and he got me chocolate ice cream. He told me when he was a boy he used to play hide-and-seek games all the time. He said he wanted me to have as much fun as he had had when he was a boy.

"Look at that funny face of yours, it's all dusty," he said and he laughed. Then he got some paper towels and wet them and washed my face. "What are you like?" he asked. He asks that a lot when he's happy with me. "You know I'd never hurt you," he said. "And I'm sorry I scared you, princess."

"I thought the ghost was going to kill me," I told him.

I started to cry—but without making any noise. Teardrops came down and I couldn't stop them.

"Princess?" Jack knelt down by my chair and grabbed my hands. I thought he was going to be mad at me but he wasn't. "I hate it that I made you cry. You've been so brave tonight."

I put my arms around his neck and my face against his shirt and I cried more. He hugged me and patted my hair like I pat your fur and then he whispered, "You know, I really am the Explorer. I didn't tell you before because it wasn't the right time."

I hugged his neck really, really hard.

"I'll always be your father and you'll always be my little girl."

That's what he said and it made me so happy that I didn't mind how scared I'd been before.

"But why didn't Mommy tell me?" I asked him. He took my hands away from his neck and sat me back on the chair and smiled at me. His eyes get more blue when he smiles.

"Mommy thinks you're not old enough to know yet. She wants to tell you when you're seven years old. She'll be really cross with me and angry if she knows I told you now. I don't want that—do you?"

"No," I said.

"So it's our secret, isn't it? Because if Mommy gets really angry with me, it will be bad. So you'll keep the secret until you're seven and she tells you, won't you?"

If Mommy got really angry with him, he might go away again, I could tell.

"I'll keep it secret."

"Good girl. And remember to act surprised when she tells you. I don't want her to guess I told you before she thought you were ready to hear."

He picked me up and carried me back upstairs to my room and put me in bed and tucked me in. He said he'd stay sitting on my bed until I fell asleep.

"If I keep the secret, you won't leave again, will you? You promise?" I asked him.

He was brushing my hair back from my face with his fingers and he said, "I won't leave. If you keep the secret, I'll never leave you—I promise. But you have to promise me something else too. You have to promise that the hide-and-seek game we played tonight is just between us, OK?"

I said I didn't understand what that meant.

"It means Mommy would be angry at me too if she knew we played a scary game so late at night and so we have to keep that a secret too. I think Henry would be angry as well, so we won't tell him either. You know, princess, fathers and daughters have secrets," he said. And then he said, "That's part of what is special. That it's just us two who know things together. You promise not to tell anyone anything about tonight?"

I nodded my head and said, "I promise."

He kissed me on top of my head then and I was all warm

and cozy and happy with him there like that. It wasn't hard at all to fall asleep.

I have a father. I have a father like everybody else and he's here, with me. Forever. So it's all right now, Bones. You can play with Jack and go up to him and let him pat you and everything. He's not going away, ever again. He promised.

18

People changed. Henry had seen it before. Some of the boys who started their stint in the Marines as scared, insecure weaklings, came out strong, secure men. Others who thought they were God's gift to the world had had the shit kicked out of them and were humbled. Over the course of seventy-five years, he'd seen many people change in many different ways, but he hadn't been prepared for the change he saw in Holly when she arrived back from the honeymoon. It wasn't only the way her beauty, which had been hiding for so many years, now shone like a bright light—he'd already noticed how she had grown into her looks with the advent of a man who loved her. No—it was the way she held herself. There was a certainty to her which translated into her posture and the way she walked. Her shoulders weren't hunched, her stride was purposeful.

Marriage, the honeymoon, having time on her own with Jack for a few days—Henry wasn't sure what it was, but something had given Holly a new confidence.

Nevertheless, he was going to have a talk with her. And he needed to do that as soon as possible. Obviously he hadn't said anything when she and Jack had picked up Katy the night before—but now he was sitting with her on the porch and

Katy was with Bones in the living room and Jack was in town getting groceries. This was his chance; yet he found himself hesitating.

"We were so lucky with the weather for the wedding, weren't we?" She smiled. "Look, the clouds have come in with a vengeance."

"Mmm."

"Are you all right, Henry? You seem preoccupied."

"What do you say to a walk on the beach? You must want to stretch your legs after all that driving."

"Sounds like a good idea. Katy," she called out. "We're all going for a walk. Bring Bones out with you."

"OK," Katy yelled back. "Just a second."

"I'll tell you all about Vermont. The inn was beautiful. But not too quaint if you know what I mean. It wasn't up itself."

"Shit, sweetie. You're talking like a Brit now. I bet you'll have the accent soon too."

"No, I won't. I tried once. Jack was rolling on the floor laughing at me."

Katy came out, followed by Bones, and they set off for the beach.

"You're being preternaturally quiet, Henry."

"Preternaturally?"

"Jack and I have a competiton going for who can use the best big words. He's winning so I have to practice."

"Right. I have a feeling you stole it from me, but that's certainly a good one."

"Henry?" She stopped. "You sound strange. What's the matter?"

"Nothing. Katy, when we get to the beach, why don't you go look for shells?"

"Which shells?"

"I don't know, bumblebee—pretty shells."

"Is there a hidden agenda for this walk?" Holly asked.

"I want to have a talk with you, that's all."

"Katy." She frowned. "Go see if you can find any angel's wings shells, OK?"

"OK." Katy ran off to the shoreline and Holly turned to Henry. "What's this about? What's so important that you need to talk to me alone? Is something wrong with Katy? Did something happen while I was away? What's going on?"

"Let's sit down." He took off his jacket, spread it on the sand, sat down on it and motioned for her to sit beside him. When she did, he said, "I'm worried, sweetie. Katy fell and hurt herself the other night."

"Is she all right? Is she—"

"She's fine. No harm done. But when she fell and hurt herself she was terrified of crying. She said that Jack hates it when she cries and that he leaves when she cries. You should have seen how frightened she was. It wasn't right."

"Jack doesn't like noise. He has to get used to her crying, but he will. It's not a problem, Henry."

"It seemed like a very big problem."

"It's not."

"Are you sure?"

"Absolutely."

The confidence with which she said this surprised him.

The new Holly, the certain Holly. He put his arm around her shoulder.

"I don't mean to be an interfering old grandfather, sweetie. But there's something else, too. The other night I came down to the beach to fish and I saw Jack and Katy playing catch. It was midnight. He said she'd woken up and he didn't want you to wake up, so he brought her down here to practice. Don't you think that's a little odd?"

She pulled away from him, away from his arm.

"What the fuck are you trying to say here?"

"Sweetie. Calm down." Her eyes were on him, accusing, enraged. "I'm the one who swears, remember? You're the prim and proper Bostonian."

"It's not funny, Henry. Just what are you implying? Tell me right now. Jesus Christ, I can't believe this."

"There's nothing to believe, Holly. I'm not saying anything— only that it's an odd time to play catch on the beach with a five-year-old."

"He's getting to know her. He's her stepfather. If he wants to play catch with her on the beach, he can. You're making something innocent and sweet really, really ugly. It's sick. You're being perverse and sick and twisted."

He stood up and strode away, heading straight toward the long grass where the ashes of John and Julia were buried. He wasn't too old to cry. The anger with which she'd said that, the words she'd used, had wounded him deeply.

Why aren't you here? You'd know what to do. You've left it to me and I can't manage any more. I don't know this Holly. My Holly would never have spoken like that to me. I was wrong, obviously. But how else could I have put it? Wasn't it incumbent on me to bring it up? Didn't she need to know?

"Henry!" She had run up beside him and was panting. "Stop. I'm sorry." She took his hand in hers. "I shouldn't have said that. I'm sorry. Come on. Let's go over to Katy and Bones."

They walked a few yards in silence.

"Henry, please. I didn't mean what I said. It's just that no one understands Jack, no one knows what he's been through or how good a person he is. But I thought you did. I mean, I thought you were on his team and then suddenly you come out with all this stuff. You don't know him, Henry. He'd never hurt Katy."

He knew he had to collect himself; he had to shake the hurt off and keep going as best he could.

"No, I guess I don't know him. That's part of my point, sweetie. We don't know about his background, really. He doesn't seem to have any friends. I'm not saying anything against him, you know I'm not. Has he told you about his sister dying?"

"Yes." She nodded. "He told me. It's awful. That's *my* point, Henry. He's been through hell and you of all people should understand that. I trust him completely. And if you love me, you'll trust him too. There are things I can't— Just trust me and trust him. Please."

There used to be mussels on the rocks that jutted from the dike. Picking them was back-breaking and the process of cleaning them and pulling off their beards exhausting, but it was all worth it once they had been steamed open. Isabella had had a special mussel recipe: after they opened, she'd take them from their shells and fry them in butter and sherry; then they'd sit out on the porch together, devour them in huge spoonfuls and laugh at how so much work went into so little eating time. A decade or so ago, they'd disappeared. The clams remained but the mussels had vanished. He could order them in a restaurant, but they'd be farmed mussels, fattened up with flour so the taste was in whatever sauce they were cooked in, not in the mussels themselves. Farmed mussels, farmed salmon—there was something inherently wrong in making creatures of the water into cows.

But the mussels weren't going to reappear magically, no matter how often he searched the rocks for traces of them.

"Henry?"

"Yes, sweetie. Of course I trust you. I'm sorry if you thought I didn't. Tell you what, I'll take Jack out fishing before dinner tonight—he's not working, is he?"

"No, he starts again tomorrow night."

"Good." He squeezed her hand. "It might take me longer than it should to make adjustments, you know. Old men get set in their ways."

"You're not old, Henry."

"As we used to say in my youth, tell it to the fucking Marines."

With all his worrying, Henry had almost forgotten how easy it was to have Jack around, what a pleasure he was to have on a fishing trip. They'd set out from the dock at five and meandered around fairly aimlessly, searching for gulls. Neither of them could see any, so they headed for the end of the dike. Going on a normal trip like this, with Jack being the same comfortable companion he'd always been, was reassuring. Perhaps he shouldn't have approached Holly first with his concerns: he should have gone straight to Jack.

Looking back on it, telling a wife just back from her honeymoon that her new husband might have been behaving in an inappropriate manner with her child was not a very smart idea. A man-to-man talk with Jack out on the water would clear the air. Why hadn't he thought of that to begin with? He could have avoided all that unpleasantness on the walk with Holly.

"Not a gull in sight." He looked over at Jack, who was still searching for signs of them. "We can cast toward the rocks, though—sometimes you get lucky and catch a striped bass that's lurking in them. There's no point in trying to find gulls when there aren't any. Plus, I brought a nice bottle of red wine. We can settle down and have a drink and cast when we feel like it."

"Sounds like a good plan."

Jack was wearing jeans, a long-sleeved blue cotton shirt and a windbreaker. He seemed slightly distracted, but then he'd been concentrating hard because Henry had given him total control of the boat. He'd managed to start it, guide it out of its berth and take it to the dike with no problems whatsoever, but even when Henry told him to cut the engine and relax, he looked tense.

"So . . ." Uncorking the bottle, Henry poured the wine into two plastic glasses. "Holly looks wonderful. I assume it was a terrific honeymoon."

"It was." Jack nodded, taking the glass Henry proffered. "Cheers."

"Cheers."

They sipped the wine as the boat drifted slowly with the tide.

"The inn was nice?"

"Very. But I prefer it here. I prefer the sea to lakes."

"I'm the same. A lake is like a suburb—neither one thing nor another. Too safe."

"Exactly."

The rain hadn't come, but it was still a cloud-covered sky. Jack kept scanning the horizon as he drank, while Henry debated when he should bring up the subject of Katy and her crying.

Do it. The sooner you get it over with, the sooner we can all return to normal.

"It must be hard having a five-year-old in your life— becoming an instant stepfather."

"No, actually." Jack stopped scanning, looked directly at Henry. "It's easy. You know Katy—it couldn't be easier."

"I know Katy, yes. But I also know children can be a pain in the ass. Especially when they cry. Katy told me you get angry when she cries. I can understand that, but I'm worried that you may be overreacting because you're not used to things like that, to children crying."

"What are you trying to say, Henry?"

"Exactly what I did say. That you might be overreacting. Katy's frightened of crying now because she doesn't want you to get angry."

"This is a joke." He took a big slug of wine. "You know how well Katy and I get along. Why are you getting on my case like this?"

"I'm not getting on your case, Jack. I'm pointing out that Katy feels very anxious about crying because of your reaction to her."

"Fantastic." He reached out, took the wine bottle from its holder on the boat's dashboard and poured himself more. "I can't do anything right, can I? OK, I don't like it when she cries. Big deal. What am I supposed to do? Say, 'Great, Katy, cry some more, I love it when you cry?' *She* doesn't like it when she cries either. She's not a moaner. She's a good girl and we have a good relationship. You're taking the piss. You and everyone else."

"There's no need to be so defensive. I'm making an observation, that's all."

"Well, cheers to you." Raising his glass, he put it to his mouth and emptied it. "So you've teamed up with Billy now, have you? What's this foreign waiter doing with Holly Barrett and her child? He hasn't gone to some fuck-off university so he must be a nasty piece of work?"

Here we go again. But it's not as if I shouldn't have been expecting it. Life lesson number one: no one likes criticism. The first reaction is almost always to defend, the second to lash out at the critic.

"You know I'd never think such a thing. And I'm not teaming up with Billy Madison. Not in the least. I don't have any time for him—you should know that. I think he's a pain in the ass."

"He's evil, that's what he is. A sneaky evil little bastard. He's been asking around about me—you know, he tried to get information on me from Charlie Thurlow. And he got hold of my cellphone somehow. Is that legal? Snooping like that? I'd call it harassment. The guy should be in jail—he sure as hell shouldn't be a lawyer. The sooner that nutter goes back to Boston and stays in Boston, the better."

"I'm with you there."

Billy lambastes Jack, Jack lambastes Billy. I suspect this is a dynamic that will never change.

Jack got up, walked to the stern, picked up a fishing rod and started to cast toward the rocks.

"It pisses me off, Henry. It fucking pisses me off. People should mind their own business."

"I agree. But part of *my* business is Katy, Jack. I want to make sure she's happy."

"Yeah. I get it." He was reeling the line in quickly. "But I'm tired of all this shit."

"All what shit?"

"Come on." He cast again. "You know what shit. Billy bloody Madison poking his fucking nose into my business because he can't stand the fact that he mucked it up with Holly. He's so up himself, that man. He deserves to be—whoa—oh, my God—I got one. Look . . ."

Henry stood up and watched as Jack began to reel in the striped bass. Bass didn't fight as hard as bluefish, but that didn't mean they were easy to land. And it was immensely satisfying to catch a fish out of the blue like that; when the gulls were circling, you knew you stood a good chance, but casting into the rocks rarely yielded a fish.

When Jack had brought the fish up close to the boat, Henry went to get the net.

"OK, I'm here. Bring him to the surface again."

Jack did, but the fish took one more deep dive before Jack reeled it back up, close enough for Henry to lean over and net it.

"Got it."

Henry scooped it out of the water, into the boat.

"This one's too small to keep. I'll get the hook out and then throw it back in."

He went down on one knee, put his hand on its head as its tail flapped wildly against the boat's bottom, steadying it so he could take the hook out.

As he wrenched it free, Jack came and knelt beside him.

"It's not too small," he said. "Get back, Henry."

"What?"

Jack's hand was on his shoulder, pushing him away from the fish.

"It's not too small."

"It is. Look—I'll get the tape measure and show you."

Standing up, he went to the tackle box, and rooted around it for the tape; when he found it, he turned back—and saw Jack, bent over the fish, whacking its head with the club so ferociously Henry was momentarily stunned, speechless.

"What the fuck? Jack? Stop it, for Christ's sake!" The words finally exploded, furiously. The fish was long past dead, but Jack was still clubbing it, relentlessly. Time after time, the club went up in the air and came down on the fish head with a sickening thud.

He rushed to where Jack was kneeling and grabbed his wrist in mid-air.

"Stop it! It's dead, for fuck's sake."

Jack's hand went limp; the club fell to the deck of the boat. Henry dropped Jack's arm and bent down to pick up the club.

"Oops. I guess I went a little overboard there, didn't I?" Jack laughed; a laugh Henry found offensive.

He straightened, tried to lock eyes with him, but Jack's eyes had floated off to the horizon.

"I thought you didn't like killing them. What the hell was that all about? I told you it was too small to keep."

Jack shrugged, continued staring off into the distance. "I was pissed off. I took it out on the fish. Sorry. Next time I catch one I won't keep it even if it's a monster. I'll throw it back. That should even things out."

Not really, Henry wanted to say, but he kept his mouth shut.

"Sorry, Henry." His eyes returned to Henry and he gave a quick, apologetic smile before zipping up his windbreaker, sweeping his hand through his hair, and going back to the bow. He poured himself the small amount of wine left in the bottle. "You should take a turn at casting now."

"No. I'm ready to go back." Henry went over to the steering wheel, turned the key and put the boat into forward. "I've had enough for the day."

More than enough.

"Henry . . ." The glass was halfway to his mouth, but Jack clearly had decided against drinking it and put it back down. Once again he gave a brief, apologetic smile. "It was only a fish. I really am sorry if I upset you. It's just that the honeymoon was so amazing and coming back here, back to the whole Billy scenario—and then you saying I've frightened Katy. I didn't know she was afraid of me, honestly. I'll make sure it never happens again. She can cry as much as she likes, I won't be angry with her, I promise."

"Good. That's good to hear."

"Still friends, yes?" Jack extended his left hand.

Henry shook it with his left.

But it couldn't have felt further from his heart.

19

The Mill Pond Diner was classic. Anyone new to town would always marvel at its "authenticity," how perfectly it matched their expectations of what a small-town diner should be. Booths with individual jukeboxes, waitresses with smudged lipstick and loud voices, the omnipresent smell of grease: all that was missing was cigarette smoke hanging heavy in the air. A decade ago, Billy had spent plenty of afternoons in it, hanging out with other Shoreham teenagers, including Holly, but he'd never been there at seven forty-five in the morning. And he'd never before had to think about what he was going to wear to go there. But then Henry had never called him at seven in the morning to summon him to a breakfast meeting.

He'd had to hunt to find an old plaid L.L. Bean shirt and a pair of worn khaki trousers, so he could fit in more with the Barrett look. Nothing new, nothing even remotely flashy. He even took off the Tiffany watch his parents had given him for his twenty-first birthday. When he walked through the Mill Pond Diner door, he saw immediately how different the early-morning clientele was from the afternoon teenage group. Older men hunched over the counter, intent on their eggs and bacon, all of them sporting baseball caps. Henry, whom he spotted over in a booth by the far wall, looked almost regal, sitting straight as a rod, a newspaper and cup of coffee in front of him. Henry glanced up, saw him, and waved him over.

Billy had no idea what had prompted Henry to call him and arrange this early-morning meeting, but he was determined not to go on a wild rant about Jack again. This time he would prove to Henry he could be a logical, mature and sober man.

As he slid into the booth, he remembered the times he and Holly had sat in the same one. Not that many years ago, but it felt like centuries.

"Thank you for coming," Henry said. "Would you like some coffee or something to eat?"

"No, thank you. I wolfed down some instant coffee and a piece of toast before I got in the car."

Henry then placed both hands on the table. He looked so much like a judge that Billy began to expect some sort of sentence to be handed down. Three weeks of community service for making a phone call while intoxicated?

"I'm trying to get something straight," Henry stated. "I've been going over it in my mind and I can't figure something out. You said you looked at Jack's cellphone, yes?"

"Yes."

Ten weeks in the slammer for stealing a look at someone else's cellphone?

"And Jack came in and saw you doing this?"

"No. No, he wasn't there. He came into the kitchen, but only after I'd put it back where it had been."

"Then how does he know you looked?"

"What do you mean?"

"I mean he knows you looked at his phone. How? Are you *sure* he wasn't in the kitchen while you were looking at it?"

"Absolutely. I heard them come in and I put the phone back immediately—right where it had been. I was careful, Henry. The last thing I wanted was for him—or Holly—to know I'd done that."

"Did you tell anyone besides me that you looked at it?"

"No. I was embarrassed that I had. I only told you because I'd had a few too many beers and was out of control."

"You might have called someone else and not remembered." A slight accusation in Henry's voice, but nothing close to what Billy had expected.

"I was drunk but not that drunk, Henry."

"Are you positive about that?"

"Positive."

"Well, somehow Jack knows you looked at his phone."

Billy now wished he'd ordered a coffee. His brain cells needed more of a caffeine push. Could Jack possibly have seen him? No. He put the phone back before Jack came anywhere near the kitchen and he had made sure he'd replaced it in the same spot on the table.

"How could he know? The only way he could know—"

"Would be if the woman you spoke to called him to tell him." Henry beat him to the conclusion. He'd obviously been mulling this over for a while.

"Which she couldn't do if—"

"She didn't know him." Henry shook his head. "There must

be an explanation. Are you sure she said she didn't know him?"

"Yes, Henry." Billy turned around, caught a waitress's eye and asked her for a coffee. He swiveled back. "Twice. She said twice she'd never heard of him."

His mind was racing with this information, but he was also aware it would be better if he allowed Henry to continue to lead the conversation. If he pushed too hard, Henry might retreat. So he sat, quietly, like a schoolboy, all the while yearning to wave his hand in the air and blurt out theories.

You're dressed like a Barrett, act like one. Don't draw attention to yourself.

When his coffee arrived, he poured some milk into it and waited.

"Jack also said you'd been asking Charlie Thurlow about him."

"True." He cradled the cup of coffee in his hands; was Henry going to give him a lecture about respecting privacy? No—right now, Henry was concentrating on Jack, not him. "I asked what was on his résumé. Charlie said he had good references from his other jobs, that everyone said how good he was at his work and how quiet he was."

"Anything else?"

"I asked about his education. Charlie mentioned a school—Compton Hall. That's all I could get from him. He thought I was being way too inquisitive."

"You were."

"But now you are too, Henry." He forced himself to remain calm, level. "Because something *is* wrong."

"Something *might* be wrong. Did you check up on the school? Did you Google it?"

"No—Charlie made me feel like a jerk for asking. And then when that woman said she'd never heard of him, I assumed I had remembered the number wrong and I was on a wild goose chase. But I have a very good memory, Henry. It's part of the reason I did well on my Law Boards. I've always had a good memory."

"Like Katy."

"Katy?" Billy smiled. "She does? Really?"

"Pretty phenomenal, actually. She's a very smart little girl."

"What else is she like? What does she like to do?"

Henry reached down, picked up his cap beside him on the booth and put it on his bald head.

"I need to get back home, Billy."

It was eight in the morning. Why did he have to get back so quickly?

"You're going to Google the school, aren't you?"

"Yes."

"I want to come with you. I'm involved in this too, Henry. That woman lied about knowing Jack. She could be his girlfriend, his wife even. They could be—"

"Slow down. You're jumping to conclusions far too fast."

"But you'll let me come over?"

"All right." He stood up. "I'll pay for your coffee and mine and I'll wait for you at my house. Walk over by the beach way, though. I don't want your car in my driveway. And when you get there, knock at the back kitchen door."

"No problem. And thanks, Henry."

"I very much doubt that we'll learn anything. And I'm not saying you're right in your distrust of Jack, you know."

"I know." Billy nodded.

But you're worried. Something has changed and I have a feeling it's not just the fact that Jack knows about me seeing the phone number. You're now saying "we," as if we are on the same team. Finally I'm not the only one who's worried.

He did as Henry had told him: drove home, parked the car in his driveway and went down to the beach before climbing the path up to Henry's house. No one saw him because no one was on the beach: it was a rainy, miserable day. When he reached the house, he skirted around the back and knocked on the kitchen door. Henry opened it immediately.

"In forty minutes, they're all coming over for coffee, so we'd better get a move on. Come on." He led him through the kitchen and into his living room where his computer sat on the desk. "I'm not proud of myself for all this secrecy," he commented, and Billy could see his discomfort. Still nervous that if he said the wrong thing Henry might change his mind, he stayed silent. When Henry sat down and brought the Google page up and typed in "Compton Hall School England," he felt a surge of relief. They were in this together now.

The results came quickly and Henry clicked on the top one, which was clearly the Compton Hall School web page; Billy peered over his shoulder as Henry began to read.

"OK—we have all the usual bunk about what a perfect school this is. Single sex—male—for boys between twelve and eighteen. A public—which means private to us—boarding school in Surrey. I wouldn't have thought Jack was a boarding school boy, although it does make sense, now that I think about it. The way he follows orders fits with that. So— boys there get good results, it does well in the league tables, whatever those are. Lots of athletics. Particularly rugby. Blahblahblah. Nothing out of the ordinary. Looks harmless to me."

"But he didn't go to college, at least he doesn't have a college or university listed on his résumé."

"Well, not everyone goes to college, do they?"

"I guess not. But at a school like that, you'd think they would. There's a phone number for the school at the top there. What about calling them?"

"And saying what?"

"You could ask for the headmaster; it might be the same one who was there when Jack was. It's a way of getting some information, at least possibly."

"I don't know."

"Henry, come on, we've come this far. It makes sense to keep going. And it's five hours ahead in England, isn't it? So someone should be there."

"But it's summer. It's probably closed for the holidays."

"It's worth a shot, isn't it?"

Leaning back in his chair, Henry appeared to be contemplating a personal dilemma. Then his hand reached out, picked up the phone from its cradle on the desk. "All right," he sighed. "But I'll probably regret this morning forever."

Billy started to pace around the room as Henry dialed. The

odds were against anyone being at the school, much less any-one who might remember Jack as a student. In a way, he was more pleased at the fact that Henry was making the call than hopeful of a result coming from it. He stopped to stare at the rain pouring down, turned abruptly from the window as he heard Henry say hello and then pause before continuing with:

"I would like to speak to the headmaster if it's possible. . . . Oh, I'm fortunate to have caught you in, aren't I? . . . Yes, I was calling to inquire about one of your alumni, as it happens. I'm in Massachusetts and he's applying for a job here and I see on his résumé that he attended your school ten years ago. . . . Yes, near Boston. . . . Oh, really? And did you and your wife enjoy the trip? . . . It is, yes. The foliage at that time of year is spectacular. Yes. . . . Anyway, I was wondering if you might be able to give him a reference. His name is Jack Dane."

Billy saw the pain in Henry's eyes as he continued the deceit. It was the first time, too, that he'd seen him slightly slouched. There was a long pause, during which Henry looked away from him, gazing up at the ceiling.

"I see. . . . Yes, of course. I'll wait."

Putting his hand over the receiver, Henry said, "He's look-ing up the records. We're lucky to have found him in—he just happened to be there because he's about to interview a prospec-tive teacher. He's very garrulous, which is also lucky for us. He didn't even ask me what job— Hello. Yes, I'm still here. . . . Fine. Of course. I understand. Did you happen to be headmas-ter at that time? . . . No, of course. I see. Thank you very much."

Henry hung up the phone, stood up, took his pipe out of his pocket.

"He said that Jack Dane was a pupil at the school, that there is nothing in his records which would reflect on a job application and that it would be inappropriate to discuss his records or his time there further."

He put the pipe in his mouth but didn't light it.

"Another brick wall." Billy sighed.

"His tone changed."

"What?"

"He was so genial at the beginning. Telling me about his and his wife's holiday here ten years ago, talking on as if he welcomed a distraction. But when he came back on the line, he was suddenly curt. Very abrupt."

"What do you think that means?"

"I don't know. Probably nothing. It was odd, that's all. Noticeable." He looked at his watch. "Do you still remember the number of the woman you called?"

"Yes."

"What is it?"

Henry wrote down the number as Billy reeled it off, then punched it in.

I'm right. Something has happened. Something Henry hasn't told me about. There's no way Henry would be making calls like this if he didn't have serious doubts about Jack. And it's not just to do with his knowing I looked at his phone—I'm sure it isn't. So what is it? What has Jack done?

"Yes, hello. I'm very sorry to bother you, but I was wondering if I could speak to you about my son-in-law, Jack Dane. . . . Yes, I'm sor—"

Henry took the phone away from his ear, looked at it briefly before putting it back down.

"She hung up. She said this was the third call she'd had about this person she'd never heard of and she hung up. So we're back to square one."

"Not exactly." Billy leaned back against the window, crossed his arms over his chest and looked Henry straight in the eyes. "There's something you're not telling me. What has Jack done? I know it's more than his knowing I looked at the phone. Or that headmaster sounding abrupt. He's done something that worries you, hasn't he?"

Henry looked at his watch again.

"You have to go, Billy."

"Why won't you tell me?"

"Because there's nothing concrete to tell."

"But there *is* something."

"I don't know if it even qualifies as something. You really do have to go, Billy."

What was it—a strange look that passed across Henry's face? Or his tone of voice? Billy wasn't sure, but he sensed that what he was about to say was right:

"Something about him frightens you, doesn't it?"

"For fuck's sake—he's walking up the road now with Holly and Katy. Get your fucking skates on and get out the back. I don't want trouble."

"All right, but I'll call you later."

"Go."

You've already got trouble, Henry, he thought as he slipped out the kitchen door and headed for the back path down to the beach. *The McCormack woman has lied again. That headmaster went all weird when he looked at Jack's file. And for some reason, you're suddenly frightened of him. We've all got a shedload of trouble.*

20

Whenever she needed to rethink her world, Anna had problems sleeping. If a guy didn't call her when he should have, if her boss didn't appreciate her work, if something was out of kilter, she would work and rework it in a night-time brain race, until it came out in some form she could deal with. She didn't really like the guy anyway, her boss hadn't understood how crucial her role was, but would soon. . . . There were ways to play with the facts and make them fit her vision of how her life should be panning out.

So at two o'clock on Saturday morning, she was wide awake, trying to get her head around the upside-downness of life; specifically the way things had changed with Holly. The new Holly. So different from the Holly she'd known all these years.

She'd more or less bludgeoned Holly into inviting her down for the weekend again, saying it was only fair after she'd been disinvited to the wedding.

"I want to see the honeymooners back in their nest," she'd said. "Come on, Holl. Let me get a little bit of vicarious bliss. Who knows? It might be catching. I might find my own tall, dark foreigner and marry him in a month. Then we can all go bowling together on Friday nights."

Holly had laughed and said, "Of course. It will be nice to see you. And I won't even mind if you flirt with Jack again."

"Hey, Holl, I'm sorry about that. You know me, I—"

"Never mind—just come down on Friday. We'll be here."

So she'd driven down after work on Friday, unhappy that the weather had turned rainy, but curious to see Holly and Jack in their new husband and wife status. As before, Jack was working that night, so she and Holly and Katy had a spaghetti supper around the kitchen table.

It was one of those hard-to-explain things. Something had changed, but what exactly? That's what kept bothering her during dinner. Holly was friendly and funny and Katy was sweet and eager and they all had fun twirling spaghetti round their forks and slurping it into their mouths. It could have been any Friday night they spent together. Except something was different.

It took until dessert for her to figure it out. She was getting ice cream out of the fridge and when she brought it to the table and put it down in the middle, then stuck three spoons in it, Holly looked at her and smiled and said, "Jack does that too—he puts the spoons in like you do," and Katy said, "Jack loves chocolate ice cream and so do I," and Holly put her hand on Katy's shoulder and squeezed it and Anna sat down and thought, *Shit. This is happiness. This is the real thing—and Holly has it. Holly Barrett. The shy, kind of awkward, very smart but not very popular girl.*

The first time she'd spoken to Holly, it was only because she felt sorry for her. There was this girl sitting on the steps by the gym on the first day of eighth grade, looking lost and lonely.

Anna had been just about to ask her if she was new to the school when she realized that it was Holly Barrett, who'd been in her class the entire year before. That made her feel even sorrier for her, so she said, "Hey," and gave a little wave to her. "How shitty is it that we're back at this dump for another year?"

Holly had blushed and mumbled, "Yeah, really," and Anna had almost walked on. Instead she sat down beside her.

"So what's the deal? Do you have Miss Zombie for math again this year?"

"Yes."

"But you're good at math, aren't you?"

"I'm OK."

"I wish I were as OK as you."

"I can help you if you need it any time."

"Thanks, Holly."

"No problem."

They sat there for another couple of minutes, not speaking, until Anna got up, said, "See you," and left.

After that, Anna began to seek Holly out. She'd sit with her at lunch often, sometimes she'd ask for help after school on her homework. None of her friends understood this new friendship and Anna wasn't sure she did, either, until her best friend Debby cornered her one afternoon, saying, "What's the deal with you and Holly Barrett? Are you hanging out with her because she does your homework for you?"

"No. I hang out with her because I like her and because she's the only person I can be quiet with."

Debby looked at her as though she were an alien and Anna

was surprised too. She hadn't realized before what it was about Holly that she liked. But Holly really was easy to be with. She listened when you felt like talking but didn't expect you to perform all the time like the other girls did. And she wasn't checking out what clothes you wore or competing to be cool. When she was with Holly, she didn't care as much as she normally did about what she looked like.

When Billy Madison showed up at their school the next year, he and she immediately started dating, and the fact that Billy had a summer house almost next door to Holly's made it natural for the three of them to spend time together. Anna hadn't known about Holly's crush on Billy—she was too wrapped up in Billy herself to notice.

It all happened so quickly: she got tired of Billy and ditched him and within a month Holly was pregnant with Billy's child. Anna couldn't believe Holly and Billy had had sex, she couldn't begin to believe Holly was going to go ahead and have the baby, but she wasn't totally surprised by Billy's refusal to be involved. She knew his parents. She knew how much pressure they would put on him. And she knew him. She knew how likely he was to bail and give in to them.

The whole thing was crazy, completely screwed up. And when Holly's parents died, it got even worse. Holly retreated to Birch Point all year round, like some kind of hermit heading for the woods. Anna had done her best to stand by and support Holly, trying to get her to Boston as often as possible. But Holly was always Holly. Reticent, responsible, rational.

Jennifer Aniston had once said that Brad Pitt was missing a "sensitivity chip"—well, Holly lacked a "socializing" chip. She wasn't the type of girl to go to a party, much less meet a man at one, so their weekends out were nothing if not tame. Anna had to admit, when she'd have a bad day, she'd sometimes find herself thinking, "Well, at least I'm not Holly. I'm not a shy, self-conscious single mother living in the boondocks with no hope of ever getting out."

But not now. Now, it felt as though Holly had gone and robbed some self-confidence bank. Now she was the one who knew who she was and what she wanted—and had gotten it. When Holly had said, "Goodnight, Anna," a few hours before, there was a tiny tinge of sadness in it. As though Holly was thinking, *You won't have the perfect man with you, but I hope you have a good night anyway.* As though the tables had completely turned and Holly was feeling sorry for *her.*

She threw back the covers, got up and walked over to the window overlooking the driveway. When was it? Their junior year? It must have been around then. She and Holly were sitting at the kitchen table, the one they'd just had their spaghetti dinner at, and Holly's parents were there too and she had made some throwaway remark about how much fun the junior dance was going to be with Billy. She knew as soon as she'd said it that it might sound as though she was gloating—Holly didn't have a date. But it was too late to take it back and anyway, Holly was used to her by now and knew she didn't mean to say anything bad on purpose.

But Mr. Barrett had waited for a while, maybe twenty minutes, and just as she and Holly were about to leave the table, he'd turned to Mrs. Barrett and said, "You know, it's interesting, Julia. How different people peak at different times."

She'd known right away his words were directed at her. She wasn't half as smart as Holly but she wasn't dumb either. Mr. Barrett came across as laid-back, friendly and quiet, but nothing got past him. He kind of scared her because it was as if he was always weighing things up, figuring things out, his brain busy working away at the important things. Almost as though he could see through you, straight into the bad parts. That one little sentence of his was a warning to her: You might be a hotshot now, but just wait, Anna—my daughter has a whole lot more to her than you do.

Well, you were right, Mr. Barrett. Holly has peaked now. But I still don't want her life, I—

A car drove up. A car with no lights on. Anna instinctively stepped back from the front of the window and stood to the side, peering down at it.

Billy? Had Billy come on some crazed two a.m. stalking mission? But it wasn't Billy's car, it was Holly's. The wipers were crossing the windshield; as they swayed to the left, she tried to see in, but she couldn't distinguish a face in the dark. The driver's door opened then, slowly, and Anna saw Katy climb out.

What the hell? Katy driving?

Jack exited right behind her, out the same door.

Has she been hurt? Did he take her to the hospital? Where's Holly?

She was about to rush downstairs, but then she saw Jack put his finger to his lips and Katy put her finger to her lips too and it was beginning to look as though they were in some crazy play. Jack closed the car door in slow motion, inching it back in place so softly it wouldn't have made a noise when it finally closed. He turned back to Katy then and they gave each other a high five.

Enough already.

Grabbing her bathrobe off the hook on the door, she threw it on over her pajamas, left her room and headed downstairs. The light in the kitchen was on, so she could see where she was going. By the time she'd reached the bottom of the stairs, she saw them both coming toward her. Jack took one look at her, put his finger to his lips again and pointed his other hand in the direction of the kitchen. Katy was nodding and started pointing toward the kitchen too.

"OK, OK," she mouthed to them both and then followed them.

"What's going on?" she asked as soon as she closed the kitchen door behind her. "Why the—why is Katy driving a car at two o'clock in the morning?"

"Hi, Anna." Jack smiled. "Nice to see you again."

"Yeah, right. You too. What's going on?"

"I was driving. Like Mommy used to drive with Grandpa when she was little. He'd let her drive down our road till the cement part started. Jack was letting me do it so I can show Mommy tomorrow when she wakes up."

"Uh huh. And you woke her up at two in the morning to practice driving?" She stared at Jack. "What's the English word for crazy?"

"Mad. And she was awake already. I passed by her room when I came back from work and I saw her sitting up in her bed wide awake. Right, Katy?"

Katy nodded, with a big smile too.

"So you took her out in the rain in her pajamas to go for a drive?"

"It was really fun, Anna. I'm good at it. Jack said I'm really good at corners."

"Boy." Anna rolled her eyes. "That's just brilliant. So what's the English word for inappropriate, Jack?"

"What's the American one for killjoy?" He was still smiling. As though nothing whatsoever was wrong.

The problem with his looks was that it was hard to get over them. She was having a tough time concentrating when she knew she should have been. His face was so supremely faint-worthy that sustaining her already dubious role as an authority on childcare was becoming difficult. Besides, Katy was obviously happy and Jack wouldn't be smiling if he'd been caught doing something he shouldn't have been, would he? Maybe this was some kind of thing English people did with children.

"So you're going to tell Holly about this?"

"Of course. Now, it's probably time for us all to get some sleep. What do you say, princess?"

Katy yawned as if on cue and Jack patted her on the top of the head.

"Time to get going, then. See you tomorrow, Anna. Or rather later today."

"Right."

They left the kitchen, went upstairs, and Katy skipped into her room, while Jack continued down the hallway to his and Holly's. Anna's room was across from theirs, at the end. She took off her bathrobe, hung it up and slipped under the covers.

OK, so I'm jealous. Holly has found true love and all is happy in her world. It doesn't mean I can't find it too. There has to be a Jack out there on some bus waiting for me to sit beside him. Anyway, he's not that perfect. I'd prefer French to English. A honeymoon in Paris would be excellent.

When she woke the next morning, she knew she had been in the middle of a dream: a dream featuring Mr. Barrett. The odd thing about it was that it had been a dream replay of an actual event. She was fifteen and in the middle of her romance with Billy. She'd come to Birch Point for the day, a Sunday, and while Billy was busy playing tennis with his father, she'd gone over to visit Holly, but Holly wasn't there. She'd gone out somewhere with her mother. Mr. Barrett answered the door, said he expected them back in a few minutes and invited her in to wait.

"So how's it going at school?" he'd asked as they both sat down in the living room.

In the dream she said, "Lousy. I'm fine in math class because Holly is helping me but I'm in the bottom of my class in most other subjects because I can't be bothered to work. I'm more interested in Billy and parties and having fun. My parents are totally pissed off at me."

As soon as she said it, she woke up. And remembered instantly that she hadn't said that to him at the time, in reality. She'd smiled and said, "It's going great, Mr. Barrett. It's going really well at school." Because she didn't want him to think she was even more shallow than he already thought she was. Mr. Barrett was one of those people you always wanted to impress.

"That's nice," he'd said, nodding his head, but his eyes narrowed a little. "You know, I had lunch with a friend the other day who is a criminal lawyer. And he said something interesting. He said that he could tell now when people were lying—after many years, he'd figured out what gave them away. Ninety-five percent of the time, when someone lies, he—or she—smiles. That says something about human nature, doesn't it?"

She remembered squirming in her chair and then being hugely relieved when the front door opened and Holly and her mother came in. A few minutes later, when she and Holly were in Holly's room together, she'd said, "Your father has a mega bullshit detector, doesn't he? He's kind of scary."

And Holly had said, "He's not scary at all. What are you talking about?"

Anna hadn't explained.

Sitting up in her bed, Anna rewound the mental tape and went over the scene of the early morning.

No way. No way a man takes a five-year-old girl out driving at a time like that. And for Katy to drive, she must have been sitting in his lap. She had to have been—he got out on the driver's side right after she did. And why all the secrecy? If he wanted to give her driving lessons, he could do it in the day—with Holly. Why did I buy that grin of his and talk myself out of waking up Holly then and there?

What is it? What's that Shakespeare quote? The only one I came close to remembering when we were doing one of those plays in senior year. I remembered it because of that remark of Mr. Barrett's.

She clenched her fists and squeezed her eyes tight and racked her brain, groping for the memory, feeling it elude her, until she finally gave up trying, got out of bed and headed for the bathroom.

"You missed breakfast. And you missed coffee with Henry. I'll get you some now," Holly said when Anna came downstairs.

Holly was sitting in the living room with a book in her lap and was about to get up when Anna said, "No, stay here. I need to talk to you. Where's Jack? And where's Katy?"

"Jack's gone to town—we're out of dishwasher powder, so he said he'd get it. And Katy's asleep. She went back to bed after we went to Henry's for coffee. She was tired."

"I bet she was." Anna sat down across from Holly. "Do you have any idea what she was doing at two o'clock this morning?"

"Yes. Jack told me. He took her on a drive. He was letting her drive the car."

"So he told you."

"Of course he did."

"And you have no problem with that?"

"She was awake when he came back. He thought it would be a fun adventure."

"Fun. Right."

"What's *your* problem, Anna?" Holly put the book on the table, leaned forward in her chair. "Is there something you want to say to me?"

"Yes, Holl, there is. You've always been the sensible one. I can't believe you think it's OK for him to take her out in the middle of the night like that. She's five years old."

"I know how old my daughter is." Holly's back was ramrod

straight. She was glaring at Anna, challenging her with furious eyes.

"He has you wrapped around his little finger, doesn't he? If it were anyone else, you'd be going ballistic."

"Anyone else? He's her stepfather. He adores her. If he wants to take her out on a drive, he can. She loved it. She can't wait to show me how good she is."

"Jesus, Holly. You're letting your feelings for him cloud your judgment. I know he's handsome and charming and all that. But you don't really know anything about him, do you? It's like he came out of thin air, landed in Shoreham and swept you off your feet. What do you really know about this guy?"

"I know everything about him. And I know something else, too. I know you're jealous. You can't stand to see me happy because you've always been the one who has everything and I've been your little sidekick who lags behind. Poor Holly, right?" She stood up. Anna could see that she was shaking.

"Poor Holly who wasn't as popular as you at school. Poor Holly who didn't have a boyfriend and tagged along with you and Billy like some poodle. Poor Holly who got pregnant by the guy who you'd ditched, a guy who didn't care about her and then ran away. Poor Holly who isn't cool or attractive or sexy. You're so used to patronizing me and feeling sorry for me, my happiness threatens you. I'm tired of this shit, Anna. I'm tired of you feeling better about yourself because you're not me. You think I don't know that about you? You think I'm not aware of how you look down on me?"

"Holl . . ." Anna stood up too. She took a step closer to

Holly, reached out and put her hand on her shoulder. But Holly shrugged it off. "OK. Fine. You're right. I've been a bitch and—"

"Oh, please. Spare me. You always do that. You admit to being a bitch as if that makes it all right to be a bitch. Like, 'Oh, look at how honest Anna is being. Isn't she great?' And everyone forgets the fact that you've been a bitch in the first place."

"Is that what I do?"

"All the time."

"And you hate me for it?"

"I hate you for trying to ruin my happiness."

"Which is what you really believe I'm trying to do?"

"Yes."

"Right. I'll leave."

"Good."

"Good."

Anna turned and went back up the stairs to her room, threw her clothes in her bag. Years of friendship had flown out the window—fine. She had other friends. She had a whole other life in Boston that Holly Barrett wasn't part of.

When she walked back down with her bag, Holly was standing at the front door, holding it open.

At the threshold, Anna turned. "Don't worry. I'm going. I won't spoil your precious happiness. But it's wrong, and you know it. Taking Katy out in the middle of the night, having her sit on his lap to drive. It's wrong. Hating me doesn't change that."

As she walked to her car, she heard the door slam with a bang behind her.

Fine, OK. Fine. I'm out of here. Forever. Leave her to stew in her idyllic little piece of heaven with her heavenly husband whom she knows nothing about and who takes her daughter out for drives and can't stop smiling. It's not my responsibility any more. If she doesn't want my help, fine.

Anna started the car, drove out the driveway, heading back to Boston and sanity. But halfway down the road, she stopped, reversed and took a left-hand turn at the sign on the tree that said Madison.

21

When Jack came back, Holly was curled up on the living room sofa, crying. She would never have imagined she'd tell anyone she hated them, much less throw them out of her house. And the fact that the person she'd said that to and the person she'd thrown out was Anna was awful. Yelling like that didn't make her feel any better. Bringing up all that stuff from the past didn't either. She'd been totally out of control; she'd said things she didn't really mean, just as she'd done before with Henry. But she'd been pushed into it—both times. They were both so wrong about Jack, she didn't have a choice.

As soon as he came in and saw her sitting there, hugging herself, Jack came over, pulled her up and put his arms around her.

"What's happened? What's the matter?"

"I had a fight with Anna. I said terrible things to her and I kicked her out. She's left."

"Is that such a bad result?" He was stroking her hair, calming her down. "I know she's a friend of yours, but honestly— she's so up herself it's not funny. In fact, I'm surprised she and Billy didn't stay together and get married. They're twins, those two. They belong together."

"I was so mean, though. I told her I hated her."

"Holly . . ." Jack took a step back, cupped her face in his hands. "Friends have fights sometimes. It happens. And I bet you had a fight with her because of me. Because she didn't think I should be taking Katy out so late at night. I'm right, aren't I?"

"Yes."

"You were defending me. Which was very sweet of you. Where's the princess?"

"She's taking a nap."

"Ah ha. I'll put this dishwasher powder in the kitchen and then what do you say to going to our room for a while? Taking a little nap of our own? I can cheer you up, I bet."

"I bet you can." She smiled.

"Go." He slapped her on her bottom. "Go get ready. I'll be there in a second."

A minute ago she had been miserable and crying. Now she was taking the stairs up to her room two at a time. Jack could do that. He could change things in an instant, make her laugh, make her happy, make Katy jump up and down for joy with some silly game or joke. Since their honeymoon, they'd been completely in sync. Maybe some day Anna would understand what that meant. Maybe.

Holly stopped at the top of the stairs and caught her breath. Could she have ever imagined six weeks ago that she'd be feeling sorry for Anna? That she'd be about to race into her room at eleven o'clock in the morning for some seriously amazing sex with her husband? A husband Katy loved too?

Good things happen. For a long time, I didn't think they did. But they do—and they've happened to me.

She was taking off her blue jeans when Jack came in.

"Started already?"

"I don't know how long Katy will sleep."

"Good point." He stripped off his T-shirt, took his watch off and put it on the bureau. "Hang on a second." He picked up his cellphone from the tabletop. "I have a message. Did you hear the phone ring when I was out?"

"No, but the door was closed and I was downstairs so I wouldn't have. Who is it?" She walked over and stood beside him as he dialed his message service.

"Shit."

"What, Jack? Who is it?"

He didn't reply. He was listening, biting his lip, his face scrunched up in what looked like pain.

"Jack?"

"Fuck. I need to hear this again." He looked at the receiver, pushed a button and put it back to his ear.

"Fuck." He threw the phone on the bed, went over and sat down on the end, shaking his head. "I don't fucking believe it. I don't fucking believe it."

"What?" She sat down beside him, put her hand on his knee. "Tell me what's going on."

"This is a nightmare." He pounded his fist against his mouth. "What the hell. I didn't think Henry would— Billy, OK, but Henry . . ."

"Henry what? Jack, tell me. Please."

"You know how Billy found the number and called to check up on me before?"

She nodded.

"Well, now Henry has been checking up on me. And he called the number too. The woman I told you about. Which means . . . which has to mean that Billy gave Henry the number. That Henry and Billy are together, trying to find out about me. Henry called the school I was supposed to have gone to."

"But he didn't find out anything, did he? I mean he couldn't, right?"

"Right. But that's not the point any more. I can't stay here. Billy's not going to stop. And if he has roped Henry in with him, well—"

"Jack, I can talk to Henry. I'll tell him—"

"No. No way. Then Henry would think he had to tell Billy to shut him up and then Billy, well, Billy could tell anyone."

"Not if I—"

"Holly. Listen." He turned to her, took both her hands in his. "You have to understand how this works. People don't keep secrets. They say they will, they say they'll never tell another soul, but then they can't stop themselves. It's human nature."

"But I would never tell—"

"You say that and I believe you but we're married. We're in love. Billy Madison isn't in love with me, is he?" Jack snorted. "You have no idea how fast news travels when it travels fast. I can't stay here. I have to go."

"You mean we have to go."

"I know you said in Vermont that if this ever happened, you'd come with me, but now that it is happening, Holly, are you sure? Because it's not going to be easy, starting a new life. And you're not going to be able to tell anyone, not even Henry, where we've gone."

"I know. But I want to go with you. I have to go with you, Jack. I love you with all my heart. And you know Katy loves you too. Of course we'll go with you—wherever."

He kissed her, a kiss so similar to the first one he'd given her that night on the beach that she could almost imagine the sand beneath her feet. When he broke it off, she opened her eyes and willed herself not to cry.

"I'm going into town. I'll make up some excuse to get my pay check early from Figs and you can start packing."

"We don't have to leave today, do we?"

"We have to leave as soon as we possibly can. Today would be good." He stood up. "And you can't tell anyone, Holly. Remember that. You can't tell anyone."

"I won't. But how can I say goodbye to Henry?"

"You can't say goodbye to him. I'm sorry." He kissed her on the side of her head. "You know that's why I walked away from you that first night. I thought this could happen someday. And it wouldn't be just your life I'd be messing around with, it would be Katy's too."

"We'll be fine. I promise. There's no way I'm not going with you."

"OK. Start packing. I'll be back as soon as I can."

After Jack walked out, Holly sank down on the bed, struggling to take in all the ramifications of what had happened. She knew she should start packing but she couldn't bring herself to. Her life had been wrapped up in this house for so long, leaving it would be another kind of death. And how would Katy cope in a brand new place? With no Henry? No Bones?

Why did this have to happen? How could Billy have convinced Henry to make those calls? Henry didn't do things like that. He wasn't a snoop, he had huge respect for other people's privacy. Yet somehow Billy had made Henry change his mind.

Billy Madison had once again come into her life and turned it upside down without even a thought for the consequences.

She wished she'd never seen him pushing that sailboat out into the water his first summer in Shoreham. His parents weren't Shoreham types; they belonged in New York, in the Hamptons, with their white tennis outfits and their flashy Lexus. How could Henry have fallen into Billy's trap? They could have gotten away with it if Billy had made that one call and dropped it, but not now, she could see. Jack was right. If they told Henry the truth, he'd insist on telling Billy to shut him up and then Billy might tell Anna and Anna would tell anyone within ten yards of her because it made such a good story she wouldn't have the willpower to resist.

Holly straightened her back, stood up. She'd have to start packing as much as she could before Katy woke up. There'd be another whole pile of problems when Katy woke up and began asking questions.

She'd deal with it, though. She'd make whatever sacrifices she had to for Jack. They belonged together. She would give up Henry, her house, everything for him and it would all be worth it.

Inside a small jewelry box she kept on the bedside table was a photograph of her parents. Holly took it out, sat with it on her lap for a moment. They were standing on the steps of the porch of Henry's house, their arms around each other. Her mother was smiling at the camera, her father was looking at her mother protectively. They'd been a perfect team; yes, they'd argue occasionally, but they were each other's best friend, she knew. They would have sacrificed anything for each other.

Holly had always suspected that her mother had driven off the road that day because tears had blinded her. The grief of losing her husband had been too much; seeing his body in the funeral home had killed her.

Until she finally laid down beside him and stayed there with him and they died together.

You couldn't bear to lose Dad. And I can't bear to lose Jack. We both mated for life.

22

"I don't believe it." Anna and Billy were at her front door, standing in the pouring rain. "What could you two possibly think you're doing here? Go away. Now."

"I'm not going anywhere, Holly. Anna told me about Jack taking Katy out last night. I can't let this happen."

"Nothing's happening," Holly shouted, feeling like that figure in the Munch painting *The Scream*. "Nothing except you two trying to ruin my life and Katy's life and coming pretty close to succeeding. Go away. I mean it. Leave."

"Holly—it's not just me any more. Henry doesn't trust Jack either. I'm not going to go away. Jack can't do something like that with Katy. How could you let him? Have you lost your mind? Has he brainwashed you?"

I promised him. I promised Jack I wouldn't tell.

"He's covering something up," Billy continued. "Let us in, Holly. We have to get to the bottom of all this. He's covering up his past. He has some woman he talks to in England who pretends not to know him. Everything about him is fishy."

"You have to admit, Holl," Anna joined in, "the fact that Henry doesn't trust him either says something. Besides, I know you kicked me out and everything, but we're getting soaked out here."

Holly didn't move or speak.

"Look, you're not seeing straight, Holly." Billy sounded as if he were a prosecutor in a courtroom. "I understand you've fallen for the guy and love can make you crazy, but you have to think about Katy."

Fury was rising in her, expanding, until her entire body was shaking with rage. They thought Jack was some kind of fraud and child molester. If she kept her promise, they'd continue to think that. If she and Jack and Katy left without saying anything, Billy and Anna and, most importantly, Henry would believe they were right about him.

And they'd also believe that she, Holly, would sacrifice Katy, lead her into a life of abuse—because she had fallen so much in love she couldn't see straight.

I'm sorry, Jack.

"Come in—both of you." She turned, walked over to where the telephone was, aware that they were following behind her, picked it up and dialed.

"Henry? I need you to come over here right away. . . . Yes, now. It's important. It's crucial. . . . Good." She hung up. "Sit down," she said to Billy and Anna as they stood in the middle of the room. "Go sit down."

"We're all wet . . ."

"Don't worry about the sofa, Anna. You know it's damp anyway." Holly waved them toward it.

They both sat, facing the television, like naughty schoolchildren, neither one saying a word.

"I'm going upstairs to check that Katy's still sleeping. By the time I come back, Henry will be here. I'll talk to you all then."

Relieved to see Katy was out for the count, sleeping peacefully, Holly sat down at the foot of her bed, watching her breathe in and out. She was so innocent, so sweet. How could anyone think Jack would hurt her?

I have to tell them. You have to understand, Jack. I can't let them think what they're thinking. I have to go tell them now.

"What's going on?" Henry had just entered the living room when Holly reached the foot of the stairs. His cap and shirt were drenched with rain; he had rushed over without putting a coat on. "What are you two doing here?" he asked Billy and Anna.

"I'll tell you what they're doing here," Holly said, and he swung around to look at her. "Sit down, Henry. Sit down and I'll tell you all what you're doing and how wrong you are to be doing it."

Henry went to the chair across from the sofa, beside the television, and sat with a puzzled look.

"This is like some Agatha Christie movie or *Columbo* or something. Everyone gathered in one room—"

"It's not funny, Anna." Holly remained standing, between the chair and the sofa. "Before you knocked on the door, I was upstairs packing my things. We're leaving Shoreham. Because of you." She fixed her eyes on Billy. "Because you came and you couldn't let me be happy and you started making phone calls and I don't know how—" she turned to Henry "—he got you involved in such a shabby enterprise, but he obviously did. You had to butt in. You had to ruin my life." She was looking at all three of them in turn. "Why?" Her voice had tears in it. "Why did you have to ruin everything? Henry?" She turned to him again. "Why did you make those calls? Why?"

He looked so stung, so pained, she felt a twinge of guilt, but it passed quickly.

"I did it out of concern for you, sweetie. I—"

"Concern for me?" She shook her head. "I don't think so. You did it because you don't trust me, you don't have any faith in my judgment. You all think I'm some little naive, pathetic girl who would fall for any man who paid the slightest attention to me, don't you? Tell me—when exactly did I become so gullible, so incapable of looking after myself, not to mention Katy? You think I'd put Katy at risk because of a man? How could you think that about me?"

"I don't think that, sweetie. Of course I don't. I was concerned about Jack's behavior, not yours, I—"

"Stop it. I can't take this any more." She held up her hand. "You have no idea what you're talking about. You all distrust Jack. You all think there's something wrong with him. What's wrong with him is *you*. You're interfering in things you have no idea about."

"Which are what things exactly, Holly?" Billy leaned forward.

"Jack got into trouble after his parents died, OK?" She said this directly to Billy. "He got involved with the wrong people. He got involved with the gangland scene in London. They did bad things, but Jack knew they were wrong and he ended up testifying against them in court. And because of that, he had to be given a new identity. He came over here and he started a whole new life. But if anyone discovers who he is, the people who he used to be with, they'll find him. And they'll kill him, Billy. OK? They'll kill him for testifying against them."

"Shut up! Like the Mafia?"

"No, not *like* the Mafia, Anna. *Actually* the Mafia, OK? Do you understand? So that's why he has no friends from the past, that's why he isn't some lawyer or corporate banker or whatever you'd think was acceptable." She was aiming her words at Billy again. "You should know what it's like to make a mistake and want to move on from it, to start again. But you won't let him do that, will you, Billy? You had to check up on him and be devious. And now we have to leave. We can't stay here. Which means you're not going to see Katy, Billy. And it's all your own fault."

"Holly, wait a second—"

Billy stopped mid-sentence and everyone's heads swiveled at the sound of the front door opening. Jack appeared. Looking like someone who had walked into his surprise party. At first, seeing the bewilderment and disbelief on his face, Holly feared he might turn around and go back out, drive away from Shoreham forever. But he came into the living room, strode straight up to her.

"So—what is everyone doing here?" he asked her. "You haven't—"

"I had to, Jack. I had to—"

"You didn't. Tell me you didn't." He put his hands on her shoulders. "Holly? Please. You know how important this is. You promised me."

"I couldn't let them think like that about you. I just couldn't. I couldn't let them get away with being so wrong about you."

Jack spun away from her, dragged his hands down his face as if he were raking it.

"Fuck." He shook his head, stared at the floor.

No one moved or spoke.

"Sorry, guys," Anna finally spoke. "But I don't get it. And don't all look at me as if I've dropped a bomb or something because I've broken the silence. I don't get why it's such a big deal, why you'd have to leave Shoreham, Holly. What I mean is, OK, Jack, so you're what? In some kind of witness-protection program? And now Billy and Henry and I know about it too. But it's not as if we're going to tell anyone. Why would we? Billy doesn't want to lose the chance of seeing Katy if you left, Henry doesn't want you to go, obviously, and there's nothing in it for me to blab either. I mean, come on. Why do you have to go?"

"You wouldn't be able to resist telling someone, Anna. I know you. It's too good a story."

"Holly." She got up, came to where Holly was and stood right in front of her. "You've said a lot of things to me today, things I hope you don't mean. Maybe you were right, maybe I was jealous of you and Jack. And maybe I did treat you like a sidekick when we were at school. But you know, your parents— and Henry too for that matter, and no offense, Henry, but it's true—treated me like an airhead. They patronized me, not in a terrible way, but still, I knew what they were thinking. I wasn't good at school, I wasn't as smart as you—I bet they couldn't figure out why you would be friends with me. But we were friends, Holl. And I am still your friend. And I wouldn't trade you in for a good story. That's not fair. If we're all about setting the record straight about people today, include me in. I'm not as shallow as you think I am."

"Oh, God, Anna. I'm sorry." All of her righteous anger disappeared and Holly stepped toward Anna and hugged her. "I didn't mean to accuse you of being shallow, I really didn't. It's been a crazy day. I'm so sorry for taking it out on you."

"Oh, come on. This is very touching, but it's not the point." Billy stood up, began to pace around the room. He stopped behind Henry's chair. "First of all, how do we know we can believe this story, Jack? You could have made this whole thing up. Gangs and the Mafia. Come off it."

"Why would I make it up?" Jack looked up from the floor he'd been fixated on. "And *how* could I make it up, even if there were a reason I wanted to? I know you called the school I was supposed to have gone to, Henry. I know you both called the woman who is in charge of my new identity because she called me to tell me you had. How would I know you'd called that school unless the school had informed her—which they have to do in cases like mine?

"And there *are* gangs in London, Billy. It's not all Wimbledon and strawberries and garden parties in Buckingham Palace. The Mafia does exist in London. And I was part of it all. I'm ashamed of it. I'm ashamed I went off the rails like that, but I have to pay for it every day of my life. I have to look over my shoulder the whole time. But I thought I could still have a life. I made a new life with Holly and Katy. I want to live that new life. Is that a crime?"

Holly went to him, put her arm around him.

"He deserves a new life, he deserves the same new life and happiness he has given me and Katy."

"Are you saying they're still after you, after this amount of time? That they'd really follow you to America if they found out you were here?" Billy pressed.

"I know of a case," Henry spoke up, "where a Mafia informer was about to testify and he was in the courthouse, on the fourth floor, waiting to go down to the courtroom, and he had a guard, but the guard must have been paid off, because he left the room and when he did, a hit man went in and threw him out the window. It happened in New York, when I was living there. You're never safe from those people. They make it their business to ensure you're never safe."

Billy looked chastened, but only for a second.

"None of this is the point, though, is it? The point is, you took Katy out for a drive at what? Two o'clock in the morning. And you can't explain that away with anything to do with the Mafia, Jack. You did something entirely inappropriate."

"That word again." Jack sighed. "Inappropriate. She was awake. We went on an adventure. She loved it. If it's inappropriate for her to have fun, I'm guilty as charged."

"She must have been sitting on your lap to drive. It *is* inappropriate. You're not her father."

"I am so tired." Holly could feel Jack's whole body sag as he spoke. "I'm too tired to play games with you, Billy. I told Holly and I told Henry—I had a sister who died when she was very young, when she was Katy's age. Amanda. One time she and I woke up in the middle of the night and got dressed and went to sit in our parents' car and pretended to take a trip to France.

Stupid make-believe, but she loved it. We used to have so much fun together. Was that inappropriate? Maybe I shouldn't play Ping-Pong with Katy either. Maybe I need to be accompanied if I walk with her down the beach just in case I do anything inappropriate. Look, I'm sure some American shrink would say I'm recreating Amanda in Katy or whatever, and if everyone thinks that's wrong, fine. I won't do anything like that ever again. But at no point did I ever do anything inappropriate with Katy."

"Of course he didn't." Holly shook her head. "Does that answer all your doubts, all your distrust and horrible suspicions? Are you all satisfied now?"

"I still want to know what all this leaving business is about," Anna said. "I mean, you don't have to leave now, do you? We can all go back to normal and promise to keep our mouths shut, can't we? Right?"

What Anna said made sense; Holly dared to hope Jack would see it that way too.

"Jack?" She looked up at him. "Can we stay?"

"Maybe. But all this digging around has to stop. Are you going to stop, Billy?"

"What choice do I have?" Billy's tone was petulant. "Anna's right. It's not in my interest for you to leave town."

"I said this morning that I knew I'd regret making those calls, Jack." Henry took a deep breath. "And I do. I only hope you can forgive me."

"It's not a problem, Henry."

"What did the Mafia guys do? I mean, what did they do that you had to testify against them?"

"I'd really prefer not to discuss it, Anna."

"I think we should go now." Henry rose from his chair. "And leave Jack and Holly in peace. We've meddled enough in their lives as it is. I'm sorry, sweetie." He walked over to Holly, leaned over and kissed her on the cheek. "I've been an old fool and I apologize."

"You should have trusted me, Henry."

"I know, I—"

"How about a fishing trip tomorrow morning, Henry?" Jack put his hand on Henry's shoulder. "I could use a trip in the boat."

"Does that mean you're not leaving?" Anna asked.

"Looks that way." Jack gave her a brief smile; Holly's heart soared.

"Of course we'll go fishing." Henry sounded relieved and grateful. "Nothing like a trip on the boat to clear the air."

"Come on, Billy." Anna motioned for him to join her. "Henry's right. It's time to go."

"Anna—you can stay here. I'm sorry about what happened before, I—"

"Holl—don't worry. Like you said, it's been a crazy day. And a long one—already. I'm exhausted. It's time for me to get back to Boston."

"Billy . . ." Jack blocked his path as he was walking to the front door. "Can we try to be more civil to each other? Isn't it time we called a truce?" He held out his right hand.

"OK." Billy shook it. "Whatever."

Jack turned, rolled his eyes at Holly, mouthed "whatever" and smiled at her.

"Come over later if you want to, sweetie," Henry said as he was walking out.

"I will."

When they'd all left the house, Holly threw herself into Jack's arms.

"I'm sorry, I really am, for telling them. I know I promised, but I had to. Do you understand?"

"Yes." Jack stepped back, took her face in his hands. "But this doesn't change anything."

"What do you mean?"

"I mean we're still leaving."

"Why?"

"Because I don't trust Billy, I don't trust Anna."

"But you said—"

"I know. I want them to think we're not going. They have to think we're not going. I want as much time as possible to elapse before they figure out we've gone. So I'll go fishing tomorrow with Henry, and you and Katy can have coffee with him afterward, make everything normal, and then we'll go—and that will give us at least a day's start on them."

"But what Anna said made sense, Jack. It's not in Billy's interest to force us out. Or hers, either."

"It may not be in his interest now, but what about further down the line? When he sees how close Katy and I are and resents it even more than he does now? He could do anything, Holly. He wants me out of the country, out of your life."

"He doesn't want you dead, Jack."

"Maybe he does. Or maybe he thinks I'm exaggerating. He'll figure out a way to spin it so he can live with it, believe me."

"Are you sure? I mean do you really think—"

"I have to leave. I told you before, you don't have to come with me. It's up to you, Holly. But I have to go. I can't take the chance. It's far too risky."

"Mommy. Jack." Katy was on the bottom step. "What are you talking about?"

"I was just telling Jack how happy we are that he's part of our family. How much we love him."

"He knows that already."

"He needs to know it all the time, chicken. He needs to know we're like wolves."

"What are you talking about?" Katy's cheek had a crease down it from her nap. She looked at them both with bewilderment. "How are we like wolves?"

Holly took Jack's hand in hers. "Jack knows how. He'll tell you."

23

The three of them stood on the road in the rain. Henry was about to turn left to go to his house, but he hesitated; Billy saw this and pounced.

"Do you really believe it, Henry? The Mafia, his sister, a new identity?"

"He told me about his sister before. He wouldn't make something like that up."

"And the Mafia?"

"Why not?" Anna felt as if it were the morning after a party and they all had to discuss what had happened the night before. "I mean, the Mafia exists everywhere, doesn't it? But how did he get involved in it in the first place? He doesn't look like a Mafioso."

"I doubt that all Mafiosi look alike." Henry knew he should go home, but he couldn't quite bring himself to.

"It's all very dramatic, isn't it? It doesn't really get more dramatic." Anna hugged herself.

"It does fit," Henry stated. "How else would he know we'd called the school? That McCormack woman being in charge of his new identity—of course, she wouldn't say she knew him, would she? It makes sense." He looked toward his house. "I feel guilty talking about it like this. I should go."

"The only reason I didn't trust him in the first place was because of Mr. Barrett," Anna said to Henry. "Because of something he once said to me."

"What did John say?"

"He said people smile when they lie. And Jack was smiling when he was talking about taking Katy out in the car. I know—it's stupid, but I couldn't help remembering. There was this Shakespeare quote it took me forever to remember—I only remembered it when I was walking out of the house now. How weird is that? Anyway, Jack wasn't smiling in there just now."

"What Shakespeare quotation?"

"It's like 'You can smile and still be a villain.'"

"It's 'One may smile, and smile, and be a villain,' to be precise. *Hamlet*. John said that to you? Why?"

"He didn't say the quote, but he said that people smile when they lie. I smile when I lie, I know. And I thought Jack was lying this morning because he kept smiling. But like I said, he wasn't smiling when he was telling us his story."

"No, he wasn't."

"And that's proof he wasn't lying?" Billy kept shifting his weight from foot to foot. He'd been uncomfortable in the house, but then everything about Jack made him uncomfortable, even that brief handshake. Henry was obviously going to believe Jack's stories. And he couldn't think of any way to challenge Jack now; he couldn't call Eliza McCormack again; and it wasn't as though he could pick up a phone and call Mafia headquarters in London.

"Billy, we should call it a day. We should stop this interfering. It's wrong. Jack and Holly explained everything in there—at some risk to themselves. As you said to me before, we all make mistakes, we all do things we shouldn't. He was wild in his youth, he is paying for that now. And he did the right thing by testifying. We should leave them be."

"I'd like to know about this testimony. What the case was, how—"

"Stop it right now." Henry put his hands up in the air. "I mean it, Billy. Leave it alone."

"But his late-night drive with Katy—"

"I think we're in danger of reading too much into things like that these days. I know I was concerned, but I can see it from Jack's point of view. I can see how it could be perfectly innocent."

"You can, Henry? Really? Because I'm not sure I can believe one word that comes out of his mouth."

"Come on." Anna tugged on Billy's arm. "Calm down. Let's get out of the rain. I'll come back to your house, we can sit and have a coffee—I'll need one before I drive back. You really do have to forget this, Billy. If you don't, the Mafia might end up coming after *you*. Or Katy, now that I think about it. If they found out where Jack was, they might go after Katy to torture him even more. I saw this episode of *Law & Order*—"

"You really trust him, Henry?"

"I trust Holly, Billy. And yes, I do. I do trust Jack. He was entirely sincere in there. He deserves a chance. As I said before, we should leave them in peace. Have a good drive back, Anna."

"Thank you."

"And I truly am sorry if I acted in a patronizing way to you. But I don't think John and Julia ever meant to."

"I'm sure they didn't. Don't worry, Henry. Besides, I *am* pretty much of an airhead. It's no big deal."

"It is a big deal. They wouldn't have wanted to hurt or offend you. Come see me next time you're down, Anna. We can have a cup of coffee."

"Will do." She began to drag Billy away. "Goodbye, Henry. And don't worry, I'll calm him down."

"Goodbye, Henry," Billy said grudgingly.

Billy allowed himself to be led off by Anna while Henry turned, walked the two minutes it took to get to his house.

At least he was busy today. Taking Bones to the vet—he'd had an upset stomach that morning—buying groceries, stopping in on an old friend in town. Unusually for him, he was anxious to get off Birch Point and into the "real" world. The whole business with Jack had been too much. The Mafia? A young man like Jack involved in the Mafia?

Well, worse things happen at sea. But then again, do they? What's worse than Holly marrying someone who was in the Mafia? Someone who has been a criminal?

But I believe in rehabilitation. I can't throw away my beliefs because the person rehabilitated is married to my granddaughter. Am I a "Not in My Own Backyard" type of liberal? Do my beliefs go only so far?

Yet it all felt so very much against what John and Julia would have wanted for Holly. And so very much against what *he* wanted for Holly. But love wasn't in the business of adhering to other people's expectations. Holly was in love with Jack, Jack in love with Holly. That's all that really mattered. That and the fact that Jack had changed, that he'd come to his senses and straightened himself out.

Anna's right, though—how does a boy like that get involved with the Mafia in the first place? What was his original identity? What was his name, I wonder? And what exactly did he do before he straightened himself out? What crimes did he commit?

Henry picked up Bones's leash from the front hall table. The disappointment and anger in Holly's eyes as she had asked, "Why, Henry?" had been a terrible thing to behold. He had let her down. And if he kept on distrusting Jack Dane, Holly and Katy might leave Birch Point forever.

"Come on, Bones. We've got to mind our own business from now on. Normal life resumes as of now. Which means there is no excuse for not going to the vet, old man. But I've got a special snack for you when you're well again."

Holly hadn't called him. When he returned to the house in the late afternoon, there were no messages. Normally, if she came over and he wasn't there, she'd write a note—but there was no note, either.

She's punishing me. And I can't say as I blame her.

He put the groceries in the kitchen, made himself a bowl of Campbell's minestrone soup and a slice of bread and butter, and then went back into the living room and sat down with the last three issues of the *New Yorker* he hadn't gotten to yet. As he read, he kept losing his place and had to start over again.

After a while, he gave up any hope of concentrating on words and went to play Hearts on his computer. Hearts could keep him occupied for hours: a small vice he kept a secret. There was no redeeming feature in sitting in front of a screen playing card games: he should have been educating himself, learning something, being productive. Instead he spent far too long trying to Shoot the Moon or offload the queen of spades, smoking his pipe as he played.

Isabella would never have let him get away with it. If Isabella were alive, they would have been sitting out on the porch chatting. What would she have thought of Jack and Holly?

Henry led the two of clubs, sat back and pondered.

"Find out, Henry. When you go out fishing tomorrow morning, find out exactly what it was he did and didn't do. We can't pretend it doesn't make a difference, no matter how much Holly wants us to. You need to find out."

All right, Isabella. That's what I'll do.

Sleep was eluding her. She'd be just about to nod off and her eyes would snap awake, seemingly of their own free will. She was facing the wall: Jack's arm was around her waist, holding her to his body. He was asleep; she could tell from the regularity of his breathing pattern. He'd been remarkably cheerful all day: smiling, making jokes, full of enthusiasm for their move. She'd had to go to the bank in the afternoon to withdraw the cash in her checking account, while he stayed home with Katy and decided where it was they were moving to.

"What about Indiana?" he'd asked when she returned and found him at the kitchen table. "I like the sound of it. It sounds anonymous. What do you think?"

"Why not?" She'd forced a smile. Katy was watching TV in the living room. She couldn't tell her about the trip until the last minute. It wasn't fair to make Katy keep a big secret like that. "I thought you loved the sea, though, the horizon."

"Good point!" he'd exclaimed—as if she had said something supremely intelligent. "Indiana it isn't!" He pulled the atlas lying on the kitchen table back in front of him and opened it. "Oregon. Oregon sounds good, doesn't it? And it's on the Pacific. There's even more of a horizon on the Pacific."

"Are you all right, Jack?"

"I'm fine. I'm sorted."

"Sorted?"

"Never mind." He shook his head, grabbed her hand, stood up and pulled her up with him. "Come here." He hugged her. "We'll have a brand new life. We can be anybody, do anything."

She tried to catch his good mood and run with it, but all she could think of was leaving Henry behind.

"Katy will miss Henry. So will I," she said.

"So will I. But it's like I said before. You have to keep looking forward. Maybe I could be a fisherman in Oregon. And you could be a schoolteacher. In a small coastal town. We should live in a cabin. Katy would love living in a cabin." He began to dance, and she fell into it with him, following him as he led her around the kitchen table. "We'll have a radio in the cabin kitchen. And dance in the moonlight." He stopped, looked at her. "It will be amazing, Holly Barrett Dane. A simple, amazing life. No television. A radio but no television. You can picture it, can't you?"

"Yes," she lied.

And she'd lied when they had sex that night, too. Pretending, for the first time, to have an orgasm. She didn't want to disappoint him or admit to him how frightened she was. He needed her to be strong and she needed to be strong for him. Saying goodbye to Henry the next day without telling him they were leaving Shoreham would be the most difficult lie she'd ever have to tell.

The smell of his warm sleeping breath in her ear made her remember that first time in the bus, how he'd whispered to her, how she'd felt so close to him, so intimate. What if someone had told her then that she'd be married to him and leaving Shoreham with him forever within six weeks? What would she have thought?

I would have thought I'd trade in anything to be with him— anything except Katy.

I'm sorry, Henry. But I don't have a choice. Love like this doesn't give you a choice.

Henry woke up sweating, drenched from his dream. He'd been walking down the dike in the blazing heat and John had suddenly appeared, standing beside the lighthouse. Not John at the age he'd died, but John when he was in his early twenties. Young and strong and handsome and his son.

"Hello, Dad," he'd said and Henry had rushed up to him to hug him, saying, "You're alive. John. My God, you're alive."

"I'm going swimming, Dad. Come with me," John had said—and then he'd broken out of Henry's hug and dived off the rocks at the end of the dike, swimming toward the canal.

"The current. Don't, John. The current's too strong. You'll drown," Henry had shouted from the rocks. "Stop," he kept shouting. "Don't go to the canal. Stop!" But John had kept swimming.

When he reached the buoy marking the canal, he turned.

"You'll love it, Dad. I promise. Come with me. Come swim with me. Dive in now."

He couldn't move. He tried to pick up his feet, to launch himself into the water, but he couldn't move.

"I can't. Not yet. I can't come with you yet," he yelled.

"OK." With the illogic of dreams, John didn't have to shout to be heard. Henry could see his face clearly, bobbing above the waves. John smiled that amused, funny smile of his, then dived down into the water.

Henry kept searching the canal, waiting to see him reappear, but he was gone.

He woke, drenched not only with sweat, but with a terrible sense of loss and incomprehension. Was that dream supposed to mean something? He didn't believe in all the dream malarkey, Freudian interpretations or whatever they called them now. But he'd been so happy when he'd first seen John standing there; so panicked and miserable when John disappeared under the water. It all felt so real and so crushing. Why hadn't he followed John into the canal? The only moments he was allowed to be with his son again were ones in dreams. Why hadn't he gone to him?

He got out of bed, stripped off his pajamas, sat back down, and allowed the tears to fall. When they'd finished, he turned on the bedside lamp; then went to the chest of drawers in the corner of the room to find a new pair of PJs. As he was opening the middle drawer, it hit him.

"I had a sister, Miranda. She died when she was young."

That's what Jack had said that night he was playing catch with Katy.

He remembered thinking, *Prospero's daughter, Miranda. A lovely name.*

"I had a sister who died when she was very young . . . Amanda."

That's what Jack had said in the house.

He hadn't misheard, either time. He was almost certain of it. Jack couldn't have had two sisters.

Would parents name a daughter Miranda Amanda Dane—or whatever their last name actually was? Perhaps. But would you refer to your sister by both her Christian and her middle name? Unlikely.

Whatever the truth of Jack's sister's name, Henry knew he couldn't go back to sleep. If there had been a big Mafia trial, it would have been reported in the English press. He could search for it on the Web. At least that would keep him occupied; he'd feel he was doing *something*. Not standing paralyzed on the rocks, a helpless onlooker.

Closing the middle drawer, Henry then opened the top one. He was going to get dressed properly, fix himself a cup of coffee and go sit at his computer and do some Web surfing. No one would have to know. He wasn't in league with Billy this time. He was simply doing some research on his own.

As he waited for the kettle to boil, he thought of the day they'd buried John and Julia. Late that night, he'd gone down to the long grass where their ashes lay. There was no moon, there were no stars. He'd taken a flashlight and Bones and found the spot where they lay and sat down beside it.

"I promise you I'll take care of them. I'll love Holly and Katy with all my heart and soul and I'll take care of them. I'll try to do what you'd do if you were here. I'll do my very best for as long as I live. That's a promise."

A foghorn sounded. Henry turned at the noise, looking for ghosts.

24

There were pages and pages of responses on Google.co.uk to the "Gangland cases London 2003–2005" Henry typed in. He combed through them, learning as he did that there were two major types of "gangs" in London: the "Yardies"—a nickname given to gangs of a West Indian origin—and the Mafia. Honing in on the Mafia-related entries was proving fruitless. He didn't know Jack's real name; he had no way of working out what case might be connected to him. There were armed robberies and murders, money-laundering and kidnappings. Henry spent hours raking through them looking for potential clues and finding nothing.

Jack's case could have been any of the ones he'd pulled up, Henry knew. What was the point of continuing? They were all gruesome and nasty. Jack had landed himself in a terrible fix, certainly, but as he continued to move from page to page, Henry began to question whether finding out how terrible that fix actually was would help. Still, he searched on, feeling as if he had the mental equivalent of something stuck in his throat. He needed to clear his mind, to breathe freely again. He couldn't stop himself from repeatedly clicking the mouse button to read the next entry.

At some point he must have fallen asleep, his head on the desk. Waking up with a start, he wiped his mouth, checked his watch and saw it was six a.m., then stood, stretched, and went to the kitchen to make a cup of coffee.

There was no point in going upstairs to bed now; Jack would be over in a little while to go fishing. The coffee would give him a second wind and the trip out in the boat would be another energy boost; if he had to, he'd take a nap in the afternoon.

Carrying the cup of freshly brewed coffee with him, he walked outside and sat down on the porch steps. The night had turned into a gray day—uninspiring and gloomy. When he looked out over the canal, it was flat and glassy; there was no wind, no movement of any kind. A good day to speed along in the *Sea Ox*, maybe even a good morning to fish. But despite the caffeine beginning to kick in, Henry was suddenly overwhelmed by a longing to sleep again; he wanted to curl up, to be like Bones and pad around in a circle and then curl up and go to sleep. And then . . . then to wake up and find the sun shining and Isabella and Jack and Julia and Holly and Katy all there, standing over him, telling him to get ready, it was time to go to the beach.

Turn back the clock. Keep turning it back until you recapture that moment of happiness you didn't appreciate fully at the time. Live it over again.

Let me have them back again. Just once, just for a minute.

Standing up, he felt suddenly faint and leaned his hand against the wooden pillar for support.

Self-pity is not excusable. However tired you may be. Go upstairs and wash your face and pull yourself together.

He turned, went back into the house, headed to his desk to switch off the computer. It was time to give up on the quest to find out what Jack may have done. He'd ask him on their boat trip. He should have learned by now that direct confrontation was always the best way to approach a problem.

As he leaned down to push the power button off, Henry caught sight of the piece of paper with a number written on it, the number Billy had read out to him: Eliza McCormack's number.

Eliza McCormack. The woman who had given Jack his new identity. A parole officer? Someone in the prison system?

He put the cup of coffee down on the desk, rebooted the Apple and typed in Google.co.uk. After the Google page came up, he typed "Eliza McCormack" in the box and sat back. The first entry was:

Eliza McCormack Wikipedia, The Free Encyclopedia

Eliza McCormack, QC, has made her name fighting cases no one else will touch . . .

Henry leaned forward, stared at it, thinking, *She's a lawyer, is this the right Eliza McCormack?* and clicked on the Wikipedia link.

The picture caught his eye first. A black-and-white head shot of a silver-gray-haired woman in early middle age. Mid-forties to early fifties, he guessed. Perfectly coiffed, strong features with a predominant nose, no-nonsense mouth and challenging eyes. Lines on her forehead which signaled a healthy distaste for

Botox. If he'd seen her across the room at a party, he'd want to go talk to her.

Eliza McCormack QC (born April 30 1962) is a well-known English barrister. She has made her name in criminal defense work, often in cases which gained public notoriety, including the Choirboy Killer, Len Houston, the Paddington 4, and the Green Warriors.

A mountain climber, skier and renowned feminist, she has been nicknamed "Extreme Eliza," and has a reputation as a fiery and witty public speaker.

Contents:

1. *Personal Life*
2. *Famous Cases*
3. *Notes*
4. *See Also*
5. *Further Reading*
6. *External links*

Henry paused. Was Eliza McCormack someone who would be involved in giving someone a new identity—was this kind of thing in the remit of barristers in England? And would she defend someone in the Mafia? He clicked on *Famous Cases*.

As well as representing 11-year-old Thomas Grainger, the Choirboy Killer, who murdered twin 3-year-old girls, Amanda and Miranda Dunne, McCormack has represented Len Houston, the television talk show host accused of—

He stopped, his eyes returning to the names Amanda and Miranda.

No. This is coincidence. No. This can't be anything but coincidence. They are names, that's all. Names any child might have. I misheard before. He didn't say Miranda the first time around. I misheard. My hearing isn't what it used to be. I'm getting old.

He leaned forward, put his elbows on the desk, covered his face with his hands. Just as he had done in the doctor's office when the oncologist had said there was no more she could do to help Isabella.

Don't let this happen. Don't let this be the truth. It can't be the truth.

Type "Thomas Grainger" into Google and find out you're wrong. Find out what a misguided, crazy old man you've become. Prove it. Because it can't be true. It can't be.

He didn't type anything in. His hands stayed where they were, covering his face.

Katy. Playing on the beach with Jack. Katy. Going for a ride with Jack. Alone with him in the car. Late at night. Katy.

In an instant, he'd sat back up straight, pulled up the Google page and typed in "Thomas Grainger."

Image Results for Thomas Grainger

There were three snapshot pictures. One of a dark-haired young boy standing in front of a board with measurements of feet and inches on it, holding a piece of paper with the name "Thomas Grainger" written on it and a date of birth.

Beside it was a photo of two little girls. Blonde-haired, identical little girls smiling into the camera, looking as if they might be posing for a family Christmas card.

The final picture on the right was of a teenage boy. An older version of the boy in the first picture.

A younger version of Jack.

No, oh my God, no.

Leaning forward, he studied the teenage boy more closely. Jack's eyes. Jack's nose. Jack's mouth.

A feeling of dizziness came over him again; he couldn't take in the text printed underneath the pictures. All he saw were parts of sentences: *viciously battered over the head with a cricket bat . . . an 11-year-old choirboy at the prestigious choir school . . . horribly reminiscent of the Jamie Bulger case . . . Barrister Eliza McCormack . . . Grainger was released from prison at 18 . . . new identity to protect . . . Dunne, father of the murdered identical twins, suffered a fatal stroke in 2007 . . .*

"Henry."

25

He turned so quickly, he knocked over his cup of coffee.

Jack was behind him, staring over his shoulder at the screen.

"I didn't hear you come in. How long have you—"

"Sorry about that. I saw you hunched over your desk as I was walking in. I didn't want to disturb you, you were so engrossed. I'll get something to wipe up that coffee, Henry. Hang on a second."

"Jack, no. Wait. Leave it. We need to talk."

"Because of that?" Jack pointed at the screen. "You don't really think that's me, do you?"

"Are you saying it isn't?"

"Of course it isn't." He smiled. "You need glasses, Henry. Should we get going, then? Off to the dock? The fish are probably out there jumping, just waiting for us."

Viciously battered over the head with a cricket bat . . .

"My vision is fine, Jack." He stood up. "We're not going anywhere right now." He went over to the armchair beside the fireplace. "Sit down in that chair across from me. We're going to talk."

"Come on, Henry. Don't be silly. Let's get going." Jack didn't move.

"No." Henry pointed to the chair. "Sit."

"What? I'm Bones now?" Jack ambled over to the chair, sat down casually. "This is a waste of time."

He couldn't fit the image of a boy who had killed two little girls to the man who was sitting across from him now—to Jack, his grandson-in-law. What he desperately wanted to do was stand back up, say, "Forget it, let's go," and head over to the dock. How could he start this conversation? How could he *have* a conversation about all this? The horror of it kept flooding his heart; yet he knew he had to push it to the side, somehow. He had to find out the truth—now.

"You wanted me to know, didn't you?"

"To know what? I'm not following you." Jack crossed his right leg over his left.

"You're following me, all right. There's nothing wrong with my eyesight and there's nothing wrong with your brain. You wouldn't have said their names if you didn't want to be found out. You would have made up some name like 'Ruth' for your sister—not Miranda and then Amanda. You said both their names, Jack. You wanted me to know."

"Do you mind?" Jack reached into the pocket of the windbreaker he was wearing, pulled out a packet of cigarettes and a lighter, showed them to Henry.

"I don't give a fuck if you smoke. I want you to tell me the truth."

Henry stared at him as he lit the cigarette, took a puff and then another.

"Jack? I'm waiting. Or should I call you Thomas?"

"Call me whatever you like, Henry."

"Are you going to tell me the truth?"

"Which truth?"

"What does that mean?"

"It means which truth? The truth the media puts out? The truth people want to believe? Or the truth, the whole truth and nothing but the truth? It's a strange word, isn't it? Truth?" Jack inhaled again, deeply. Blew out the smoke, stared at it, flicked the still-burning cigarette into the fireplace. "The truth is, Henry . . ." He uncrossed his legs, sat forward. "I did something awful. Unspeakable. Monstrous. I can tell you that I was eleven years old and I didn't know what I'd done. I can try to explain what happened. But that won't make any difference, will it?

"The truth is I killed Amanda and Miranda Dunne and I went to prison for it. I was released from prison when I was eighteen and I was given a new identity. But I was found out. Someone recognized me and sold the story to the papers and they camped outside my flat and I was about to be strung up and lynched by a baying mob. But I was allowed to flee in the middle of the night and then I was given another identity— and guess what? The same thing happened. Someone recognized me and sold me out again. I had three identities, Henry. Three times I came close to being killed by some enraged member of the public. They finally realized I couldn't live in the UK. My lawyer, well, she helped do a deal, a special deal, to get me here to America."

If I could leave. If only I could leave this room now. If only Jack could disappear forever. I don't know how to deal with this. I don't think I can continue to look at this man.

"That's one truth. Another truth is that there is a justice system. And there is this theory about the justice system. The theory is that if you go to jail and do your time, you have paid your debt to society and are rehabilitated and let out to live the rest of your life. Except that's not the truth. Because no one wants you to live your life when you've done what I've done. I can never repay the debt, Henry. I thought I could, with Holly and Katy. I really thought I could live a life and give them all my love and make up for the terrible thing I'd done. Why do they bother with this so-called truth of theirs, Henry? That's what I want to know. Why do they tell you that you can be rehabilitated when they won't let you be?"

"*I* want to know why you . . . why you killed those girls. Why, Jack? They were three years old. How could you possibly have killed them?"

"It was an accident, Henry. We were playing. Up in a tree-house in the back of my garden. I used to play with them all the time. Their mother came to clean our house and would bring them with her and on holidays from school, I played with them. They were like little sisters to me. I had my cricket bat. A new one I'd been given for my birthday. I was showing off, swinging the bat, and it flew out of my hand. I lost control and it slipped and it hit Amanda in the head. She fell down and didn't get up. She wouldn't get up. I kept trying to wake her up but I couldn't. And Miranda started screaming and crying and I was so frightened, I hit her to stop her from screaming. I hit her. I wasn't trying to kill her, Henry. I was trying to stop her crying. I expected them both to get up. You have to believe me. I didn't mean to kill them. I was eleven years old.

"But I was this public-school boy. I was a choirboy, a privileged kid, from a privileged background. I hadn't grown up on an estate or watched nasty videos. So I was evil incarnate. I was the devil in a choirboy's robe. Everyone could hate me; everyone *wanted* to hate me. The only person who understood was Eliza McCormack. She was the only person who believed in me."

"Your parents?"

"They disowned me. I had besmirched their good name, you see. My mother couldn't go to the golf club any more. My father couldn't keep his fancy job at his fancy bank. I ruined their lives. They wanted nothing to do with me."

"They're alive."

"They're alive. But as far as they are concerned, I'm not. I'm dead."

"I can't—" He shook his head.

"You can't what, Henry?" Jack rose from his chair, came toward him, kneeled at his feet. "You can't let me live my life? Every child psychologist in the country came to see me in prison. They all wanted to know why I'd done what I'd done. As if I had a *reason*. As if I'd *planned* it. I had shrinks, I had social services people, I had counselors. But the only person who ever made any sense was Eliza. She said the only way I'd have a fair trial was if I was judged by a jury of my peers. By a jury made up of other eleven-year-olds. Because they were the only ones who might know what would be going through my mind—my fear, my terror. Amanda wouldn't wake up and Miranda was screaming and I was scared witless. I wanted her to stop screaming. I didn't want to kill her. I hadn't meant to kill Amanda. I didn't even understand what death *meant*. I sat there in that tree-house afterward and waited for them both to wake up. They were supposed to wake up, Henry."

Jack began to cry; he was looking up at Henry, his eyes imploring, tears dripping down his cheeks.

"They were supposed to wake up." He threw himself forward, buried his head on Henry's knees. Reaching out, Henry put his hand on Jack's head.

An eleven-year-old boy. He didn't know what he was doing. He couldn't have known or understood.

They sat, Jack sobbing on Henry's lap, Henry patting his head, until the sobs started to slow down and Henry could feel Jack beginning to gain some control.

"I'm sorry." Jack pulled back, wiped his face with the sleeve of his windbreaker. "I haven't talked about it for a long time. I hate talking about it."

Henry stayed silent until Jack composed himself, went back to his chair, pulled out his cigarettes again and lit up.

"Not exactly the fishing trip you'd expected, is it?" A thin smile appeared momentarily on his face before being replaced by a grimace. "I know this is a mess, Henry. I didn't mean to get Holly involved. I walked away from her, as you know. And then you took me on that fishing trip and I saw her again and I knew I was in love. You know, Eliza once said to me, 'Everything is redeemable.' I thought she could be right. I thought I could be with Holly and Katy and redeem myself. And then Billy butted in—"

"This is not Billy's fault, Jack."

"I know, I know. But if he hadn't—"

"You would have had to tell Holly anyway. You couldn't live a lie like that with her."

"I can't tell Holly."

"You can tell Holly. You *have* to tell Holly."

"She'll leave me. You know Holly. She would never be able to live with me knowing what happened."

"She has to know."

"And that will help? How? Holly's still scared of some boy who might have stolen a bicycle once. You think she'd forgive me? People don't forgive. Not something like this. It will kill her."

"It won't. She has to know."

"She doesn't. Billy will back off now. She doesn't have to know. Knowing will only hurt her. We can be the way we were before. We can live here and be the way we were before."

"You know that's not possible."

"Why not?"

"Because it's a lie, Jack." Henry sighed. He didn't think he'd ever been as tired as he was now.

"So you don't believe in rehabilitation? You don't believe in second chances? I thought you believed in the law, Henry. I thought you believed in liberal causes."

"I believe in the law. But I also believe in the truth. And you cannot live with Holly and Katy without Holly knowing."

"You think I'd do something to Katy? Hurt her? Henry, you are so wrong."

"You were out with her late that night on the beach and—"

"And I was playing catch with her. I wasn't hurting her. Jesus." Jack pitched the second cigarette into the fireplace. "You see what happens? You know about my past so you assume I'm going to do something evil again. And Holly will assume it too. Why didn't they kill me when I was eleven? It would have been easier."

"You have to tell her."

"All right, all right. I'll tell her. I'll go over there now and tell her and ruin her life and mine at the same time."

"You don't have any choice, Jack."

"Fine. I'll do it. I have no choice." He stood up. "I'll come back when she throws me out of the house. I'll come back and say goodbye to you and see if you feel better. And you can ring me when I'm gone and tell me if *she* is better off for knowing. Because she won't be, Henry. She'll be miserable and unhappy and she'll hide away on Birch Point for the rest of her life. Is that what you want?"

"I want her to know the truth."

"Yeah, right. It has nothing to do with the fact that you want to have them to yourself again, does it? You want to be the most important person in their lives."

"You killed two children, Jack."

"I was a child myself."

"And Holly is my grandchild. Katy is my great-grandchild. I have to protect them."

"From me. Of course." He shook his head. "The Bad Boy, right? You have to save them from the Bad Boy."

"I—"

"Forget it, Henry. I told you I'll tell Holly. I'll go back now and tell her." He walked to the doorway. "You'll probably hear her crying from here."

"I'm coming with you." Henry rose too, went to where Jack was, at the threshold to the hall. "I'll be with you when you tell her."

"I want to do it alone."

"No. I'm coming with you."

"Because you think I'll run away without telling her."

"Because she'll need me there when she hears."

"I don't think so."

Jack had turned, was heading back into the house, toward the kitchen.

"Where are you going? Jack?"

"We're going fishing, Henry."

"What?"

He had stopped at the back of the hall where the fishing gear and tackle box lay.

"What the hell are you doing? Come back here."

He had crouched down by the tackle box, opened it.

"Leave that alone and come here. I mean it."

He stood up again, turned to face Henry.

He was holding the fishing knife.

"For Christ's sake—put that down." Henry stepped back a pace.

It happened too quickly for him to react. Jack was suddenly running at him, had tackled him to the floor, was on top of him, sitting astride his chest.

He tried to move, but he couldn't. Jack was kneeling on top of him; his weight was pinning him down. If he'd been younger; if he'd been stronger . . .

"Don't, Jack," he gasped.

"I'm sorry, Henry."

But Henry saw the face looming above him: there was no emotion in it, only blank detachment.

"You don't have to do this. This isn't you. Put that knife down. Get off me. We can talk." He was using what felt like the last bit of air left in his lungs to speak.

"Talking's over, I'm afraid. I know you, remember? You'll tell. You'll tell because you think it's the right thing to do."

The knife was in the air; the knife was hovering in the air above him. Jack was waving it in a circle.

The game Isabella used to play with John when he was a toddler. She'd lean over John when he was in bed, wave her finger over his chest in a circular motion, saying, "Bore a hole, bore a hole, don't know where. Bore a hole, bore a hole, right in . . . there!" and push her finger into his chest, John squealing that child's squeal of fear mixed with delight.

The knife arced down. Henry closed his eyes against the excruciating pain, felt the steel twisting inside of him, tearing into him.

Not now. I can't die now. I promised John and Julia. I can't die now. Please. Holly . . .

"Katy."

26

The only way to tell them apart physically was the small birthmark on Amanda's face, on her forehead, actually. A little red splotch. Otherwise they were identical. And Enid, their mother, used to dress them in the same clothes too. Which I personally thought was stupid. Because they were so different in personality. Totally distinct. So why dress them up like matching dolls, like two little Barbies in the same outfits? Sometimes I wondered whether Enid cared about them at all. She'd come over and clean and they were supposed to sit quietly and watch her. Or else she'd turn on the TV and put them in front of it. All they wanted to do was go outside and play but if I wasn't there, I swear, she kept them locked up—prisoners. It was all wrong. I think she had them just to show off.

They were, as Holly would say, seriously cute. Tow-headed, I think it used to be called—you know, that super-blonde hair, flaxen almost. Lighter than Katy's. Another way you could tell them apart was that Amanda used to suck her thumb, but Miranda didn't.

And what's that all about, anyway? Naming them like that? It's like dressing them the same. If Enid had had her way she'd probably have given them both the same name. You know those cabs that have air fresheners in them, usually shaped like little Christmas trees? Enid smelled like those cabs.

But the girls didn't. Amanda seemed younger than Miranda. More dependent. When I'd say, "Let's go play outside," Miranda was always, "Yes!" but Amanda would stand there sucking her thumb. So Miranda would go, "We're playing. Now. Come on, Amanda." Ordering her. Amanda did whatever her sister told her to. Within five seconds or so, she would be running around the garden laughing and chasing me, totally forgetting she was ever shy.

I saw Holly was shy the minute I sat down next to her on the bus. She blushed the biggest blush I'd ever seen. Nobody's shy any more, Henry. Not the women I meet, anyway. They're like Anna, you know. Brash and full of themselves and pushy. I'm not trying to big myself up here, but I can't tell you how many women tried to hit on me when I was waiting on them. It was truly embarrassing. They think if they throw themselves at you, you'll catch them. And that the easier they are to catch, the more you'll like them. When I was let out of prison, I spent a few months up in Leeds, with my first new identity, hiding. That was the worst time. Getting used to being out but not being out. Because I've never really been out of prison. But my point is, in Leeds there were all these girls out on the streets on Friday and Saturday nights. In winter. Dressed in nothing, and I mean nothing. High, high heels. Make-up plastered everywhere. And drunk. Totally slaughtered. Looking to get fucked. Sorry—but I know you're OK with me saying that. And I kept thinking, *What are they going to feel like tomorrow morning?* Hungover, yes. But in the midst of that hangover, are they going to be proud of themselves? For getting fucked by some man who doesn't give a shit? Would this be how they'd want their own children to behave?

Miranda had lipstick on that day. Can you believe that? Enid had given them both lipstick. Amanda hadn't put any on, but Miranda must have spent some time in front of a mirror at her house because it was all neat and tidy and not smudged. "What are you doing, shrimp?" I asked her as soon as they came in. "What's that junk on your face?" And she giggled and said, "Lisstick. Mummy gave it to me." "Never too young to get the hang of make-up," Enid said as she was taking off her jacket. I wanted to belt her. Miranda looked so fake. It was disgusting. Can you imagine Katy wearing lipstick? No way is that going to happen. "I don't think the lipstick looks pretty on you," I said to Miranda. Enid was out of the room then; she'd headed straight for the kitchen like she always did when she came in. Looking back on it, I wonder if she was hitting the bottle. Making a beeline for the kitchen and tanking up before work.

It wouldn't surprise me. She was all over the fact that my mother left me home alone sometimes. "You're too young to be home alone," she'd say and I'd say, "But I'm with you. Mummy knew you were coming so it was OK to leave me." "OK." She'd hunch her shoulders up and wrinkle her nose. "But what if I couldn't make it today. *Then* you'd be alone." "You'd call if you couldn't make it," I answered. "Right?" She looked at me like I was a smartarse she wanted to hate but couldn't hate because my mother employed her. And because I played with her kids and they loved me.

They did love me. And no. Not in some perverse way. Ask the fucking coroner. It wasn't like that. Never. They'd do finger-paintings for me at play school; once they insisted on bringing over those balloons like animals that you get at birthday parties. They wanted to give me the one that looked like a duck. I kept everything they gave me up in my room in case they ever asked to see. I didn't want to hurt their feelings, throw something away that they'd given to me specially. Miranda was upset that I didn't like the lipstick. She tried to get it off with the back of her hand, but it looked even worse then, so I took her into the loo and wiped it off for her with a washcloth. Amanda was with us, of course. She wanted me to wipe off her face too, so I did. Miranda wanted to be the only one who got her face wiped, but I couldn't play favorites. I was really careful about that.

I didn't tell you I have an older brother, did I, Henry? Nine years older. He did everything right. But don't jump to any conclusions here. The shrinks in prison wanted to make a big deal of it too. When I was eleven, he was at Oxford, a scholar and a gentleman. They thought his success might have twisted me up somehow. But here's the interesting bit: I did everything right too. Until I became a killer.

It was an incredibly sunny day. The weather had been terrible before; England at its worst. Rainy and cold and gray. But it changed overnight and the sun came out. Not unlike our wedding day, actually. Perfect. The girls came outside with me and I chased them around the garden for a while. They wanted to go up in the tree-house. At least Miranda did. Amanda was a little frightened by being up high: she'd get scared climbing the ladder. The tree-house was there when we moved in. My father would never have been able to make one. He wasn't a DIY type of man. Notice I talk about him in the past tense? I figure if he ever talks about me, it would be in the past tense, so why shouldn't I relegate him to the fucking grave too?

It was school holidays and I'd just been given a new cricket bat. Yes, I was a choirboy, but I wasn't a pansy. I was a decent athlete, not a bad batsman at all. I tried to get them to play with me in the garden, but Miranda kept pointing to the tree-house at the end of the garden, and saying, "Up. I want to go up." She loved it when we went up there. What I'd do was put one of them on my back, climb up, put her down, and then go back and do the same with the other. I'd stockpiled fun things to eat up there. Chocolate and cans of coke. We'd be up there looking over the garden, as if it were our kingdom. That special place where no grown-ups ever bother you. Miranda always wanted to go up first, and I'd let her because then Amanda could see it was safe. Miranda hopped on my back and I climbed up with her and then when I brought Amanda up, I took my cricket bat with me. I'd just been given it. By my godfather. He came to my trial, by the way. My trial which was not conducted by a jury of my peers. No eleven-year-olds on my jury. Old people. Ancient people who couldn't remember what it was like to be a child.

Climbing the ladder with a little girl on my back and a cricket bat in my hand wasn't easy, Henry. But I managed.

Where was Enid during all this? Working. Or hitting the bottle. Or both. She wasn't watching her twins, that's for certain. They talk about me, they should talk about her too. She has some responsibility in all this. Handing her daughters over to the care of an eleven-year-old: some people might call that delinquent mothering. I do.

We used to sing songs up there. You know, those nursery-rhyme type of songs: "Incey Wincey Spider." That kind of song, so they could sing along with me. I had a shit-hot voice. A voice that made mothers weep at Christmas carol services. You know that one, "I'm Walking in the Air?" That Christmas I sang that as a solo.

You know, I wish Holly had heard me sing. I never dared sing again after that day. Holly told me she never answers her phone, her landline; she will never answer it again after she had the calls about her parents. Well, I never sang again. It didn't seem right.

So "Incey Wincey Spider" was the last song I ever sang. We were all sitting down on the wooden platform of the tree-house, singing it together. But when Amanda asked to sing it again, I said, "No." I was already getting tired of the choirboy tag. It's ironic, isn't it? Because I was tired of being a choirboy, I refused to sing; instead I stood up and started practicing my cricket swings. And the result of that was that I'm forever branded as the Choirboy Killer.

They were sitting there, their legs crossed beneath them, and I swung the bat in a practice drive, showing them how to do it and the bat flew out of my hand. It slipped. It flew. It went straight into Amanda's head. She toppled over. Like a bowling pin. One second she's sitting up, sucking her thumb, watching me swing the bat, the next she's down on the wood, sprawled out, blood pouring from her head. And you know what my first thought was? Is my bat going to be OK? Have I damaged my new bat?

Because I thought she'd get up. I went and knelt beside her and I took off my shirt and wiped the blood off her head and said, "Wake up, wake up, Amanda." The bat hit her on her birthmark. How strange is that? Right on her birthmark, as if it were a target.

"Wake up," I said, kind of shaking her and at the same time wiping off more blood, but she didn't move.

And that's when Miranda started screaming. Screaming her head off. I had to shut her up. She was screaming so loudly and she wouldn't stop. It turns out that Enid was hoovering the living room then so she didn't hear, but I heard, Henry. It was an awful, terrible noise and she wouldn't stop. I reached out to where the bat had landed and I picked it up. It was the only way I could get her to stop. I wasn't thinking, *I'll kill her.* I swear I wasn't. I was thinking, *I can't stand this noise.* And I was terrified. Amanda wasn't moving. Her head was a mess.

I don't remember the rest. I don't remember actually hitting Miranda. In prison I used to wonder what would have happened if it had been the other way around. If the bat had hit Miranda. I don't think Amanda would have screamed like that. She was quieter. I don't think she would have screamed. I think she would have sucked her thumb harder and closed her eyes. And I wouldn't have hit her. And people would know it was a mistake, an accident. They would have believed me.

Hang on. I need to light another fag . . . OK. I know you think I'm justifying myself and the point is not who was hit by the flying cricket bat and who wasn't—the fact is that both girls died. What would you say, Henry? Probably, "Worse things *don't* happen at sea, Jack." And you'd be right.

But at the risk of sounding self-pitying, which I know you hate, I have to say I've been seriously unlucky. If I hadn't been given that bat as a present, if it hadn't been a nice day, if I'd kept singing songs instead of practicing my swing. Well, everything would be different. But all those things happened together and Miranda and Amanda died and I was sitting up in the tree-house crying when Enid came wandering out into the garden calling for the girls. I didn't answer. I watched her go back in the house. I knew she'd go up to my bedroom and look for them there. And I'm not sure how exactly I did it; I can't remember. But somehow I carried them down. One after the other. Like always. Miranda first, then Amanda. And I laid them down on the grass. I went into the house and Enid was walking downstairs because obviously she hadn't found them in my room. I said, "Enid. They're lying down outside."

And she smiled and went outside and then she started screaming. I sat down and turned the television on. You can imagine how that played out afterward. The Monster Choirboy is so callous he turns on the TV after he has murdered two innocent little girls. But I don't remember doing it—no, that's a lie, I remember doing it. What I don't remember is *why* I did it. I never watched television. My father didn't approve of it. So why did I turn it on? I don't know.

You don't need to hear the rest in any detail. I became notorious. I was tried. I went to prison. I was quote rehabilitated unquote. That's such an American word—rehabilitated. Are people ever habilitated, I wonder?

The way I've been telling you this sounds glib, doesn't it? Emotionless? Believe me, that was never the case. I loved those girls. I loved them so much I was sure after what I'd done I'd never be able to love again. When I came to America as Jack Dane, I kept myself to myself, Henry. There was no way I was ever going to get involved with someone. I could talk to women, even flirt with them if I wanted to, but I never let myself get close to anyone.

I wish I knew what it was exactly about Holly that changed everything. I knew no one could help me but I thought I could help *her*. Maybe that was part of it.

And then there was this moment—out in the car park of the Lobster Pot. I threw her a T-shirt I'd bought her. And her face, the look of pure pleasure mixed with bewilderment on it. Before that, even—the way she told me about her parents, the sadness in her voice. I recognized that sadness. I wanted to help. I wanted to save her. I wanted to give her a normal life and in the giving of it get a normal life for myself in return.

And then, of course, there is Katy.

When I first found out about her, I thought, *No*. The last thing I wanted in my life was a little girl. I told Holly I couldn't see her again and I meant it. And then there she was, running up to me on your porch. She looks like them and she doesn't look like them. She's older, obviously. As soon as she ran up to me like that, I knew I couldn't leave her, ever. I wanted to be a part of her life. To play games with her and not hurt her. You have no idea what it was like for me to play a game with Katy and have her still be alive at the end of it.

I know the last thought you had was Katy. I heard you say

her name at the end. I'm so sorry you had to die like that. But what were you thinking, Henry? Honestly? Did you really believe I could tell Holly? What would happen then? She'd kick me out. She'd banish me from her life. And if I tried to see Katy, she'd take a restraining order out on me. How was I supposed to never see Katy again? My princess? You were taking the piss, Henry. I had to stop you.

Oh, right. I could have knocked you unconscious, couldn't I? Then walked back home and not said a word and left the way we planned to. But how long would you have been unconscious for? Long enough to give us a decent head start? How could I be sure how long you'd be out for? I suppose I could have tied you up and gagged you—but I didn't think of that, did I? The second I saw you hunched over that computer, I knew I was in trouble. I tried to talk you out of it. I thought I had. But you insisted on coming with me. Like I said, a big mistake.

When you saw the knife in my hand, you looked incredulous. That's a good word. Incredulous. Holly would like that.

There's so much in life that's ironic, isn't there? You were the one who made me comfortable using a knife. You finally convinced me I could help clean the fish, you taught me how to use it.

You left me no choice, Henry. I know—this wasn't an accident. I know what death is all about now and I know I killed you. It's not like before. This wasn't an accident, but it *was* self-defense. If you told Holly about me, I wouldn't have a life. I wouldn't have Katy. I'd be effectively dead. Katy wouldn't have a father. She wouldn't have *me*.

You can't say you believe in the law, in the justice system, and then turn around and say, "Not when it comes to my grand-daughter. You're not allowed to have a life, Jack, to be a normal person again, because you married *my* granddaughter." That's hypocritical, Henry. Wrong. Either you believe in the justice system and redemption, or you don't.

I'm every parent's worst nightmare, aren't I? Wake up one morning and discover that nice man your daughter—or grand-daughter in your case—married is actually a child killer. Do you tell her or do you let her live happily ever after? Because that's the way it would have been, Henry. Your blood wouldn't be all over the hall floor. I wouldn't have had to get a sheet from your bed and wrap you in it and then pick you up and carry you up here to your bed and lay you down so you looked peaceful. It's lucky I became so fit in jail. That was not easy, Henry. A dead body like yours is, well, it's deadweight.

But I hated how sad, how *distraught* you looked downstairs. So I had to make you comfortable.

No. If you'd only let us live happily ever after, we would have. No problem. We were all about happy endings.

We like, seriously, like totally, were.

27

When Holly opened her eyes, she saw Jack sitting beside her, looking down at her, smiling.

"What time is it?"

"Eight-thirty. I just got back from fishing with Henry."

"Is Katy up?"

"Mmm. She's in the kitchen, eating some cereal."

Holly sat up, put her hand on Jack's arm. "Your jacket's all bloody. Were there a lot of fish?"

"We caught eight, can you believe it? The boat was a mess, and getting all the hooks out, then cleaning them all, we got splattered. I'm going to take a shower in a second. But first I wanted to tell you some good news."

"What? What good news?"

"We're not leaving. We're staying here."

"You're kidding! Jack! Why? What made you change your mind?"

"I decided you were right. No one is going to shop me. Henry helped convince me too."

"This is so great." She kissed him. "Whoa—you've been smoking. It's early for a cigarette, isn't it?"

"Celebratory one. Sorry."

"One day I'll get you to stop. But right now you can do anything and I won't mind. I can't believe it. This is amazing. You've made me so happy, Jack. I promise nothing bad will happen. We'll be fine. I'm sure."

"So am I. You look like you're still tired."

"I didn't sleep well last night."

"Sorry—my fault."

"You don't have to apologize to me for anything. I can't believe we're staying! I can go have coffee with Henry as usual. And I thought I might never see him again. I can't believe it."

She made a move to get out of bed, but Jack gently pushed her back.

"You should get more sleep. You don't have to worry now. And Henry's gone into town anyway. He said to tell you he's sorry to miss coffee, but he has to pick Bones up from the vet and then he has a load of errands he has to do. He'll be out for a long time. You've had a bad night. Go back to sleep. I'll have a quick shower and then I'll take Katy into town. You can have total peace and quiet. Bask in it."

"Really?"

"Really."

"OK. I am tired. Even though I'm excited. Another hour or so in bed would be great."

"You've got it." He stood up, made a move to leave, turned back and sat down on the foot of her bed. "What do you think Katy will be like as a teenager?"

"It's hard to imagine."

"I don't want her to be like those girls sitting in front of us on the bus."

"Neither do I. I don't think she will."

"But innocence is so fragile now. What happens when she wants to wear make-up? When she hangs out at the mall with girls her age who corrupt her?"

Jack looked so serious, so worried, sitting there in his fish-bloodstained jacket. Holly imagined him waiting for Katy to come back from her first date, pacing the floor with paternal anxiety, and had to suppress a smile.

"I honestly don't think we'll have to worry about that. Katy has a strong personality and she'll have a stable, loving family. She won't let herself be corrupted."

"Life corrupts. It taints people. We start off as innocent, sweet children and life taints us. I couldn't stand to see that happen to Katy."

"If we have any problems with her, we'll deal with them, Jack. We can deal with whatever life throws at us as long as we're together."

"You're right." He nodded. "As usual."

Standing up, he came over to her and kissed her on the forehead.

"Goodbye, Holly Barrett Dane."

"Bye." She curled into the sheets, pulled the pillow under her head. "See you later. I guess we'll be having fish for lunch."

"I guess so."

"I'm so unbelievably happy we're staying. And thanks for taking Katy and letting me sleep. It's really sweet of you."

"No problem. I'm here to serve."

Holly smiled, closed her eyes.

My third and final present from you, Mom and Dad—we get to

stay, we get to live happily ever after in Birch Point. Thank you,
thank you, thank you.

Eric Haffner drove down the Birch Point Road, wishing he
could have lived there himself. It was such a secluded spot and
so beautiful, even in the drizzle. If he'd gone into a different
kind of medicine, if he hadn't been a vet, he might have been
able to afford a house there. But then he wouldn't be doing
what he felt called to do in this life: taking care of animals.

Henry Barrett would be pleased to see Bones safe and healthy.
Bones had quite a few good years left in him, Eric reckoned. He
was a good dog and he had an owner who loved him. Bones
would stick around for a while. The little stomach upset he'd
had was over and he was ready to go home. Eric liked having a
personal relationship with the owners of the animals he treated;
he particularly liked Henry—an old codger who spoke his
mind, had a keen sense of humor and a sharp tongue. Eric was
looking forward to delivering Bones to him and sitting on that
porch of Henry's shooting the breeze and having a cup of coffee. He'd left Jacob in charge of the surgery; he could take at
least a half-hour break before he went back.

When he reached Henry's house at the end of the Point, he
was pleased to see Henry's car parked at the side. He hadn't
bothered to call before to say he was coming, assuming Henry
would be in. And he'd assumed right. Parking beside the red
Audi, Eric got out, let Bones out of the back. As soon as he
climbed out, Bones wagged his tail.

"Yes, Bones. You're home. Come on, let's go see Henry and
scrounge a cup of coffee."

He walked up the porch steps and knocked at the door. There was no answer, so he knocked again, louder. And waited. But Henry didn't come to the door.

He's probably taking a walk, Eric thought. *Damn. But my bet is he leaves the door unlocked.*

Opening the screen door, he then turned the door handle of the main door and pushed. Unlocked. Sticking his head inside, he called out, "Henry!"—no response.

"OK, Bones, I'll leave you here. He'll be back soon. And he'll find you waiting for him."

Bones padded inside. Eric Haffner shut the front door after him and returned to his car. He hadn't looked down. He didn't see the blood on the hall floor.

Billy Madison had barely slept. Something was wrong about Jack's Mafia story. In fact, *everything* was wrong about the Mafia story, but he couldn't say why he was so convinced it was a lie. And yes, Jack's story about his sister dying was a sad one; it might have explained why he felt so close to Katy, but it didn't excuse that late-night drive.

At eight-thirty he got out of bed, made himself a cup of coffee, and tried to take his mind off it all by turning on the television. But he couldn't concentrate on any program—he kept flipping the channels, searching, hoping something would distract him. He was tired of thinking about Jack Dane, or whatever the guy's real name was. The whole point of coming back to Birch Point had been to connect with Katy. Instead he'd spent his time obsessing over some English dude who had muscled in on his daughter.

Katy. She'd been asleep upstairs when Holly and then Jack told their story. How late had Jack kept her up the night before? How much sleep did a five-year-old need normally anyhow? It wasn't as if he knew.

Face it. You don't have any idea what happens in the life and brain of a five-year-old. Even if you were allowed to see Katy, how would you begin to get to know her? Take her out for ice cream? How predictable and forced is that?

At Stanford, whenever the concept of Katy came to his mind, he'd take out a mental shovel and bury it. He'd then pat down the ground on top by deciding Katy was better off without him, so what was the point of even thinking about her existence? The technique worked. He'd have a brief flash of "I have a daughter," but it never lasted more than a few minutes. He'd get back to work, or call up a friend and suggest a beer: he could always figure out a way to walk away from being a father.

He wouldn't call it a revelation, exactly. He wasn't St. Paul on the road to Damascus—or was it some other saint on the road to some other city? He couldn't remember. In any event, that wasn't what happened. He wasn't struck dumb with the desire to find his daughter and be a father. More like it crept up on him. He began to notice women pushing buggies. When he'd go running in the park, he'd see children in the playground and stop for a minute or two to watch them. He didn't think *Katy*. Not at first, anyway.

But as time went by, he stopped *noticing* and began to *look*. Especially in restaurants. He had a female friend who wouldn't go into a restaurant unless she was sure they had a chocolate dessert on the menu. Gradually he started to judge the suitability of restaurants by how many kids were in them. Other people, normal people, hated screaming, loud, messy kids when they were trying to have a nice meal out. Billy wanted them there. He loved to watch mothers and fathers trying to negotiate the problems of feeding toddlers in a public place, silently congratulating the ones who showed their love and attention, scolding the ones who didn't seem to give a damn. It got to the point where he once went over to a man who was being mean to his little son and told him he should treat his child better.

The scene that ensued from that was a fiasco. The father yelled at him, told him to mind his own business; the whole restaurant turned to stare as the man screamed, "You can tell me what to do when you have a kid yourself. Like you know one thing about being a parent. You don't know jackshit."

"OK, OK." Billy had backed off quickly, his palms in the air. When he got back to his table, a male friend who was with him said, "Jesus, Madison, that was a whack-job thing to do. Are you on something?"

Not long after that, he decided he needed to find Katy. Or he'd be doing whack-job things more and more regularly. The way he watched children in playgrounds, he'd probably get arrested for being a pervert.

He couldn't kid himself any more. It was all about Katy.

After forty-five minutes, he turned off the cartoon he was half-watching, stopped himself from calling Anna to discuss the weirdness of Jack's story again and decided to go down to

the Back Beach. He wasn't going to swim, just get some air
and stretch his legs. On the way down, he tripped, swore and
swore again. Chances were he'd brushed into some poison ivy
and would be sporting a killer rash by the end of the day.

There is no mastery without ease.

*Sure. But how am I supposed to be easy about some supposed
Mafioso being my child's stepfather? Tell me that, Mr. Barrett.*

The tide was coming in, he could see. If he hadn't had such
a bad night's sleep, he would have jogged, but he didn't have
the energy for anything more physically strenuous than a walk.
As he made his way across the beach, he heard barking.

Bones must have found a skunk or something.

He kept walking. The barking didn't let up.

Is Bones trapped somewhere? And Henry can't get him out?

Billy turned left, started to climb the path that led to Henry's
house.

When Holly woke up and looked at the bedside clock, it was
twenty past nine—she'd slept almost an hour. All the anxiety
she'd felt the night before had evaporated; she jumped out of
bed, went to take a shower, and found herself singing "Dancing in the Moonlight" as loudly as she could. She used to sing
along to the car radio, too, but now she felt self-conscious about
it: not only because Jack never joined in but also because on
their trip back from Vermont he'd said, "Oops—a little off-key
there, Holly."

It didn't matter if she was totally off-key in the shower. Jack
was in town with Katy and she had the house to herself. If she

wanted to, she could sing and dance and yell. Scream with this happiness that was feeling uncontainable. She hadn't dreamed it—Jack *had* come back and told her they didn't have to leave. She didn't have to try to imagine herself and Katy in some cabin in a strange place, or their life without Henry. Everything was going to be fine.

"Everybody's feeling warm and bright. Everybody's dancing in the moonlight . . ."

After the shower, she toweled herself dry, put on a pair of blue jeans and the Lobster Pot T-shirt Jack had given her on their first date, brushed her hair and decided she would try actually skipping to the kitchen. *"Grown-ups don't skip, Mommy,"* she could hear Katy say. And she would have replied, *"But right now, I'm five years old too, chicken. So I'm allowed to skip."*

The entire morning was a special one. She wasn't cooking the usual breakfast, she wasn't making sure Katy finished her orange juice, she wasn't even having coffee with Henry. Everything about the day was different.

"Slow down, you move too fast. You've got to make the morning last . . ."

A Simon and Garfunkel song her mother had liked popped into her head; she forgot the rest of the words, but hummed the tune as she made a cup of coffee and peeled a banana.

Fish for lunch. How should I cook it? Grill? Bake? Maybe grill it—put some bacon on top.

We can stay. Nothing has to change. We can work things out with Billy better now that he knows the truth. It wasn't a mistake to tell him. He'll be more reasonable with Jack now.

Jack talking about Katy growing up was weird. What does he think? She'll be a mall rat with dyed hair and a nose ring? I wonder if she'll find someone like Anna for a friend. She's starting real school in September. How crazy is that? She'll be in first grade.

Holly picked up her coffee mug, wandered into the living room.

He hasn't talked about it, but I bet he wants a baby.

Her hand went up to her mouth, she stared out the window.

A baby. How amazing would that be? To have a child, with someone I love who loves me? Katy would love a little brother or sister, I know. She wouldn't be jealous—she knows how much Jack loves her, how special she is to him. Maybe I should talk to him about it—tonight. Why not? Or maybe I should wait for a while. We've been through so much in the past forty-eight hours. It might be better to wait. I'll play it by ear.

The drizzling rain had stopped. She went out onto the deck, sat in a chair, pulled her knees up to her chest.

Four children. A big family. I'm young—that's the advantage of having a child so young. I can have more. I can have three more, definitely. Kids running all over the house, playing. God—it would be so perfect.

Putting her mug down on the deck, she noticed that the wood needed repainting.

We can trim some of the trees to get a better view, we can clean up the deck, sand it down, repaint it. There's so much to do. I should make a list.

The air had a quiet heaviness to it. Not muggy, exactly, but damp. Holly was about to get up and go back into the house to get a pad of paper and pen when she heard barking.

Bones is back from the vet. So Henry must be back—I guess he didn't have as many errands to do as Jack thought.

She picked up the mug and walked down the porch steps, heading to Henry's, singing.

"Dancing in the moonlight, everybody's feeling warm and bright. It's such a fine and natural sight . . ."

28

As she walked up the drive to Henry's house, Holly was surprised to see Billy coming around the side, heading for the porch.

"Billy? What are you doing here?"

"I was down on the beach and I heard the barking. I thought Bones might be stuck somewhere, that he might have gotten under the porch somehow, but the noise is coming from the house. Where's Henry?"

"He must be inside with Bones. Hey—what's with the old shorts? Are you losing your branded look?"

Seeing Billy didn't upset her; she could even joke with him. Nothing could upset her, not today.

"I'm trying to lose it, you know, become one with the ethos of Barrett Point." He smiled. "I'm surprised Henry hasn't helped Bones out by now; he's been barking for a while."

Climbing the porch stairs and opening the screen door, she said, "Bones has probably found a mouse and he's scared to death of it. Henry might be scared too. Maybe he's standing on a chair, cowering."

Billy, a step behind her, laughed.

Who knows? Maybe this will all work out now. Maybe Billy

will be civilized and, OK, we won't be best friends, but we can get along with each other. This may be the day for new beginnings for everyone.

"Henry?" she shouted amidst the barks, which were clearly coming from above them. "Where are you? What are you doing up there?" She headed for the staircase.

"Holly." Billy's voice was low, urgent. "Wait."

"What?"

"The floor. There's something strange on the floor here."

"What do you mean?" She looked down, saw large dark red splotches, small dark red speckles. "Henry must have spilled some paint. Bones, shut *up*! Henry?"

"Holl—I'm not sure—"

But she was already heading upstairs.

"Holly."

He took the stairs two at a time, clearly determined to get in front of her. When he was a few steps up on her, he turned to face her and took her by the shoulders. "Look—just let me go first, OK? Stay here and let me get the dog and Henry."

They heard it simultaneously. Bones's bark suddenly switched, became a high-pitched moaning whimper. An unearthly sound; a bad, desperate sound.

They looked at each other, unease mirrored in each other's eyes.

Holly was swamped by an attack of the same sick feeling she'd had as soon as she'd answered the phone both those times her parents had died and heard the authoritative, serious voice on the other end. The harbinger of bad news. Bones's whimpering made her want to run out of the house and hide.

Bones is dying. It's a whimper of death, I know. How will I tell Katy? Poor Katy. This will hurt her so much. And Henry. He loves that dog so much. Where is he?

"You stay here—I'll go," Billy said, but she had already pushed past him and was rushing to Henry's bedroom door.

When she opened it, the first thing she saw was Bones on the bed, lying stretched across Henry's chest, his nose pointing toward her. He had stopped whimpering; his eyes were closed.

Henry was lying face up, a sheet covering him up to his neck. His eyes were closed and his face was pale and his nose looked different: longer, thinner.

"They're both asleep," she said in a hushed voice. She stared at Henry's nose. Why did it look so different? "They're taking a nap together."

"Holly." Billy had come up behind her. "Holly. I don't think Henry's asleep."

Of course he's asleep, you idiot. There's no other possibility. He has to be asleep.

She took a step toward the bed, and as she did, Bones opened his eyes.

"Why are Bones's eyes so sad, Mommy?"

They were looking at her now—the saddest eyes she'd ever seen. Deep, dark circles of ineffable sadness.

Henry's eyes didn't open. Henry didn't move.

"You know, sweetie, I heard once that in World War Two, the RAF fighter pilots were allowed to bring their dogs with them to their base camps. And the dogs would go out at the end of the day and stand on the runway waiting for their masters to fly back from their bombing missions.

"But sometimes a dog wouldn't go to the runway. A dog would stay in the barracks.

"And that's how they knew who wasn't coming back that day. The pilots whose dogs didn't go out to meet them had been shot down. Somehow the dogs knew.

"They're loyal as hell and they're smart fuckers. They know when something's wrong."

"Holly."

She felt sick: sick in her stomach, sick in her mind, sick in her heart.

"Shut up. Just shut up."

She closed her eyes because she knew when she opened them, she'd see Henry sitting up in bed. Sitting up saying, *"Shit, sweetie, why are you looking so goddamn scared? I'm fine, for Christ's sake."*

She opened them.

"Holly, the sheet's covered with blood. Something bad has happened."

"All you have to do is love Katy. With all your heart. Stop worrying. You worry too much. Listen to an old wise man and take a chill pill."

"Someone has killed him. Look at the blood. This wasn't an accident or a hemorrhage—someone killed him and wrapped him up in the sheet."

"Red Slobs are playing this afternoon. You and Katy come over here and let's listen to them beat the crap out of the damn Yankees."

"Holly. Come away from the bed. Don't look at the sheet. Please."

"You're not supposed to get over death, sweetie. You don't forget

and you never stop feeling the loss. You never make peace with grief, you just work out a way to live with the war grief wages in your heart."

Her eyes moved down from his face.

Blood was splattered all over the white sheet that covered his body. So much blood. Too much blood.

It's not your blood, Henry. This can't be your blood. It's like some kind of bad modern painting, the ones you hate so much. It's not real.

"Get off the bed, Bones." Billy was at her side now; he was taking Bones by the collar, forcing him to get off the bed. "Down, boy."

Bones barked once, turned his head to look at Henry.

"Down." Billy dragged him to the floor.

She had to get rid of it. The sheet. The terrible bloody sheet. She couldn't let Henry lie under this sheet.

"Holly, you can't. Don't touch any—"

She took hold of it, swept it off the bed, threw it on the floor.

"Because it's closer to the heart. I shake hands with my left hand because it's closer to the heart."

Your chest. Oh, my God, the blood. That knife. This can't be happening. It can't be.

Oh, Henry, what have they done to your heart?

Winds of rage and torrents of tears were swelling in her, a hurricane about to hit land and wreak havoc. She doubled over, threw up on the floor. When she stood up again, wiping her mouth, she turned away from the bed.

I can't look. I don't understand. This isn't happening.

Billy was staring transfixed at the terrible, bloody mess which was Henry's chest and the blood-soaked knife which rested on top of it.

"We need to call the police. Right away. Now. We should go downstairs. You shouldn't look at this, Holly. Go downstairs."

"I'm not leaving him alone. No way."

But I can't look at you again. I can't see it again. Where are you? Where have you gone? How can you leave me like this? I can't leave you. I'll never leave you. I'm going to be sick again. I have to—

"Holly—where's Katy?"

"Katy." A jolt of terror stopped her rising nausea. "Oh, my God. What if she comes back and comes over here? What if she—? I have to go home and see if she's back. If she's not, I'll call Jack. Make sure she doesn't come over here. Then I'll come back."

"I'll call 911."

"I'll be back . . ." She was talking to Henry, she was promising Henry; knowing he couldn't hear but not believing it, not really. Henry wasn't really dead but still—Katy couldn't see this. The two thoughts were flipping back and forth, paralyzing her with their contradictory messages.

None of this was real. It couldn't be. But Katy couldn't see it. This had to be a nightmare but she had to control this nightmare somehow, she had to make sure she kept Katy out of it.

Holly turned from the bed, broke into a run; when she reached the bottom of the staircase she tore out the door, the screen banging with a crash behind her.

OK, OK, call 911, Billy told himself, as he ran downstairs and into the living room. He had tried to bring Bones with him, but the dog wouldn't leave Henry's room. *Find something to pick up the phone with so you don't mess up any fingerprints. That's what you're supposed to do, right? It's a crime scene. Think* Law & Order, *think like a lawyer.*

He pulled his T-shirt over his head and used it to lift the phone on Henry's desk, then punched in 911 with his covered fingertip.

"There's been a break-in, there's been a murder. My name is William Madison. The man murdered is Henry Barrett. On Birch Point Road in Shoreham, at the very end of Birch Point Road. Please send the police and an ambulance as soon as possible."

The woman on the other end of the line made him repeat what he'd just said, took the details, then told him she'd get the police there immediately.

When Billy put the phone back down, his stomach began to roil.

Don't. Stay calm. Stay focused. Pull yourself together. Get a glass of water. Can you touch a glass? Drink from the tap. Just get some water. . . . What's that? Henry must have spilled a cup of coffee over his desk. Why? Was he at his desk here when whoever broke in came? Sitting here having a cup of coffee before . . . all that blood. That knife . . . Jesus. His chest . . .

His stomach churned again, and with it came a fuzzy feeling clouding his head. Yellow and black circles flooded his brain and he swayed forward, threw his hands on the desk to stop himself from toppling onto it.

Don't. Don't faint. Take a deep breath—what's that noise?

He had braced himself on the desk, his hands splayed out in

front of the computer, when it suddenly whirred and came to life, the screen flickering and then lighting up inches from his face.

I must have hit the mouse. The computer must have been asleep and I hit the mouse.

A page appeared with *"Image Results for Thomas Grainger"* written across the top and pictures underneath it. The colored circles receded; his vision cleared.

Who the hell is Thomas Grainger? What are those pictures? What was Henry looking at? Some small boy, identical twin girls and . . . Jack? Yes—Jack at a younger age. What's Jack doing there?

Billy started to read the text underneath the pictures, his eyes drawn immediately to an entry beginning:

Did upper-class upbringing contribute to the callous nature of 11-year-old Thomas Grainger, the "Choirboy Killer?" / UK.

In the days after the arrest of Thomas Grainger, the media de-bated whether distant parenting and a too-privileged lifestyle played any part in Grainger's seemingly motiveless murder of 3-year-old twins, Amanda and Miranda Dunne. Now 18 and having been given a new identity, will Grainger try to con-tinue living life as he knew it before, or has he—

The screen door slammed again and Billy jumped. *Shit, no. I'm alone, shit . . .* but it was Holly who burst into the room.

"They're not at home and he's not answering his cell, but I left a message for him on it and I left a written message—I taped it on the front door so he'll have to see it when he drives up. Katy won't come here. I'm sure he'll get one message—or the other. The police must be on their way, right? I know this is my nightmare and I know it will end and I'll wake up but meanwhile I have to stay in it, don't I? Unless I make myself wake up. Wait—I could do that. I could make myself wake up."

She began to punch herself on the arms with her fists wildly flailing.

"Holly—stop." He went over to her, grabbed her wrists. "I'm sorry. I'm really, really sorry. But this is real. I wish it were a nightmare too, but it's not."

She tried to yank her arms away but he wouldn't let her. "It has to be."

"Listen to me. I know you must be in shock, but try to listen to me. It's important. It's crucial." He tightened his grip on her wrists. "Have you seen Jack this morning?"

"Of course I have." She looked relieved to be answering an easy, normal question. "He came in after he'd gone fishing with Henry."

"And then?"

"Everything was going to work. We were staying and it was all going to be good again. We were going to have fish for lunch. I was going to get Henry to come over and eat with us. I was sitting out on the porch having a coffee when I heard the barking." Holly's body sagged; her face collapsed. "It's lasted too long to be a nightmare, hasn't it? And it's sequential. Nothing has happened out of sequence. And I always wake up after the worst part. The worst part has happened and I haven't woken up. Why haven't I woken up?"

"Come on." He put his arm around her shoulder, led her to the chair. "Sit down. Take a deep breath."

What's going on? What do I do? Could Jack actually have been the one that writing was referring to? Could Jack have killed those two little girls? Was that what Henry—

"That's not Henry upstairs, you know. It never is when someone dies. They leave their bodies. You can tell it's not them any more. They've gone somewhere else. Did you know that?"

Billy shook his head. The pained, bewildered look in her eyes pierced his heart.

"I don't understand. Who would want to kill him, Billy? Why Henry? I have to go back up there. I have to be with him."

"No. You just said that's not him, Holl. He's gone. I won't let you go up there again. I don't mean to seem callous—"

Callous—the callous nature of 11-year-old Thomas Grainger . . .

"But I need to know what happened. I mean, did Jack say anything to you? When he came back from his fishing trip?"

"He said they'd caught a lot of fish, but I knew that already."

"How?"

"Because of his jacket—it had a lot of fish blood on it. Anyway, he said Henry was going to go pick up Bones from the vet and then do chores in town so there was no point in coming here for coffee. It must have happened when he got back from his chores. It's weird . . ."

A lot of fish blood. A lot of fish blood. Shit, no. This can't be happening. What did Holly just say? "It's weird." What's weird?

"What's weird?"

"It happened before, with Mom and Dad. I had this weird reaction, this calm came over me. You know, as if I didn't have any emotions at all. I was rational and calm. About a half-hour after I found out that they'd . . . Anyway, it's the way I'm beginning to feel right now. It won't last long." Her hands fluttered in the air briefly. "It's really weird. I have to call Jack again." She pulled out her cellphone from the pocket of her jeans, dialed. "No answer. Straight to voicemail. I can't say what's happened in a message. Where is he?"

"Where the hell are the police?" Billy looked out the window before turning back to Holly. "Listen, this is important. There's something on Henry's computer. He was looking—"

"I can't believe I was mad at him yesterday. That never changes. I mean, you always want to take back whatever you last said. Even if you said, 'I love you,' like I did to Mom before she went to see Dad in the funeral home. I don't mean I'd take it back, what I mean is I'd add to it. I'd say so much more. If you know someone you love is dying, you have a chance. Henry yelled at me once when I didn't finish the peas on my plate. That's the only time he was ever really angry with me." She looked up at the ceiling. "How could I ever have been angry with him?"

She's in shock.

A lot of fish blood.

But maybe they did fish. Maybe that's not a picture of Jack or maybe I read it wrong. I have to go look at that computer again.

He walked back to the desk. The page was still up, the photos still there. He leaned forward, stared at the last one. It was

Jack. It was definitely Jack. He switched his gaze to the young boy holding the piece of paper with his name written on it in front of him. A juvenile mugshot. Which could easily be Jack as a young boy. But maybe it wasn't. And maybe Jack's picture when he'd been involved in the Mafia somehow got mixed up and ended up on this page by accident.

Be careful, Billy. This is one time you can't afford to make a mistake. There's way too much at stake here.

"Billy? What are you doing?"

"Just a sec, Holl."

OK—say Henry was looking at this page when Jack came in. But what led him to it?

He heard it then, a siren in the distance. Halfway down the Birch Point Road by the sound of it.

The T-shirt he'd taken off was on the back of the desk chair. He picked it up, used it to push the "Back" symbol at the top of the page—the name Thomas Grainger came up on the Google page. He pushed "Back" again.

As well as representing 11-year-old Thomas Grainger, the Choirboy Killer, who murdered twin 3-year-old girls, Amanda and Miranda Dunne, McCormack has represented Len Houston, the television talk show host accused of—

McCormack. Eliza McCormack?

He looked up from the screen as a police car screamed up on the lawn, looked back at the screen and pushed "Back" yet again.

Eliza McCormack, QC, has made her name fighting cases no one else will touch . . .

He saw two policemen get out of the car; he heard Holly's voice saying, "Jack—I can't get you on your cell. If you're home please pick up. I need to talk to you. Right away. Call me. Please. I need you."

Two doors slammed shut; two men started walking up the steps.

Eliza McCormack is a lawyer. She represented Jack. And Jack— Jack is Thomas Grainger. Jack killed those little girls when he was eleven. And he went to jail . . . and then he got out and was given a new identity and somehow he ended up here. Henry put it all together . . . all of it . . .

"Where's Katy?" He whirled around to face Holly. "Where's Katy?"

"I told you—she's with Jack, in town."

"No, no, no. He didn't take Katy. Tell me he didn't take Katy."

"I told you before." She frowned. "Now isn't the time to talk about Jack and Katy, Billy."

He sprinted to the door, opened it. They were there. Two officers, one short with red hair who looked about nineteen; the other older, dark, tall and stocky. The taller one looked authoritative. He chose him.

"Officer, you have to find Jack Dane. His real name is Thomas Grainger. He killed two girls and he killed Henry Barrett and he has my daughter."

"Are you the person who called 911?"

"Yes, but that's not the point. This man has my daughter. He's a killer and he has my daughter."

"We're responding to your call, sir. You said there's been a break-in and a murder here. Would you tell us where the body is, please?"

"We don't have time to go through all this shit. You have to find Jack Dane. Now."

"Billy?" Holly had come up behind him. "What the hell are you doing?"

"I'm telling the truth, Holly. I'm telling the fucking truth. Jack killed Henry. He killed two girls before. He has Katy. We have to find him. Now."

"You're crazy. You're out of your mind. I can't stand this. Henry's lying upstairs. How can you be saying this when Henry's lying upstairs? How *dare* you?"

"I'm Lieutenant Garth Galloway and this is my partner Walter Farley." The older one gestured to the red-haired younger man. "What exactly has happened here?"

"My grandfather, Henry Barrett—he's . . . someone has killed him. He's upstairs. My name is Holly Dane. My maiden name is Barrett. Someone broke in and killed him. There's a knife. Don't listen to anything this man is saying. He hates my husband. He'd do anything, he'd say anything, to destroy my husband."

"Jack killed him. Look at Henry's computer, Holly. Jack killed him."

"Why don't we come inside now and I'll go upstairs and my partner can stay down here with you two while you both calm down, all right?" Galloway took a step forward.

"Jesus," Billy shouted. "We don't have time for this."

"Calm down—it's Mr. Madison, isn't it? That's the name you gave when you called."

"Yes. You need to listen to me. You need to look at the computer."

"We will, all right? But for now, I'm going upstairs. I'd advise you to calm down. I'll be back in a few minutes."

"His bedroom is upstairs on the left. There's a dog up with him. His dog, Bones," Holly said.

"Does the dog bite?" the one named Farley asked.

"This is a fucking joke," Billy shouted. "We don't have time."

"You're a monster. You're a fucking monster." Holly turned on him, began to pummel his chest with her fists. Farley grabbed her, dragged her away.

"Stop this right now, both of you," Galloway barked. "Or I'll be forced to restrain you both. Wait here now with my partner. Both of you. I'm going upstairs. When I come back down I'll need to ask you folks some questions and I expect you to stop this fighting."

When Galloway headed up the stairs, Holly and Billy followed Farley into the living room. Holly sat in Henry's chair, refusing to look at Billy while Farley went and stood in front of the fireplace; he had his hand on his gun, Billy could see. Waiting for the madman and woman to start shouting again? He had to restrain himself before they restrained him, but he had to tell them what had happened. He had to get them to find Jack and Katy. He had to make Holly understand even if she wanted to kill him for doing it.

"Holly, please, just look at the computer. That's all I'm asking. This is about Katy, not me and Jack. Just look at Henry's computer."

She didn't respond, but she did stand up and walk over to Henry's desk.

"Eliza McCormack, QC, has made her name fighting cases no one else will touch . . ." she read out loud, then turned back and faced him.

"So what? You knew she was involved with Jack's case. He told you that."

"He told us she was in charge of giving him his new identity, not that she was his lawyer. But forget that—press the 'Forward' button on the computer, look at what comes—"

"She can't touch anything," Farley interrupted. "This is a crime scene."

"She can use something—a Kleenex, my shirt. Whatever. She needs to go forward, she needs to see the pictures, the text."

"She can't touch anything. She can't contaminate the scene."

Dumb cop/dumber cop and I'm stuck here with dumber. Somehow I have to make them see. I have to get them to pull up the page with the photos.

"I know you," Farley said, staring at him. "Billy Madison. Of course. You were at that beach party Charlie Thurlow threw—what was it? Ten years ago?"

Billy shook his head in despair.

"Great party. Awesome. You don't remember?"

"Yeah, it was awesome. Look, there must be a way to access

the pages Henry was looking at on the computer without *con-taminating* the crime scene, OK? You can do it, you must be able to—"

"It would be a good idea if you sat down, Mr. Madison." Galloway had returned, was standing at the threshold. "And you too, Mrs.—what is it again?"

"Dane," Holly replied. She'd wandered away from the desk and was by the window, staring at the cellphone in her hand. "My daughter and husband must be back by now. I need to go over to my house. It's a two-minute walk."

"You need to answer some questions first. You two sit down in those chairs across from each other and we'll get started. I've called the crime scene investigators. You know, the CSI folks who get all the publicity." Galloway tilted his head. "But wouldn't you know it, in a one-horse town like this we don't qualify for them being on the spot. They'll have to come from Fall River. It's a hike, but if they put their skates on they'll be here soon enough."

"You need to look at the computer, Lieutenant."

Galloway wants to be in the movies. He wants to play the part of a folksy cop in a movie. Shit. How do I get this through his thick head?

"Henry Barrett was at that computer on his desk before he died, before he was killed. He was finding out the real identity of—"

"So what time did you find the body, Mrs. Dane?"

Billy saw her flinch at the word "body."

"Around nine-thirty, I think. Henry's dog was barking and I came over to find out why. He doesn't usually bark like that."

"Lieutenant—"

"You heard the dog barking, you came over here and then you . . . ?"

"I saw Bill— I saw Mr. Madison. He had heard Bones the dog barking too. We came in the house and we went upstairs. I don't—there's nothing more. Can I go home now? I need to get to my daughter."

"Holly, where did Jack take Katy? Did he tell you where he was taking her?"

"Oh, for God's sake." Holly shook her head, closed her eyes. "I can't take this from you any more. You need help. Go get help."

"From now on, Mr. Madison, you're going to shut up. And when I say that, I mean it. Understood?"

Billy nodded, faking an apologetic air. *Galloway's like my father. He'll only believe the truth of something if he gets there himself. If someone else tells him black is black he'll shout, "No, it's white." I have to shut up and hope he has at least one brain cell in that bulky head of his.*

"Do you know who might have been the last person to see your grandfather alive, Mrs. Dane?"

"My husband Jack went fishing with him early this morning. When he came back he said Henry was going into town to get Bones from the vet and do some errands. So I guess the vet or someone in town would have been the last one to see him." She glared at Billy. "You see how stupid you're being? How crazy? Henry went to pick up Bones, and Jack left with Katy, so Jack has nothing to do with anything. I fucking hate you. I hate you for doing this. I knew you were bad, but I never thought you could be this bad. You're evil."

"Dr. Haffner—the vet—sometimes delivers the animals home." Walter Farley took a step forward from the front of the fireplace. "He delivers my mother's cat to her. I think he likes getting out of that surgery, getting free cups of coffee."

"Call him," Holly said, but she was looking at Billy, challenging Billy as she said it. "Call him. Go ahead. You'll see. He didn't come here. Henry went to him. Like Jack said."

"I have his number on my cell. My mother put it there." Farley's face reddened slightly as he brought his cellphone out of his pocket. "In case something happens to her she wants me to call him about the damn cat. OK, here it is. Do you want me to call?" he asked Galloway, who nodded.

He punched a button, put the phone to his ear. "Yes, hello. This is Walter Farley, Dr. Haffner. I'm in the middle of an investigation and I have a question pertaining to the investigation I want to ask you. Did you deliver a dog, name of —"

"Bones," Holly and Billy said simultaneously, Holly looking at him as if he had no right to say it, to mention anything connected to her or Henry.

"Bones—to Birch Point Road, Mr. Barrett's house ? Right. I see . . . This morning? What time was that? Right . . . Right . . . Thanks. No . . . I can't talk to you about it at the present time . . . Thank you. Goodbye." Farley whipped the phone shut, pocketed it.

"Haffner brought the dog to the house here. Mr. Barrett's car was in the driveway but he didn't respond to Haffner's knock, so Haffner opened the door and let the dog in. He assumed Mr. Barrett was taking a walk. So he left."

"Which means that your husband was wrong, Mrs. Dane." Galloway crossed his arms in front of his chest. "And that he may have been the last person to see Mr. Barrett alive."

"Ask her about his jacket. Jack's jacket."

Galloway shot Billy a look, but it wasn't as withering as Billy had expected.

"Is there something special about your husband's jacket?" He had turned his attention back to Holly.

"No."

"Holly . . ."

"It had fish blood on it, OK?" She gave an exaggerated sigh. "Because he and Henry caught a lot of fish and cleaned them. So Jack's jacket had blood on it. Mr. Madison doesn't understand it's possible to get messy sometimes."

"Look, Jack was the last one to see Henry, his jacket was bloody, Henry had discovered about Jack's past on the computer—is that enough for you now, Lieutenant? Will you please look at the computer?"

"Hold on, that's the ambulance pulling up now. They won't be able to do anything and we can't move the . . . we can't move Mr. Barrett until the crime scene people arrive. I'll go tell them what's what. You stay right where you are." Galloway strode to the front door.

"I'm not leaving." Billy sat, his heart pumping so hard he felt he'd run five miles at full speed. *Jack has Katy. What's he doing with her? He's just killed Henry. Why? Because Henry found out. OK—Katy doesn't know. She's no threat, but . . . but those two little girls. What threat would they have been?*

Tears had started to cascade down Holly's cheeks; her head hung down; she was staring at the cellphone which she had in her hand again, her body shaking.

"Holly, you need to—"

"I'll be all right." Her head snapped up. "I'll be all right," she repeated between sobbing breaths. "I'm not talking to you. Leave me alone." She looked at her watch. "Where are they? Why hasn't he called?"

Because he's a fucking murderer, Billy stopped himself from screaming.

"Your grandfather was a smoker?" Farley asked Holly. She had covered her face with her hands; she didn't respond.

"He smoked a pipe," Billy answered for her.

"There are cigarette butts in the fireplace here."

"Jack—Holly's husband. Jack smokes."

"Right." Farley nodded. "So where are the fish, Mrs. Dane?"

"What?" Holly raised her head, palmed off tears.

"You said they caught a lot of fish. Where are the fish?"

Smart cop. I was wrong. Smart, smart cop.

"Are you in it too? You went to a party with him ten years ago and now you believe him and you think Jack—? They're in the fridge." She wiped more tears away. Billy watched her, saw anger taking over from her grief again. "The fish are in the fridge. After Henry cleans them he puts them in the fridge. I'll show you." Not looking at either of them she stood up and started out of the room toward the kitchen. Farley nodded at Billy and they both followed her, neither speaking. Holly waited until they were all standing in front of the fridge.

"Am I allowed to open it?"

"I'll do that." Farley glanced back at the kitchen door—obviously checking to see if Galloway was there—before picking up a napkin from the kitchen table and using it to open the fridge door.

"See?" Holly said to Billy. She wasn't looking at the fridge, she was glaring at him, enraged.

"Eggs, milk, bacon, butter, orange juice." Farley catalogued the contents. "I don't see any fish." He put his head nearer, drew out two shelves, pushed them back. "No fish."

Holly stepped forward, crowding Farley so that he stepped back. She peered in, scanning the contents, biting her lip.

"They must be in the freezer on top." She ceded her place in front of the fridge to Farley. "Go on, open it." He did.

"Ice cream. Ice cubes. Frozen peas," he stated. "That's it."

Holly stood on her tiptoes, looking in, then turned back. Billy could see that her brain was furiously at work, trying to figure out was going on; he could see from her face that she was coming to conclusions but stopping just before she reached them, like a horse refusing to jump a fence.

"Jack must have brought them home. They must be in my fridge."

Galloway walked into the kitchen, stopped beside Farley.

"What's going on here?"

"We were looking for the fish Mrs. Dane said her husband and Mr. Barrett caught this morning," Farley explained. "They're not here. No fish."

"They must be in my house."

"Well, Mr. Barrett's car hasn't been moved this morning. I just went to check it out. It's been raining—it's muddy and there are no tire tracks visible. Is Mr. Barrett's boat accessible from the beach, Mrs. Dane? Does he have a mooring in the bay here?"

"He keeps it at the dock, at the marina. Look, they probably took my car to the dock. Or they fished from the rocks on the beach. And the fish is in my fridge. This is so stupid. This is just ridiculous."

"Look at the computer. You'll understand everything if you look at the computer." Billy wanted to grab one of their guns and force them back into the living room, stand over them as they read.

"Say that again and I'll kill you, Billy Madison. You *know* Jack loves Henry. You *know* he wouldn't hurt him."

"Folks . . . I know this is a stressful time. But can we concentrate on what's going on?" Galloway sighed. "Did your grandfather smoke, Mrs. Dane?"

"A pipe. We've done this already. He smokes a pipe."

"Well, there are a couple of cigarette butts ground out on the floor in his room, underneath the window."

"What kind?" Farley asked.

"Marlboro."

"Like the ones in the fireplace, Lieutenant. I noticed them before. Is that your husband's brand, Mrs. Dane?"

"I don't know. I don't know if he has a specific brand."

"I think we should look at the computer, like Mr. Madison says." Farley backed away from the fridge.

I remember him now. The little red-haired kid at the party who looked about ten years old and didn't say a word. Maybe he was smart even then.

Lieutenant Galloway stood, seemingly deep in thought.

Hurry up. Don't stand there like a lump. Listen to Farley, for fuck's sake.

Galloway turned and lumbered back to the living room. When he reached Henry's desk, he hesitated for a moment.

"OK, Mr. Madison. Show me what you're talking about," he said as he pulled out a pair of gloves and put them on.

"Click on the 'Forward' arrow there." Billy pointed. Galloway clicked, the Google page with the name Thomas Grainger came up. "Click on it again. OK. See those photographs. The boy in both of them is Thomas Grainger—he killed those two girls in the middle. And Thomas Grainger is the real name of Jack Dane, Holly's husband. He's English; it happened in England—the murder of the girls, I mean. Go ahead, read what's beneath. Henry must have been reading it when Jack— when Thomas—came into the house. And he saw it or Henry said something. I don't know; but he couldn't let Henry live knowing what he'd done, don't you see?"

Both Galloway and Farley leaned forward, scanning the text and the pictures. After two minutes, Galloway swiveled to Holly, who was sitting in the chair again. The chair Henry had been sitting in that night Billy had come to question him about Jack Dane.

"Can you come over here, Mrs. Dane, and tell us if this photograph is your husband?"

She didn't move.

"Look, Holly. Please. Just look at the pictures."

"This is ridiculous. It's a waste of time. If you'd just come with me to my house you'll see the fish there, you'll see Jack and Katy. His cellphone must be out of batteries and he didn't pick up my message on the home phone. They're there right now, wondering where the hell I am."

"Look at the photographs, ma'am. Then we'll go to your house."

"All right. If that's what it takes to stop this craziness, all right." She stood up, walked over to the desk; Galloway and Farley made room for her and she was sandwiched between them as she studied the screen.

"Mrs. Dane?"

Her eyes kept traveling, up and down—from the text to the photos, from the photos to the text.

"That can't be Jack. It looks like him, but it can't be him." She stepped back. "It's just someone who looks like Jack. You're wrong, Billy."

"Why was Henry looking at it if it's not Jack? Why is Henry dead, Holly?"

"He got it wrong too. Like before when everyone was wrong about Jack. And then someone broke into the house and robbed him and killed him. That's not Jack. He wouldn't hurt anyone. Especially little girls."

"Your grandfather's wallet was on the dresser, Mrs. Dane. Cash and credit cards are in it. Nothing appears to have been taken," Galloway said.

"Well, they took something else then. Or they were interrupted or something."

"So . . ." Farley put his hands in his pockets, rocked slightly. "What we're supposed to assume is that someone came into the house after your husband and grandfather came back from fishing, Mrs. Dane, stabbed your grandfather for no apparent reason, took nothing from his wallet, smoked a few cigarettes and left?"

"I don't know what they did. I don't know." Her eyes traveled, resting on all three men, then back to the computer and quickly away.

"Holly, Holly." Billy clenched his fists. "Listen to me. What did Jack say this morning? Did he tell you where he was taking Katy? Tell us exactly what he said."

"He said he hoped Katy wouldn't turn into a difficult teenager—you know, wear too much make-up and stuff. He said Henry had to pick up Bones from the vet and then do some chores. And that he'd take Katy into town so I could get some more sleep. He said we wouldn't have to leave Shoreham. That everything was fine." Relief flooded into her eyes. He could see her mentally grab hold of something, the drowning woman reaching out for the life jacket.

"You see? It's not him in the picture. It looks like him but everyone is making a mistake, like they made about him before. He wouldn't say everything was fine and we could stay in Shoreham if he'd just done . . . done that to Henry. He wouldn't say that, would he? Why would he say we could stay, that it was all fine now? He wouldn't have said that."

Billy looked at her hopeful face. He didn't want to do it, but he had no choice.

"Jack wouldn't have said that unless he wanted you to go back to sleep, unless he wanted to have some time before you realized what he'd done. He wanted time to take Katy with him and escape. That's Jack in the picture. You know it is. He killed those little girls. And Eliza McCormack was his lawyer. He wasn't in the Mafia, Holly. He killed those girls. Henry found out about him and he killed Henry. It wasn't fish blood, it was Henry's blood. You said you were on the porch having coffee this morning, right?"

She didn't respond.

"And you have milk in your coffee, right?"

"You're crazy. I refuse to have this discussion."

"So you opened your fridge to get the milk when you woke up and made yourself coffee. Was there a pile of fish there, Holly? In your fridge?"

He knew, he could tell: she was thinking back, remembering.

"You would have noticed a whole pile of fish. But it wasn't there, was it? Henry didn't go into town to pick up Bones or do errands. Jack's not answering his phone. And he's not calling you to tell you where they are. Jack's the smoker. And he's gone, Holly. He's gone and taken Katy with him."

"No."

"Look at the picture again and tell me that's not Jack."

Her eyes went back to the computer, the photograph.

"No."

"He couldn't tell you what he'd done. He knew if he did you'd never let him anywhere near Katy. He knew, Holly. He made up that story to cover himself. He told you to go back to sleep because he wanted to take Katy. Who is going to come down this private road where you have to stop to let other cars pass—where you can be identified *easily*—who is going to randomly come into this house and stab Henry and not take anything? And carry him up to bed. Would someone who didn't know him, who didn't care about him in some twisted way, do that? He told you to go back to sleep, that everything was going to be all right, because he wanted time. He's got Katy, Holly. He has Katy."

She kept looking at the photograph. He saw her struggling; he saw her face as she tried to digest the truth—the horse running up to the fence. But this time the horse didn't shy. This time the horse jumped.

"No!"

Her scream ripped through the room.

29

It was like a coyote's scream, like a terrible howl of pain, the cry of a young woman who was being horribly tortured and raped.

Walter Farley had heard a coyote once on a camping trip; he'd never forgotten the sound. Now he was hearing it again, at the same time seeing Holly Dane's contorted, terrified face. Everyone else in the room involuntarily took a step back, away from her. It seemed like a long, long time before the scream stopped. When it did, she ran up to Galloway.

"Where is she? I have to go home. Let me go home. She might be at home. I have to go, I have to find her. I have to find Katy." She ran for the door, but Galloway blocked her, standing in front of her.

"Calm down," he said.

As if. No way is she going to calm down. We've never dealt with a case like this. This is nuts. This is out-of-the-ballpark crazy and we're both winging it. But Garth is even more out of his depth than I am here. Garth is all about routine. He wants a rulebook for this. Fat chance.

Galloway wouldn't move. Holly Dane kicked out at him but didn't connect.

"What are you doing? I have to find her. Please," she sobbed. "Please. I have to go home."

"Calm down—"

"She's my *daughter*. She's five years old. She needs me. Let me go."

"You're not going anywhere, Mrs. Dane, until you calm down."

"Two minutes. One minute. My house is just there." She pointed out the window to the left. "I'll calm down, I promise. Just let me go home. Please. She's my daughter. She's my baby. I have to find her. Please."

"I could go over to the house with her, Lieutenant," Farley volunteered.

"Or I can go," Billy Madison said. "If Holly needs to stay here, I can go."

Garth was thinking. It always took him forever to think. Like some slow-moving freight train.

Meanwhile Billy Madison was straining at the bit. He'd been that way the whole time; desperate to be listened to. Walter recognized his frustration.

Try being a red-haired guy who looks younger than he is. You get used to not being taken seriously.

Billy Madison—always the cool kid. The one people looked up to at parties. With the gorgeous sexy girlfriend Ann or something. Billy Madison's jumping out of his skin now, a long, long way from cool.

"All right." The freight train was picking up some speed. Galloway had made a decision. "You go with them both, Farley. I'll stay here with the body."

Galloway was exasperated with these two, Walter could

see. And also probably scared of Holly Dane, how crazy she was looking. He was still chewing over the computer information too, trying to figure out what was going on, playing catch-up.

But then he didn't know some of what Walter knew—the relationship between Billy Madison and Holly Dane, what had gone down in the past. Walter knew—thanks to a coffee with Charlie Thurlow a long time ago. Charlie saying, "Hey, did you hear Billy Madison got some girl on the point pregnant and skipped town?" And Walter's feeling of . . . what? A small twisted pleasure that Billy Madison, who hadn't even said hello to him at that party, that Billy Madison who went to some hot-shot private school in Boston and had the sexy girlfriend, had screwed up.

Galloway stepped aside, obviously not anticipating the speed with which Holly Dane ran out of the room, out of the house. Walter raced off after her, Billy right behind.

She could run. It took until she reached the door of her house for Walter to catch up to her.

"Wait," he panted, but she didn't break stride—tore through the door, into the house. He pulled out his gun, said, "Wait," louder. There was no car in the driveway, but this Jack guy could be in the house. Probably not, but he had to be careful.

"Katy!" she was yelling. "Katy! Sweetheart, are you here?"

"Mrs. Dane, stay here."

She wasn't listening, wasn't going to listen.

"He's not in the house." Billy was beside him now, all of them in the living room. "You can put that gun away. He's not here. He's gone. That's the whole point. He's gone."

Right. I wouldn't be here either if I'd just killed Henry Barrett.

Walter put his gun back in its holster; he and Billy followed Holly into the kitchen.

"Katy! Chicken—are you here? Sweetheart—it's me." She searched the room, ran back out, made a dash for the stairs. He and Billy in her wake again.

"Katy?"

She was in what was clearly the kid's room, on her knees, searching under the bed, then off them, up and opening the closet door.

"She's not here, Holly. Jack's taken her."

She was in hysteria mode. Not about to listen, off and running into another room, another bedroom. Hers and the guy's, it looked like. Her eyes going around every corner wildly then suddenly stopping, hugging herself.

"He wouldn't hurt her. He couldn't hurt Katy. He loves her. There's an explanation. There has to be. This is all wrong. He's innocent. He didn't kill those girls. Or Henry. It's a huge mistake."

Billy, about to say something, stopped. Like he didn't want to hurt her any more, kick her with the truth. Hear that coyote scream again.

"Wait." Her whole face changed, some ray of hope sneaking into it. "Jack must have left a message on the phone—the house phone. He must have." She rushed out back downstairs, back to the living room, making a beeline for the phone.

It was feeling like a surreal game of sardines in the can.

As soon as he saw it, he was pissed at himself for not having noticed before. He was the cop. He should have seen the blinking light on the telephone message machine.

She looked at it like a lighthouse in a storm.

"He's left five messages, *five*. It's OK, it's all going to be OK." She pressed the "Play" button. "Get back!" she shouted at him and Billy when they came up to her. "I need to listen. Get back!" They both moved forward to hear.

"*Message Number One received at 9:42 a.m.: 'Jack—I can't get you on your cell. If you're home, please pick up. I need to talk to you. Right away. Call me. Please. I need you.'*"

Click.

"*Message Number Two received at 10:01 a.m.: 'Mrs. Dane, this is Southeast Telephone. We have a special offer on long distance—'*"

She swore, pushed "Skip."

"*Message Number Three received at 10:15 a.m.: 'Holly?'*"

"Jack!"

'*Holly, if you're in, pick up . . . OK. You're not.'*"

Click.

"Don't—don't hang—"

"*Message Number Four received at 10:26 a.m.: 'Holly? . . . Pick up if you're there.'*"

Click.

"Jack! Jack! You see—he's calling. It's going to be OK. It's all a big mis—"

"*Message Number Five received at 10:30 a.m.: 'Holly. I heard sirens before. I have to think they've gone to Henry's house, don't I? You see, the thing is, I was going to tell you before that Katy and I will be out for a while. Not to worry about us. We're having fun. But I'm guessing that now, well now, you're not there because you've been over to Henry's. How'd that happen so quickly, I wonder?*"

Well, it has, so it has. Nothing we can do about that, is there? Anyway, I don't want you to worry. Katy is now my traveling companion. And you know I'm a good traveling companion. I might even sing to her. You never heard me sing, did you? I'm not bad. I'm pretty bloody good, to tell you the truth.'"

There was a pause. Walter could hear him inhaling a cigarette. The upbeat tone he'd just been using in that English accent of his suddenly changing.

'Holly. Listen to me. Believe me. None of what happened was supposed to happen. You have to believe me. He was going to make me tell you. I couldn't. I couldn't stand the look I knew I'd see in your eyes.

'I don't want to use up all your tape and I'm about to throw my cellphone away so I have to say goodbye now. I really do love you, Holly Barrett Dane, but the salient—good word, right?—the salient point here is that you can take care of yourself, I know you can. You're much stronger than you believe. Katy can't, though. She's a child. Katy needs me.'"

Click.

"We need to put out an APB," Walter stated. "What's your license plate number, Mrs. Dane?" He checked his watch. "That call came in ten minutes ago. He said he heard the siren so he can't have gotten too far."

She stumbled to the sofa, fell onto it, her body shaking, her eyes closed, whispering, "No," over and over and over again. Shut down. She'd shut down, cracked. Billy Madison went and sat down beside her, looked up at Walter.

"3786. It's one of those old family plates; they've had it forever," he said. "Holly?" He put his hand on her knee, but she didn't open her eyes; instead she sat there, crumpled up in a ball, still saying, "No," like a mantra.

"She's in a state of shock. I should get someone medical here."

"No—I'll deal with it. You have to find Jack, the car. I'll get her out of this somehow."

Walter called Galloway, gave him a quick rundown, told him the license number, watching Holly as he spoke. Her expression set off a weird chain of thought, making him remember an old toy from his childhood. A wooden box with little wooden pins standing in it and a keyhole at the front. You wound up a wooden peg with string, placed it into the keyhole, twirled the string to set the peg loose. It spun wildly around the box, careening off the walls, knocking down the pins.

He could see that's what was happening in Holly Dane's head now. It was spinning wildly, knocking into walls, unwound, unhinged.

"Right." He flipped the phone shut. "Lieutenant Galloway is putting out an APB. We'll find him, Mrs. Dane, and your daughter."

Her body was shaking so much she looked as if she were sitting naked in a deep freezer. And still that "No, no, no . . ."

"Traveling companion. He said traveling companion." Billy Madison turned to him again. "You need to check the buses too, the planes. The trains. Whatever. He's taking her somewhere. Where would he take her? Think, Holly." He put his hand on her arm, squeezed. "*Think*."

Billy Madison had been the blond-haired blue-eyed boy

wonder, great at sports, sure of himself. He would have been prom king if he'd gone to Shoreham High. Now that arrogance had drained out of him. The man was desperate, trying to find the kid he'd abandoned. Trying to get Holly Dane to surface from the dark hole she'd gone to—but she wasn't coming up for air. She was catatonic.

"Mrs. Dane, we have the APB out." He approached her, trying his most official voice. "Finding the car is the important thing now. Try to concentrate here if you can. You have any idea where he'd go?"

The "No, no, no" suddenly stopped, but she didn't open her eyes, didn't respond to his question. Walter looked at Billy. "Do *you*? Any idea at all?"

"We weren't exactly friends. No, I don't. Listen, I need time alone with Holly. I can snap her out of this, I know I can. And maybe I can get her to remember something. Figure out where Jack might have gone. She knows him."

"Not that well, apparently." Billy shot him a dark look; Walter ignored it, continued talking. "I'd get her a blanket. And something hot to drink. She's shivering like crazy. Give me her cellphone number and the number here. And I'll give you my number. There's nothing either of you can do now except try to figure out where he's gone. If you have any ideas at all, call me. And I'll call you if I hear anything. OK?"

"OK." Billy nodded.

"When she comes out of it, she'll want to get out there and look for them herself. Which is not a good idea. She should be here in case he calls again. I'll get a tap on the phone, OK?

And if she doesn't come out of it soon, you call me. She'll need a doctor. She will need professional help. I'll be back here as soon as I can."

Walter looked at her, looked away. Holly Dane's face was too painful a sight, too lost, as if she'd been standing on a pier and the whole structure had crumbled, every single thing she believed in falling away, taking her with it to the bottom of the sea.

His eyes landed on a photo on the table beside where she was sitting, a family photo, taken on the beach. Jack Dane was a handsome guy. A little older obviously than he was in the computer picture, but he'd been good-looking then and he was even better-looking now. And Katy—she was pretty with that blonde hair and shy smile. A really cute little kid.

Those twin girls on the computer had been really cute too.

What makes an eleven-year-old boy kill two little girls? he asked himself, knowing he didn't have even the beginning of an answer. And what was Jack Dane doing with Katy now?

He'd take the photo with him so he'd have a description to send out.

If they didn't find Jack Dane and the girl soon there probably wouldn't be enough professional help in the world to make Holly Dane all right.

It was that "We're having fun" comment of Dane's, that and the "I might even sing to her" line. The way he'd said it, in that happy-go-lucky tone of voice with the Brit accent.

After Walter Farley had switched numbers with Billy Madison, told him to stay put whatever happened, reminded him about calling if Holly didn't come around soon, he headed for the door, feeling a little guilty relief about getting out of there. He couldn't stand to see her face. He didn't want to hear that scream of hers, not ever again.

And after that message, he was beginning to think he might have to hear it: because Jack Dane had sounded like a natural-born psychopath.

30

Farley left the house and Billy was alone with Holly. Who wasn't opening her eyes. Who wasn't speaking. Who was sitting shivering, completely non-responsive. He had to figure out a way to reach her. Before, when she'd screamed at Henry's, she'd been thinking of Katy; she'd been focused entirely on finding her, but Jack's message had tipped Holly over the edge. It was a "fight or flight" response to threat, he realized. Her first reaction had been to fight, but once Jack had confessed, she'd flown to some form of unconsciousness.

That statement of Jack's, the fact that he'd said, "I couldn't stand to see the look in your eyes if you found out"—she must have understood then that her whole life with him had been a lie of gigantic proportions. He wasn't confessing to an affair or a gambling problem. Or a stint in the Mafia. He'd admitted to killing two three-year-old girls and the grandfather who had been like a father to her.

Farley was right: she needed a blanket and something hot to drink. Billy went into the kitchen, found some instant coffee, put the kettle on. He went upstairs while it was boiling, went into Holly's bedroom, grabbed a crocheted blanket off the end of the bed. On his way back downstairs, he stopped outside

Katy's bedroom. Then entered it, looked around, and found a stuffed animal on top of her toy chest in the corner. Grabbing it, he went back downstairs, wrapped the blanket around the still-comatose Holly, put the stuffed animal on the sofa beside her, before going into the kitchen and fixing her and himself mugs of strong black coffee.

The fog was beginning to roll in; Billy waited for the kettle to boil and stared at its mist, feeling a malevolent force in it, as if it were here to take hold and envelop Birch Point forever, as if it would never clear.

"OK, Holl." He sat down beside her, took a quick swig of his coffee. "Here." He blew on the top of her mug to cool it down, put it up to her lips. "You have to swallow a little of this." Forcing the mug between her lips, he tilted it a tiny bit. She swallowed. "OK. We're getting somewhere." She was still shivering, but not quite so much.

"Here." He grabbed the stuffed dog, placed it in her lap, put her hands around it. "That's Katy's, Holly. Katy's stuffed dog. I don't know what she calls it. But I guess it reminds her of Bones. Does Katy love Bones? See, I don't know. Katy might not like dogs. Maybe she doesn't play with this one." He made her swallow another sip of coffee. "When's Katy's birthday? I should know, but I don't. Does Katy like birthday parties?"

Say it enough times. Say Katy's name enough times and Holly might respond.

He leaned forward, spoke directly into her ear. "Katy needs you, Holl. Katy. Katy needs you. Katy."

"Katy." It was soft, but he heard it, drew back, took hold of her shoulders, gave them a small shake.

"Yes, Holl. Katy."

"Oh, my God." Her eyes flew open. "Oh, my God. I don't know what—" She looked around the room, her eyes searching every corner. "What happened? Billy, where's Katy? Have they found her? Where was I? What happened?"

"You shut down for a while. You short-circuited. After you heard Jack's message."

"No. Oh, God." When she closed her eyes, Billy thought she'd gone back, was going to blank out again. But she opened them. "I killed Henry. Jack killed Henry because of me."

"No, Holly. You're wrong. Jack killed Henry because he was trying to save himself. We need to find out where he's gone. Where he's taken Katy. We have to think, Holly. You have to start thinking now. Have some coffee—it's right there on the table. Take another whack of coffee and think, OK?"

She reached out for the mug.

"Where is the cop?"

"He's gone back to Henry's. He's put an APB out on your car."

"I have to go. I have to go look for her." She started to stand up, but he pulled her down gently.

"No. Farley said that's a bad idea and he's right. They're looking for the car, they're the professionals. And Farley said Jack might call again—you should be here if he does. You have to try to think where he might have gone. You might remember something he said. Tell me again everything he said before he left."

"He said . . . wait a second." She took a big gulp of coffee, put the mug down, pulled the blanket tighter around her. "I'm sorry. I'm so cold. I can't stop shivering. He said he was her traveling companion. That means he won't hurt her, doesn't it? Doesn't it, Billy?"

"Probably, yeah." He didn't want to send her over the edge again. "But we have to find them."

"I know." She took a deep breath.

"So what did he say this morning?"

"He said he had good news, that we didn't have to leave Shoreham, that—"

"Wait. I thought that was the whole point of yesterday—didn't he decide yesterday that you didn't have to leave?"

"No, he just said that to make everyone think we weren't going. He didn't trust you. Last night he was all excited about going."

"Going where?"

"Oregon. He talked about finding a fishing village on the coast of Oregon. At first he said Indiana, but he switched to Oregon."

"Jesus. Oregon."

"He likes horizons, the sea."

"So why Indiana?"

"I don't know." She shook her head. "But then he switched, like I said. To Oregon."

"Some fishing village? What's that all about?"

"He likes fishing, being out in the boat. I told you—he likes the ocean, the endless horizons. He said . . . he said on our honeymoon that he wouldn't mind dying, that he'd be happy to die, if he could see an endless horizon."

"There are places everywhere where you can see an endless

horizon. Give me your phone, I'll tell Farley about Oregon."
She handed it to him and he dialed Farley's number. "It's Billy
Madison. Any news? . . . OK—Holly—yeah, she's talking
now—she said he might be headed for Oregon. . . . No—no
specific place in Oregon—somewhere on the coast."

Lame. This sounds so lame. Some coastal town in Oregon, for
fuck's sake. Shit. But how would he get there—in Holly's car or some
other way? And wouldn't he think twice about going there after he'd
told Holly that's where he wanted to go? Dane's not dumb.

Think. I have to think.

"Right, call me the second you know something. Right.
Thanks."

"OK." Billy stood up, began to pace. "There's no news yet.
Let's come at this in a different way. What does he like?"

"What do you mean?"

"I mean, what does he enjoy doing, besides fishing?"

"He likes the Lobster Pot. Mini golf."

"I doubt he's going to show up at the Lobster Pot with Katy
and order fried clams. Or be putting his way around the Windmill."

"I'm sorry, Billy." He saw tears in her eyes. "It's all my fault.
This is all my fault. I believed him. I trusted him. With Katy. I
trusted him with Katy. How could I have?"

"This is *not* your fault, Holl. Stop it. If we're going there, I
can say it's all my fault for leaving you two in the first place.
We don't have time for this, OK?"

She nodded, wiped away the tears.

"Why?" Billy stopped pacing. "Why was he talking about
dying on your honeymoon? That's bizarre."

"I don't know. I don't know why. We'd had that fight that afternoon. Just after the ceremony. You know. You saw us when we came in."

"What was the fight about?"

"We'd been out in the Sunfish. He wanted to go to the Bad Boy's Island, land there. I said I thought it was bad luck; you know, that old story about the Bad Boy. He hated that whole thing, that whole story. He said I was stupid and cruel for believing in it, being superstitious."

"OK. And then, later, he's talking about dying. I don't get it. That doesn't link up. Forget that, anyway. Let's go back to what he said this morning. He said you could stay here. Then what?"

"He was talking about Katy. How he was worried about her being a teenager and hanging out at the mall. He said children are innocent and then they get tainted by life. I don't know. It was strange but it wasn't. I mean, I know how much he loves Katy. He didn't want her to get tainted. Wear too much make-up or get a tattoo or whatever. It was like he didn't want . . ."

"He didn't want what? Tell me."

"He didn't want her to grow up."

The way they were looking at each other was the way they'd looked when they'd heard Bones whimper.

Her cellphone rang. He saw it was Farley's number, answered it.

"Yes? . . . Right. OK. I guess that makes sense. Good. OK— I'll tell her." He pressed "End Call." "They've found your car parked at the Mill Pond Diner. So it looks like they've taken a bus. Farley says it should be easy to track them from there.

He must have taken Katy to Boston. En route to wherever, I guess. But they'll be easy to track."

"Thank God." She began to cry again but different, relieved tears. "Thank God. I should have thought of that—it's where we first met, on the bus."

"Right."

But this feels all wrong. He's not that dumb. Jack's not that dumb. He'd know how easy it would be to find them.

He walked over to the window, stared out into the trees.

"Billy?"

"He's smart. He's too smart to get on a bus."

He doesn't want her to grow up. Maybe he didn't want those other little girls to grow up. Think. Put yourself in his shoes. Try. You park the car at the Mill Pond but you don't get on a bus. So what do you do? Where do you go?

"Billy? What's going on? You said that's where the car is. And that's where the bus stops."

No car. No bus. No train anywhere near—the freight trains don't come often enough to think of hopping on one and even if you wanted to, you have Katy to deal with. Harder. You can't stand by a train track with her, waiting for a train that might not come for an hour. You could steal a car. That's possible. That makes sense. But are you thinking of running away with her—or something else? Taking her into a forest? Too long a hike back to the woods here. You and your fucking endless horizons . . .

"Billy?" She was standing beside him now.

"You have a local phone book, right?"

"Yes." She was puzzled, scared.

"Can you get it for me?"

"Yes. But—"

"Please, Holly."

She went over to a table in the corner, opened a drawer, brought the phone book to him, handed it to him, searching his face for a clue. He opened it, thumbed through it until he found the number. Flipped the cellphone on and dialed.

"Hello, this is Lieutenant Galloway. I need to know if Henry Barrett's boat is still in the dock or whether it's been taken out. Could you check that for me, please?"

He waited. Holly was staring at him, her hands clasped as if in prayer.

"Right. Thank you." He ended the call. "The boat's gone. Jack's taken Henry's boat. He must have parked at the Mill Pond, walked back to the marina, taken the boat."

"The boat?"

"Like you said, endless horizons."

"I don't understand."

"He's happy to die if he can see an endless horizon. He doesn't want Katy to grow up. He knows we've found Henry. He's feeling cornered, trapped. It adds up to bad, however you play it out. I'm calling Farley."

"Wait a minute."

He could see she was thinking, remembering something.

"We can't wait, Holly."

"Oh, my God, the wolf story."

"What?"

"The wolf who curled up to die beside his partner who'd been trapped. The wolf story. He told me on the honeymoon. I thought he was talking about us, about the kind of love we had. The kind of love where you'd give up your life for the other person. But it's not about me and him. It's about Katy and him. He's trapped and he wants Katy to . . . he wants her to . . ."

"I'm calling—"

"No. Wait." She straightened; something significant had shifted, he could tell. For the first time he saw in her a strong resemblance to Henry. "I can talk him out of it. He's gone to the Bad Boy's Island—I know he has. I understand now—I see it. You're right. But if the police get there first, he'll kill her. If I go there, I can talk him out of it. Please, Billy. We've got to get out of here—you still have a boat, don't you?"

"Yes. But look at the weather. The fog's coming in fast. It will be imposs—"

"I can find it. I know it. I could find it blindfolded. It's her only chance, Billy. I understand now. Of course that's where he's gone. He's taken her there. I can feel it. And if the police find him first . . . Listen to me—I know I didn't listen to you before and I was wrong. But I'm right now, I swear I am. I have to save her. I can do it. Believe me. I can do it. I have to."

"I don't know. He could be anywhere out on the water. He could be headed to Martha's Vineyard for all we know. A police boat could—"

"He's on the Bad Boy's Island. I know he is. I remember now—the way he said, 'Goodbye.' It was final, Billy. I didn't get it then, but I do now. He admitted he killed Henry—he knows he won't get a second chance if he's found—he knows it's over. We have to go find them, now. I'm the only one who can talk him out of it. He said he loves me, remember? He'll listen to me. But if he sees the police . . . You know what he'd do, Billy. You know I'm right."

"OK. All right. We'll go to my house, get the car and go to my boat. But this man is dangerous, Holly, we have to—"

"I'll be right back. Wait here. I'll be right back and then we'll go. Promise me you won't call Farley."

He looked at her. Back in fight mode. Determined and focused. More determined, more focused than Farley or Galloway could be, he knew. She was right: one look at a policeman and Jack would feel even more cornered. She was the only person who could possibly stop him.

"I promise. Where are you going?"

"Upstairs. I need to get a compass for the fog. There's one upstairs. I'll be right back."

She ran for the stairs, leaped up them, looking, for a split second, like a little girl.

Like Katy.

Jack had had Katy for a while now. If Holly was right and they'd gone to the Bad Boy's Island, they'd have been there for a while already. He saw the blood on the sheet, Henry's mangled chest, the awful, bloodstained knife.

Don't go there. Don't go there until you have to.

31

They set out for Billy's house, but before they'd gone two minutes down the road, Holly heard the sound of a car approaching them.

"Quick, get down," she whispered, taking his hand and dragging him with her into the bushes bordering the road. "Hide. It could be Farley or the other one."

They crouched together as a police car came around the corner and passed them.

"Shit," Billy swore. "I think it was Farley. He might be going to find us."

"We have to run. Come on." She stood, set off racing toward his house. He overtook her a hundred yards before the beginning of his drive; by the time she reached his car he was in the driver's seat and had started the engine.

"Great. Good." She was panting. "We just have to pray we don't run into another car on the road here. Once we hit the paved road we should be OK. No one will be looking for this car."

They took a left-hand turn at the end of the driveway onto Birch Point Road.

"We hope. If Farley came looking for us and didn't find us—"

"I know. But he might have gone to Henry's."

"Why the huge windbreaker? It swamps you."

"I told you—I'm cold."

"Where's the compass?"

"In the pocket. But I won't need it. I can find my way there. And I know how to steer a Whaler. I'll be fine."

"No way, Holly. Not I. We. I'm going with you."

"That's the same as having the cops with me. You know how much Jack hates you. It won't work. The minute he sees you—"

"I've already thought of that. Because of the fog he won't be able to see us until we get really close. If he's there."

"He's there all right. I know it. I can feel it." She kept checking the road ahead and behind, listening out for any sound of a car.

"Anyway, as soon as we see Henry's boat, I'll slip off the stern of the Whaler into the water. I can swim around the side; he won't see me. You know how good a swimmer I am. I can go around the side of the island, sneak up from behind. If it goes wrong, if you can't talk him down—I'll be there."

"It's not a good idea. It's not safe."

"It's happening, Holly. I have the keys to the boat. You're not leaving without me."

She clenched her fists. It could be the worst possible idea ever. But what choice did she have? She could see how hard he was gripping the steering wheel of the car; she knew she couldn't dissuade him.

I'll figure out how to make him stay in the boat when we get there. I'll figure it out then.

They'd reached the end of Birch Point Road: no cars had passed them. She turned around: no car was following them. Billy pressed on the accelerator.

Six, maybe seven minutes to the dock if they drove fast enough. And then? It was calm. The boat could go full throttle. Twenty minutes and they'd be at the Bad Boy's Island. If she was right and could find it in this fog.

Shit.

"Does your boat have gas?"

"Yes. I filled it up a couple of days ago. Full tank."

Thank God.

"Billy. Thank you. Thank you for doing this."

"As if I wouldn't?" He was racing down the road, looking straight ahead. "I'm not as much of an asshole as you think I am."

"I never—"

"Yes, you did. Forget it, OK? It doesn't matter. None of it matters now."

No, it didn't. Nothing mattered. Nothing except Katy. How had Jack explained it to Katy? "*Princess, we're going on an adventure. A little boat trip like our car trip that night.*" Is that what he'd said?

Why hadn't she listened? To Billy—to Anna. To Henry most of all. How could she have thought him taking her out like that was innocent, harmless? Why hadn't she listened?

"You fucking idiot." She pounded her forehead with her fist. "You've been such a fucking idiot."

"Stop it, Holly."

They were going past the graveyard now, turning left to head for town.

What did you wish for that first night, Jack? I wished for you. Do you believe that? I wished for you.

"What are you going to say to him?"

"I don't know. I have to make him understand he can't hurt Katy, that hurting Katy won't help him."

"Shit—that's your phone. Is it Farley?"

Holly had pulled the cell out of her pocket.

"Yes. What do I say?"

"Give it to me."

"Hello? . . . Yes. Yes. She got worse again. Like before. I'm taking her to the hospital. I know, I know you said that but Jack knows her cell number too if he wants to call and she's in bad shape. Have you heard anything? . . . Really? I see. OK. Thank you." He closed the phone, handed it back to her.

"They were seen in Cumberland Farms—Jack was buying food. And they're getting in touch with all the buses that left from the Mill Pond."

"Did he buy the hospital story?"

"Yes. He still thinks they're on a bus. They're concentrating on the Boston buses."

"That gives us a little more time. When was he seen in Cumberland Farms?"

"He didn't say."

Within minutes they were at Cumberland Farms themselves. Billy signaled, took a sharp left-hand turn toward the marina, so fast the tires squealed. When they reached the car park he cut the engine and they both leaped out, not bothering to close the doors, racing to the pier.

"Jump in," Billy yelled when they reached the Whaler. She leaped on board, immediately began to untie the ropes holding the boat in its berth while Billy put the engine down, started the motor. "OK—we're going. Hold on."

He reversed so quickly she lurched forward, but got hold of the side, righted herself until he put it into forward, gunning it so hard she lurched to the other side.

He wasn't paying attention to any speed limits, was blasting through the calm waters, heading out of the Shoreham River. People on board boats coming in the other direction were yelling at him to slow down, but he kept going, zigzagging between the buoys marking the channel.

There had been some visibility when they were near the land, but as soon as they got out of the channel into open water, the fog became so dense it was palpable.

"*A real pea-souper,*" Henry would have said.

Henry. I need you. How could he have done that to you? I thought I knew him. I thought he loved me. And you. And Katy. How could he have done that to you? He must have known he was killing a part of me when he murdered you. And now he has Katy, Henry. Our Katy. I will not let him hurt her. I won't let him.

Peering through the fog, trying to see the end of the dike, she felt sick. It was a joke. She couldn't see more than a few feet in front of her. There were no more buoys marking the channel.

"Where's the compass? I'm thinking if we head northwest we'll be in the right direction." Billy stood at the steering wheel, straining to see ahead.

"I couldn't find it."

"But you said—"

"I know. I couldn't find it."

"Shit."

"Keep straight ahead. I know the way. I can remember. I know I can."

"We don't have a prayer. Jesus."

"Just go straight—we'll see the dike in a little while. A few minutes. Go straight and to the left a little."

"Fuck!" Billy swerved the wheel. "A fucking lobster pot. Shit. I almost ran over it. And then the engine would have been fucked."

"It's OK, it's OK, you're doing well."

"We should call the harbor police. They can get out more boats, they can—"

"No. Just a few more minutes, you'll see. We'll see the dike. If we don't you can call."

They were silent as the boat plowed ahead. Holly kept staring, looking and looking for the familiar sight of the dike, but there was nothing. A lone seagull flew above them, flapping its wings, gliding.

Like some albatross. I wish it would make a noise. It's deathly. This fog is gray and deathly. It's like a shroud. What is he doing with her? What is he doing with her on that island? Is he on the island? Am I right? Or has he taken the boat into the middle of nowhere, stopped in the middle of the ocean and . . .

"Holly—I can't see it. I can't see anything. We have to call—"

"Wait. Wait." She could see it. Or was she imagining it?

A shape of something ahead. Something real, solid, looming in the distance. Or was it a mirage? "Keep going. I think I see something. Head a little to the left. That's it. Now straight. It's there—see?"

"No."

"Look—the lighthouse. The lighthouse on the end of the dike. Do you see it?"

Billy leaned forward, concentrating.

"I think—wait. Yes. I see it. You're right. I can see it now. We're heading straight for it."

"Swing the boat around so we're parallel to it."

He turned the wheel. Holly stood beside him, reached out, turned it a fraction more. "That's it—if we keep on straight now, we should get there in about . . ." She checked her watch. "In about ten minutes if we keep at this speed."

"There's nothing between here and Nantucket except that island. If we miss it . . ."

"We won't. I sailed there so many summers. I never landed on it, but I know it. I know this is the right course."

"How could Jack find it in this fog?"

"It wasn't that foggy before. Remember? It was drizzling but the fog didn't really set in until just a while before we left."

They were silent for a few minutes, until Billy said, "What's she like?"

"What?"

"Katy. I want to know about Katy."

"Why?" She already felt as if she were stretched out on a rack; this comment of his turned the notch even tighter. "Because you don't think you'll ever *get* to know her?"

"No. Because I want to know."

"She's . . ." Holly thought of adjectives. So many adjectives, none of them coming close to doing justice to Katy. "She's perfect, Billy. She's the best, the most perfect girl in the world." She paused. "It's this love. I don't know how to say it. It's not just that I'd die for her. Mothers say that, parents say that, I know. And it's true. It's a given. But that doesn't begin to cover it. The love I feel for her is in every bone in my body, every cell in my body. A world without Katy—it's—it's not possible. But I can feel her. I know she's alive. I'd know if she weren't, you know?"

"I guess I can imagine."

They kept going, silent again now, both of them constantly scanning the horizon.

"A little . . ." She reached over again, turned the wheel a tiny bit to the left.

"Are you sure?"

"I think so."

Nothing. Absolutely nothing was in sight. Turning around she looked back to the lighthouse but it had disappeared.

"I don't know." Her eyes went to the left, to the right. Where were they? They must be on the right course, but now she wasn't sure. Now she had lost all sense of direction. "Wait a minute. Slow down."

He pulled back on the throttle.

"I think this is right. It must be. We've gone straight from the lighthouse, right? A little to the left but straight. I don't know." She spun around in a circle. "It has to be right. Unless we're too far to the left." She checked her watch. "We've been going seven minutes. So we should hit it in three. But shouldn't we be seeing it? At least an outline?"

"This fog is unbelievably thick. We might not see it until we hit it—literally. Or if we miss it by a few feet we'll miss it totally. What do you want me to do?"

"Put her in neutral. Just for a second. I need to get my bearings again."

She could see from the look on his face that he didn't think it was possible. He slowed the boat further, put it in neutral; they sat on the still, glassy water, adrift.

"We're lost, aren't we?"

"I don't know, Billy. I know we were headed in the right direction. I don't know." She wanted to throw herself off the boat into the water, swim for it. But swim where?

Katy. Where are you? Katy?

If she called out Katy's name would Katy hear her and call back? Or if Jack heard her? What would he do?

Why? Why is this happening? How could this have happened? How could I have done this to Katy? If only I hadn't gotten on that bus. If only he hadn't sat down beside me. If only I'd listened to people when they told me. I've been so selfish. So disgustingly selfish.

What have I done to Katy? How can I save Katy?

The seagull had caught up with them; she saw it hovering above them with its beaky little eyes. Still gliding soundlessly, another harbinger of doom, this one a silent one. The image of Bones lying across Henry's chest assaulted her, that sad, lost look in his eyes.

"Oh, my God, Billy. I don't know where we are."

"We have to call the police now."

As she reached for the cellphone in her pocket she heard the familiar cry of a seagull. Looking up, she saw that it wasn't the one following them that had cried out, but another, a smaller one. It circled around the boat then headed off, flying off to the right, the first one following it.

"Go after them. Quick. That second one came out of no-where. It might have come from land. It might have come from the island and it might be going back."

"That's a lot of 'mights'—are you sure?"

"It's our only hope now. Yes. I'm sure. Go—quickly."

He pushed the stick forward, took off after them.

They'd gone thirty seconds when Billy said in a hushed voice, "Look, I think that's a boat. Look ahead—to the right."

She saw it: a form in the water, a hull, like a ghost ship stranded for centuries. Henry's *Sea Ox*.

"Cut the engine," she whispered back.

"I see the island now. I see it. I'm going off the stern. I'll get in the water without making any noise and swim around, OK?"

"Billy, no . . ."

But he'd already stripped off his shirt, moved to the stern; without even a splash he'd gone off the back. She watched him dive down, then quickly turned and stood at the wheel as the forward momentum of the boat brought it closer to Henry's and then past it, slowly gliding onward to the shore.

Where are they? I can't see them. Where are they?

The bow of the boat hit sand. Holly grabbed the anchor, jumped off onto shore with it, ran up onto the sand, all the time searching for them.

"Holly."

She swung around to the right. Jack was sitting on a rock; she could just see him. About ten feet away from her. He held up his hand, waved. She threw down the anchor, ran. With every step she could see more, until she could see Katy.

Katy, curled up on his lap, her head against his chest.

"Katy! Katy!"

But Katy didn't raise her head. Katy didn't move at all.

32

"Stop right there, Holly."

She was five feet away from them.

"Stop."

The menace in his voice brought her to a halt.

"What have you done to her, Jack? She's not moving. What have you done? Katy!"

"Don't yell, please. She's not going to hear you."

"No, no. Please God, no."

"She's not dead, Holly. She's asleep. Out for the count."

"What have you done to her?"

He was dressed in jeans and the Lobster Pot T-shirt. They were both wearing the shirts he'd bought on their first date. He was sitting calmly on the rock. Holding Katy.

"Good work finding me, Holly."

"What have you done to her?"

"Step back, Holly. I mean it."

"What have you done to her?"

"I gave her a little sleeping pill. Told her it was a different kind of sweet—sorry—candy."

"What are you doing? Jack, please. Let her go."

"Can't do that. Not possible, I'm afraid."

"What do you want? Tell me what you want. I'll do anything, Jack. If you let me have her, I'll do anything."

"I know," he sighed. "Of course you'd do anything."

"I will. I promise. I'll help you escape. I promise." She took a step forward.

"Not a good idea, Holly." He picked something up from beside him. "I have a knife. I left the other one behind, but we took a trip to Walmart. Amazing how much they sell there. I mean, they have everything, don't they? Most of it's crap, but it is bloody cheap."

"Jack." She stepped back at the sight of the blade. "You're talking like a crazy person and I know you're not. I know you're not crazy. I know what you did . . . I know you felt you had to. You felt trapped. Like the wolf, right? Like the wolf you told me about on our honeymoon. Remember telling me? Remember Vermont?"

"Oh, please. You were right the first time. I'm not crazy. And you can't change anything by bringing up nice memories. The past is over, Holly. Do *you* remember? The past is jettisoned."

"You said you still loved me. You said it on that message. If you love me, if you really do love me, you'll let Katy go."

"True." He nodded and her heart leaped. "But something else happened. What I mean is, I love Katy more."

"Then let her go."

He appeared to be thinking.

Please, please, please.

"But here's the problem. If I let her go, what happens?

What's her future, Holly? No father, a mother who—well, I don't think you're going to have a normal life, if you don't mind me saying so. And I won't be around, will I? One way or another, I'll be dead. And she'll grow up and she'll become—she won't be Katy any more."

"Is this that whole teenage mall thing you were talking about before? Katy getting tainted by life? I'll make sure she doesn't. You know me, Jack." She paused. *Think. Think fast.* "You know I'm old-fashioned, right? That's what you liked about me. I'm not going to change, I won't let Katy change. You *know* me. You *love* me. You know I wouldn't let anything bad happen to her. I'm her mother."

"And I'm her father. I told her that, you know. She was so happy when I told her I'm her father." He shifted position slightly, but she still couldn't see Katy's face; it was still pressed against his chest. "She grows up and finds out her father killed her great-grandfather. That her father killed two little girls. Shit, Holly, *I'd* take drugs or get off my head every night if that were my history."

"But you're not her father."

His face changed, his eyes hardened.

"I really wish you hadn't come here. It was a stupid thing to do. It's the Bad Boy's Island, Holly. You never come here, remember? Bad luck."

"But you're not the Bad Boy. I know you're not. You don't want to hurt her. I know you don't."

"I wasn't planning on hurting her—"

"Then let her go. Give her to me."

"I was planning a nice swim. The two of us, into the water

together. Look—look how calm it is. I wanted some time to sit, to think, to look at the horizon. Hard to do in this fog, but it's the principle of the thing, right? I know the horizon is out there, don't I? Besides, the fog is a kind of horizon too, in its own way. I just needed some quiet time. And then a swim."

"A swim?"

"A nice long swim."

"How long?"

He shrugged.

"How long?"

"I've been thinking about the Bad Boy. What it must have been like for him camping out here. I *channeled* him. He must have hated Shoreham so much. One fucking bicycle and that's it. That's the end of life as he knew it. One mistake. He's branded forever. People shun him. You know, I overheard a girl talking once in Bristol, at a bar, when I had my first—no, hang on—I think it was my second—yeah, my second new identity. She was talking with her girlfriends at the next-door table to mine. I was alone, having a pint. She was saying, 'Remember that Choirboy Killer? The one who killed those twins? I saw some twins in the shop today and it occurred to me that he's out of jail now with a new identity and all and we're around his age and that some girl, somewhere, someone like us, might be hooking up with him right now and she wouldn't even know who he was. How fucking scary is that?'"

He patted Katy's head as if she were a dog.

"What do you say, princess? Should we ask Mommy? Yes,

I think we should." He kissed Katy's head. "So how scary is it, Holly? Now that you know. I'm curious. Tell me. How scary is it?"

She could feel the tears running down her face, but she didn't wipe them off. She couldn't move.

What if Katy wakes up? What will he do if she—

"And tell Billy Boy if he takes one step closer to me, I'll use the knife."

"What?"

"He's behind me. Look—about fifteen yards behind me on the left."

"What are you talking about?" She stared over Jack's shoulder. "I can't see anything, there's nobody—"

"He's there, Holly." Jack didn't take his eyes off her. He raised his voice and called out, "Billy, I can hear you there. You know how if you're blind your hearing gets sharper? Well, one of the only advantages of jail is that it heightens your senses too. I can hear the proverbial pin drop yards away. I know you swam off the boat, Billy. Come a step closer and I'll have to hurt Katy. I don't want to. I hate blood. I really do."

"Billy!" she yelled. "Billy, if you're there, don't move. Please. He has a knife. Don't move."

"Drop the knife, Jack. Put it down," Billy shouted.

"For fuck's sake, shut up. I'm talking to Holly. Leave us alone. You never could leave us alone. If you don't now, you'll force me to hurt Katy."

"Don't move, Billy! I'm begging you, don't move."

"Are you listening to her, Billy?"

"Yes. I'm not moving, OK? I'm not moving."

"You said you wouldn't hurt her." Holly was begging, pleading. "Did you ever love me? Ever?"

"I always loved you. I still do. He doesn't have a clue." Jack tilted his head backward. "Billy Madison doesn't have a clue how happy we'd be right now, how happy we would have been *forever,* if he hadn't stuck his fucking nose in."

"Then kill him. Kill me. Just don't hurt Katy."

"I don't think Katy would appreciate me if I killed you. And to tell you the truth, I honestly can't be bothered with Billy Boy. He's insignificant, always was. I like that word insignificant. You wouldn't believe how much I read in jail. I read and I watched *Neighbors.* Great teenage years. Awesome, right?"

"Are you sure she's breathing? I can't see if she's breathing."

"I can feel her heartbeat, Holly. Right next to mine."

"What are you going to do? Tell me how I can fix this. Please. Please. Tell me how."

"There's nothing you can do. You shouldn't have come."

"You didn't mean to kill those girls, I know you didn't. It must have been an accident."

"It was." His face softened. She could see—what she'd said had made an impact.

"It was an accident. You didn't mean to. We can work something out, I promise. You wouldn't hurt a child on purpose. You wouldn't hurt Katy, not Katy. Let her go, Jack. Give her to me."

His eyes narrowed. He was thinking again.

Don't say a word, Billy. He's going to let her go if we don't say a word.

He stood up, carefully, holding Katy with one arm, the knife in his other hand, took a step toward her.

He's going to give her to me. Katy. My baby.

"We're going around in circles here, Holly. I'm tired. So bloody tired. That whole thing with Henry . . ." He shook his head. "It was messy. Wrong. It shouldn't have happened."

"I know. I know you didn't mean to hurt him."

"I didn't want to have to hurt him. He gave me no choice."

"I'm so sorry, Jack."

"Really? So am I." He took another step forward. She held out her hands. For Katy. He was going to put Katy in her arms.

"Hang on." He hoisted Katy with his left arm so that her face rested on his shoulder. "That's better."

"Jack?"

"We're going for a swim now. If you or Billy come within five feet of us—no, make that ten—ten feet of us, I'll use this knife. You won't want to see that, believe me. I hate blood. It's so messy. Henry's boat after a big fishing trip? It made me want to throw up. It's better this way. We'll go for a swim. You won't have to see anything messy. There won't be anything messy."

Billy came charging out of the fog, running at Jack, who whirled to face him, at the same time raising his knife, pointing the blade straight at Katy's head.

"Stop right there, Billy Boy."

"Stop!" Holly screamed. "Stop!"

He did. He stopped on the sand, put his hands up.

"Don't do it. Jack. Don't hurt her. I won't interfere any more. You can go away, you can escape. We'll let you leave the island, we won't tell the police. I can drive you anywhere you want to go. Put her down."

"What are you like?" He smiled, a rueful, twisted smile. "As if I'd want to escape without Katy. But you wouldn't understand that, would you? You're her father? That's a joke. You were right to run away. You should have stayed away. I'm tired of this. I'm hot. We're going for a swim. Ten feet or I'll use the knife."

"Don't kill her, Jack. For God's sake, please, please don't kill her. You love her. If you love her, let her live."

"Holly, God doesn't come into it. I learned that a long time ago. God's been on vacation for centuries. I'd let Katy go, I really would. Maybe she would have a decent life with you. Maybe she would stay innocent and sweet, the Katy she is now. I don't think that's possible, but—"

"Then let her go, let her—"

"But the problem is this. She's part of me now. She's mine. And I can't die without her."

He turned, headed for the water, Katy in his arms.

Billy was standing beside her.

"Don't move. Don't move an inch," she ordered him.

In case you run over a deer, sweetie. It can happen so easily on our road. In case it doesn't die. You'll have to put it out of its misery and I might not be here to help. Here it is. I'll teach you how to use it.

She reached into the inside pocket of her jacket, pulled out the gun, took off the safety catch.

He was wading in, the water was up to his thighs, his back was to her. She took a few steps toward him.

"I told you—ten feet," he shouted, but she took another step closer.

He swung around to face her. The water was just above his waist.

"She's going for a swim, Holly. That gun's just stupid."

He took Katy off his shoulder, put her in the water, his right hand on her head, pushing her down.

"Let her go!"

She took another step toward him, raised the gun, her hands shaking crazily, pointed it at his head. She had to keep the bullet high, away from the water, away from Katy.

"This is silly." He said it as if they were having an argument about what to have for dinner.

She fired. He didn't move. Not an inch. She'd missed. She realized she must have unconsciously closed her eyes when she fired and the shot had gone way up in the air above him.

Katy's body was thrashing underwater; Jack's hand was still on her head, pushing it down.

She moved another step forward, pointed the barrel directly at the top of his chest, willing herself to keep steady and to keep her eyes open.

"I want you to know something, Holly." Jack smiled at her. He smiled straight at her. The same smile he'd had on his face when he'd raced her on the beach and turned to kiss her for the first time. "I don't mind."

Henry, help me do this.

She pulled the trigger.

He kept smiling. He was still smiling and she thought she'd

missed again until she saw a burst of blood come from the middle of his forehead.

Jack fell backward into the ocean; Katy's head surfaced. Holly ran to her, ran splashing through the water, her heart exploding.

33

Sitting in Henry's chair on his porch, looking out over the water, staring at the sailboats and the tankers and the buoys and the glistening sea, she still heard it. She couldn't get it out of her head. Even when she managed to get some sleep, she'd wake up and it would be there.

Lady Macbeth kept washing her hands; Holly kept hearing the song. Coldplay's "Fix You." On an endless looping soundtrack, accompanied by the image of Jack's body floating in the water in a pool of blood.

Five days had passed since it happened. Everyone kept telling her she had nothing to feel guilty about. She'd saved Katy from Jack. She'd had no choice. At breakfast this morning, Anna had even called her a heroine.

"Jesus, Holl. You never told me you knew how to use a gun. You never even told me you *had* a gun. You're a real-life heroine. Just think what would have happened if you hadn't figured out where Jack was, if you hadn't had the gun."

"Shooting a human being doesn't make me a heroine."

"It does when that so-called human being was going to kill Katy."

"How do you think Katy is? I know she doesn't say much, but how do you think she is?"

"Quiet, like you said. It's hard for me to tell, I've only been here one night. But listen, there are good child shrinks in Boston. You have to get Katy to see someone. You really do."

"I know," she replied. "I've talked about it to Billy. I will. In a while. I just want her to settle back down in the environment she's used to. And at least she talks to Bones. Bones is here for her—he sleeps in her bed. I hear her whispering to him for hours every night."

"I wouldn't call that healthy," Anna remarked.

"Nothing's healthy." Holly shook her head. "Nothing's healthy, Anna. But right now, I think Bones helps her. I know he does."

Anna had given her a quizzical look then dropped the subject. An hour later, she'd offered to take Katy and Bones down to the beach.

"It's a beautiful hot day. A swim would be good for her. And you've got to let her out of your sight for more than a minute. You have to give her some space, Holl. You can't keep sitting holding her on your lap forever."

"I know, but it's hard."

"Let me take her to the beach. Please. That will be at least semi-healthy."

"OK." She knew Anna would keep pushing until she gave in. "OK. Thanks."

As soon as they'd left the house, Holly had walked over to Henry's. Sat down on the deserted porch and wept.

"I remember once when I went to visit your grandmother in the

hospital and she had just been having a talk with someone else there, another woman with cancer.

"Isabella said to me, 'Henry, I know how hard this is for you. And I know how wonderful you've been. But no one really understands what it's like—they can't. Not unless they're going through the same thing. I can't tell you what a relief it was to talk to Sarah.'

"It made me realize, sweetie, that there are times when sympathy doesn't really do the trick. You need empathy. You need someone who really has walked a mile in your shoes."

You're right, Henry, but how do I find someone else who has killed someone? Killed the husband she loved? And if I did, would it help? Really? And who could Katy find? What child has been through what she's been through?

Katy was alive. That's what she kept telling herself. Katy was alive. Holly had spent hours trying to explain to her what had happened: how Jack was sick, how he'd done bad things, but that didn't mean he hadn't loved her.

It was so confusing, all of it. Holly couldn't understand, so how could Katy? She asked so many questions, all of which Holly did her best to answer honestly without terrifying her. What she could never tell Katy was that Jack had tried to kill her. The look of fear and incomprehension and pain in Katy's eyes when she'd told her Jack was responsible for Henry's death was terrible enough. She couldn't go further, tear Katy's world apart any more than it had been torn already. Henry dead; the man she'd thought was her father dead.

And in the midst of it all, learning from Holly that Jack had lied and that Billy Madison was her father. Which of course meant that Holly, her mother, had lied to her too. The Explorer wasn't an explorer. The world Katy had lived in her whole life had been blown to smithereens.

"When you feel so tired but you can't sleep. Stuck in reverse . . ."

Katy was alive: that's all that mattered. She had time, years and years, to try and cope with the awful things life had thrown at her. Holly would take her to Boston, get her counseling. She'd do everything she could to help Katy through this.

But right now she couldn't move further than a walk to Henry's house. Exhaustion overwhelmed her. She couldn't sleep more than an hour at a time; she couldn't eat, either.

I killed Jack. I killed another human being. I know I had to but that doesn't change the fact that I killed someone.

Jack.

Why didn't you tell me about your past to begin with? Why did you murder Henry instead of leaving, taking off by yourself? And why, really why, did you take Katy?

Everything he said on that island was burned into her soul and yet none of it made sense. Did he love her? Had he ever loved her? If he loved Katy so much how could he possibly want to take her with him to oblivion?

Answer me, Jack.

People tiptoed around her. She didn't blame them. What could they possibly say? Friends of Henry dropped by to pay their respects. And left as quickly as possible. A few mothers from Katy's kindergarten came too, maybe to offer support, but it felt more as though they were there to gawp, driven by a gossipy desire to see a cause célèbre. But they never mentioned

Jack. No one wanted to, no one could bring themselves to say his name.

Even the police had treated her with kid gloves. They knew Jack Dane had murdered Henry, they established that Jack had bought a knife at Walmart, they found the knife on the ocean floor, ten feet out. Billy and Holly's stories were identical; they knew, too, from Katy's short stay in the hospital, that she'd been given a sleeping pill and had had water in her lungs. Plus, of course, they'd delved further into Jack's past, read all about the killing of the twins. So they weren't going to make Holly go to jail or to trial. It was a clear case of a mother defending her child's life, a child who was in the hands of a self-confessed murderer, one who had already killed two children.

Billy was the only one who dared mention Jack's name. He'd come over a few times, sat down with her in the kitchen, had a cup of coffee. Katy stayed in the living room watching television, but he was good about not trying to push his way into her life. "She needs to get used to me," he said. "I think she still believes Jack is her father. It will take time."

"I know I should take her to see someone, a child psychologist."

"It's only been a few days since—"

"I know. I can't do anything right now. I'm so tired, Billy."

"I bet you are. And you'll do the right thing with Katy. She'll be fine, I know she will."

"I'm not sure. I'm not sure about anything. *I* need to see someone."

"It would be a good idea, Holl. Listen, maybe we can all go

together. But then the shrink would need to see a shrink. Way too much crazy information. Major overload."

She almost smiled.

"Why didn't you tell me about the gun?"

"I don't know. Honestly. I don't know."

"Thank God you had it."

"Because of Henry. He gave it to me in case I ran over a deer on the road and had to put it out of its misery. He taught me how to use it."

"Thank God."

"I wouldn't have been able to—if he were any further away, I would have missed the second time too."

"But you didn't."

"No. I didn't."

He never stayed long, but she was relieved to see him when he came. He hadn't killed someone he loved, but he'd been there with her; he'd been at her side from the moment they'd found Henry until the end. He *knew*.

He knew and he didn't throw any of it back in her face; he never reminded her how stupid she'd been not to listen to him.

"When you love someone, but it goes to waste, Could it be worse?"

"Stop it!" Holly shouted, covering her ears as if the music were blaring from a speaker system on the porch. "Leave me alone!"

He was haunting her. In her dreams, in reality, all the time. Jack was always with her; fragments of conversations they'd had coming back to her, memories of the sex they'd shared, his body melting into hers; images of him alive and laughing, images of him dead, floating on the sea. And that song. That song.

Holly got up. The smell of Henry's pipe had been embedded in the chair; she breathed it in, trying to capture him.

Were you in pain, Henry? God, please, no. Please let it not have been painful. I love you so much. I'm so sorry. So, so sorry.

When she walked back home, she saw a car traveling down the road toward her.

Oh no, not a reporter. I can't take it.

The first couple of days had been a zoo. This wasn't just a local story, it was big news. Huge news, especially in England. The house phone only stopped ringing when she unplugged it. Hordes of reporters tore up and down the Birch Point Road and camped outside her house. She and Katy had had to hide inside until Billy got rid of them all. It was a private road, they were trespassing on private property. He set up a gate at the beginning of Birch Point, a gate with a lock, and made keys for all the residents. He also paid for a security guard to man it. They were no longer prisoners in their own houses, only on the Point. Billy had worked on that, too. He'd had neighbors do their food and essential shopping for them in town.

But whose car was this and what was it doing here? And why was it turning into her driveway?

It pulled in, stopped and a woman got out. She was tall, with silver hair; an older woman. Holly felt herself relax. This wasn't a journalist, probably a friend of someone on the Point who had gotten lost.

"Hello, can I help you?" she said as she walked up to her.

"I'm looking for Holly Barrett." The woman shut the car door. She was wearing black linen trousers, a white blouse, a black linen jacket.

"I'm Holly Barrett," she said, fear punching her in the stomach. The woman spoke in an English accent.

"My name is Eliza McCormack." She put her hand up to shade her eyes from the sun. "I'd like to speak to you about Thomas Grainger."

Holly couldn't move, couldn't respond.

"I was Thomas's lawyer. I'd like to speak to you for a few minutes. I won't take up much of your time."

"I don't know. I'm not . . . I'm not—"

"I know this must be hard for you, but I'd appreciate it hugely if you could just give me a few minutes of your time. Please?"

"All right."

Holly walked up to the door, opened it, and Eliza McCormack followed her inside.

"Thank you very much," she said as they went into the living room. "And what a lovely house you have. People these days spend so much money and time trying to put their stamp on a house. I think it's nicer if you let the house put its stamp on you."

"Thank you." Everything about this woman made her nervous.

"Do you mind if I sit down?"

"No. Please. Go ahead."

"I don't mind."

Those last words floating across the water just before she pulled the trigger.

Eliza McCormack sat in the armchair Henry had sat in when he'd come over the last time she'd seen him alive.

"Would you like some coffee or something?"

"No, no, thank you. I'm fine."

Holly sat down on the sofa across from her. Eliza McCormack looked so chic and pulled together, Holly felt suddenly embarrassed by the fact that she wasn't wearing shoes, had on an old pair of shorts and a T-shirt.

"I should tell you. I came over from London to identify Thomas's body. I couldn't come immediately because of a case."

"What?"

Identify his body? They knew it was Jack. Why . . .

"The authorities needed someone from England, you see. Someone who knew him in his original identity. And of course his parents weren't about to—"

"His parents?" Holly's hands flew up in the air. "What do you mean, his parents? His parents are dead."

"Is that what he told you?"

"Yes. Yes, I don't—"

"I see. But haven't you looked him up, read the cuttings? But of course not—you'd know if you had. His parents disowned him. Completely. It was dreadful, but, given those two, not unexpected. I'm surprised though. Don't you want to know?"

"Know what?" She could feel herself shriveling under this woman's intense stare.

"All about Thomas. His history."

"No." She shook her head. "No."

"Why not, if you don't mind me asking?"

"Could you please stop saying that?"

"Saying what?" Her eyebrows arched.

"That word—'mind.'"

"I'm sorry, of course I will."

"It was a private thing between Jack and me. I can't explain."

"No need to. This must be so distressing for you."

Holly nodded.

"And I know you haven't given any interviews. But I want to assure you that what we say here is strictly between us. I have no interest except a personal one."

"What do you mean?"

"I'd like to know what happened at the end. I understand it may be painful for you." Eliza McCormack frowned. "And I don't want to cause you any pain. But I knew Thomas—Jack—well. He was . . ." She paused. "Special. Intelligent. Thoughtful. He used to say to me he could never have a 'normal' life again, but I made him believe he could.

"So you see, I feel responsible for what happened to him. Because I made a tragic mistake. I told him that everything is redeemable, that he could go ahead and live his life and, yes, marry this woman he'd fallen in love with. He had paid his debt to society. He had a right to a life. And I was instrumental in getting him here to America. He'd been hounded, hunted to the ground *three* times after getting out of jail. He couldn't possibly live in England.

"It wasn't easy to get him here, but his life was in jeopardy. Tabloids in the UK offer money to people who spot the so-called 'villain'; and under the Human Rights Act, Thomas could not legally be denied the right to live freely and safe from torture or inhumane treatment. He was given anonymity in perpetuity and as his was such a serious case, he was granted permanent relocation to another jurisdiction.

"Getting him here to the States, where he wanted to be, well, that was slightly tricky. But speaking hypothetically, of course, the UK government is nothing if not keen to allow the USA to remove its citizens or guests from our sovereign land for the purposes of extraordinary rendition or extradition to the States for criminal proceedings, and with a little help from people with whom I have a fair amount of clout, it may have been possible to come to an agreement with your government to take this endangered, so-called child-killer off our soil in return for, shall we say, the disappearance of some paperwork and perhaps the handing over of a high-priority terror suspect.

"These things can be done on an informal basis. I'm not saying they were, of course, but hypothetically, it's possible."

"I don't understand what you're saying."

"I'm sorry." She smiled. "It's the lawyer in me. We never stop, unfortunately. Anyway, all of that isn't relevant. What is relevant is my own misjudgment, my mistaken belief that he could put down roots here. I told him, as soon as I received that first telephone call, I told him to get out, to leave. I only wish he'd listened to me. But he loved you too much."

"He loved Katy, my daughter. That's what he told me. At the end. He said he couldn't die without Katy. He wanted her to die with him. He was drowning her when I, when I . . ."

"Is that right?"

"What?"

"I mean, was he actually drowning her when you shot him?"

The question was fired like a bullet straight to her heart.

"Yes. Yes. He had her head underneath the water. He had his hand on her head. I could see. He was drowning her. He told me not to get within ten feet of him or he'd stab her. But he was drowning her. She had water in her lungs when we took her to the hospital afterward." The words were flying out of her mouth, she needed desperately to speak them. "He was going to kill Katy because he didn't want her to grow up, or because he loved her too much to die without her. I don't know. I didn't understand then and I don't understand now, but I couldn't, I couldn't let him—"

"Did he say anything?"

"What?"

"At the end. Did he say anything?"

"He said, 'I want you to know something, Holly. I don't mind.'"

She leaned further forward. "So he knew what you were about to do. He wanted you to shoot him."

"No, no, he said the gun was stupid. I don't think he believed I'd use it. I don't know. I don't *know*."

"Holly?"

Neither of them had heard the front door open. Billy was on the threshold of the living room, but the armchair was hiding Eliza McCormack from his sight.

"Holl—what's going on? Whose car is that outside?"

"It's my car." She stood up, turned to face him. "My name is Eliza McCormack. I came to speak to Holly about Thomas—about Jack Dane. And you're the man who rang me to begin with, aren't you?" She stepped forward toward Billy as he approached them. "I recognize that voice."

"Hello." He looked doubtful as she extended her hand to shake, but he shook it. "I'm Billy Madison and yes, I called you. What's going on here? Holly, you look really upset. What's going on?"

"I was just asking Holly a few questions about what happened." She returned to the armchair, sat down.

"Why?" Billy remained standing.

"Because I need to know."

"I don't think you have the right to upset her. She's been through enough."

"I don't mean to upset her, really I don't. I only wanted to learn what actually happened. You can never trust newspaper reports. At least not in England." The wry way she said it reminded Holly of Jack.

"He didn't think I'd use the gun. I'd never even told him I had one."

"But wouldn't he be fairly sure you'd use it when your daughter's life was at stake?"

"What is this, a cross-examination?" Billy came and stood beside Holly, put his hand on her shoulder.

"He couldn't have known I knew how to shoot."

"Perhaps your grandfather might have told him?"

"What's your point, Ms. McCormack? Who cares if he knew she could shoot a gun or not? He was about to kill our daughter."

"Of course." She stared up at Billy with her sharp, light blue eyes. "But I know Thomas. I knew him. He was very intelligent.

I suspect he knew Holly had a gun and that she knew how to shoot it and that he wanted her to come to that island and shoot him, kill him."

"Why?" Billy asked.

"To put him out of his misery."

"Oh, for fuck's sake." Billy's voice had risen. "What misery? That's absurd. The miserable person was Holly. She'd just seen her grandfather with his chest ripped apart. She'd just found out her husband had murdered two innocent children. And that he'd taken her daughter, *our* daughter, to an island. And had a knife. How dare you talk to her about Jack's, or whatever the fuck his name was, misery?"

"I'm sorry for the loss of your grandfather." Her gaze went back to Holly. "Honestly, I am. But Thomas must have felt cornered, trapped. To do what he did to him. From the age of eleven that boy was trapped. He made a terrible mistake and he paid for it, and he wanted to redeem himself. He told me that he had finally found himself here. That the love of you and Katy was redeeming him. Threatened with the loss of that, well, he did something horribly wrong. But I do not believe he was going to kill Katy. He wanted you to think he was so you would kill him. Why else would he say that, Holly? 'I want you to know something. I don't mind?' He wanted you to know it was all right to kill him. He wanted you to put him out of his misery."

"Like a deer," Holly whispered.

"She's nuts." Billy squeezed Holly's shoulder. "Don't listen to her. She's nuts. She wasn't there. She doesn't know. I saw him too, you know, Ms. McCormack. I saw him start to drown

Katy. He was definitely going to kill her. That's the most far-out, implausible theory I've ever heard. What? You think Jack knew we'd find him? Knew we'd get to the island and confront him? Bullshit. He left his car at the bus stop. If he'd wanted us to find him he would have left it at the marina. If he wanted to die so much and be put out of his misery he could have bought a fucking gun in Walmart and blown his head off. He didn't have to take Katy with him."

Holly couldn't take her eyes off Eliza McCormack. She knew so much about Jack; she knew what Holly had always wanted to know—what he'd been like as a child, what his family was like, everything Jack had at first refused to tell her and later lied about.

"Were his parents awful to him?"

"Holly . . ."

"No, Billy. I want to know."

"Yes, they were awful." Eliza McCormack nodded. "They never loved him. They sent him to a boarding school, a choir school, when he was seven. They idolized his older brother and they didn't give two hoots about him; all they cared about was their social life, their social standing. They'd leave him alone constantly. Alone most nights in a huge house while they went off to parties. They pressured him constantly. He had to be first in his class at school, he had to be the best chorister, he had to perform for their friends at drinks parties and keep his mouth shut the rest of the time. There was no love, none. They proved that when they disowned him. They never came to the trial, never visited him in jail. Nothing. They cut him out of their lives entirely. He was only eleven years old."

"He had an older brother?"

"Yes, and he also cut him out of his life entirely. Thomas was left alone, abandoned. It was scandalous."

"No." Billy marched over to her chair. "*This* is scandalous. Leave. I mean it. You're supposed to be a hotshot lawyer? What a joke. You're in love with your client. It's obvious. Obvious and unprofessional and scandalous."

She rose, stepped aside from Billy, fixed her startlingly clear light blue eyes on Holly.

"He's right. I did love Thomas. Not in that way, though. He was a boy when I met him. My heart went out to him, I admit. Yours would have too. He didn't understand what he'd done, not really. He hadn't meant to do it. When he told me how much he loved those girls, I believed him. And let me tell you, I don't believe many of my clients. But Thomas was different. He was a child. A neglected, unloved child.

"Once again, I'm sorry about your grandfather. But I'm also very sorry I told Thomas he could lead a normal life. I should have known better, I really should have. And I truly believe he wasn't going to actually kill your daughter. Nevertheless, Mr. Madison is correct. This was a very unprofessional visit. I shouldn't have bothered you. It's my responsibility, not yours. I'll leave now."

She turned and walked out the door. But not before Holly saw the tears in her eyes.

"Jesus Christ!" Billy came and knelt before her on the sofa. "I can't believe you had to go through that. I should report her to the bar or whatever they have in England. That was unbelievable."

"I need to get out of here, Billy. I can't be in this house any more. Katy and I need to get away."

"Absolutely. You're right. You shouldn't be here. People can find you here. Listen, I've rented an apartment in Boston. It has two bedrooms—you can stay there, at least for a while. I'll stay down here, I won't bother you. You can get away from this place. These memories."

"You're sure?"

"Absolutely."

"We can't leave Bones."

"You can take Bones with you. Being a prospective lawyer, I checked the lease over with a fine-tooth comb. I remember, there wasn't any 'no pets' clause. And Anna's place isn't far away. You'll have a friend close by. It's a really good idea."

"OK." She nodded. "Thank you. Yes."

"Tell me you didn't believe any of that bullshit she was saying about Jack wanting you to shoot him, did you?"

"I don't know."

"You know it doesn't add up. None of it."

"I know."

"So . . ."

"Billy, all I want is to get away. I don't want to think about it. I need to concentrate on Katy. I need to get out of here."

"It's a done deal. I'll go get the keys to the apartment. You can leave tonight if you want."

"Good. Thank you."

Holly got up, walked over to the window, looked out into the trees.

"Lights will guide you home, And ignite your bones . . ."

"What do you think that means? 'Ignite your bones?' Come on, tell me."

"Stop tickling me, Jack, and I will."

"No deal. You have to think while I'm tickling you. It's like walking and chewing gum at the same time. I want to see if you're capable of it."

"OK . . . 'Ignite your bones.' Let me think . . . Stop it! You're making me laugh. I can't concentrate . . . OK—'ignite your bones' means set your whole world on fire. Light you up from within."

"Not bad, Holly Barrett. Passing mark. And the next line?"

'I will try to fix you.' I guess it means make you happy again, like you said on the bus."

"Mmm-hmm. Or . . . or it could mean I will try to tickle you until you're too weak to resist and then I'll have my wicked way with you. A slightly different kind of fixing, but still . . ."

"But still good."

"Still great. Still, like, totally awesome."

34

Autumn always had a sense of loss in the air, that back-to-school feeling, a Sunday-night kind of melancholy. However beautiful the leaves were, however renowned the New England foliage in the fall, the truth was that those leaves were dying. A spectacular burst of color and then the drop to death.

Holly sat out on the deck, taking a break from packing, and looked at the view, expanding almost every minute as leaves drifted down to the ground. She could see a big chunk of the canal; if she stayed until tomorrow, she'd probably be able to see the railroad bridge.

I never put it together before. How stupid am I? I never put the word "fall" as in autumn together with the verb "fall" as in the leaves falling. I'm not so hot at putting things together when it comes to anything.

Going to Boston had been a good move, though. That had been a smart decision. Billy's apartment was clean and comfortable and roomy enough, even with Bones in it. She'd found a therapist for Katy, and one for herself too.

How did you ever know if therapy was working? Well, Katy was talking a little more to her and a little less to Bones. And she'd started first grade at a new school in Boston without any huge problems. Holly had had a long talk with the headmistress before she'd enrolled Katy and had liked her take on the whole situation.

"We'll treat her normally," Mrs. Woodfin had said. "If at any stage she appears to be reacting abnormally, we'll tell you immediately. Children are resilient, but in my experience they are also secretive and keep a lot to themselves if they're frightened. As you know, this is a small school. We can keep an eye on her without keeping too much of an eye on her and making her feel different, if you see what I mean."

On the first day, Katy had cried huge, heaving sobs at the prospect of being separated from Bones. But Holly made her go; she had to. Since then it had been easier. And she hadn't had a phone call from Mrs. Woodfin. But Holly yearned, ached, for the day when Katy would show some sense of joy again. And when she'd share with her whatever it was she was sharing with her therapist. Did she talk about Jack with her? Katy hadn't mentioned his name to Holly since the first week after it happened. Katy's therapist had said she'd allow Holly to attend the fifth session. They'd had four now. Holly was desperate to get to the fifth and dreading it at the same time. She wasn't used to finding out what was going through Katy's mind from someone else, from a stranger.

She's talking more. About general things, but still—that has to be a good sign. And she's spending the day with Billy today. Her therapist thought it was a good idea. So did mine.

How totally bizarre is it to have two women we don't know deciding what's psychologically good for me and Katy? But if I'd had any clue about what was good for us, we wouldn't be in this position in the first place.

This deck was where she had been sitting when she heard Bones barking. Which was why she was going to sell the house. Every single room, every corner of it reminded her of something to do with Jack. She'd thought before that he was haunting her, but it was worse than that because haunting was done by the dead and Jack wasn't dead here, he was alive. She could feel him in her skin, in every pore. She could hear his voice, she could see him sitting at the kitchen table eating his breakfast.

You needed your meals exactly on time like that because that's what you got used to in jail. I'm right, aren't I, Jack? You got used to that routine.

Packing up his clothes this morning had been agony. She could smell him then. And whatever anyone said, smell was the most powerful of senses when it came to memory. He was there in the room with her, telling her to fold his shirts more neatly.

Did you want me to kill you, Jack? I haven't dared talk to my therapist about that yet. In case she looks at me the way Eliza McCormack did. Did you know I'd figure out you went to the Bad Boy's Island? Were you waiting for me? Knowing I'd bring a gun? Willing me to shoot you to put you out of your misery? Is that why you smiled?

It doesn't make sense, Billy's right. But it does. That's what's so crazy. It does.

Her cellphone rang and Holly took it out of her pocket, answered it.

"Hey, Holl." Anna's voice was chirpy. "How's it going?"

"OK. I'm taking a break right now."

"Good. I wanted to tell you, Billy and Katy came over here for lunch. I think he wanted to make her feel more comfortable, you know?"

"How was she?"

"She was pretty good, talking more. She told me about her school, she sounded pretty chilled about it. And she was OK with Billy. I mean, she was keeping her distance, but it wasn't like she was avoiding him. And when he asked her questions about school, she'd answer. Once he even made her smile. I can't remember what the joke was, but she smiled."

"That's good. That's great."

"Yeah. And I have to tell you, he's not the dufus he used to be. He's grown up a lot. And he has the hots for you. He kept talking about you."

"Because Katy was there."

"No, Holl. You know how when you have a crush on someone you always want to bring their name up, talk about them? That's what it was—believe me, I know this behavior."

"People have crushes on you, Anna, not the other way around."

"That's true. But listen, none of this is what I really called about. Have you done it yet?"

"No."

"You have to, Holl. You know you do."

"I know."

"Maybe I should be with you when you do."

"Maybe. I'll think about it."

"Promise you'll do it soon, with me or without me."

"Yes."

"OK, I'll get off your back. It must be hell packing all that stuff up. His stuff too."

"It's not good."

"You should have let me come with you and help."

"I wanted to do this alone. Hold on . . ." Holly stood up, went to the corner of the porch. "A car just drove up. I have to go."

"Who is it?"

"I don't know. I have to go. I'll call you later."

She heard the knock on her front door, went inside and debated with herself whether to answer it. Her car was in the driveway; whoever had come would know someone was here. It couldn't be Eliza McCormack again. It just couldn't.

Another knock.

Holly walked to the door. If it was a reporter, she'd get rid of him or her. Say she had no comment, would never have any comment and they were trespassing on private property; if they weren't gone in a minute, she'd call the police. She opened it.

"Hello?"

A woman, but not Eliza McCormack. A younger woman, probably in her early forties, with big blonde hair, wearing jeans and a pink sweatshirt, a huge denim handbag slung over her shoulder.

"Hello. Sorry, I know this is rude and I wasn't really expecting . . . I mean, I came on the off chance because I was hoping . . . but it is you, isn't it? Holly Barrett?"

Her heart nosedived at the sound of the English accent, even though it was a different accent than she was used to: any time a word ended with a "g," the woman pronounced it as if it were a "k."

"Yes. What do you want?"

To stare at me? To ask me what it was like to shoot him? What?

"My name is Enid."

Holly looked at her blankly. She was wearing a huge amount of blue eyeshadow and bright pink lipstick.

"Enid Dunne. My husband died and I remarried a little while back and now I'm Enid Parker but I was Enid Dunne. I'm their mother. Amanda and Miranda's mother."

"You're . . . ?"

"Yes. Can I come in?"

"Of course. Yes."

Holly stepped aside and Enid went past her, trailing a strange smell, the scent of one of those room deodorizers or air fresheners.

"Sit down, please." Holly had no idea what to say as Enid Dunne took the bag from her shoulder, put it on the sofa and sat down beside it.

"It looks like you're packing up here."

"Yes. I'm selling the house. I'm so, so sorry about your daughters. I don't know what to say."

"That's all right. Nobody does."

An awkward silence followed.

"Can I get you coffee or tea or something?"

"No. Thank you. I told Gary—my husband—I told him I wanted to go shopping. I think he guessed. I mean, when I said

I wanted to come to New England, see the leaves and everything, he said, 'Are you sure that's all you want to see?' and I
said, 'Yes, Gary. That's all.' But I think he knew. We flew in
two days ago. And today, when I said I was going shopping, he
looked at me like . . . well, I think he knows, but what's he going to do, right? As long as I don't bang on about it to him. He
doesn't like me talking about it. He's not a talker, Gary. But
he's a good man."

"I'm sure he is."

Enid Dunne was so nervous, all Holly wanted to do was
help her relax.

"I didn't think you'd be here, to tell the truth. It was a mission finding this place. I asked at a store in town and they said
they thought you'd left but I wanted to see the place anyway. I
don't know why." She shifted on the sofa, crossed her legs, uncrossed them. "People bang on about closure, you know. Like
that's possible. It wasn't like I thought I'd get closure coming
here. But I did want to. I mean, if you were here which I didn't
think you'd be, but if you were, I wanted to thank you."

Holly couldn't speak; nor could she take her eyes off Enid
Dunne. All the make-up couldn't hide the defeat in her face.
Holly saw the wrinkles a woman her age shouldn't have had,
saw years of pain and loss and unbearable grief.

"My heart went out to him," Eliza McCormack had said.

*What happened to your heart when you saw her? Didn't it break
like mine is now?*

"It's not like his dying . . . I mean, it doesn't bring them
back, you know? But his being alive. That wasn't right. Him
being alive and having a life and all, it was wrong. All the

time, I used to wonder, *Is he laughing? Is he having a good time somewhere right now, laughing?* Like it was fine for him to be alive? Like he deserved to be alive and to laugh? Because he didn't." She shook her head. "He didn't. I don't care what they say about having done his time. They're taking the piss when they say that. Like he has a right to have time to do. Like he has a right to anything. He didn't give them any rights. He took it all away. Everything. Their whole world, my whole world and everything. Look . . ." She reached over, picked up her denim bag, unzipped it. "Look."

"Mrs. Dunne. I mean, Mrs.—"

"Enid. It's an old-fashioned name, I know, but it's mine. I'm stuck with it. Look, I have them right here. I brought them in case you were here." She pulled out a packet from the bag, a packet of photographs, opened it and began to lay them out carefully in rows on the coffee table in front of the sofa. "Look at them. Come here." She patted the sofa seat beside her. "Come look at my girls."

She couldn't not do whatever Enid asked. Sitting down beside her, she looked at the pictures.

"They're beautiful."

"Aren't they?"

"Absolutely beautiful."

"Most people couldn't tell them apart. They were that alike."

"Yes. And they look so happy. They're always smiling."

"They were good girls. Never trouble. Miranda, she could be stroppy sometimes, but never for long. And Amanda was a quiet little thing, but don't get me wrong, she had plenty of character."

"I bet she did."

Some of the pictures looked posed, as if they were taken by a professional photographer in a studio. But most of them were informal. Holly could see, in the informal ones, a slight difference between the girls. One looked a little more shy, serious, and she had a small birthmark on her forehead. She must have been Amanda. The other, Miranda, seemed to be clowning for the camera more.

"I was thinking . . ." Enid kept gazing at the photos, her eyes moving from one to the next in the rows she'd made, then starting at the beginning again, as if she were afraid she had missed something. "On the drive here. I couldn't think much being on the wrong side of the road and trying to get the directions right and all, but when I could think, I thought, *I wonder if she saw it. He was that charming. He must have charmed her too. She might not have seen it.*"

"Seen what?"

Enid looked up, away from the pictures, straight at Holly.

"The evil in him. He was a charmer, all right. My girls loved him, worshipped him. But I saw it. Not very often, mind you, but I'd catch him with that look in his eyes when he didn't think I was watching. I saw the evil in him. I should have left that job. I shouldn't have brought the girls with me. We needed the money. I couldn't afford to have someone else look after them while I worked. I keep saying that to myself but it doesn't help. I knew. I didn't know he'd do it to them, though. I *never* thought that."

"What look in his eyes?"

"Like he hated the world and everything in it. Like he

would enjoy punishing the world. I never saw him do anything bad, not until . . . But I saw the look. Like he couldn't wait to do something evil."

"But he was only a boy."

"And children can't be evil?" she snorted. "That poncey lawyer of his was all over that. 'He had a bad childhood, he didn't know what he was doing, poor, poor Thomas.' That was her excuse for him. He didn't know what he was doing? Fucking hell, he didn't. Pardon my French. He knew exactly what he was doing. 'It was a mistake, the cricket bat slipped and he panicked, it was all an accident.' That's what she tried to say. But no one was buying it. An accident? Slipped out of his hand? Look at the coroner's report. Amanda was hit three times by that bat, not once like he tried to say."

Enid picked out a pack of cigarettes from her bag.

"Do you mind?" She waved them at Holly.

"No, please, go ahead. I'll get an ashtray."

Like he couldn't wait to do something evil.

Was that the way it really was, Jack? Is it true? Can an eleven-year-old child be evil?

When she returned and put the ashtray in front of Enid, she sat down beside her again; their thighs were touching.

"Blame the parents," Enid said, at the same time lighting the cigarette. "That's what that bitch of a lawyer tried to do. If she had children of her own, she wouldn't have, I promise you that. But no, she says, it's not his fault, it's his parents." They didn't love him.

"I'm not saying they were good people, the Graingers. They were snooty, full of themselves. They didn't have any time for him. But they didn't beat him or nothing. They didn't lay a finger on that boy. He had everything he could want or need. Other children, they're much worse off, and do they do what he did? No. No, they don't. So the parents didn't kiss or cuddle him—does that give him the right? Does anything on this earth give him the right?"

She blew out the smoke forcefully.

"I'm so sorry, Enid."

"All I'm saying is don't you go feeling any guilt. He shouldn't have been allowed out, never. They made this song and dance about him not having touched them, you know, in any bad way.

"I'll tell you something. I wouldn't have wanted anyone touching my babies like that, I would have gone mental, but if that had happened and whoever had done it had let them live? I've asked myself that question and I've answered it. I'd rather it was that way. As long as they were still alive. Still with me."

She swept at her face with her free hand in an angry gesture.

"You can cry. Go ahead. Please."

"No—I said I weren't going to do this." Grabbing her bag again, she fished out some Kleenex. "I promised myself. If I found you, I'd be strong. I talk too much. No one wants to listen. Gary, he's tired of it. He wants us to have a baby, you know? He says I'm not too old, but I will be soon." She dabbed at her face, took another drag of her cigarette. "He thinks that will help. But me? I know I'll spend my whole time worrying. Never letting the baby out of my sight. Gary says that the worst has already happened, it won't happen again. But he hasn't been through it, you know? He doesn't know what it does to you, how it tears you up. It tears you into pieces. It killed my husband.

He killed my babies and he killed my husband. And he's killing me. Bit by bit, he's killing me."

She stubbed the semi-smoked butt into the ashtray.

"He's dead, Enid."

"I know, I know." She grabbed her bag again, brought out a comb and swept it furiously through her mass of hair. "That's why I came. To make it more real and everything. Gary saved his money for this trip. He's a good man. He doesn't want to hear me go on about it but he wasn't going to stop me from coming. He knows. He's not saying anything but he knows."

"Do you think it has helped?"

"Fucked if I know."

The way she said it startled Holly—it could have been Henry. *"Fucked if I know, sweetie."*

"I should be going." She began to gather all the photographs, put them back into their packet.

"You don't have to go. You could stay, have a coffee."

"No. No, Gary'll be waiting. It's a drive back." She stood up, began to speak, stopped, then said, "Tell me something. Did you love him?"

"Yes." Holly had stood up too. Enid's face was close to hers. "I did."

"So did my girls."

"I didn't know at the end. I mean, I still don't know if he was going to actually kill my daughter or not. I think he loved her."

"He said he loved mine too. What a load of rubbish." Once again her hand delved into the bag, brought out the cigarettes and a lighter. Holly watched as she lit up, inhaled, exhaled. Jack had smoked in what was almost a tender way, lovingly inhaling, taking his time with each cigarette; Enid's smoking was harsh, angry, fast.

"You have to have a heart to love someone. No offense or nothing but you still have a daughter to love and you're wasting your time thinking about *him* and whether he was going to kill her or not kill her. He was going to kill her all right but if he weren't, what's the frigging difference? He killed your grandfather, I read. He kills people. That's what he does. That's what he *did*. Your daughter's the one you should be thinking about, not him. You saved her, you should be jumping up and down. You should be the happiest woman on this earth."

The next puff of smoke blew straight into Holly's face but she didn't wave it away.

"Look, I'm sorry. I can see his charm got to you, like, but it makes me mental. I *have* to think about him, you don't. That evil little bastard didn't kill your babies. You don't have to feel the guilt I do for letting him kill your babies. You have no clue how that would feel. That guilt. And you're sounding worried like he may not have killed your daughter so why did you shoot him? You shot him for *me*, if you want a reason. You shot him for *me*."

She sank back down on the sofa, burst into tears. Holly sat beside her, put her arm around her shoulders.

"Enid, I'm sorry. I can't tell you how sorry I am."

She cried, pushing her left hand through her hair over and over again, smoking with her right. When the cigarette was down to its filter, she put it out in the ashtray, straightened up, pulled out the little blue-and-white pad of Kleenex, and wiped her face.

"This must be so painful for you. I'm so sorry."

"Don't be sorry. I didn't mean to go off on one like that, give you a hard time. It's just I don't want anyone to give that monster another thought, ever. He don't deserve that. I can't ever forgive him, no fucking way. But maybe I can forget him. No, I can't forget him either. But at least I don't have to think any more that he's having a good time, laughing. And that's a blessing. I mean it." She reached out, touched Holly on her thigh. Her make-up was smudged, her hair a mess. "I can't ask you to see a photo of your daughter. Do you understand that? I can't."

"Of course I understand."

"I can tell you're a good person." Out came a compact from her bag, and the comb again. "I'm in a right state, aren't I?" She shook her head. "I have to fix myself up here. If you let one thing go, then it all goes, you know? It's why I can't have a drink, not even one any more. If I had one, I'd have a million. Like the fags. I should give them up too but I can't." She concentrated on her image in the mirror of the compact, spent five minutes putting her face back together while Holly went and got her a cup of coffee.

"Here." She handed it to her. "Please."

"No. No, I've got to be going. Thank you but I need to leave now. I've talked too much. I only came to make it seem more real, and to thank you. I never meant to start talking."

"It's fine, honestly. I'm glad you talked. If there's ever anything I can do, please let me know. Can I talk to you again some time? Can I have your phone number?"

"I don't mean to be rude or nothing, but no." She was up and heading for the door, Holly following her. At the threshold she stopped.

"I have to go back to Gary now and try to . . . try to . . . I don't know. But no more of him. If I keep letting him into my life like I have been, it'll be the end of me and Gary too. He'll kill that too. I wanted to thank you and I did but I talked too much. It's the last time. I have to stop. Do you understand?"

"Yes. I understand."

"I can tell you're a good person, Holly," she said again.

"You're the good one."

"No. I used to be, but no. Still . . ." She shrugged, shifted the bag from one shoulder to the other. "I can try to make Gary happy."

"I'm sure you do."

"You should talk to Gary about that." She let out a half-laugh. "And now I have to drive on the frigging wrong side of the road again."

"Be careful, drive carefully."

"Yeah, and you too, OK? You take care of yourself and that daughter of yours."

"I will. I promise."

"Bye." She stepped forward, gave Holly a kiss on both cheeks.

"Goodbye, Enid."

She watched as Enid got into the car and drove off. And then she walked over to Henry's house.

It was up for sale too. The Barretts would no longer be on Birch Point. This was the end of an era, an era that had begun as a family's search for an idyllic spot to relax and spend summers in. She sat down on the top step of the porch. All Henry's furniture had gone; it had been auctioned in a sale Holly hadn't attended.

Holly looked up at the sky: there wasn't a cloud in it. When she lowered her gaze, stared out to sea, she saw only one boat: a boat that looked like the *Sea Ox*, with a lone figure steering it. A tall bald man, standing up straight at the wheel. She waved. Even though there was no chance at all that he could see her, she waved and whispered, "I love you," watching the boat until, when it was out of sight, she stood and walked back to her house.

As she was making herself a cup of coffee in the kitchen, she heard her cellphone ringing in the living room. She took her mug, went and answered it.

"Holl?" It was Anna. "Who was in the car?"

"Enid Dunne. The mother of the girls Jack killed."

"Christ. What did she want? Are you all right?"

"She wanted to thank me. For killing him."

She heard Anna draw in her breath, let it out in a gust.

"That's heavy-duty. Are you OK?"

"Yes. I'm fine. It's hard to explain, but I feel . . . I don't know . . . I feel like it was fate in a way—that she came here today when I was here. I was supposed to see her."

"Your voice sounds different. Stronger."

"He's left, Anna."

"Who's left?"

"Jack. He's gone. He's not in the house any more. I was just making a cup of coffee and I realized it: he's gone."

"Yeah. Well, he *is* dead, Holl."

"Now he is."

"OK, whatever. I'm glad. I'm glad he's gone."

"I'm going to do it now."

"Are you sure? Are you sure you don't want me with you?"

"I'm sure."

"I know you're going to be OK. You'll be fine."

"I'll be fine whatever happens. Katy's alive. That's all that matters."

"OK, but call me, will you? Promise?"

"I promise."

"Bye. And Holl—I'm not a dyke or anything, as you know, but I love you."

"I love you too."

Returning to the porch, she sat down with her cup of coffee. This was the last time she'd ever sit here. The fact that she couldn't feel Jack in the house as she had before didn't change her mind: she had to leave Birch Point, start again in another place. What Enid had just said kept running through her mind.

Was there such a thing as an evil child? Could a child be born evil, was there an evil gene, passed down through generations? Or did evil strike randomly in the crib, the devil infiltrating a baby's soul? Was it nature or nurture? Did Jack's parents shape his personality, make him violent with their lack of love, their non-parenting?

If she'd been given an essay to write at school on the nature-versus-nurture question, she would have sat down and done a good job on it, arguing all the points in a rational way. But life didn't allow you to answer questions like that. It was too complicated, too subtle and confusing. Enid had seen the evil in Jack, but Holly hadn't. No matter how she looked back on their past together, even knowing what she now knew, she couldn't say he had been evil. Not to her—until the end. As much as she wanted to, she couldn't deny that she had loved him and that he had given her joy.

How could an evil boy who had murdered two innocent children and spent years in jail have a sense of humor? Be so tender in bed, so loving? But then how could Jack have killed Henry, stabbed him to death? And taken Katy with him like that? Wasn't that pure evil? Could any excuse justify that? No.

Life may taint us, but Jack wasn't just tainted, he was steeped in blood.

"Your daughter's the one you should be thinking about, not him. You saved her, you should be jumping up and down. You should be the happiest woman on this earth."

I'll never know the answers. Do I have to know them?

"You can never make peace with grief, sweetie. You just work out a way to live with the war grief wages in your heart."

And I have to learn how to live with what Jack did. Who he was and what he did to us all. Somehow, I have to live with it and move forward, for Katy's sake.

"All you have to do is love Katy with all your heart."

You know I do, Henry. If that's all I have to do, I'll be fine, we'll all be fine.

Do I have to know the answers?

She looked up at the cloudless sky.

That man was wrong about the three presents. That was his way of making the brother he loved still alive and with him. I know that now. But that doesn't mean I can't pray to you.

Mom. Dad. Henry. Please, God, please. I'm praying now. Make Anna right. Make it not have happened. Make this be over. Make him be really dead.

Holly took a slug of coffee, walked upstairs to her bedroom, picked up her bag, took it with her into the bathroom, pulled out the pregnancy test and unwrapped it.

A⁺

AUTHOR
INSIGHTS,
EXTRAS &
MORE...

FROM

**BROOKE
MORGAN**

AND

AVON A

Q&A with Brooke Morgan

What drew you to the subject matter of this novel?

I'm an American living in London. Two young boys who murdered a three-year-old named Jamie Bulger in Liverpool were let out of jail a few years ago and were given new identities. This was big news in the press and my daughter turned to me one afternoon and said "What if I fell in love with one of those boys years from now?" Immediately, I thought: yes, absolutely, what if? Because some girl probably will. And will she know what he's done? Will he tell her? Will she ever find out if he doesn't?

I was struck by all the psychological reverberations and began to think in terms of writing a novel on those lines. The plot took shape fairly quickly, but the turning point in terms of writing was when I realized that Holly would not only fall in love with Jack, but also have a young child of her own.

The book was first published in the UK, but what drew you to the Cape Cod setting?

I spent my childhood summers in a town very like Shoreham, and as it was a special place for me, I wanted to set *Tainted* there. Although most of my time there was idyllic, on foggy wet days I always had a sense of the sinister lurking. Boats would pass by in the Canal blowing their foghorns eerily, like ghost ships, and the whole atmosphere was unsettling.

In many ways the setting echoes the themes of the book: What appears perfect on the surface can have frightening undertones.

Did you do any psychological research as you were writing the novel?

I read nonfiction books on children who have killed, and I spent a long time discussing the nature of children who commit "evil" acts with two child psychiatrists.

Jack, especially, is a frightening character. While we really don't get into his head, you certainly managed to create a vivid villain who started out as quite charming. How did you manage to do that?

I've met a few very charismatic people who have a dark, frightening side which reveals itself over time. And people, too, who seem charming and easygoing, but who hide very scary tempers. Jack was based, to a large degree, on them.

We can choose, especially with people who don't know us, to present ourselves the way we'd like to be seen, but the question is always whether we can change, hide, or suppress our essential natures.

Are there writers or movies that inspired you?

Dennis Lehane novels always inspire me. And in the middle of writing *Tainted*, I watched *Sleeping with the Enemy* again, which reminded me of what it's like to fall in love with and marry a man whom you don't really know.

What's next for you?

I'm working on my next psychological thriller, entitled *Trapped*.

Photo by John Rickwood

BROOKE MORGAN is a Bostonian who now lives in London with her two children. *Tainted* is her first novel.

Brooke Morgan